ALSO BY KATHLEEN MCGOWAN

The Expected One

THE

Book
of
Love

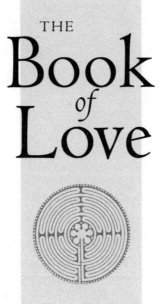

Book Two of The Magdalene Line

KATHLEEN McGOWAN

A Touchstone Book

Published by Simon & Schuster

New York   London   Toronto   Sydney

Touchstone
A Division of Simon & Schuster, Inc.
1230 Avenue of the Americas
New York, NY 10020

First Touchstone hardcover edition March 2009

TOUCHSTONE and colophon are registered trademarks of Simon & Schuster, Inc.

For information about special discounts for bulk purchases,
please contact Simon & Schuster Special Sales at
1-800-456-6798 or business@simonandschuster.com.

Designed by Mary Austin Speaker
Art by Patrick Ruffino
Map by Paul J. Pugliese

Manufactured in the United States of America

10 9 8 7 6 5 4 3 2 1

Library of Congress Cataloging-in-Publication Data is available.

ISBN-13: 978-0-7432-9997-8
ISBN-10:   0-7432-9997-3

This is for Easa

The world was never as worthy
as on the day that the Song of Songs
was given to the people;
for all the writings are holy,
whereas the Song of Songs is
the holiest of the holy.

—RABBI AKIVA, FIRST CENTURY CE

North
Sea

●Knock
Where holy visions were witnessed
by the local people

GREAT
BRITAIN

BELGIUM

Abbey built by Matilda of Tuscany
to house and protect the secret
teachings of the Book of Love
Orval

English Channel

A t l a n t i c
O c e a n

Matilda's home while married
to Godfrey the Hunchback
Stenay●

●Chartres
Location of the most important
Gothic cathedral in the world
and a legendary mystery school;
the home of martyr Modesta

Bay of
Biscay

F R A N C E

Bérenger Sinclair's
Château des Pommes Bleues
Montségur● ●Arques

PORTUGAL

Montserrat●
Resting place of
the Book of Love for 300 years

●Fátima
Where three young shepherd
children witnessed visions in 1917

S P A I N

M e d i t e r r a n e a n

0   50   100 miles
0   50   100 kilometers

Baltic
Sea

GERMANY

Speyer
Primary residence of Henry IV

Worms
Where a council was held in 1076 to
depose Pope Gregory VII and
declare Matilda an adulteress

Matilda of Tuscany's childhood home
Mantua
Canossa
The impenetrable castle of Matilda's family
where Henry IV was forced to do penance

Lucca Florence
Matilda's birthplace and the primary
location of the Order of the Holy Sepulcher
for more than a thousand years

Rome ITALY

Salerno
Pope Gregory VII died here in exile

Sea

Calabria
The first location of the Order of the
Holy Sepulcher, where the tradition descended
from Saint Luke began and endured

THE
Book
of
Love

In the beginning, God created the heavens and the earth.

But God was not a single being; he did not reign over the universe alone. He ruled with his companion, who was his beloved.

And thus in the first book of Moses, called Genesis, God said, "Let us make man in our image, after our likeness," as he is speaking to his other half, his wife. For creation is a miracle that occurs most perfectly when the union of male and female principles is present. And the Lord God said, "Behold that man has become one of us."

And the book of Moses says, "Thus God created man in his own image, male and female created he them."

How could it be that God created female in his own image if he did not have a female image? But this he does, and she was first called Athiret, and this name meant She Who Treads Upon the Sea. But it is not only the seas of our earth that this refers to. It is also upon the sea of stars, the band of light we call the Milky Way.

She treads on the stars as this is her domain, for she is the Queen of Heaven.

And she became known by many names, and one of these is Stella Maris, the Star of the Sea. She is the Mer Maid, for mer means both love and sea, and this is why the water is often seen as a symbol of her compassionate wisdom.

Another symbol used to represent her is a circle of stars that dance around a central sun, the female essence enveloping the male in her love. Where you see this symbol, you will know that the spirit of all that is divine in femininity is present.

Later, Athiret of the Sea and Stars became known in the Hebrew as Asherah, our Divine Mother, and the Lord became known as El, our Heavenly Father.

And so it was that El and Asherah desired to experience their great and holy love in a more expressive physical form and to share such blessedness with the children they would create. Each soul who was created was matched, given a twin made from the same essence. In the book called Genesis, this is told in the allegory of Adam's twin being created from his rib, which is to say his own essence, as she is flesh of his flesh and bone of his bone, spirit of his spirit.

Then God said, as it is told through Moses, "And they shall become as one flesh."

Thus the hieros-gamos was created, the sacred marriage of trust and consciousness that unites the beloveds into One. This is our most holy gift from our father and mother in heaven. For when we come together in the bridal chamber, we find the divine union that El and Asherah wished for all of their earthly children to experience in the light of pure joy and the essence of true love.

For those with ears to hear, let them hear it.

EL AND ASHERAH, AND THE HOLY ORIGINS OF
HIEROS-GAMOS, FROM THE BOOK OF LOVE,
AS PRESERVED IN THE LIBRO ROSSO

La Beauce, France
AD 390

*H*eavy beeswax candles dripped along the perimeter of the cavern, illuminating the cramped meeting space. The small community prayed with soft devotion, following the lead of the ethereal woman who stood before them at the stone altar. She finished the prayer and held the treasure of her people before her, an aged manuscript, bound in leather.

"The Book of Love. The only true words of the Lord."

Candlelight glinted off the copper-gold hair of Lady Modesta as she kissed the book. The faithful in attendance responded in unison.

"For those with ears to hear."

A reverential silence ensued, as if the words from the Book could not be followed with common talk. It was one of the young men, a devout and earnest follower named Severin, who broke the peace within the sacred environment.

"How fares our brother Potentian?"

Modesta answered, her voice as calm and lyrical as when she prayed. "I was able to see him in prison today and bring him bread. He is well. His faith is unshakable, as ours must be."

Severin could not control his growing agitation, despite his best efforts to overcome the fear that swelled within. "You say he is well, but for how long? Rome kills more of our people as heretics each day. They will come for all of us next."

There was a hesitant, murmured agreement in the little community. But Modesta, both wise and patient, never missed an opportunity to teach the truths that she held close.

"It is indeed a sad time when the persecuted become the persecutors. Christians suffered so many years of torture, and yet now they save their greatest violence for each other. We must forgive them for they know not what they do."

Modesta's sentence was punctuated by a sharp whistle at the mouth of the cavern. Too late, the lady and her congregation realized that they had been discovered by the very men from whom they were hiding.

Within moments, the tranquility of the religious gathering was shattered by chaos as a retinue of armed men burst forth through the only opening in the cave. No escape would be possible. These soldiers were all identically dressed, in dark robes and full hoods that covered their heads completely, with sinister slits where their eyes would be. Their leader stepped forward and removed his hood, revealing a shaved head and a carved wooden crucifix at his neck. Focused on Modesta, he spat out his contempt of a female leader while quoting from the epistles of Paul.

"Permit no woman to teach, but to keep silent. Lady Modesta of La Beauce, you are under arrest for heresy."

Modesta eyed him calmly and with recognition. "Brother Timothy. You come for me, and I will go with you. But leave these innocent people in peace."

The distressed young Severin panicked at the prospect of losing their leader and jumped forward to block Brother Timothy's advance. "You will not take her!"

Hooded men flooded forward. Modesta took the distraction as an opportunity to maneuver the sacred book behind her back and out of sight of her accuser. She did not yet realize how grave the danger was to her followers. A woman devoted to the essence of love and compassion cannot fathom the minds of violent men quite so quickly.

The hooded militia drew their weapons and began to make use of them without hesitation. A double-edged sword plunged first through the heart of Severin; his life burst forth from the wound, baptizing the congregation in his blood.

Chaos transformed the small space as the remaining faithful attempted to scatter, the terrible realization of their predicament now a full reality. Their exit was blocked by the ruthless violence of an attacking force that showed no mercy for the remaining congregation.

"Madeleine!"

Modesta searched for her child in the melee, but the little girl was already running to reach her mother on the altar. Uncommonly petite at eight years old, Madeleine appeared much younger, which Modesta prayed would be to her advantage.

She had to save her child. She had to save the Book.

Hugging the girl close, Modesta hid the treasure in the folds of Madeleine's dress, pulling her cape over the garment to create further cover. She yelled over the chaos to Brother Timothy.

"Stop! Stop! I will go with you. Please, no more bloodshed."

There was nothing left to stop. The hooded soldiers had slaughtered all the others in attendance, leaving the cavern floor drenched with the blood of the innocent faithful. Brother Timothy sniffed with distaste as he stepped fastidiously over a blood-soaked corpse on the way to capture his quarry.

"Spare the life of this little child," Modesta pleaded with him. "You are a man of God. You cannot visit the sins of the fathers upon the children."

"Is she yours?"

"No. She is of the peasantry, and simple."

Brother Timothy stepped forward to run a lock of the child's dark brown hair through his fingers.

"She does not have the unholy hair that is the mark of your kind. If she did, I would kill her myself. But a female peasant child is hardly worth the effort. Let her go."

He dismissed the girl with a wave and turned his back on the females to assess the carnage.

Modesta hugged Madeleine as the little girl clutched her hands against her tiny body, holding on to the concealed book for dear life. Realizing this time with her daughter would be her last, Modesta whispered in her ear. "Be not afraid, Madeleine. I will love you again. The time returns."

She kissed her daughter quickly and sent the little girl running out of the cavern, watching her go with a tragic mix of maternal pride and unutterable heartbreak.

❂

"My beloved. I would give anything if it were not you in that cell."

Potentian grasped at the bars that separated him from his wife. His time in prison had taken its toll, and he was wasted to flesh and bones. His face and hair were filthy, but to Modesta, he was the most beautiful man in the world. She wished only that she could touch him, but they were both bound and the distance between them in the dank prison was too great.

"And yet we are together, which is a blessing in any form. Do not fear death, my love. We cannot, as we know it is not the end."

Potentian was desperate. "Do not give up. You are kinswoman to Bishop Martin of Tours. We can petition his intervention. He can stop this!"

Modesta sighed her resignation. "My blessed cousin has been unsuccessful in saving heretics, much as he has tried. The Church is most determined to be rid of us, and quickly. Brother Timothy will see us dead before sunset tomorrow."

"And what will become of our Madeleine?"

"She was spared in the massacre. I had to deny her, to say she was not ours. Thanks be to God that it is your coloring she has, or our mourning would be beyond bearing. She will go to my brother. You know he will protect her."

"And the Book? Is it safe?"

"Madeleine hid it in her cloak. She was so brave."

His expression in the low candlelight was full of admiration. "She takes after her mother. By saving the Book, she will be the savior of us all. The teachings of the Way will continue."

Modesta nodded her agreement, before musing out loud.

"The truth is once again saved by a girl child. So has it always been, so shall it ever be."

❊

A somber crowd gathered on the ancient hilltop for the execution, where an ominous wooden chopping block perched atop the scaffold. Two axes leaned against the block, crossed in an *X* formation.

Side by side with hands bound behind them, Modesta and Potentian trudged up the hill. They were surrounded by heavily armed and hooded men, who goaded them to move faster. Modesta's once glorious hair had been hacked off, harshly and unevenly, to expose her delicate neck to the blade that would separate it from her body.

Potentian looked at her, his heart filled with love and sadness. "We shall die as we have taught and lived. Together."

Modesta returned the expression. "And we shall come back to teach together again. As God wills and the time is determined."

Potentian slowed his pace to prolong their precious time together. His wife matched his stride to stay as close to him as possible in these minutes. He whispered his final request.

"Will you sing it for me? One last time?"

Modesta smiled at him, the final earthly gift she could give to her beloved, and began to sing in her sweet voice:

I have loved thee a long time,
Always, I will not forget thee . . .
I have loved thee forever,
God has made us one for the other

As Modesta completed her song, a muscular man with a reddish glint to his hair emerged from the crowd and came toward them, holding Madeleine safely in his arms. Catching a glimpse of her daughter, Modesta froze. Potentian, following the gaze of his wife, stopped beside her. They did not dare acknowledge the child, but in that moment there was a profound exchange of love and loss between this little family.

Madeleine looked at her mother intently, with wisdom well beyond that of any eight-year-old, and nodded. The slightest hint of a smile played at her lips. Her mother, proud and relieved in this terrible moment, managed to smile back just as a hooded guard pushed her roughly from behind and toward the scaffold. Modesta leaned close to her husband and whispered.

"Both of our treasures are safe."

A guard on either side of the chopping block approached to position the prisoners. Modesta asked her question loud enough for the crowd to hear.

"Good sirs, will you allow us just one moment to pray together?"

The guards looked over to where the baleful Brother Timothy stood, squirming in anticipation of the coming spectacle. He was entrapped. As a man of the Church he could not deny a prayer request.

"The Church is merciful and will allow a brief prayer if the heretics wish to repent."

Modesta moved to her husband, turning her face up to him for the final time. In this moment, there was no scaffold, no axe, no terrible injustice. There was only love as they repeated the most sacred prayer of their people in soft unison.

I have loved you before,
I love you today,
And I will love you again.
The time returns.

Modesta reached up to touch her lips to those of her beloved in one soft, ultimate kiss.

"Enough!"

Brother Timothy's ire shattered the moment. Angry now, the guards ripped the couple apart and pushed them to their knees, side by side at the block.

With the deep calm that comes from knowing that only God awaits, both Modesta and Potentian lowered their heads to the block. They continued to pray softly in unison as the first axe fell with a sickening thud. The second followed a moment later.

The crowd did not stir. The sense of mourning and tragedy was thick in the atmosphere. It was not the celebrated execution of heretics that Brother Timothy had hoped for. He allowed his unpopular perspective to ring out: "Let this be a warning to all that heresy will not be tolerated in the Holy Roman Empire!"

The townsfolk dispersed in the wake of this harsh cautionary instruction, faces solemn and more than a little afraid. Brother Timothy ignored them all. He approached the chopping block to address the executioners.

"Do not leave any martyr's relics for the heretics to mourn over. Throw them in the depths of the well. It's the closest I can come to sending them to Hell myself."

Brother Timothy took a long, satisfied look at Modesta's mutilated body as the executioners began their grim task. Obsession overcame his face as he pulled something out of the pocket of his robe surreptitiously: a lock of Modesta's vivid red hair.

With their shepherdess dead, the sheep would be easy to control.

He shoved the fetish back in his pocket and walked through Modesta's pooled blood without looking back.

CHAPTER ONE

New York City
present day

*M*aureen Paschal, ensconced in the six-hundred-thread-count
luxury of the Manhattan hotel room provided by her publisher,
thrashed about in the oversized bed. As restless in her sleep as she was
in her waking life, Maureen had not slept through the night for nearly
two years. Since the unfolding of supernatural events that had led her
to discover the secret gospel of Mary Magdalene, Maureen was a
woman haunted, both in her sleep and in her waking.

When she was fortunate enough to doze for several consecutive
hours, she was plagued by dreams—some surreal and symbolic, others
vivid and literal. In the most disturbing of these recurring dreams she
encountered Jesus Christ, and he spoke cryptically of her promise to
search for a secret book written in his own divine hand, something he
referred to as "the Book of Love." In her waking hours, Maureen was
tormented by these dreamtime experiences; the Book of Love had thus
far proved completely elusive. There were no traceable historical references to such a document other than a handful of vague legends that
emerged in France in the Middle Ages, before disappearing completely.
She had no idea where to begin her quest to fulfill this promise and
find such a phantom. She wasn't even sure what *it* was. And to date,

her Lord was not forthcoming with any clues that would assist her in this search.

Maureen prayed fervently every night that she would not fail in the mission given to her, and that she would somehow be guided to find the starting point for such a strange journey. The supernatural events of her life over the past few years were all the proof she needed that such divinely inspired magic existed all around her. She would just need to be patient in her faith, and wait.

Tonight, her prayers would be answered as the first clue surfaced in the bizarre and surreal world of her dreaming.

�֍

The mist of evening fell gray and heavy on the ancient ruins. Maureen walked through them slowly, thick with the dream and the fog. She was in a monastery of great antiquity, or what was left of it after centuries of desolation. A crumbling wall to her right was once a majestic masterpiece of architecture; it now held the shell of what had been a stained glass window, the Gothic style that is cut into stone as a rose with six petals. The last of the light filtered through tree branches before reaching the skeleton of the ruined window and illuminating the space where Maureen stood. She continued on to where soaring Gothic arches remained, connected to nothing as the walls they once upheld had long ago been reduced to rubble. They were disconnected remnants of a faded and former glory. Once the hallmark of an exquisite and majestic nave, the arches were left now, spare and alone, like haunted doorways to the past.

The last vestiges of light appeared to follow her through this threshold as she emerged into the wreckage of an ancient courtyard. The iridescent beams illuminated a porous stone sculpture of the madonna and child set into the niche of a cobbled wall.

Moving to the sculpture, Maureen ran her fingers gently, curiously, over the cool stone face of the lovely little madonna, who was no more than a child herself in this portrayal. Tradition indicated that the Virgin was a young teenager when she conceived, so perhaps this childlike image was not so unusual. And yet this madonna, with her enigmatic little smile, appeared more like an eight- or nine-year-old girl holding a baby. And the infant was also carved in an unusual way. He appeared to be squirming out of the girl's hands and smiling with the mischief of it all. The sculpture looked more like that of an elder sister attempting to contain her baby brother than that of a mother and her child. Maureen was considering this strange portrayal when the statue spoke to her in the sweet voice of a young girl.

"I am not who you think I am."

In the hallucinogenic and imaginary world of the dream state, it is not unusual for a statue to speak, or even to giggle, as this one did now. Maureen responded, "Then who are you?"

The little girl giggled again—or was it the baby? It was impossible to tell as the sounds were blending together now with the low drone of a church bell tolling through the abbey.

"You will know me soon enough," the child said. "I have much to teach you."

Maureen looked at the statue closely, and then at the stone wall of the niche, then at the ruined arches, trying to take in the details of the abbey. "Where are we?"

The child did not answer. Maureen continued to move through the grounds, stepping carefully through overgrowth and around the large hunks of ruined stone. The moon was rising now, full and bright in the darkening sky. She caught the lunar beams glittering in what appeared to be a pool of water just ahead. Enticed, she moved toward it, through the space in a ruined wall and across the crumbling stone threshold to where the water awaited her. It was a well, or a cistern, wide enough for several men to bathe in at once. Leaning over to gaze at her shimmering reflection in the water, Maureen was struck by the feeling of fathomless depth. This well was sacred and ran deep into the earth.

The little girl spoke again. "In your reflection, you will find what you seek."

Maureen's reflection shifted, and for a brief moment she saw another image, not her own. She reached in to touch the water, and as she did so, the copper ring on her right hand slipped off and fell down into the well.

Maureen screamed.

The ring was her most prized possession. It was an ancient relic from Jerusalem that had been given to her during her search for Mary Magdalene. The size and shape of a penny, it was engraved with an ancient stellar pattern of nine stars set in a circle around a central sun. The pattern was worn by the earliest Christians to remind them that they were not separate from God, and to correlate with the line in the Lord's Prayer "on earth as it is in heaven." The ring was a material symbol of Maureen's newfound faith. That it had fallen irretrievably into the black depth of the water was as heartbreaking as it was shocking.

Kneeling down at the stone edge of the well, Maureen searched, desperate to see if she could catch a glimpse of the ring somewhere within. It was hopeless. She had been right about the depth—it was utterly fathomless. Rising slowly to her feet in resignation, she caught a sudden glimmer of something flashing in the water. Splash! An enormous fish, a type of trout glittering with golden scales, leaped from the water in the well, then back into the depths. Maureen waited to see if the remarkable fish would return. Another splash split the water, and the trout leaped in the air again, this time seeming to move in slow motion. Protruding from the fish's mouth was her copper ring.

Maureen gasped as the fish turned in her direction. He released the ring and sent it sailing toward her. Holding out her hand, she felt the ring drop safely in her open palm. She closed her hand tightly around it and clutched it to her heart, grateful that it had been retrieved by the magical fish, which subsequently retreated into the depths of the well. The water went still, and once again, the magic was gone.

Returning the ring to her right hand, Maureen carefully peered into the well one final time to see if there were any more miracles to be had in this strange monastery. The water was quite still, and then the tiniest ripple broke the surface. A wave of golden light began to suffuse the well and the area surrounding it. As she looked into the water, an image began to take shape. The scene was a beautiful valley, lush and green with trees and flowers. She watched as a rain of golden drops fell from the sky, gilding everything in the vision. Soon the valley was flowing with rivers of gold, and the trees were covered with it. Everything glittered all around her with the rich warm light of liquid ore.

In the distance she heard the girlish voice, the same that had emanated from the impish little madonna.

"Do you seek the Book of Love? Then welcome to the Vale of Gold. Here you will find what you seek."

The sweet giggle was heard once again, as the vision faded, returning Maureen once and for all to the darkened ruins of a mysterious abbey in the moonlight. It was the last thing she heard before the alarm went off in the twenty-first century, returning her to a predawn New York City.

Early morning network television is not for the faint of heart.

The tap on Maureen's hotel suite door at precisely 4:00 a.m. was the hair and makeup artist who had been hired to prepare her for an interview on one of the popular national morning shows. Thankfully, the woman was sympathetic to Maureen's sleeplessness and had the presence of mind to alert room service to the need for coffee before making her way upstairs.

Maureen Paschal was in New York on the heels of her international best-selling novel, *The Truth Against the World: The Secret Gospel of Mary Magdalene*. Based on her own life experiences, the book merged Maureen's personal journey of discovery with the often shocking revelations of Mary Magdalene's life as the most beloved disciple of Jesus. Although she was an accomplished journalist and successful nonfiction author, Maureen had elected to write this book as fiction, which in itself was the subject of controversy. The press was relentlessly skeptical, even mocking. Why, if this story was based in fact, did she decide to write it as fiction?

Maureen's answer to this perpetual question, while honest, was unsatisfying to the ravenous international press. She answered the same questions on talk shows the world over, explained as patiently as her increasingly frayed nerves would allow that she had to protect her sources for reasons of their safety, and her own. When she recounted how her own life had been endangered during the search for this ancient treasure, she was widely ridiculed and accused of exaggerating, even lying, for the sake of publicity.

In the press whirlwind that followed *The Truth Against the World*, all semblance of peace and privacy in her life had evaporated. Maureen was exposed to every kind of public scrutiny—the good, the bad, and the truly awful. She received both commendations for her courage and death threats for her blasphemy, with just about every other reaction in between.

Nevertheless, *The Truth Against the World* had captured the popular imagination. While critics and the press found attacking Maureen made sensational copy, a growing worldwide readership was responding to the achingly human story of the life of Jesus as told from the perspective of Mary Magdalene. Maureen was unapologetic in insisting that Jesus and Mary Magdalene were legally husband and wife, that they had children, and that they ministered together—and that none of these things in any way diminished the divinity of Jesus. The values of love, faith, forgiveness, and community were the cornerstones of Jesus' teachings, and yet the attacks against her book in the name of religion dismissed or overlooked her real message in order to focus on its controversial messenger. During her research, Maureen had almost been killed by those who wished this gospel's message to remain secret, so she needed no one to assure her of its authenticity.

Still, Maureen was happy that her book was proving to be popular with men and women the world over who felt they had been let down by traditional religious institutions that were more focused on politics, power, economics, and even war than they were on true spirituality.

Maureen was satisfied with the book and with the story as she had told it, and she was certainly fulfilled by the flood of supportive mail that she received from around the globe. Each letter she received from a reader who emphasized that "Mary Magdalene brought me back to Jesus" fortified her and increased her own faith. Yet she struggled daily with the responsibility of communicating the true story of Mary

Magdalene as she had discovered it in a way that would do justice to the material, to reach still more people who remained skeptical. This was the reason for her appearance on television this morning.

While the press junket around her book had been something of a circus, Maureen had higher hopes for this morning's interview. The producers had done due diligence, interviewing her extensively in advance, asking truly intelligent questions, and even sending a camera crew to her home in Los Angeles for background information. If nothing else, she believed that this time there was at least a chance that the questions asked of her would be fair and informed.

She was not disappointed. The interview was conducted by one of the show's anchors, a national personality known for her intelligence and poise. She could be tough, but she was fair. And she had done her own homework, which impressed Maureen.

The setup for the piece showed photographs of Maureen around the world, doing research on the life of Mary Magdalene. Here she was on the Via Dolorosa in Jerusalem, here she was climbing the peak of Montségur in southwestern France. These images created the lead-in to the first question.

"Maureen, you write about an alleged lost gospel of Mary Magdalene that was discovered in the south of France, and the cultures in France that believe Mary Magdalene settled there following the crucifixion. Yet you have been attacked by highly regarded biblical scholars here in America who insist that there is no evidence of any of this. They insist that there is no proof that Mary Magdalene was ever even in France. How do you respond to them?"

Maureen was grateful for the question. Newspapers and magazines always gave scholars the last word. Virtually every article written about her closed with some academic somewhere discrediting her with customary scholarly disdain, saying that there was no proof and that all these legends surrounding Mary Magdalene had less substance than most fairy tales. Maureen decided to pull no punches while she had the opportunity finally to answer her critics on national television.

"If scholars are looking for the evidence in their ivory towers, conveniently written in English and accessible through their air-conditioned libraries, then they certainly won't find it. The kind of proof that I seek is more organic, human, and real. It comes from the people and the cultures who live these stories, who incorporate them into their lives every day. To say that these traditions don't exist or don't matter is dangerous—perhaps even xenophobic and racist."

"Whoa!" The anchor reeled in her chair. "Don't you think those are pretty harsh words?"

"No, I think they're necessary. There were entire cultures in the south of France and areas of Italy that were eradicated for believing exactly what is in my book. They believed that they were descended from Jesus and Mary, and they practiced a beautifully pure form of Christianity that they claimed came directly from Jesus himself, brought to them by Mary Magdalene following the crucifixion."

"You're talking about the Cathars."

"Yes. *Cathar* comes from the Greek word for 'purity,' as these people were the purest Christians to live in the Western world. And in the only crusade ever declared against other Christians, the Catholic Church of the thirteenth century massacred the Cathar people en masse. The Inquisition was founded to destroy the Cathars. These people had to be eliminated because they didn't just know the truth, they *were* the truth. And make no mistake, it was ethnic cleansing. Genocide. Harsh words? Of course they are. But butchering an entire people is harsh, and we can't hide behind words that try to justify it anymore. The word *crusade* carries a connotation that it was somehow acceptable to murder people in the name of God. So let's stop calling it that and call it what it was. Mass murder. A holocaust."

"So when you hear modern scholars say that these people don't exist or that the traditions of their culture don't matter—"

"It breaks my heart to think that such evil has the last word. *Of course* there's very little physical proof left of Mary Magdalene's presence. Over eight hundred thousand people were slaughtered to ensure that there would be no physical proof left to find. Ever. And the worst of the massacres took place on July twenty-second in 1209 and a year later in 1210. That's Mary Magdalene's feast day, and it's not a coincidence. Inquisition documents from that time indicated that it was 'just retribution for these people who believed that the whore was married to Jesus.' "

"Which brings me to the question on everybody's lips. You claim that the story you tell about Jesus marrying Mary Magdalene comes from a lost gospel you recently discovered in the south of France. Yet you refuse to divulge your sources or tell any more about this mysterious document. What are we to make of this? Your harshest critics say that you have invented the entire story. Why should we believe you when you don't come forth with more proof that this gospel even exists?"

This question was tough but important, and Maureen had to answer it with great care. What she could not yet reveal to the world was the rest of the story: that the gospel had been taken to Rome by her own cousin, Father Peter Healy. Father Peter and a Vatican committee were now working to authenticate the gospel. Until the Church ruled officially on the priceless manuscript, which could take years given its explosive content and the ramifications for Christianity, Maureen had agreed not to divulge any of the facts surrounding its discovery. In return, she had been allowed to tell her version of Mary Magdalene's story without fear of reprisals—if and only if she phrased it as fiction for the time being. It was a compromise she had had to make, but one that cost her dearly. She felt real sisterhood with Cassandra, the prophetess of Greek legend: doomed to know and tell the truth, yet equally doomed never to be believed.

Maureen took a breath and answered the question to the best of her ability.

"I have to protect the people who aided in the discovery. And there is a lot more information to be revealed, so I can't risk those sources at any cost if I want to continue to have access to them. Because I can't disclose the sources behind my information, I had to write this book as fiction. I am hoping that the story will speak for itself. My job as a storyteller is to awaken audiences to the idea of alternate possibilities to one of humanity's greatest stories. This is why I call it the greatest story never told. And certainly, I believe it to be the truth with all my heart. But let people read it and judge it on its own merits. Let readers decide if it feels like the truth to them."

"We'll leave it at that—let the reader decide." The lovely blond anchor was holding up a copy of the book. "*The Truth Against the World* indeed. Thank you, Maureen Paschal, for joining us. A fascinating subject to be sure, but I'm afraid we're out of time."

It is the great dichotomy of television that it takes many hours to prepare for a segment that lasts three or four minutes. Still, Maureen was satisfied that she had made her points succinctly and forcefully and was grateful to both the producers and the anchor for their fair and intelligent treatment of the subject.

Now it was all of 7:15 a.m. and Maureen was dressed, made-up, and coiffed to the nines—and wanted nothing more than to go back to bed.

*Marie de Negre shall choose
when the time is come for The Expected One.
She who is born of the paschal lamb
when the day and night are equal,
she who is a child of the resurrection.
She who carries the Sangre-El will be granted the key
upon viewing the Black Day of the Skull.
She will become the new Shepherdess of The Way.*

THE FIRST PROPHECY OF *L'ATTENDUE*, THE EXPECTED ONE,
FROM THE WRITINGS OF SARAH-TAMAR,
AS PRESERVED IN THE LIBRO ROSSO

Château des Pommes Bleues
Arques, France
present day

BÉRENGER SINCLAIR stood before the encased artifact that dominated his expansive library. The case was mounted above a massive stone fireplace, the hearth currently dormant owing to the late spring warmth that had come to the rocky foothills of the Languedoc. Lord Sinclair was a collector of the highest order. He was a man gifted with the political power and financial resources to obtain most anything he desired. The object in this case was of immense value to him not only because he was a serious collector of historical pieces, but because it was a symbol of his deeply held spiritual beliefs.

To the casual eye it could have been any medieval banner, tattered and faded almost beyond identification. The bloodstains that lined the edges had turned a muddy shade of brown, over five and a half centuries since the soldier who carried this banner had been put to death. Her death.

Closer inspection of the fabric showed what had once been a richly embroidered motto emblazoned across a background of golden fleurs-de-lis. It was a simple yet powerful conjunction of names that read "Jhesus-Maria." The bold and visionary soldier who had carried this banner was executed for heresy, burned at the stake until dead in the town square of Rouen in 1431. While the official records of her trial indicate a number of convenient charges created by the Church leaders in France at the time, this banner represented her true crime: belief that Jesus had been married to Mary Magdalene, belief that their descendants belonged on the throne of France at any cost, and the subsequent conviction that the original and pure practices of Christianity could be restored under the appropriate king. This was the reason that the names were connected: they were the names of man and wife, conjoined in love and law.

What God has put together, let no man tear asunder. Jhesus-Maria.

This was the banner carried by Saint Joan in the siege of Orléans, the standard of the maid of Lorraine, the emblem of the visionary soldier known to the world as Joan of Arc. Beneath the case inscribed in gold was one of the saint's more famous quotes. For a girl of nineteen, she had been astonishingly eloquent. And uniquely courageous.

> *I am not afraid . . . I was born to do this. I would rather die than do something which I know to be against God's will.*

Bérenger Sinclair ran his hands through his thick, dark hair as he stood before the artifact in careful thought. On days like this, when he was tired and strained, he came into his library to pay homage to this brave teenage girl who had been instilled with a faith so great that she feared nothing and sacrificed everything. She inspired him and gave him strength.

He felt a strange closeness to her, for reasons that were complicated within his family and tradition. History recorded that Joan was born on the sixth day of January, although insiders within his heretical culture knew that this was not true. Joan's actual birth at the vernal equinox had to be obscured to protect her from the dangerous and watchful eyes of the medieval Church. Specifically, she had to be shielded from those who monitored female children from select French families who were born on or near the vernal equinox. January the sixth had been chosen as a "safe" date for Joan's birth; it was celebrated on the liturgical calendar as the feast day of the Epiphany, the day when light comes to the world. Bérenger knew this well, as it was his own birthday.

Sadly, obscuring her birth date had not saved the little maid of Lorraine from her fate. For some, destiny is inescapable. Joan had embraced her legacy as the daughter of a potent prophecy, all too publicly.

The prophecy, referred to as *l'Attendue* in French and translated into English as "The Expected One," referred to a series of women in history who would come forward and preserve the truth—the truth about Jesus and Mary Magdalene and about the gospels that were authored by each of them separately. According to the prophecy, these Expected Ones would be born within a certain period surrounding the vernal equinox, come from a specific bloodline, and be blessed with holy visions that would lead each to the truth, and to her destiny.

As The Expected One of her time, Saint Joan paid the ultimate price, as many others had before and since.

And that was why he was here, in the library today, in contemplation before Joan's precious artifact. Because he knew in his heart that it was time for him to fulfill his own legacy. For this was where he held something else in common with brave Joan: he had his own prophecy to contend with. And he knew that God had given him extraordinary resources to do just that, knew that all the blessings he had accumulated in his life were provided so that he might fulfill his own promise, in this place and this time in history. He had done this by aiding Maureen in her search, playing an integral role in the discovery of Mary Magdalene's magnificent, untold story. But that treasured gospel was now out of his reach and in the hands of the Church. Further, it appeared that Maureen was also out of his reach. While he knew he had the ability to assist in her latest quest for the illusory Book of Love, she did not currently share that sentiment.

It was his own fault that Maureen did not want to include him in this. After the Church commandeered the gospel, Bérenger had behaved like an insensitive dolt toward her, something for which he now did heavy penance.

At a loss to determine exactly what his role was currently, he was feeling rudderless and alone. This thing called destiny was a complex and often inscrutable taskmaster.

"Bérenger, may I speak to you?"

Turning to the door, Bérenger smiled at the hulking, masculine form of Roland Gélis, his closest friend and confidant. Roland had lived at the château since he was a child, when his father was majordomo during the life of Alistair Sinclair, Bérenger's grandfather and the fearsome family patriarch who built a billion-dollar fortune in North Sea oil. Together, the boys had been raised in the traditions of *Pommes Bleues*, the French phrase that translated to "blue apples." It was a reference to the large, round grapes found in that region of

France, grapes that, for centuries, had represented the bloodline of Jesus and Mary Magdalene. The association was derived from the verse in John fifteen, "I am the vine and you are the branches." All descendants of Jesus and Mary Magdalene, either genetically or spiritually, were branches of the vine. The Languedoc was high heretic country.

Though the Gélis family had worked in service to the Sinclairs for several generations, they were not subservient. They were nobility in their own right, in the quiet way that so many families in the Languedoc and Midi-Pyrenees region were, carrying the secret traditions of their people with extraordinary grace and dignity, even when subjected to the greatest persecutions. The Gélises were of Cathar heritage, and they were pure.

"Of course, Roland. Come in."

Roland sensed immediately that the Scotsman was not himself.

"What is bothering you, brother?"

Bérenger shook his head. "Nothing. Everything." He took a breath and managed to look embarrassed as he confessed, "I fear I am something of a lost sheep without my shepherdess."

"Ah." Roland understood immediately. Bérenger had been self-flagellating over Maureen since the argument that had trounced their fledgling relationship before it had ever had time to grow. Prior to that explosion, they had all assumed that given the immense adventure they shared during the search for Magdalene's lost gospel, they would remain inseparable: Bérenger Sinclair and Maureen Paschal, Roland Gélis and Tamara Wisdom, who was Maureen's best friend and Roland's fiancée. They were the Four Musketeers, bound by honor and a common mission—to defend the truth against the world. They had even installed a wood plaque inscribed with the famous quote from D'Artagnan over the library door:

ALL FOR ONE, ONE FOR ALL—THAT IS OUR MOTTO, IS IT NOT?

But when Maureen returned to California to work on her book, some of that intimacy began to erode. Maureen was consumed with the passion to tell Magdalene's story, and to chronicle their adventures in finding it while they were still so fresh in her mind. That was her mission and Bérenger respected her for it. They had all left her alone and hoped she would return to the château when she was ready. But since the release of the book, Maureen was busier than she had ever been. She had time only for the work that Mary had given her.

And then there was Peter.

Father Peter Healy was Maureen's cousin and closest confidant. He was also the reason for the crack in the foundation of Bérenger's relationship with Maureen. It was Peter who had stolen the Magdalene gospel and taken it to the Vatican. This betrayal had shocked them all, but Maureen had forgiven Peter quickly. She had defended him to the others, saying that he had only done what he felt in his heart was best for Mary Magdalene's message. Still, Bérenger believed that the priest's loyalties pointed far more clearly to the Vatican than to Maureen and the truth that she had uncovered.

The events that followed outraged Bérenger Sinclair. The Church tightened the restrictions on what Maureen was and was not able to reveal regarding her discovery of what they referred to as the Arques Gospel. Bérenger blamed Peter for surrendering the priceless document to the Vatican in the first place and putting Maureen in a position that forced her to compromise. Further, he was increasingly frustrated by the distance that separated him from Maureen and annoyed by what often felt like her blind loyalty to Peter. In the most heated argument of their relationship, a frustrated Bérenger accused Maureen of spiritual weakness for allowing Peter and his Church to walk all over her and suppress the truth. Maureen was shattered by his accusation. The crack in their relationship had become a chasm.

When Bérenger Sinclair met Maureen Paschal, he believed he had discovered something he had searched for yet despaired of ever finding: the woman who was his equal. Maureen was his one and only soul mate, the partner who could not only share in his visions of a better world but who had the passion and the courage to make those changes with him. There was tremendous strength in that petite body, and like him, she possessed a Celtic warrior's spirit that was an uncommon force of nature. Thus his accusation of weakness cut her to the core in a way that he was keenly able to understand. He often had reason to repent the Celtic aspects of his own nature, particularly when his passion manifested itself in the warrior's approach favored by his Scottish ancestors. His DNA was a double-edged sword, as was Maureen's. That they were so alike in their heritage and spirit was equal parts blessing and curse as they tried to forge a relationship. If they could learn to work together in harmony and harness their shared passions for the work and for each other, they could create an unstoppable energy toward positive change in the world. But those same passions had the power to be singularly destructive.

That Maureen had included his name most tenderly in the dedication to her book, alongside those of Tamara and Roland, was the only thing that had made Bérenger Sinclair truly smile since the argument that had separated them.

"I pray that we will see Maureen soon," Roland said in his gentle way. "And something has just occurred that makes me believe that it might be sooner than we think."

"What? What happened?"

Roland smiled at him. "Tamara has just received a strange package, addressed to you. Stay here. We will bring it to you. But while you're here"—Roland pointed to the far library wall where the Sinclairs' illustrious family tree, painted from floor to ceiling, spanned a thousand years of history—"take a close look at the mural of your family's lineage."

And so it was that the Queen of the South became known as the Queen of Sheba, which was to say, the Wise Queen of the people of Sabea. Her given name was Makeda, which in her own tongue was "the fiery one." She was a priestess-queen, dedicated to a goddess of the sun who was known to shine beauty and abundance upon the joyous people known as Sabeans. Their goddess was known as "she who

sends forth her strong rays of benevolence." Her consort was the moon god and the stars were their children.

The people of Sabea were wise above most others in the world, with an understanding of the influence of the stars and the sanctity of numbers that came from their heavenly deities. They were called the People of Architecture, and their structures rivaled those of the greatest Egyptians, so astonishing was their understanding of building in stone. The queen was the founder of great schools to teach such art and architecture, and the sculptors that served her were able to create images of gods and men in stone that were of exceptional beauty. Her people were literate and committed to the written word and the glory of writing. Poetry and song flourished within her compassionate realm.

A virtuous people were the Sabeans. Their fiery sun queen reigned in her kingdom with warmth, light, and love, and they were therefore possessed of every kind of abundance: love, joy, fertility, wisdom, as well as all the gold and jewels anyone could require. Because they never doubted the existence of abundance, they never knew a day of want. It was the most golden of kingdoms.

It came to pass that the great King Solomon learned of this unparalleled Queen Makeda by virtue of a prophet who advised him, "A woman who is your equal and counterpart reigns in a faraway land of the South. You would learn much from her, and she from you. Meeting her is your destiny." Solomon did not, at first, believe that such a woman could exist, but his curiosity caused him to send an invitation for her, a request to visit his own kingdom on holy Mount Sion. The messengers who came to Sabea to advise the great and fiery Queen Makeda of Solomon's invitation discovered that his wisdom was already legendary in her land, as was the splendor of his court, and she had awareness of him. Her own prophetesses had foreseen that she would one day travel far to find the king with whom she would perform the hieros-gamos, the sacred marriage that combined the body with the mind and spirit in the act of divine union. He would be the twin brother of her soul, and she would become his sister-bride, halves of the same whole, complete only in their coming together.

But the Queen of Sheba was not a woman easily won and would not give herself in so sacred a union to any but the man she would recognize as a part of her soul. As she made the great trek to Mount Sion with her camel train, Makeda devised a series of tests and questions that she would put to the king. His answers to *these would help her to determine if he was her equal, her own soul's twin, conceived as one at the dawn of eternity.*

For those with ears to hear, let them hear it.

THE LEGEND OF SOLOMON AND SHEBA,
PART ONE, AS PRESERVED IN THE LIBRO ROSSO

Château des Pommes Bleues
Arques, France
present day

BÉRENGER, ROLAND, AND TAMMY sat around the large mahogany table in the library. The object of their scrutiny was what appeared to be an ancient document, a long scroll on a type of parchment that was badly deteriorated with age. The scroll was sandwiched between two panes of glass in an effort to preserve it and to hold together the crumbling segments of what looked like a medieval jigsaw puzzle.

The box containing the fragile document had been delivered in the early morning to the château, addressed to Bérenger Sinclair in care of the Society of Blue Apples, and left by an anonymous courier who did not wait to be identified. The housekeeper who received the package said she believed the courier may have been Italian because of his clothing, car, and accent, but she was uncertain. He was most assuredly not local.

"It's a family tree," Tammy commented first, as she ran her hand from the name at the top of the glass. "There's some Latin here at the top, and then it starts with this man. Guidone someone or other. Born in 1077 in Mantua, Italy."

Bérenger, gifted with an aristocrat's classical education, squinted to read the fading Latin at the top of the scroll. "It looks like it says 'I, Matilda . . . ' At least, I think it says Matilda. Yes, it does. It says, 'I, Matilda, by the Grace of God Who Is.' Strange phrasing, but that's what it says. The next sentence says, 'I am united and inseparable with the

Count Guidone and his son, Guido Guerra, and offer them the protection of Tuscany in perpetuity.' And it says that this son Guido Guerra was born in Florence at a monastery called Santa Trinità. Why would the son of a count be born in a monastery? It's . . . odd."

"It's not the only thing that's odd," Roland commented. As he did so, he pointed out a name on the lineage. "Look at these names, Bérenger."

Bérenger stopped short as he followed Roland's finger on the glass. On a line from the thirteenth century, there were names he recognized. A French knight by the name of Luc Saint Clair married a Tuscan noblewoman. The same names were listed in his own family genealogy as his own ancestors. But this would not be common knowledge outside their immediate and protected circle. Whoever sent this package knew, at the very least, that it had relevance to Bérenger Sinclair and that somehow these family trees intersected.

Tammy's attention was drawn to a card that was enclosed with the document and tied to a tiny, gilded hand mirror. The paper on the card was elegant, a heavy parchment, embossed with a strange monogram at the bottom center. A capital letter *A* was tied to a capital letter *E* by a tasseled rope that knotted in the center of both letters. That in itself was not so unusual; what made the monogram strange was that the *E* was facing backwards, almost as a mirror image of the *A*. The card was inscribed with a handwritten poem of sorts:

Art Will Save the World,
For those with eyes to see.
In your reflection, you will find what you seek . . .
Hail Ichthys!

"Art will save the world," Tammy repeated. "We've seen this concept in action a few times." In their search for Mary Magdalene's lost gospel, the four of them had deciphered a series of maps and clues found within European paintings from the Middle Ages and the Renaissance and Baroque periods. It had been a map painted into a fresco by Sandro Botticelli that led Maureen to find the priceless documents written in Mary Magdalene's own hand. In the complex world of Christian esoterica, searching for symbols in art was the starting point for many a great journey. When the truth could not be told in writing for fear of fatal persecution, it had often been encoded in symbolic paintings.

Bérenger picked up the mirror and looked in it briefly before repeating the third sentence of the poem. "In your reflection, you will find what you seek. Hmm." He did not have time to consider this further, as Roland interrupted him, uncharacteristically animated by what had caught his eye.

"Look at this!" Roland was pointing to the bottom of the document. "The last name on the lineage. Am I seeing this clearly?"

Tammy put her arm around him as she leaned in to see what generated the excitement in the gentle giant. But it was Bérenger who verified it for all of them as he peered carefully at the final name at the end of the family tree, arguably the greatest name in the history of the art world.

"Michelangelo Buonarroti."

Chapter Two

New York City
present day

"*M*aureen! Ms. Paschal . . ."

Maureen entered through the revolving door off Forty-seventh Street and into the lobby of her hotel where Nate, the bell captain, recognized her. Her publisher and publicist often left packages for her here and vice versa, so she and Nate had become fast friends on a first-name basis. Maureen tipped well and Nate was vocal in his appreciation for redheads; it was a good combination for a working relationship in New York City.

"There was a package delivered for you this evening. I just got in and noticed it in the back room."

Nate emerged from the back, balancing an elegant gift box in both hands. It was easily two feet long, flat and deepest red in color. Affixed to the box with wide scarlet satin ribbon was a huge bouquet of white flowers, fragrant Casablanca lilies mixed with long-stemmed white roses.

Maureen looked over the box carefully before taking it from him. "Was there a card?"

Nate shook his head. "No, nothing. Sorry."

Maureen smiled at Nate and thanked him, anxious to get upstairs and see what the red box contained.

She was still smiling as she entered her room, intoxicated by the heavenly scent of the lilies. There was only one man in the world who knew that these were her favorite flowers, because lilies and roses were symbolic of Mary Magdalene. There was only one man who would have sent such an elaborate display.

Bérenger Sinclair.

In spite of herself, Maureen felt that nearly indescribable electric thrill that runs up the spine and covers the skin with goose bumps. God help her, she was still madly infatuated with him, if not in love, and who would blame her? He was good-looking in that darkly charismatic Celtic way, charming, brilliant, *and* extraordinarily wealthy and powerful. But he was also infuriating in his arrogance and had displayed a propensity toward being harsh and judgmental. Bérenger had wounded her deeply, which was something she could not allow to happen again anytime soon.

Still, after all they had been through together, he understood her more than any other man on earth.

Throughout Maureen's quest, Bérenger had protected her, sheltered her, and even educated her in the folklore and traditions that surrounded the Magdalene mysteries in France. There was no doubt that he had dramatically influenced and altered her life, no doubt that they were inextricably connected in their destinies. However, everything about him was potentially dangerous. Bérenger was a notorious European playboy and a confirmed bachelor. At the age of fifty, he had never been married and had never been inclined toward a serious commitment of any kind that she was aware of. He explained his years of bachelorhood as not wanting to settle for any woman who was not expressly made for him. Upon meeting Maureen, he said, he was certain. She was the one, the reason no other woman had ever held his interest.

It was a pretty explanation. Perhaps too pretty. There were a lot of warning signs with a man like Bérenger, even prior to their terrible argument. He had apologized, but Maureen remained wary.

And yet her stomach turned over at the thought that these flowers had come from him.

Untying the ribbon carefully, Maureen removed the blooms and lifted the lid on the box. There was a card in a sealed envelope that read "Miss Paschal." Strange, Bérenger would not address her that way. Perhaps it was simply the florist's formality. Maureen looked back down into the box and removed the tissue paper that covered the contents. She wasn't sure what she had expected, but it was most certainly not this. Contained within was what appeared to be an ancient document. Whether it was real or a replica was impossible to tell at first. However, it was carefully encased between panes of glass: some effort had been taken to protect it. Gently, Maureen lifted it out of the box. It was nearly two feet long, terribly yellowed with time or else a very good copy, and frayed around the uneven edges.

The text of the document, written in a flowery yet exacting Latin script, filled three quarters of the page. Glancing through it, noting the ancient form and the elaborate handwriting, Maureen didn't think she would be able to decipher it. Her Latin was serviceable, but this was a challenge for a scholar with skills far beyond her rudimentary vocabulary.

It was the signature at the bottom that was most arresting. Bold and elaborate, it was clearly hand-drawn with ink, and yet it resembled a seal of some type, with a Latin cross drawn between the letters:

Maureen took out her Moleskine notebook and wrote out the letters from the medieval signature in a linear way. It read

MATILDA DEI GRA SI QUO EST

It appeared to say "Matilda, by the Grace of God Who Is."

Beneath the letters there were two additional symbols: one looked like a stylized version of the letter *H*, if the vertical lines were wavy; the other looked immediately familiar to Maureen. Her hand flew to the necklace she was wearing, a gift from Bérenger on her last birthday. It was a delicate diamond-encrusted symbol, a spiral of ram's horns—the astrological glyph for the sign Aries. Maureen was born on the twenty-second day of March, in the first degree of the first zodiac sign on the edge of the vernal equinox, as the sun passed through Pisces and entered Aries. The symbol of ram's horns had been emblematic of the vernal equinox since antiquity. But what could it mean on this document? And the more pressing questions, who sent this to her and why?

Maureen opened the card carefully. The elegant paper was embossed with a strange monogram at the bottom. A capital letter *A* was tied to a capital letter *E*, the letter *E* facing backwards as in a mirror image. The card was handwritten:

> *As you travel through the Land of Flowers,*
> *You will come upon the Vale of Gold.*
> *Do you seek the Book of Love?*
> *Then here you will find what you seek . . .*
> *Hail Ichthys!*

Maureen sighed, half with relief and half with agitation. This was how her search for Mary Magdalene's gospel had begun—with a strange gift and a mystery to be solved. She had prayed for clues, and now they were appearing. Clearly, whoever sent this knew something of her personal history, which was a little disconcerting. That the phrasing on the card was identical to the words spoken by the little madonna in her dream was downright disturbing. She shuddered at the strange intimacy of such a note. While she had faith that she would be guided by God on her path, as she had always been, there was something unmistakably ominous about an unknown correspondent who could see into her dreams. Was it possible that someone was actually influencing them? She wasn't sure which of those scenarios was more menacing, but both worried her.

She did the only thing she could think of to do. She got down on her knees and prayed for protection and guidance on the journey that was about to commence.

❖

Maureen did a quick mental inventory. There were only three people in the world she could consult with on this immediate mystery, all of them in Europe. The first was her cousin, Peter Healy, the Jesuit scholar who was currently based in the Vatican. Peter would be able to translate the document and perhaps even identify it. Maureen was willing to bet that whoever sent the mystery package was well aware of her relation to such a resource. Otherwise, they likely wouldn't have left her to her own devices to translate something so elaborate. She would call Peter, of course, although she knew that his first reaction would be to worry. Better to do a little more investigation before dumping this on him quite so blindly.

That left Bérenger Sinclair and Tamara Wisdom, both currently in residence at the Pommes Bleues headquarters in the Languedoc. Bérenger, like Peter, would immediately worry and demand that she come to France while he investigated. That was not the reaction she wanted or needed at the moment.

That left Tammy.

Tamara was Maureen's closest friend, confidante, and partner in heresy. A brilliant and acerbic independent filmmaker from L.A., Tammy had lost her heart while making a documentary about the Magdalene legends in France—both to the magnificent landscape and to the gentle Languedoc giant named Roland Gélis, to whom she was now engaged. Tamara, Roland, and Bérenger all lived in the magnificent Château des Pommes Bleues, the French estate of the Scottish Sinclair family that served as headquarters to their beloved society of the same name. While a call to one was a call to all, perhaps Maureen could get Tammy on her own by ringing her cell phone first.

Midnight in New York. That made it six a.m. in France. It was early, but this was important. She dialed Tammy's cell number and heard the international double ring on the other end. Then a click as Tammy answered, not sounding the least bit sleepy as she quipped, "Hail Ichthys!"

"You got one too?"

"Addressed to Bérenger. It arrived last night."

"An ancient document about someone named Matilda?"

"That would be the Countess Matilda of Tuscany."

"You know this Matilda?"

"Yes, and so do you. She shows up in esoteric legends throughout Europe. A type of warrior queen who ruled half of Italy. And most important for our purposes, she was the founder of the Abbey of Orval."

Maureen gasped. There were two major revelations in Tammy's last sentence. She would deal first with the one that pertained to the clue in her card. "Orval. Or-Val. It means Golden Valley, right? As in, 'You will come upon the Vale of Gold'?"

"Yes. You realize that this means we have half the puzzle and you have the other half. Clearly somebody wants us to work on this together. Or perhaps I should say that someone wants you and Bérenger to work together, given that the packages were addressed to the two of you. Significant?"

Maureen ignored Tammy's implication momentarily and returned her attention to a more pressing issue. "Orval. As in . . . the Orval prophecy?"

Tammy laughed. "But of course, my petite Expected One. It looks like someone wants us to go to Belgium to get a closer look at your own personal prophecy. How fast can you get here?"

Maureen sighed with the realization that the call to adventure must be heeded. There would be no turning back. First she would call Peter in Rome and fill him in on the events of the last twenty-four hours before making arrangements to ship the document to him overnight. Then she would call Air France and get a flight out to Toulouse.

France. Bérenger. Complicated.

❁

Restless sleep came to Maureen that night, and brought with it another dream. It was the recurring theme that had been haunting her for some time. But tonight it was longer and more complete than ever before.

❁

A figure in shadow huddled over an ancient table, the scratching of a stylus as words and images flowed from an author's pen. As she watched over the shoulder of the writer, an azure glow seemed to emanate from these pages. Fixated on the illumination shining from the writing, Maureen didn't see the writer move at first. As the figure arose and stepped forward into the lamplight, Maureen caught her breath.

She had been given glimpses of this face in previous dreams, fleeting moments of recognition that were over in an instant. He now fixed the full force of his attention on Maureen. Frozen in the dream state, she stared at the man ahead of her. The most beautiful man she had ever seen.

Easa.

That was the name by which Mary Magdalene referred to him in her gospel, and therefore the name which Maureen felt most comfortable with. It was in finding Easa through the eyes of Mary Magdalene that she discovered her own faith. To the rest of the modern world, he was Jesus.

He smiled at her then, an expression of such divinity and warmth that Maureen was suffused with it, as if the sun itself radiated from that simple expression. She remained motionless, unable to do anything but stare at his beauty and grace.

"You are my daughter, in whom I am well pleased."

His voice was a melody, a song of unity and love that resonated in the air around her. She floated on that music for an eternal moment, before crashing down to the sound of his next words.

"But your work is not yet finished."

With another smile, Easa the Nazarene, the Son of Man, turned back to the table where his own writing rested. Light from the pages grew brighter, letters shimmering with indigo light, blue and violet patterns on the heavy, linenlike paper.

Maureen tried to speak to him, but the words would not come through. She could only watch the divine being before her as he gestured to the pages and spoke with gentle precision.

"Behold, the Book of Love. Follow the path that has been laid out for you, and you will find what you seek. Once you have found it, you must share it with the world and fulfill the promise that you made. Our truth has been in darkness for too long. Try to remember that destiny and destination come from the same root."

Although his speech was definite, his words were a mystery.

Easa held her gaze for an eternal moment before rising to glide effortlessly across the space that separated them. He came to stand directly in front of Maureen, paralyzing her with his intense, dark eyes.

"The time returns. If you remember nothing more when you awaken, remember those three words."

Maureen was struggling in the dream, desperate to hold on to everything he was saying. She tried to repeat the three words. This time, speech did not elude her. She managed to whisper in response, "The time returns."

Easa rewarded her by leaning forward and placing a single, paternal kiss on the top of her head.

"Awaken now, my child. You must awaken while in this body, for everything exists within it. And be not afraid, for I am with you always. Now go forth without fear and do all things with love. Be ye therefore perfect."

Maureen awakened with a start, gasping for air as she reached for the bedside lamp to bring light into the room as quickly as possible. Her heart was pounding in her chest as she reached for her notebook where it lay on the nightstand. She scribbled his words as quickly as they came, starting with his reference to the Book of Love, and praying that she wasn't forgetting anything. She underlined the sentence "*Destiny* and *destination* come from the same root." What could that possibly mean? She shook her head at the near absurdity of it: Jesus was giving her a lesson in etymology.

There, again, was mention of a promise. Keeping a promise she made? When? In this lifetime? Another? She was relatively certain that she didn't believe in reincarnation, and more certain that such a concept was contrary to Christian teachings. What else could it mean? A promise made before she was born?

Maureen reflected on the blue light for a moment. It was shining from the pages, as if Easa's words had a life of their own and it was contained within this gorgeous, shimmering indigo-violet color. Something pulled at Maureen's consciousness: this light, this color was important somehow. It was something she needed to understand, but the meaning was a mystery to her in this time and place.

She wrote, "Be ye therefore perfect." This sounded like scripture. She'd turn that over to Peter; he'd know instantly if it was or not. But the line that preceded it certainly did not appear typical of scripture: "You must awaken while in this body, for everything exists within it."

She turned another page and wrote in large, emphatic letters

THE TIME RETURNS.

She looked at her notes again, realizing that she had forgotten one sentence. While Easa's other words puzzled her, these—which he had spoken to her in a previous dream—were completely disconcerting. Ominous. Inescapable.

"*But your work is not yet finished.*"

Her work, it would seem, was just beginning.

Makeda, the Queen of Sheba, arrived in Sion with a very great retinue, a train of camels the length of which had never been seen, bearing spices and very much gold and precious stones, all as gifts to the great King Solomon. She came to him without guile, for she was a woman of purity and truth, incapable of pretense or deception. Such things as lies and falsities were unknown to her. Thus it was that Makeda told Solomon all that was in her mind and her heart and asked if he would answer the questions she had for him. They were not, as some have told, riddles to test his wisdom. Rather they were questions of the heart and soul. His answers would allow her to determine if they were truly born of the same spirit and destined to celebrate the hieros-gamos together. And yet in the end, she did not need these questions. She knew upon coming into his presence and looking in his eyes that he was a part of her, from the beginning to the end of eternity.

Solomon was mightily taken by Makeda's beauty and presence, and disarmed in total by her honesty. The wisdom he saw in her eyes reflected his own, and he knew immediately that the prophets were correct. Here was the woman who was his equal. How could she be else, when she was the other half of his soul?

And so it was that when Makeda, the Queen of Sheba, had seen all the greatness of Solomon, all that he had created in his kingdom, and most of all, the happiness of his subjects, she said to the king, "The report was true which I heard in my own land of your affairs and of your wisdom, but I did not believe the reports until I came and my own eyes had seen it; and, behold, your wisdom and prosperity surpass the report which I heard. Happy are your men! Happy are your subjects, who continually stand before you and hear your wisdom! Blessed be the Lord your God, who has delighted in you and set you on the throne of Israel! He has made you king, that you may execute justice and righteousness.

"And blessed is the Lord your God who has made you for me, and me for you."

And it was then that the Queen of Sheba and King Solomon came together in the hieros-gamos, the marriage that unites the bride and the bridegroom in a spiritual matrimony found only within divine law. The Goddess of Makeda blended with the God of Solomon in a union most sacred, the blending of the masculine and the feminine into one whole being. It was through Solomon and Sheba that El and Asherah came together once again in the flesh.

They stayed in the bridal chamber for the full cycle of the moon in a place of trust and consciousness, allowing nothing to come between them in their union, and it is said that during this time the secrets of the universe were revealed through them. Together, they found the mysteries that God would share with the world, for those with ears to hear.

And yet neither Solomon nor Sheba became a consort of the other, for they were equals, each a sovereign over his and her own domain and destiny. Both knew the time would come when they must separate and return to the duties of their respective kingdoms, each to stand alone yet again, in newfound wisdom and power. Their triumph and celebration was in what they brought, each to the other, to use well and wisely in their individual destinies.

Solomon wrote over a thousand songs following the inspiration of Makeda, but none as worthy as the Song of Songs, which carries within it the secrets of the hieros-gamos, of how God is found through this union. It is said that Solomon had many wives, yet there was only one who was a part of his soul. While Makeda was never his wife by the laws of men, she was his only wife by the laws of God and nature, which is to say the law of Love.

When Makeda departed from holy Mount Sion, it was with a heavy heart to leave her one beloved. Such has been the fate of many twinned souls in history, to come together at intervals and discover the deepest secrets of love, but to be ultimately separated by their destinies. Perhaps it is love's greatest trial and mystery—the understanding that there is no separation between true beloveds, regardless of physical circumstances, time or distance, life or death.

Once the hieros-gamos is consummated between predestined souls, the lovers are never apart in their spirits.

For those with ears to hear, let them hear it.

THE LEGEND OF SOLOMON AND SHEBA,
PART TWO, AS PRESERVED IN THE LIBRO ROSSO

Vatican City, Italy
present day

"THANKS, MAGGIE."

Margaret Cusack placed the tea tray carefully on Father Peter Healy's desk. She clucked around him and the tray like the Irish hen that she was, pouring his tea, measuring the sugar, adding the milk just so. Maggie was what Peter's mother would have referred to as a spinster, a woman of a certain age with "neither chick nor child of her own." Instead, she had made a life and career as a priest's housekeeper, beginning with her years as a teenager in County Mayo. When the priest she worked for was transferred to Rome, she came with him, and never left. She had been here for fifty years.

When Father Bernard passed away last year, Maggie had proven herself so loyal and indispensable a fixture that she was kept on until a new position could be found for her. Her absolute devotion to the Church knew no limits.

She had written to her family to tell them that it was her blessing from the Lord that this lovely man, Father Peter, had come to Rome at just the right time. That he was young and charming—and Irish—was an even greater boon to her. Maggie missed Ireland tremendously and often hummed the folk ballads of her native land while cleaning up after Father Peter's busy day.

Today she was humming something that startled Peter with recognition. He hadn't heard it in years. It was a hymn written in the Irish language that he had learned as a boy at the Christian Brothers school. He surprised Maggie by joining in with her.

"*Céad mile fáilte romhat, a Iosa, a Iosa . . .*"

A hundred thousand welcomes, Jesus. It was a song about welcoming Jesus into our hearts and our lives. It was traditional, but Peter thought he remembered that it came from an ancient hymn dating back to the dawn of Christianity and the time of Saint Patrick. The Irish pronunciation of his name, *Iosa*, sounded like *Easa*.

"Such a lovely song, isn't it, Father?"

"It is, Maggie. And it only just now occurred to me that *Jesus* in Irish is pronounced *Easa*. Did you know that he is called Easa, or Issa, in a number of languages?"

"I can't say that I knew that, Father, other than the Irish part. And only because of the song. I haven't much Irish anymore, but the songs and poems stay with you."

"Aye, they do."

He let the subject drop. Maggie wasn't one for discussions on anything alternative in her Catholicism. She was staunch in her orthodoxy, like many Irish countrywomen of her age and time, and like virtually everyone else whom Peter was surrounded by here in Rome. She likely wouldn't want to hear about why Mary Magdalene called him Easa in her own gospel—that it was a familiar form of his Greek name, familiar because she was married to him. In fact, Maggie would probably inflict a penance of ten thousand Hail Marys on herself just for hearing such blasphemy from his lips. Her previous employer, Father Bernard, was an old-school traditionalist just as she was.

Maggie was happiest when she was mothering Peter, delivering his food and tea and tidying up his living space, which doubled as his office. As long as he restricted their conversations to daily living and reminiscing about home, she was happy as a little lark.

In addition to her duties as a Vatican housekeeper, Maggie was also a committed member of the Confraternity of the Holy Apparition, a group devoted to the understanding and promotion of the Virgin Mary's appearances around the world. She carried a number of booklets and small paperbacks with her so that on her breaks she could study the accounts of these apparitions. At this particular moment, as she fussed over Peter's tea, she had a dog-eared paperback sticking out of the wide pocket in her apron.

"What are you reading?" Peter was always curious.

"The life of the Holy Sister Lucia," Maggie replied, pulling the book out of her apron to show it to Peter. *Lucia Santos: Her Life and Visions.*

"Ah, Fátima. Are you preparing for the anniversary this year?"

"We are, Father. Ninety years since the Blessed Virgin appeared before the little children of Fátima. We are having a special commemoration for it."

The phone rang in the adjoining hallway, and Maggie ran to answer it while Peter sipped his tea. He needed some peace now, to think about the earlier phone call he had received from Maureen. He was not only her closest living relative, he was and had always been her spiritual counselor. They had lived through some trying times together, and both had endured extraordinary tests of faith during her search for Mary Magdalene's gospel. There was not an hour of the day that passed when Peter didn't wonder if he had passed or failed those tests.

After Maureen had risked her life to obtain the ancient documents from their hiding place in a French cavern, Peter had taken it upon himself to remove the gospels from France and turn them over to the Church. To do this, he had been forced to deceive Maureen and all her friends at the Château des Pommes Bleues who had aided and protected her during the adventure. Essentially, he had stolen the documents like a thief in the night. While he now wallowed in self-loathing for that decision, his reasons for making it at the time were manifold. Primarily, he had convinced himself that he was protecting Maureen. Unfortunately, she and her associates didn't see it that way. It had taken the better part of the last two years to completely mend their relationship, and that was much to the credit of Mary Magdalene herself. Because her gospel emphasized the power and importance of forgiveness, Maureen had decided that she would be the ultimate hypocrite if she didn't forgive Peter under the circumstances.

But Peter had yet to forgive himself. At the time of the discovery and as he translated the gospel, he was shaken to his core by the revelations within it. He simply could not accept that such a critical link to the history of Christianity should not be in the hands of the Church, where every expert available could be utilized to analyze the material and authenticate it. So he did what he thought was best by turning over the originals to authorities in Rome. In return, he was allowed to participate in the ongoing investigation into the controversial gospel.

It was a miserable existence. Peter was immersed daily in the red tape and hierarchy of a Vatican structure that viewed him as an out-sider. He was not a hero for delivering this priceless document. In fact, the opposite was true. He was suspect at all times as a participant in a potent heresy. Because Peter had translated the material first, prior to turning it over to the Vatican authorities, he was problematic. He knew precisely what the gospel said and, worse, had shared that translation with his cousin, who was a best-selling author as a result. And in his own heart he was convinced of its authenticity without so much as a single test. There were many here who opposed that idea, and Peter was often stymied and silenced in his attempts to be heard. There were mo-ments when he felt far more like he was under house arrest than an ac-tive participant in the authentication process. He had only one ally in all of Rome whom he could really depend upon. Thankfully, it was a very powerful ally. Peter prayed for hours each night that the other members of the Vatican council would allow the light of the truth to enter their hearts during this process. He lived for the possibility that he might one day be able to tell Maureen that Mary Magdalene would be authenticated—and vindicated.

But now he had a new complication. Maureen was on the verge of another spiritual breakthrough, whether she knew it yet herself or not. Peter had watched this all happen before: the increase in the visionary dreams that led to a rapid series of synchronistic circumstances, all of which were inexplicable outside of divine intervention. Such events had led Maureen to the Magdalene gospel two years ago. So here she was having the dreams again, and this time Jesus was quoting scripture to her.

Be ye therefore perfect.

The line was from Matthew, chapter five. It was a commandment from the Sermon on the Mount that followed the instruction to love your enemies and bless those that curse you. Certainly, this was foun-dational to Christianity, but what did it mean in the context of her dream?

Stranger still was this line: *You must awaken while in this body, for everything exists in it.* Peter knew the context of that sentence immediately. It was from one of the controversial Gnostic Gospels that were discovered in Egypt in 1945. He knew with certainty that it came from the Gospel of Philip. He was even more certain which line came next within the ancient text: *Resurrect in this life.* He had participated in a number of heated debates over the meaning of these lines while living in Jerusalem in the earlier days of his Jesuit studies. Part of the controversy over the Gnostic material came from this very idea that life on earth, here and now and with an emphasis on this body, was as important as the afterlife. Perhaps more important. This was a concept not generally embraced by orthodox Catholicism for obvious reasons; some would assert that it was heretical. Yet it was key in the Gnostic texts. Peter had long been fascinated by the Gnostic perspective, and he argued with his more conservative brethren that the fact that these gospels had not been altered, dissected, edited, and translated to death over the last two thousand years made them pure and ultimately worthy of serious consideration. The opponents of the Gnostic material took the position that they were written too many generations after the life of Jesus to be considered valid, given that some of them were dated to the mid-third century.

Peter thought it was unfortunate to the point of tragic that the Church had taken such a harsh position against the importance of the Gnostic codices. Why was it always black and white, either/or? Why did the Gnostic Gospels have to stand in opposition to the canon? Could they not be read together, as complements to each other, to see what greater learning they might take us to about who Jesus was and what he was trying to teach us?

Maureen was dreaming about Jesus again, and the Lord himself was quoting from both the canonical and Gnostic Gospels. Fascinating. And given her history, it was very likely significant in ways he could not even dream of yet.

And now, there was a pair of medieval scrolls to consider.

Peter wouldn't have time to consider them much longer. Maggie waddled into the room, flustered as she always was when a high-ranking member of the clergy had business with Peter.

"Father Girolamo rang. He says he needs to see you in his office immediately on business, something regarding Cardinal DeCaro and an ancient document."

Confraternity of the Holy Apparition
Vatican City
present day

Father Girolamo de Pazzi was tired, with the kind of bone-weary exhaustion that comes from a very long life given in service to something more important than one's own comfort. In his case, that service was to the Immaculate Heart of the Blessed Virgin Mary through his tireless dedication to the Confraternity of the Holy Apparition. His public work focused on understanding the visions and visionaries who had been sanctified by the Church as authentic over five hundred years.

But his private work had a different focus. Behind closed doors, he was preoccupied with another, more intriguing kind of prophet—or more accurately, prophet*ess*. This was a lineage of women, connected by blood and birth rights, who through time had experienced visions of exceptional clarity and power. They had been called by different titles through history, some more heretical than others. They were known alternately as Magdalenes, shepherdesses, black madonnas, popesses, and Expected Ones. Father Girolamo studied the details of their biographies; some of them were scant in their antiquity, like the elusive Sarah-Tamar and Modesta; others were well documented, like Teresa of Ávila. He combed through their lives in search of the answer to the questions that burned within him:

Why? Why was it that these particular women were gifted in such a way by the Lord?

And *what?* *What* was it that they knew that was out of the reach of even the holiest of men?

He looked down at the aged manuscript that covered his desk, the one that preoccupied his days and his nights. It had once been in the highly prized personal collection of Pope Urban VIII, and it contained a series of prophecies. Written like poetry, the verses—sometimes in French, sometimes Italian—had been committed to paper over many generations. Because the verses were quatrains, consisting of four lines each, some scholars before him had credited these verses to the famous French prophet Nostradamus. Indeed, this manuscript had been filed in the Biblioteca Apostolica as the work of Nostradamus for a hundred years until Father Girolamo rescued it. He knew that this document was potentially priceless, and certainly not the work of one author. Rather, it was a work that appeared to span centuries. And while the verses had been translated over and over again, he still did not have the key to their true meanings. The quatrains were written in a type of code, a prophetic language that could not be interpreted except by those who were born to comprehend it.

And still, he tried. He took the lines apart, one by one, for hours at a time. There was a specific prophecy that had become an obsession for him, the French one that began with "*Les temps revient.*" The time returns.

Father Girolamo studied the page, willing the meaning of the phrase and the prophecy which followed to come to him. In one hand he clutched a lovely and delicate crystal case, shaped like a locket, which contained the relic of a visionary. He prayed that the reliquary would aid him in his translation, but thus far the words had not revealed their secrets to him.

The old priest sighed and sat back from his task. While Father Girolamo was based in Rome and had been for the majority of his long life, his confraternity had had its origins in Tuscany, in the Middle Ages. Today he felt as though he had been running it since the Middle Ages. Yet there was more work to be done, and he had another document that must occupy his time for the moment. Gently, he replaced the book of prophecies in the locked drawer that was its secret resting place.

Peter Healy was on his way over, and Father Girolamo must be prepared to address him regarding this fascinating new development.

☸

Peter stood before the enormous tapestry that covered one wall of the confraternity's private offices. It was created in the Netherlands in the late fifteenth century, as were the more famous unicorn tapestries that were now housed in museums in New York City and Paris. This one, called *The Killing of the Unicorn*, illustrated an elaborate hunting sequence. The mythical beast was surrounded by hunters wielding lances, and several in the hunting party were thrusting their spears into the trapped creature's body. The unicorn bled profusely from those wounds, and others inflicted by the hounds which were viciously tearing at its flesh. A trumpeter announced the death of the beast with great ceremony and celebration, in the foreground of the textile. While the tapestry was a masterwork of Flemish craftsmanship, the subject matter might appear disturbing to the uninitiated.

"Profoundly beautiful, no?" Father Girolamo de Pazzi's voice, raspy with nearly seven decades of preaching, greeted Peter as he entered the room behind him.

Peter nodded, smiling in greeting. "I have always loved the unicorn tapestries. This one is harsh, but it is beautiful."

"The death of our Lord was harsh, and that is what this work of art is meant to remind us. He died for our sins, in a terrible way." The old priest waved away the lesson. "But that is nothing you do not already know, for you are wise and learned beyond your years. Come in to my study, Peter. There is something I need to show you."

Peter followed the old priest in comfortable silence. Since coming to Rome, Father Girolamo had befriended Peter. They met via Maggie Cusack, who was the most committed member of the elder man's confraternity. While Peter had spent a fair amount of time in Girolamo's presence, he had never been here, to the inner sanctum of the confraternity offices. This was a private place, and as the old man closed the door behind them, Peter knew that there was a secret about to be revealed here. It no longer surprised him. He had come to the understanding that Vatican City was built on secrets, with secrets, by secrets, and for secrets.

Resting in a central place on Father Girolamo's antique desk was the document Maureen had received in New York. Peter wasn't clear on what was happening here; he had not given the document to *this* priest. He had given it to Tómas Cardinal DeCaro, his mentor.

"Sit." It was a gentle command, and Peter took his seat across the desk from the old man. "You brought this document to Tómas, and he has brought it to me. He would be here himself but he is in Siena on Church business. But he trusts me, and so can you. Now, here is why he brought it to me. I am a Tuscan. And my passion through eighty years of life has been the study of Tuscan history and how it relates to the Church. And so when this rare and important document surfaced, our friend knew that I would understand its import. And I do. This relates to the grand contessa Matilda Toscana. Matilda of Tuscany. Do you know who she is?"

Peter shook his head.

"You will now. Tell me, how many times have you been inside the Basilica of Saint Peter?"

Peter shrugged. "I don't know. Hundreds."

"Then you have walked past Countess Matilda hundreds of times. She is buried in a place of honor, under a great marble tomb designed by the Baroque master Bernini and within fifty meters of the first apostle himself."

"She's buried inside the basilica?" Peter was incredulous. He had no idea that any woman was buried in Saint Peter's, much less in a place of such enormous honor. "Why?"

Father Girolamo gave a small, soundless laugh. "That depends on whom you ask. But as you are asking me, I will tell you that it is because she was a pious woman and generous donor to the Church who left all her property to the pope."

"Why do you think someone sent Maureen a document about this Countess Matilda?"

"I have deep concerns about the intentions of the person or persons who sent such a document anonymously, and until we can determine identity or intention, it is critical that we stay very close on this."

"You think this is dangerous?"

The old man nodded. "I do. Peter, you are one of the finest linguistic scholars that the Jesuits have ever produced. You did not deliver this document for translation. You already know what it says. Am I correct?"

Peter nodded. "I was hoping to have it authenticated, just to be sure."

"It is indeed authentic. Which is why it concerns me. Be very careful here, my son. I know that such a gift may appear benevolent, but I do not believe that it is. I believe that someone may be using your cousin. Tómas believes this too, which is why he came to me."

"Using her in what way?"

"Think, Peter. Our friend Tómas came to me because, in addition to being Tuscan, I am also an expert in visionary experience. And if there is one thing I have learned over my many years of study, it is this: true visionaries are born, not made. You can't aspire to it or study to be one. You are or you are not, and there is nothing in between. Therefore an authentic prophet, or prophetess, is both rare and valuable. And your cousin is something of a celebrity here, as you know."

Peter smiled. Maureen was mostly notorious within the walls of Vatican City, where she was a curiosity—a heretic and a renegade, and worse still, a woman—but also a force that could not be entirely discounted. She had, after all, made the most remarkable Christian discovery of the era as a result of following her dreams and visions.

"So whether or not the more conservative elders of the Church approve of your cousin makes no difference. The undeniable fact is that her visions have led her to achievements that are unmatched. I believe that someone is using her as a result—to find the book that is referenced in that document. And once it is found, I don't believe they will want her around to tell the tale of its existence. She must take extreme care, and so must you."

The old priest sat deep in thought, eyes closed, for so long that Peter feared he had fallen asleep. When he opened his ancient eyes finally, they were clear and bright with intention.

"Peter, I need you to keep me posted on your cousin's movements in relation to this document, and certainly inform me if she has any further contact from this . . . source. I promise you, it is for her own protection. And yours."

Peter assured him that he would do so. But the old priest's words of warning had rattled him and he was anxious to get out of there and call Maureen, who would be arriving in France momentarily.

"Now go with God, my boy. And may his blessed mother watch over you on your journey."

CHAPTER THREE

The Languedoc
France, present day

Maureen was starting to feel the tension rising in her body as they drew closer to their destination. The drive took well over an hour, allowing time for her to catch up with Tammy on all the events and their mutual research over the past few days. They talked through clues and theorized on possible sources for the documents.

"Bérenger is very uneasy about all of this," Tammy explained. "As fascinating as it is, he doesn't like feeling that he is out of control of this situation, and it concerns him that none of us have been able to come up with a substantial theory as to who is leading this heretical scavenger hunt."

"Whoever it is knows a lot about both Bérenger and me. That's certainly disconcerting. But they also know what's occurring in my dreams, which is completely beyond explanation. Therefore, it's either something divinely inspired . . ."

"Or something truly sinister."

"Yeah, thanks for that reassurance. Because I wasn't nervous enough already."

Even without the recent, unexplainable events, returning to Arques today had Maureen on edge. This was where she had discovered the

Magdalene Gospel, where she had both endured and enjoyed an adventure that was beyond the imagination of most. But it was also the home of Bérenger Sinclair, and that fact brought with it a whole series of complications.

Tammy took a detour through Montségur for lunch because she knew that Maureen loved this part of France. It was one of the earth's great places of spirit, and the location of the last stand of the Cathar people against the armies of a Church determined to exterminate the entire culture. Maureen knew this story well, having spent some memorable hours learning about the legacy of Montségur on her last visit to France.

By the end of 1243 the Cathars had suffered nearly fifty years of torture by the Inquisition. The populations of entire cities had been eradicated until the streets very literally ran red with the blood of these innocent people. One of the last Cathar strongholds left in France was Montségur, the castle located forty miles or so from where the Château des Pommes Bleues was located in Arques. For nearly half a year, the last French Cathars were sequestered together in the fortress of Montségur.

Languedoc legend said that four members of the Cathar party were able to escape Montségur two days before the remaining population were captured and burned alive for heresy. It was told that one of these, a young girl called *La Paschalina*, "the little Paschal Lamb," carried a priceless object strapped to her body—the Book of Love. This girl was instrumental in the protection of the most sacred treasure of their people. She was also Maureen's ancestor, and the source whence the name Paschal came.

As they took their leave of the ruins of the mountain fortress, Maureen whispered a prayer of thanks to her brave ancestress, and Tammy joined in on another for the two hundred souls who perished in the flames on March 16, 1244.

They headed into Couiza to take the turn in the direction of Arques as Maureen's cell phone interrupted their conversation. She answered with anticipation when she realized that it was Peter, calling from his office in Rome.

"I have some important info to share with you. Are you alone?"

"Tammy is with me. We're on our way to the château."

Peter made a slight, irritated noise, then cleared his throat and continued. "Right. The document. It's dated 1071 and is signed by Matilda, as the countess of Tuscany."

"What does the document say?"

"It's a demand letter of sorts, from a very angry and imperious Countess Matilda, requesting the return of her 'most precious red book' immediately, and at the risk of her personally leading an army of invasion and even threatening a 'holy war'—against her own husband, whom she clearly despises."

"A precious red book? It's the Book of Love, isn't it?"

"I have reason to believe that it is, or at the very least a copy of it. The letter insists that the book be put immediately into the custody of someone named Patricio, who is the abbot of the monastery . . . in Orval. Maureen, this is important as it is possibly the only authenticated evidence that such a book ever existed."

"And it is last known to be in Orval. And Orval is where we're headed tomorrow."

Peter interrupted her before she could continue. "You need to be very careful. I think this is dangerous. There's more, but I will need you to call me later, when you're alone."

"Okay." She was trying not to be irritated, but Peter's refusal to share all his information because Tammy was in the car just increased her discomfort. She would have to find a way to bridge this gap and get them all on the same team again. She needed all of them, and they would have to work together and learn to trust each other again.

After all, they were searching for something called the Book of Love. Wasn't it time for everyone to find some forgiveness? Could she?

Tammy activated the remote control to open the gates, and they drove up the serpentine path to the magnificent château. Maureen caught her breath at the sight of it; she had forgotten just how grand and beautiful it truly was. Strangely, though she had only spent two weeks of her life here, this return suddenly felt like a homecoming to her. She did love this place and the people attached to it.

The front door flew open as the car pulled to a stop, and Roland came bounding out. The huge grin splitting his angular face made him look unusually boyish as he lifted Tammy off her feet in an enormous hug. She was laughing that deep, throaty laugh that Roland loved as he kissed her soundly, if quickly, for the sake of decorum. Releasing Tammy, he stood before Maureen to take her hands in his and kiss her on both cheeks in a more formal European greeting.

"It is our great joy to have you back with us, my lady."

For Roland, Maureen was more than a friend or a visitor. She was an honored guest, and one who had accomplished something monumental in his eyes. She would always be the woman who had found the Magdalene Gospel, and that set her above mere mortals. He treated her with a respect that bordered on reverence.

It was too much for an exhausted and overwrought Maureen. When she opened her mouth to reply to him, the words would not come out. Her voice was trapped in her throat, caught on a sob that had been building for the better part of two years.

Dispensing with the formalities, Maureen threw herself against this gentle giant who was her friend, a great man who treated her in a way that she was sure she did not deserve, and cried as though her heart would break.

She was home.

Bérenger Sinclair had watched the car make its way toward the house. He could not know that the fear and trepidation he was feeling—fear of rejection, anxiety over the initial moments of meeting—was identical to what Maureen was experiencing. He did not come down immediately to greet her. He chose to wait and gauge her reaction to Roland and the environment, hoping it would prepare him for whatever she might be feeling. He had not expected the emotional outpouring that had come with her arrival. Neither had she.

Roland and Tammy escorted Maureen to her favorite room in the château, the Magdalene room, to give her time to settle down and prepare before dinner. The exquisite bedroom, well suited for a queen, was draped in crimson velvets and took its name from the Ribera painting, *Magdalene in the Desert*, that dominated one wall. Today the room was filled with the heady scent of Casablanca lilies. The copious white blooms spilled out of crystal vases throughout the room.

The tap on her door an hour later was gentle, causing Maureen to think it was one of the housekeepers coming to alert her to dinner. She was ready, having changed into evening dress and repaired the makeup that had been smeared by the crying jag. Opening the door, she stopped cold. Bérenger Sinclair leaned against the door frame, tall and beautiful and smiling at her with such warmth that she could only wonder just what defect in her psyche had made her behave like such an unforgiving idiot.

She only had to wonder for a moment. After that, she was in his arms as the world melted away around them.

❁

They were very nearly late for dinner, but it was Maureen who came to her senses and called a halt to their unexpectedly passionate reunion.

Bérenger was the essence of chivalry, even as he ran his hands through the silken copper strands of her hair, relishing her physical presence. It was with reluctance that he agreed to go downstairs, where he would have to share her company.

She was here. For now, that would have to be enough.

❁

Dinner passed companionably as Maureen answered all the curious questions about her life since the release of the book. She relaxed quickly, contented to be in the presence of these three people whom she trusted entirely. Everyone had a story to tell; there was much catching up to do on all sides. By dessert, the topic had turned to the legend of the Book of Love and how it had been preserved in the Languedoc.

Bérenger took the lead. "The Book of Love is the gospel, the good news, as written by Jesus himself. It represents his true teachings in their purest form. His parables, his prayers, his commandments. Everything we as human beings need in order to find God through the Way of Love."

"It is everything we need to know to become perfect," Roland explained. "In Cathar tradition, those who reached an exalted level of understanding these teachings were called *perfecti*, or *parfait*, in French, one who had become perfect. That doesn't mean 'perfect' in the sense that we know it today. It means that they had learned to live entirely as love expressed, through love and without judgment. That is the end goal of Jesus' teachings. In becoming beings who love, we are modeling our lives after our father in heaven, who *is* love."

Maureen was still for a moment before responding. She had not yet shared this part of her dream with Roland and Bérenger, yet they seemed to grasp it already. "Be ye therefore perfect."

"Exactly," Bérenger said. "Thankfully, some of the true teachings did make it into the canonical gospels, like that one from the Gospel of Matthew, and certainly the entire Sermon on the Mount and the Lord's Prayer with it."

"Back up for a minute," Maureen said. "So we know that Jesus writes this in his lifetime and he gives it to Mary Magdalene, who is not only his wife but his successor as a teacher and minister. And we know that there are copies of it, because she refers to one written by Philip. But the original then, the one written in Easa's hand, comes here."

"Correct. Magdalene arrives on the shores of France with her children, a handful of loyal followers, and the Book of Love. She teaches from it, first in Marseille, and then later she comes here to the Languedoc. Where we live here in Arques is sacred ground because, legend says, she built a school here as her base of operations, her first mission, if you will. It is called Arques because of the word *ark*, as in Ark of the Covenant. In other words, the new covenant, the word of Jesus, was brought here and this village was the receptacle of it—the ark that contained it. Sadly, all the ancient monuments to Magdalene are long since demolished, and done so with the intention of wiping out her presence in the Languedoc, as you already know."

Maureen did know, but she dug into her training as a journalist to play devil's advocate for a moment. "Which leads me to the crucial question, which every skeptical and incredulous person in the world would ask if you told them this story. And that is simply this: how is it possible that something so important to human history could have been completely erased? This has to be one of the best-kept secrets of the last two thousand years, if not *the* best-kept secret. How is it that no even knows such a thing existed?"

Roland was first to answer, passionate about his subject. "Because our people were murdered to ensure that no one would know that it existed."

Bérenger added, "Nothing could be more dangerous to the Church than a gospel written in the hand of Jesus Christ, particularly if that gospel proved that everything they stood for was completely opposed to his true teachings. It is the most dangerous document in human history."

"But they didn't get it. At least not from Montségur," said Maureen.

Roland answered, "No, as you are well aware, your ancestor was one of the reasons that the Book of Love was saved. At least for a while. It disappears from our history following Montségur. So much does. All that is left is what has been passed down orally, and time has sadly erased much of that as well."

Bérenger joined in. "The Cathar culture had been decimated by the holocaust against them. Those who were left were scattered all over Europe, and we lost the thread of history there."

Returning to Roland, Maureen asked, "And yet some of you survived. Your family, the few who escaped the massacre at Montségur. My ancestress. Wouldn't they have done something to preserve the Book of Love?"

"Yes, of course, but they were in no position to talk about it. Even when the Cathars lived here in peace, before the massacres, they did not discuss the Book of Love openly, not ever. You can certainly understand why they would not have been able to do that."

Bérenger made the key point. "So the Cathars protected it by never speaking of it. And the Church certainly didn't want anyone left alive who knew what it was and the explosive nature of its contents. So what you have is something that is by its nature so great a secret, to those who revere it and those who despise it, that its very existence is eliminated from history."

Maureen nodded her understanding. "Of course. So its last known resting place . . ."

"Was officially Montségur," said Roland. "Although legend says that it was taken into northern Spain by your ancestor, La Paschalina, where it was installed at the monastery of Our Lady of Montserrat. After that . . . is anybody's guess."

"And while there was only one, the true Book written in Jesus' own hand," said Bérenger, "we are quite certain that there were copies made at various times in history. The idea of copies is interesting because at least there is a possibility that the content is alive somewhere, even if the original has been lost."

"And do you think it has been lost?"

They were all silent, contemplating. Roland said finally, "It's in Rome somewhere. They were so committed to the idea of obtaining that book that they committed genocide. The Church would not have stopped until they found it. It is the dark secret behind the Inquisition. The Inquisition was founded to root out all the Cathars and their sympathizers, and then it spread like the terrible plague that it was for humanity. And yet something now tells me that all is not lost. If you are having dreams again, and someone here in the physical world is trying to contact you . . . perhaps there is a copy left somewhere that we can find. This is a new hope for us all."

Maureen used the extensive resources in Bérenger's library for research after dinner. She was hoping to find some material, no matter how scant, on the enigmatic Matilda before departing for Orval in the morning. Bérenger's book and manuscript collection was a subject of great pride for him, and he specialized in rare books on European art and history. The others aided Maureen, searching through various volumes on the Middle Ages and sharing what tidbits they found. There was precious little written about their Tuscan countess, and virtually none of it was in English. A few antique books in Latin and Italian appeared to mention her, but without Peter here to translate quickly, they were too difficult for novice linguists to wade through.

Maureen was scanning a British volume from the eighteenth century about Gianlorenzo Bernini when she cried out, "Here! I found something. Listen to this: 'In 1635, Pope Urban the Eighth requested that remains of the Countess Matilda of Canossa be removed from where they had rested in the monastery of San Benedetto Po for five hundred years, and transferred to Rome. The monks from this Mantua monastery refused to relinquish Matilda, as they believed that doing so would be a violation of her last earthly wish, which was to remain near her childhood home for eternity.

" 'However, during the new construction of Saint Peter's, the pope commissioned Bernini to create a magnificent marble tomb and monument to the Tuscan countess. He would not be denied his prize relics and bribed the abbot at the monastery of San Benedetto with an enormous sum of money, one that would sustain the monastery and allow them to continue their good works in Matilda's name in perpetuity. While the abbot agreed to the bribe, he could not tell his brother monks for fear that they would rebel. Thus it was that in the dead of night, specifically selected priests from the pope's personal entourage delivered the bribe to the abbot and, like thieves on a mission, broke open her sealed, alabaster tomb.' "

Maureen stopped reading for a moment.

"What's wrong, Maureen?" Bérenger was watching her face. Whatever she had just read had shaken her a bit.

Maureen looked up at him for a moment, took a breath, then continued. " 'What they found was a perfectly intact skeleton, wrapped in gold and silver lengths of silk. Although Matilda has been depicted as an Amazon in medieval legend, the remains were those of an unusually petite woman with near-perfect teeth. Most exceptional were the long strands of hair still attached to the skull, hair of a rare red-gold color. Satisfied that this was indeed the legendary countess so coveted by their pope, they removed the contents of the casket while the monastery slept and retreated to Rome before the sun came up. Matilda of Tuscany thus became the first woman buried in Saint Peter's, in the very heart of the church.' "

"Well, well." Tammy was the first to speak. "Clearly, I'm not the only one who senses a pattern here. It appears that our Matilda was a petite redhead, the most obvious and visible genetic marker of women in the Magdalene lineage, certainly the most legendary. Can we ascertain that she was an Expected One in her own right?"

Maureen sat back in her chair. The personal aspects of her connection to Matilda were certainly fascinating and unexpected. Perhaps they even explained in some way the fish dream and her deepening need to get to Orval as soon as possible. She responded, "But I still want to know why. Why was this particular pope—Urban the Eighth—so emphatic about having Matilda's bones there?"

Bérenger had a theory. "Did he believe that she may have been buried with something of great importance and therefore developed a ruse to open her coffin in the dead of night? Was he searching for the Book of Love, or something other than Matilda's bones, and that's why it had to be done in such secrecy?"

Something caught in the back of Maureen's mind at that. "Was she buried with some kind of document? Some information or proof that the pope wanted?"

They were not going to solve this mystery tonight, and there was an early start ahead of them tomorrow. Maureen was exhausted, both by jet lag and the emotional content of the day. She bid everyone good night and made her way to bed. Bérenger saw how tired she was. He kissed her gently, then held her face in his hands for a moment, gazing into her eyes before reluctantly letting her go. Thankfully, Bérenger hadn't asked to accompany the women to Orval. Maureen had made it clear before arriving in France that she wanted to make this journey solely with Tammy. She needed to concentrate on the mission at hand, and dealing with the complex issues of her relationship with Bérenger was not conducive to her sharpest focus.

They would return to the château following their excursion to Belgium, and then she would begin the task of rebuilding her relationship. But in that moment of fleeting intimacy, she wished he was coming with them.

And so it was that the daughter of our Lord and Our Lady, the princess known as Sarah-Tamar, began to grow into her destiny. She had the glory of both great parents and became a leader of the people in Gaul. It is told that she had the beauty and feminine strength of her mother and could heal ailments in humans and animals with the touch of her hands, much as her father before her. Upon her birth, she was declared so beloved by God that she was laid in the same wooden crèche that once held her father.

As she grew to be a woman, she was known to fall into trances and speak in rhythms and verses. These were taken to be great prophecies and were recorded by the scribes of the Holy Family. Through time, these prophecies have come to pass to prove her divine inspiration. Yet there are others reserved for the children of the future.

She is not remembered by history because the persecutions of the people of the Way began in earnest as she came of age. It was necessary for her to teach in secret, and this she did until the day she died.

Sarah-Tamar had many children. Some stayed in Gaul, others came to Rome and Tuscany to search for their brethren and to create safe communities during the persecutions, so that the teachings of the Way of Love would endure and spread. Look to the legends of the saints, of Barbara and Margaret, Ursula and Lucia, if you would find what has become of her legacy.

For those with ears to hear, let them hear it.

THE LEGEND OF SARAH-TAMAR, THE PROPHETESS,
FROM THE LIBRO ROSSO

The Belgian border
present day

TAMMY AND MAUREEN began their journey across the Belgian border and into the lush Ardennes forest, where Orval had been nestled since Matilda placed the first foundation stone there herself in 1070. It was a beautiful day for a journey into a forest that had been called enchanted for many centuries. Maureen was happily relaxed in anticipation of the adventure. The only thing that nagged at the back of her mind was that she hadn't called Peter back yet. He was insistent that she call only if she was alone, and she hadn't found a minute to herself. After visiting Orval later this afternoon, she vowed that she would take a solo walk and call him on her cell. Tammy would understand.

As they headed north on the motorway, they discussed all that they did and didn't know about the enigmatic medieval countess of Tuscany, of whom so little has been written in English.

"We have a historical blackout where much of Matilda is concerned, partially because it happened a thousand years ago," Tammy observed.

"And partially because she was a woman, so her achievements would not have been readily recorded by the scribes of her time," Maureen added.

"We do know that the Orval prophecy—your Expected One prophecy—comes from a series of documents that were held in the monastery there, protected for centuries. And that they were part of something bigger—a whole collection of prophecies that date back to the time of Mary Magdalene herself, virtually all of which have been lost outside of those few that were preserved in the oral traditions by the Cathars or similar heretical sects. Our people."

"And these prophecies, we think, were written by Mary Magdalene's daughter, her daughter with Jesus who became the little prophetess we know as Sarah-Tamar."

Maureen had come face-to-face with this legend and its power two years ago during her search for the lost gospel of Mary Magdalene, because the prophecy of The Expected One emanated from the ancient abbey of Orval. In discovering the Arques gospel, Maureen had learned that she was herself an Expected One, having fulfilled all the criteria of the prophecy. It was an identity she was still struggling to own. To be considered a prophetess by your peers was more than a little daunting for a woman in the twenty-first century.

The subject of infamous prophets reminded Maureen of something Tammy had told her early in their search for the Arques gospel. "These are the same prophecies that you believe were stolen by Nostradamus? The ones that became the basis of his famous works?"

"The very same. We know that Nostradamus was studying in Orval, as well as several other Belgian abbeys, all of which have heretical ties. And we know that when he left, documents were reported missing. And then, all of a sudden—ta-da! He wakes up one day and is a stellar prophet and publishes these remarkable predictions. So he gets points for recognizing how important the prophecies were but loses them all for declining to tell the world that they weren't his predictions to begin with. It was the Renaissance version of plagiarism."

"Was it?"

"What do you mean?"

Maureen shrugged. "I'm not sure. Something tells me there's more to Nostradamus if he was involved here at Orval. Maybe he was one of us? Maybe . . ."

Maureen dropped it as she saw the first signpost for Orval. The drive became increasingly bucolic and beautiful as the Ardennes forest thickened, enormous pines hugging the road and following the curves in a velvety green ribbon. A quaint and aged sign indicated "Abbaye d'Orval" with an arrow for a left turn. Turning that corner, both Tammy and Maureen gasped as Tammy hit the brakes. If the Abbey of Orval was designed to overwhelm the pilgrim who sees it for the first time, the architects were indeed successful. A restoration in the last century brought a modern façade featuring a deco-style madonna and child statue that was of megalithic proportions, reminding the visitor that the full name of this place had always been *Notre Dame d'Orval*. The enormous madonna was several stories tall, resembling nothing so much as an Egyptian goddess from an ancient temple in Luxor. The grand exterior was monumental and modern, giving almost no indication of the thousand-year-old hallowed ruins that stretched beyond it.

The sweet girl who sold them their admission tickets gave them pamphlets in English. The girl wore the symbol of Orval around her neck—the golden fish with a wedding ring in his mouth. By the end of the day, they would have seen this symbol everywhere in the abbey and its surrounding area: on beer bottles, cheese packages, souvenirs, and café signs.

"Hail Ichthys," Tammy whispered to Maureen. They had discussed this clue in depth on their drive from Paris. *Ichthys* was certainly a reference to a fish, specifically the fish as it symbolized Jesus to early Christians.

"You know, the Jesus fish, like the kind you see on the back of people's cars. That's an ichthys," Tammy said.

Maureen nodded. "It's an anagram. Peter taught me that. *Ichthys* represents the first letters in Greek that spell out *Jesus Christ, Son of God, Savior.* Iota, chi, theta, upsilon, sigma. And the word itself actually means 'fish.' So I think we can assume that *Hail Ichthys* is a reference to Jesus, with maybe some nod to Greek culture or legend. This specific fish is in both our clues, so he is trying to tell us something."

Tammy read through the pamphlet as they made their way to the abbey ruins.

"Whoa! Listen to this. It says, 'Matilda gave the abbey and the region its name—Orval. While touring her lands in Lorraine, Matilda stopped to refresh herself at a natural wellspring in the forest. As she did so, her gold wedding band slipped off her hand and fell into the depths of the well. Before the good countess could become agitated at her loss, a golden trout leaped from the waters with her wedding ring in his mouth. Retrieving her ring from the obliging fish, Matilda exclaimed, "This truly is a Valley of Gold!" And the place has been called Or-Val, the Vale of Gold, ever since.' Stop me if you've heard this."

Maureen shook her head in amazement. She had been dreaming of

Orval—prior to the delivery of Matilda's document to her hotel in New York City.

Here you will find what you seek. Dear Lord, she hoped so.

Tammy continued. "They claim that Matilda immediately built the monastery here as a result of the magical event with the fish, and in eternal gratitude for retrieving her wedding ring."

Maureen thought about it for a moment. "Yet we know that Matilda's letter was a threat to lead an army of invasion against her hated husband. That doesn't sound like she would have treasured her wedding ring all that much, now does it?"

"She probably threw it in the well intentionally," Tammy cracked. "And that damn fish kept bringing it back to her."

"It's allegory," Maureen stated. "It has to be. It's obvious, hiding in plain sight as it is . . ."

As they walked around the corner to the abbey ruins, Maureen stopped in her tracks. It was all here, just as she had dreamed it. The exquisite Gothic arches, the ruined window with the six-petaled rose cut out of the stone. She had a momentary flash that the six petals were not random, that the number meant something, but she didn't hold on to the thought. Even the light as it filtered through the tree branches was exactly the same as she had dreamed it.

"This is it. Exactly. Come on, I have to find her." Maureen grabbed Tammy and ran through the ruins. She retraced the steps from her dream, noticing the ruined marble hunks on the ground as she passed, moving through the remains of a doorway. Ahead of her in the niche of the wall was the sweet little madonna.

"There she is." Maureen walked slower now, approaching the statue with a type of reverence. The statue was even more beautiful—and whimsical—in person. Her face was distinct and special—wide-set eyes and a high forehead emphasized both intelligence and innocence. The stone girl was dressed simply in a robe with a veil; long braids carved in the rock fell along the sides of her head. She was clearly a child, a little girl holding a baby that was most certainly not her own. Maureen gazed in silence, until Tammy broke it with a whisper.

"What did she say to you in the dream?"

"She said, 'I am not who you think I am.' "

"So who do you think she is?"

Maureen smiled, feeling a strange communion with the little girl depicted in the statue. It was like seeing an old friend again. "I know who she is. She's Sarah-Tamar, and the baby is her little brother, the baby Yeshua. This whole place, we think it was built as a monument by Matilda to the bloodline family, right? And whose prophecies were held here? Sarah-Tamar's. She would be represented here."

Tammy was piecing it together. "Let's go back to that allegory."

"Okay. Think about the story." Maureen hypothesized out loud. "A fish, which symbolizes Jesus—the ichthys—leaps from the depths of a well. Now first we start with the fact that Jesus taught in this same way, right? He taught through parables, storytelling with symbolism."

"So you think that *Hail Ichthys* is to remind us that there are layers to the story here? That it's a type of parable?"

"Exactly! Now, the well is an ancient symbol of secret knowledge. And our fish holds a wedding ring in his mouth. Look around you, that symbol is everywhere. Jesus, the ichthys, is emerging from the depths of secrecy to show the world his wedding ring. Every telling of the story emphasizes that the ring *is* a wedding ring. And he places it securely in Matilda's hand, because Matilda is trustworthy and will protect it. It all just seems so obvious. And this is a vale of gold because it is here that all the knowledge of his family is kept, knowledge that is worth more than gold. The entire story is an allegory for what Matilda knew and how she preserved it."

Tammy was nodding. "It's how all of the bloodline legends were preserved, through codes and symbols when it was death to speak of these things openly."

"Art will save the world," Maureen observed. "And I think the definition of art covers a lot of territory in this case. Not just paintings, but architecture, literature, statuary . . ."

As they rounded the next corner, they came upon a wide well encased with ancient stone. A small sign indicated that this was the *Foun-*

taine Mathilde. Matilda's fountain. Maureen covered her right hand with her left, protecting the Jerusalem ring. She was taking no chances of losing it as she had in the dream, magical fish or no.

The well was a place of serenity, truly peaceful. A gentle spring trickled into the well, coming somewhere from deep within the Ardennes. It reminded Maureen of the holy wells in Ireland, sacred places that were devoted to goddesses for thousands of years before being converted to Christian sites of Marian devotion. To Maureen, everything about Orval felt female, filled with pure and ancient goddess energy that sprang from the earth. Maureen was falling in love with the place and its natural beauty; it felt truly sacred. It was also stirring her growing desire to know more about the mysterious Matilda who had been the force behind this structure and its community almost a thousand years ago.

Tammy leaned over to peer in the well, looking at herself in the dark water. "In your reflection, you will find what you seek."

Maureen joined her, and they both gazed into the water. She gasped as a third reflection appeared above their own. In the water looking back at them was a face identical to that of the little madonna in the statue. But this face was not stone, it was that of a flesh-and-blood child.

Maureen and Tammy both turned quickly. Standing immediately behind them was an ethereal and beautiful little girl. Like the child in the statue, she was clothed in a very simple dress, and her hair was plaited on both sides of her face. It did not escape the notice of either woman that the girl's braids were a lovely golden red color. Her hands were behind her back, where she was concealing something as if it were a surprise.

"*Bonjour,*" Maureen ventured softly.

The child didn't speak. Instead, she let out an excited giggle, identical to one that Maureen had heard before. She brought her arms around to reveal that she was carrying a thin canvas bag which appeared to contain something—something that looked like a large book. She held the bag out to Maureen, a sweet smile illuminating her wide-set eyes. As Maureen took the bag, the girl turned immediately and ran, without saying a word. She rounded a corner into the ruins and was out of sight almost immediately.

Tammy looked around to see if anyone had witnessed the exchange, but they were alone at the well with no witnesses. "What's in the bag?"

Maureen opened it and they both peered inside, neither wanting to draw attention to the item by removing it. But it was immediately clear to both of them that what was inside was indeed a book—an ancient-looking book, covered in red leather.

✸

The two women rushed out of the abbey, anxious to get to the privacy of Tammy's car and get a close look at the red book.

They left the abbey grounds and made the trek to the dirt clearing that was the parking lot. Tammy had her keys in hand but stopped suddenly. Something was wrong. Her car appeared to be leaning to the left. Approaching carefully, she noticed that the front and rear tire on the driver's side were flat. Maureen came up behind her, looking over Tammy's shoulder as her friend knelt for a closer look.

Deep Xs were carved into the sidewalls. The tires had been slashed.

Tammy kneeled to get a closer look, pointing out the perfectly cut X shapes to Maureen. She didn't think that the carvings were random. The letter X had been used for centuries as a symbol for heresy by both its proponents and its opponents. The Cathar Gnostics had used it as an emblem of enlightenment. Xs could be found carved into the stone walls of Cathar castles and the more ancient caverns that were their hiding places during the persecutions. An X on the wall indicated that Gnostic teachings were at work in that location and that it was subsequently a haven for those who would pursue the true teachings. Later in Renaissance art, the masters who were sympathetic to the bloodline heresies were fond of incorporating X shapes into their paintings.

It was the symbol of truth in issues of God.

In this case, it appeared that the Gnostic X was being used as a symbol of hostility by an enemy.

So engrossed were the women in examining the marks that they did not hear the steps behind them until it was too late.

"Stand up very slowly. Both of you."

The voice was low, menacing yet soft. Maureen did as she was told, turning slightly to see a very tall man wearing a black hooded jacket and dark sunshades. Only his mouth was visible, and it was twisted in a snarl. Tammy let out an involuntary yelp as she felt his gun jammed in between her shoulder blades.

"I will only ask once," he said to Maureen in accented English. She was struggling to identify the accent for future reference. It was a strange European polyglot, which in itself made it memorable. "Give me the bag, or I will shoot her through the heart, right here, right now. And you will be next."

The area around them was deserted. Orval was located in the center of a forest and there was no one to hear them. Maureen did the only thing she could. She handed the bag over, praying all the while that the man wouldn't hurt Tammy.

He snatched it from her and continued to issue orders. "Now get in the car and stay there. Do not move for thirty minutes. Look up there," he pointed to the rise above them, where the Ardennes forest stretched out. "I have a man in those trees. If you move one second too early, he will shoot you both, and he does not miss. Understand?" There was movement in the shadowed forest above them. Their attacker was not bluffing.

Maureen and Tammy got into the car, hearts pounding. As the doors closed, the man walked quickly away from them and toward the forest, never looking back.

❋

It was the longest thirty minutes of their lives, and both Maureen and Tammy spent it praying and whispering quietly about their dilemma. For safety they gave themselves an extra few minutes before leaving the car and heading back to the abbey. When the sweet girl told them that they were closing for the day, Tammy explained to her that their car had been vandalized. She left out the bit about the gunmen and the robbery. They were hoping the monastery would offer them lodging for the evening, as it was known to house pilgrims of both genders on a regular basis, but pilgrims pursued by hooded thugs might not be the most welcome guests.

It was a wise decision not to elaborate on their ordeal. The poor Belgian girl was so distraught by the report of vandalism in the idyllic beauty of Orval that she looked as if she would cry. One of the younger monks, Brother Marco, was called in to help in the crisis, and he set to finding rooms for the women as well as contacting a garage in Florenville to repair the car. There was an air of comfort and concern from the monks and the staff at Orval, and both women began to relax in the relative safety of the monastery. It was as if Matilda's spirit still permeated the place, and while Maureen and Tammy were within her grounds, they were safe. Brother Marco invited the women to supper, which was taken in silence in the monastery's dining hall. They were too exhausted and overwrought by their ordeal to accept, and he packed them some bread and cheese, as well as the Orval beer with the golden fish on the label, to take back to their room.

The room was typically monastic and spotlessly clean, containing two single beds, a nightstand, and a washbasin. Maureen was grateful for every inch of it. She needed to call Peter and sort through the events of the day. Who attacked them and stole the book? What *was* the book? She felt sick at the thought that she may have had one of the treasures of human history in her hands for a few brief minutes, and now it was lost to . . . to whom?

When Tammy left to take a shower in the shared bathroom down the hall, Maureen found Peter via cell phone at his home in Rome.

He became understandably agitated as she recounted the events.

"Didn't I tell you to call me back and that it was important? I wanted to warn you that you were in potential danger."

Maureen was tired and prickly. "You should have told me everything, even with Tammy present. I trust her. And if Tammy had been injured . . ."

She let the sentence drop. It was plain and implicit that Peter would have borne some responsibility if anything had happened to Maureen or her friend.

"I'm sorry. Very sorry. And I'm just grateful that you're both all right. Maureen, I want you on a plane to Rome in the morning. There is someone here you need to meet. I think he can help us to sort through everything. We can have a car pick you up at the monastery and get you to the airport in record time. Tammy can come with you if it makes you feel better."

"Thanks, Pete. Ah, the irony. You know, sometimes I am truly grateful for the power of the Vatican."

If ever there was a place to dream, it was within the magical monastery of Orval.

Maureen was moving through the ancient ruined nave of the monastery. The filtered light shone through the skeletal rose window as she stepped carefully over the scattered stones. This time, she knew where she was going. She was heading toward the fountain.

Then she heard the giggle.

Maureen followed it, not surprised when the little girl with the bright copper braids was standing by the well, gesturing emphatically for her to come forward. She had yet to speak, although she looked supremely pleased with herself as she continued to laugh. The child pointed to the water, indicating that Maureen should gaze into its depths.

As Maureen peered into the well, the surface shimmered as images began to take shape, coming into a crystal clear, cinematic focus. Maureen gasped at what she saw. Their attacker was entering a room, holding her precious book in his hands. She watched as the scene took place in what appeared to be a stone chamber or a basement. The room was filled with men, dressed ominously in strange, hooded robes that covered their heads completely and appeared to be midnight blue in color. All faces were obscured, with only narrow slits where the eyes should be. The men sat at a long, rectangular table; the central chair was larger and more ornate, indicating that its occupant was somehow the leader of this strange order.

Maureen's attacker, still wearing his more modern clothing and sunglasses, presented the book to the central figure, who examined its cover, which was encircled with a heavy leather strap and a lock. The man seemed prepared for this, as he reached into the sleeve of his robe and pulled out a dagger. A quick slice of the blade over the strap and the book fell open.

The chamber appeared perfectly still and no one moved as the leader flipped through the pages of the coveted book.

They were blank.

As he turned to the final page, there was one single Latin word scrawled across the parchment. It said simply INLEX.

The leader of the hooded men threw the book with apparent disgust at the henchman who had acquired it. While Maureen did not know what INLEX meant, it was clear that this was not what any of these men had expected.

The little girl's ubiquitous giggle returned Maureen's attention to her surroundings. The child stood before her exactly as she had earlier that day, hands behind her back. With another sweet smile, she handed Maureen a canvas bag with a large book.

"It is not what you think it is."

And she laughed as she ran off around the corner, leaving Maureen to wonder just exactly what her attacker had stolen from her.

❋

The first light of day broke through the window of Maureen and Tammy's monastic cell. Maureen rubbed the sleep out of her eyes and looked over to where her friend was still deeply dozing. After the dream last night, she had gotten up long enough to jot down her notes of the experience, focusing on the word *INLEX*. If it was a Latin word, then she was in the right place. Every brother in Orval would have a classical education and should be able to translate a single word for her.

She threw on her clothes and went in search of the helpful Brother Marco, whom she found preparing the dining hall for breakfast.

"*Inlex?*" He gazed in thought for a moment. "Definitely Latin, but a strange word. Follow me to the library and we'll look it up to be certain."

Maureen accompanied the monk into a marvelous room filled with aged tomes. She was grateful that he hadn't asked her any questions about why she needed the meaning of this particular word. He was simply gracious and accommodating to his guest. Removing a Latin dictionary from one of the shelves, Brother Marco flipped through it until he found what he was looking for.

"Here we are. *Inlex*. It means decoy. A ruse or a lure. Does that help?"

Did it ever. Maureen resisted the urge to grab him and kiss him on the cheek. She thanked him politely instead and hurried back to the room to wake up Tammy.

⚜

"It was a decoy, Tammy!" Maureen burst through the door of their little cell, waking Tammy with her exuberance.

"What?" Tammy sat up, confused.

"The book. The book that was stolen from us yesterday. It wasn't the real one, it was . . ."

Maureen stopped. In her excitement to tell Tammy about the meaning of *inlex*, she had nearly missed it. Sitting in the middle of her unmade bed was a canvas bag.

"What's that?" Tammy was waking up now. "And . . . dare I ask where it came from?"

Maureen's heart was pounding as she shook her head. Where indeed, and from whom? Who was reading her dreams and sending her mysterious heretical relics? Who had access to the very bed that she spent the night in, next to her sleeping friend? And then there was a most disturbing question: Who had robbed them at gunpoint, and what was he looking for?

She walked to the bed and picked up the sack. Opening it, she removed the very heavy book contained within. It was different from the stolen tome in that the crimson leather was more weathered and cracked, and it was far weightier. This one looked truly ancient, as if it had been hidden away for a thousand years. Unlike the decoy book, this one did not have a strap or a lock on it, and Maureen opened it very gently. There were hundreds of parchment pages bound within it, and an exacting Latin script filled them all. The first page was emblazoned with an illuminated emblem, one that Maureen had come to recognize recently. It was the Latin cross with the strange signature:

Matilda, by the Grace of God Who Is.

CHAPTER FOUR

"*T*hat whore Matilda eludes me again!"

The leader of the hooded men growled his outrage as he threw the decoy book across the hidden basement room in a fit of uncontrolled rage.

One of the brothers responded, venturing into troubled waters. "How can you be so certain that it is Matilda's book that was to be delivered to the Paschal woman?"

The elder hissed. "You dare to question me? Is there a man among you who would challenge my knowledge or my authority on this matter?"

When silence met the question, the leader continued his tirade. "Because of the painstaking and tireless efforts of our brothers through history, we have successfully eradicated all known references to the Book of Love in writing. There is no evidence that it ever existed outside the fantasies of dead heretics. During the Inquisition, we confiscated every known document that alluded to it and destroyed them—the documents and the heretics. There is only one manuscript that has escaped our grasp in all of these centuries, and that is . . . Matilda's."

He spat her name, his voice dripping venom. All the women in history who claimed the title of prophetess infuriated him. But none more than the hated countess of Canossa, who had evaded attempts to silence her for almost a thousand years.

The young henchman who had attacked Maureen and Tammy stepped forward. "What would you like me to do, Your Holiness?"

His leader snarled the command. "Go to the source. Find Destino."

Of all the male followers, only the blessed Nicodemus and Joseph of Arimathea were present on the hill of Golgotha on the Black Day of the Skull. It was they who extracted the nails and they who removed our Lord from the cross. In the presence of the women, they carried the body of their messiah on a stretcher made of linen. Their destination was a nearby tomb that had been commissioned for the family of Joseph of Arimathea. Joseph provided this resting place out of both reverence and kinship as Jesus was not only his teacher but also his nephew by blood.

Upon arrival in the sepulcher, Maria Magdalena began to wash the wounds of her beloved, praying fervently over his body all the while. She worked tirelessly to apply salves and ointments, instructing everyone else in the cramped tomb to pray along with her, to pray with all their might that their heavenly father would restore his son to them. And pray they did, but none as passionately as Maria Magdalena. Even with sweat and grime and blood smeared over her face, she had the dignity and presence of a queen. She was pale beneath it all, faint from exhaustion and grief, but she would not cease her ministrations, nor her prayers, except to check on the health and welfare of the others in the tomb. That she had the capacity to worry about all of them at such a time was most emblematic of her remarkable compassion.

Maria Magdalena worked through the night while the others slept, never losing faith that God would restore their messiah to them. But his body remained lifeless and there was no sign of hope within the sepulcher. When the first rays of sun filtered in on that Saturday morning, she wrapped the body of her beloved in the burial cloth. The symbolism of this act—the finality of it, the necessary surrender—overwhelmed her. She collapsed to the floor, still clutching the alabaster jar that held the healing ointments.

The men carried Madonna Magdalena, on the same linen stretcher that had held Jesus the day before, slowly and gingerly to the estate of Joseph of Arimathea. Luke, the blessed doctor, attended her and he was worried. Magdalena's breathing was shallow, and beyond everything else she had endured, she was also heavy with child. She would have to be watched carefully. Now their prayers must be for her. When she was settled comfortably in a bed with her women around her, the men took their leave and met in Joseph's private chambers.

The purity of Maria's love and devotion to Jesus moved all three men through the searing pain of their grief. She helped them to realize that the loss of their messiah did not have to equate with the loss of his message. Maria Magdalena had mastered and embodied the teachings of the Way, proving through her actions that love was stronger than death. She lived this truth every day of her existence. Together, Joseph of Arimathea, Nicodemus, and Luke pledged to protect her and to support her and the holy teachings in every way possible for the rest of her life, her children's lives, and beyond. On that Holy Saturday, a bond was formed as the three men blended their blood and faith together in an unbreakable oath. They formed an alliance, one that would come to be known to the people as the Order of the Holy Sepulcher.

The following morning, when the risen Jesus announced his resurrection to Madonna Magdalena, the three men knew they had taken an appropriate vow. All earthly remains of the master had disappeared.

The men believed that this momentous occasion proved that Magdalena was his chosen successor to continue the teachings of the Way. Perhaps her extraordinary ministrations in the tomb had somehow aided in the holy and utterly awe-inspiring process of resurrection. Could it be that the pure power of love was all that was needed to create such a miracle? Who could know for sure? Such things were a matter of faith, and each man must come to his own understanding of God in his own way and in his own time.

But these men were unique witnesses. The traditions and understandings that they would pass on to subsequent generations were based on their own experiences combined with the pure teachings of Jesus himself. They were the blessed founders of our Order.

THE FOUNDATION OF THE ORDER OF THE HOLY SEPULCHER,
AS TOLD IN THE LIBRO ROSSO

PANTHEON SQUARE, the Piazza della Rotonda, is one of the iconic tourist sites in Rome, dominated on one end as it is by the exquisitely domed ancient structure for which it is named. Over the course of two thousand years the Pantheon evolved as a place of worship, first by the Roman pagans and then by the devout followers of Catholicism. And while it had been consecrated to a number of gods through time, the feminine curvature of the magnificent dome for which it is justly famous was a tribute to the ancient goddesses.

Divine female energy flows through the piazza. The center of Pantheon Square contains one of Rome's great fountains, this one dominated by a 3,300-year-old Egyptian obelisk made of red granite. The monument was brought to Rome from Heliopolis to grace a temple of Isis, in honor of the goddess who was the mother of all life.

Maureen's hotel room overlooked this square, and it was at this fountain that she stared from her window while she waited for Peter to arrive with a verdict on the mysterious red book. She had been here for two days since leaving Orval. Tammy had stayed in Belgium, where Roland came to claim her so she would not have to make the long drive back to the Languedoc alone following her ordeal. She would be with Roland and Bérenger now. Maureen sighed, thinking of her unfinished reunion with Bérenger. She'd been a fool to dread it so and put it off for as long as she had, and she wondered if his patience with her and her wanderings was wearing thin.

From her window now, she spotted Peter crossing the square, briefcase in hand.

"*Buona sera,*" she called out to him, waving vigorously, then went downstairs to greet him at the elevator. Her heart was in her throat now. She could tell by the look on his face that their discovery was indeed an important one, but they had agreed for safety's sake not to discuss it over the phone or in public.

As they entered the elevator on the way to Maureen's room, Peter asked her, "Remember what the little girl said to you in the dream? It is not what you think it is?"

Maureen nodded. "It's not the Book of Love."

"No, it's not. But it appears to contain elements of the Book of Love, and certainly a number of references to it."

Maureen was digesting this, trying not to be disappointed as she opened the door to her room. She had to trust the process, and she knew better than to think the Book of Love would simply fall into her lap. Such a treasure must be earned.

Peter smiled at her as he opened his briefcase and extracted a series of Xerox copies of the first set of parchment pages, and his preliminary translations of them.

"Maureen Paschal, meet Matilda of Tuscany. What we have here is a previously undiscovered version of her life story, one written in her own hand."

Maureen squealed with delight, no longer disappointed. Her passion for the role of women in history was one of the driving forces in her life. To discover something of this magnitude was true treasure, worth more than gold.

"Apparently, this is a family tradition," Maureen observed as she scanned the pages. "We're making quite a hobby out of discovering bloodline autobiographies."

"Don't laugh. I think it literally is a family tradition, and an important one. It ultimately became necessary for certain high-ranking members of the bloodline to set the record straight because they were aware that the truth was going to die if they didn't. And this is exactly what happened to Matilda, it seems. As you know, for centuries the 'heretics' didn't commit anything to writing because it was too dangerous. But Matilda wasn't just any heretic. She was a fearless one, and clearly a woman with a profound devotion to her spiritual mission, which was to preserve the truth. There is a biography of her in the Vatican archives, written by a monk called Donizone who was her contemporary and claimed to be her personal biographer. But he was a Benedictine and recorded history with an agenda, as all monks of his order did, and some of this biography is suspect. It reads like a polished PR piece straight from Rome. So ultimately I think she made a major decision to commit her own life to paper in her own hand as she was by all accounts incredibly well educated. Donizone refers to her as *docta*, which means exceptionally learned. And it wasn't a term used loosely, and never for a woman. So she was very capable of recording her own life, with her perspective and feelings. But . . . it's highly controversial, to say the least."

"You have read the entire document?"

Peter shook his head. "Enough to know that what awaits us could be earth-shattering, but not enough to be able to tell you definitively who she was or what she had in her possession."

"But she talks about the Book of Love?"

Peter nodded. "She does."

Maureen had a thousand questions and began to rattle them off at Peter, who laughed. "I'll let Matilda tell you about it in her own words. Ready?"

Peter picked up the translations and began to read.

Mantua, Italy
1052

"NOT THAT STORY, Isobel! Tell me the other story. The one about the labyrinth."

Though she was six years old and uncommonly petite, Matilda possessed a will that completely belied her physical appearance. She stamped a tiny foot and tossed her mass of red hair imperiously as she continued to give orders to her nurse. "You know I love that story the most. I don't want to hear any others. But stop before the bad part. I hate the bad part."

As the tiny countess of Canossa made a face to punctuate her distaste for the bad part, the lovely Lady Isobel of Lucca nodded patiently at her charge. Her delicate hands had wiped the birthing blood from this child's face when she was a mere five seconds old, then had swaddled and cradled the baby as her own. Matilda had been in Isobel's care since that early spring evening when the fiery infant drew her first bold breath and shrieked her arrival to the Tuscan countryside. For her father's people, descended from the fierce Lombard warriors of northern Italy, the birth of a child on the vernal equinox was a particular blessing from God. The cry of this babe was so hearty that her father, waiting with his men in a neighboring courtyard, was certain he had been given a son blessed by a benevolent birth. Duke Bonifacio was only temporarily disappointed that the sanctified child was female. As Matilda grew and began to take on the characteristics of her noble parents—the exquisite features and grace of her slender mother, combined with the determination and strength of her father—she rapidly became the precious and adored daughter of the most terrifying man in Italy.

"Why do you love that story so, Tilda? I should think it would bore you by now as you know it by heart. And I have so many others to tell you."

"Well, it does not bore me. So start from the beginning." It was an order.

Isobel smiled benignly but did not begin the story, causing Matilda to look momentarily rebellious before caving in.

"*Please*, Isobel. Please will you tell me my favorite story? I shall play the part of Princess Ariadne and spin my magical threads while you tell it. And I did say please."

"Indeed you did, but I should not have to beg you for manners, Matilda. Your good mother is descended from the noblest household in the world, a direct descendant of the blessed Charlemagne himself, and yet she does not behave so, even to the servants who clean her chamber pot. Have you ever seen her snap orders thus? No, you have not and you will not. And outside of your good father, who has his own reasons, you won't see any true native of Lucca behaving thus, either. It is not our way, child. It is not *the* Way."

Matilda was momentarily chastised. Her imperious impulses were born of her natural high spirits combined with her father's influence. For while the Lady Beatrice was indeed a most gentle and highborn woman, Bonifacio was pure Tuscan soldier. Her father's lineage combined descent from the sanctified and holy city of Lucca with the fierce Lombard warrior blood that had integrated the house of Tuscany. Where Beatrice was the graceful and cultured product of the German royal family, Bonifacio was the often ruthless and always power-mad feudal lord; he was far more a son of his warlike Lombardi blood than of his spiritual Lucchesi birth. The Lombards had invaded Italy in the sixth century, wreaking havoc on what was left of a crumbling Roman Empire. Their influence gave to the region of northern Italy the name that would one day take permanent hold: Lombardy.

While Bonifacio had inherited significant wealth and power, he worked tirelessly to increase his own fortunes by his own merits. The rivers surrounding Mantua, the Po and the Mincio, were trade arteries to northwestern Europe that began to thrive during Bonifacio's rule. Prior to his superior leadership, merchants had feared the lawlessness of northern Italy and avoided trade there. Critical pathways from the great ports, like Venice, for importing luxury goods from the Orient and elsewhere had been completely cut off.

But the duke of Tuscany governed the Po river valley with an iron hand, stringing up brigands after seeing to it that they were brutally mutilated as a sign to approaching pirates that such behavior would no longer be tolerated. Strong bands of fearless and well-compensated men were organized into an elite force to patrol the river regions in the name of the grand duke.

Bonifacio's strategy secured the trade routes and succeeded in bringing merchants from the Adriatic via the rivers, as well as the Germans, who now were more willing to cross the Alps with their valuable wares from the northern kingdom of Saxony. In return, he exacted taxes and fees for use of the routes by merchants, who were only too glad to pay for the right to trade safely in this lucrative region. His wealth and his power grew to legendary proportions, aided by the beautiful, blue-blooded wife at his side. She was the jewel in his feudal crown, the legitimacy he required and craved.

Bonifacio's only weakness was his precious daughter, whom he often carried on his horse with him while inspecting his territories. At six years of age, Matilda had more experience on a horse than most adult males in her day. Yet after Matilda spent time in her father's commanding company, Isobel needed many hours of patience to correct the child's behavior.

"I am sorry, Isobel." Matilda managed to look somewhat sheepish, if only briefly. "I shall work to be a good and noble countess."

"That's much better. Now, remind me. Where does this tale begin?"

"Crete!" Matilda shrieked excitedly.

"Ah yes. The mighty and golden kingdom of Crete. A long, long time ago there lived a great king named Minos . . ."

The Minotaur was a great monster, born into the family of the king of Crete, the powerful ruler known as Minos, and his wife, Queen Pasiphaë. He was half man, half bull, and had the appetite of ten wild beasts. It is said that the Minotaur was the result of Pasiphaë's illicit encounter with a god, or worse, with a great white bull. This has likely been misunderstood by judgmental men who could not grasp the great mysteries of the ancients. It is likely that Queen Pasiphaë was a priestess of the moon and the embodiment of the sacred feminine and that her mating with a priest, in his guise as a bull to represent the sacred masculine, was the enactment of a ritual that has been considered a holy mystery since the dawn of mankind: a ritual of the union of masculine and feminine energies, necessary for the balance of life on the earth.

Thus the history of how the Minotaur was conceived is shrouded in mystery, but we know this: he existed as a combination of the human and the divine, and he was half miraculous and half terrible as a result. Perhaps it is the mysterious existence of the Minotaur wherein lies the secret of the Fall. Perhaps he is a symbol of the great loss of understanding that occurs when humans are no longer able to accept our divine natures and, most of all, the loss to our humanity when we abandon the necessity of honoring the masculine and feminine together in its most divine form.

The given name of the Minotaur was Asterius, which means "star-being," as a result of his divine origins. He was revered as one of the gods at the same time that he was the object of terror and fear amongst the humans. His body was covered with a pattern of stars as a reminder that all creatures come from heaven, even those who appear to have only a base nature. It is from heaven that we come, and to heaven we will return. For that which is above is also below.

Was Asterius born a monster, a terrible creature who would demand human sacrifice and terrorize the peace of Crete? Or was he made a monster because he was denied love and subjected to ridicule, cruelty, and judgment? He was most certainly a source of shame for King Minos, who could not bear that his wife had conceived without him, even if it was with a divine being. Minos was driven to the brink of madness by jealousy and wanted nothing more than to destroy Asterius, but he dared not put the monster to death because of his divine paternity. Instead, the king devised an underground prison in which to house this unwanted creature and shield him from his sight.

There lived in Minos a refugee from Athens named Daedalus the Inventor, who was summoned by Minos to create a prison in which to house the Minotaur. It was in devising this terrible structure that Daedalus became a master builder. What he conceived was the labyrinth, an enormous and circuitous type of maze that led to a midpoint; here in the midpoint was the temple in which the creature would dwell. The construction of this labyrinth was such that once one was inside, it was impossible to find the way out. This served to contain the Minotaur but also to entrap his unfortunate victims—for the construction of the labyrinth was such that once they were inside, they would not be able to escape. As his monstrous due, the Minotaur demanded a sacrifice of seven girls and seven boys to be sent into the center of the labyrinth every nine years, all of whom he devoured without a trace.

Thus Asterius the Minotaur lived the life of a god-monster, out of the sight of the people of Crete and trapped in his subterranean labyrinth, yet as a shadow cast over the land every nine years. King Minos and Queen Pasiphaë went on to have human children, among them the lovely and kind princess called Ariadne. The Minoan princess was renowned for her radiant beauty and was referred to throughout the lands as "the Clear and Bright One" and was also known to be "utterly pure of spirit and heart."

It came to pass that Crete was at war with Athens. The brother of Ariadne and the only true son of Minos, a hero called Androgeos, was slain by the Athenians in a battle. King Minos howled in his grief at the loss of his son and declared absolute terror on Athens in revenge. As part of his conquest, Minos demanded that the Athenians supply the tribute to the Minotaur from their own children, and henceforth the fourteen sacrificial innocents were taken from Athens.

The youngest son of the Athenian king was a beautiful and heroic youth called Theseus. And so it was when it came time for the Athenians to send their terrible sacrifice to the Minotaur, Theseus volunteered to go in as the first of the fourteen, determined as he was to face the Minotaur and slay him, thus saving the lives of future innocents and liberating the people of Athens from this terror. For even in his youth, this hero was wise beyond all years. He understood that the offering of sacrifices to the Minotaur was a choice. It was a tradition that did not need to be kept, but it would take someone with great courage to stop it.

The princess Ariadne was walking on the beach near the harbor in Crete when the ship from Athens landed to unload the sacrificial victims. It is said that she caught sight of Theseus and fell immediately in love with him, recognizing him as the bright hero who could defeat the darkness that lurked below the surface of Crete in the guise of her half brother, the terrible Minotaur Asterius. She had been haunted throughout her life by the slaying of innocents to satisfy his inhuman hunger, and yet the compassion in her heart also gave her great sympathy for his monstrous suffering.

Ariadne arranged a secret tryst with Theseus on the eve prior to the sacrificial ceremony. Here Ariadne vowed her aid in return for his own promise to marry her and take her away with him.

As it was, the fair Ariadne had been promised by her father as a bride to the debauched god Dionysus. It was said that the god, driven half mad by his passion for the pure beauty of Ariadne, had demanded her as tribute from Minos in exchange for military victories over the Athenians. Minos had relented with some reluctance, but the deal had been struck. But the pure lady Ariadne was a devoted disciple of Aphrodite, the goddess of love. As such, she could not bear the thought of marrying for any reason other than true love, and certainly not in submitting to a fate as the debased concubine of the god of hedonism.

Upon setting eyes on Theseus, Ariadne fell in love with him and knew that he could change her destiny. Theseus would rescue the people from the Minotaur, and Ariadne from the dark god, and both salvations would happen through the force of *love. It is said that Ariadne and Theseus joined together that night in passion and purpose, flesh and spirit, trust and consciousness. In that way she shielded him within the pure power of her love.*

Because Ariadne was the half sister of the terrible beast, she knew the secrets to slaying the Minotaur and exiting the labyrinth. All these she shared with her new love. Ariadne then wove strands of her own silken hair into a skein of golden yarn, to create a magical thread, called a clue, in which to aid her love's escape from the labyrinth. Finally, she presented him with a miraculous sword, a weapon once forged for the sea god Poseidon himself; it was crafted of silver and gold to represent the light of the sun and the moon as they reflect off the sea. Ariadne knew that this weapon would kill her half brother without causing him any suffering. Theseus would not fail to kill the Minotaur with a single true and merciful blow and emerge as a hero of the light if he followed her instructions perfectly.

The following morning, as he was being led into the labyrinth as the first sacrifice, Theseus fastened one end of Ariadne's thread to an iron ring at the entrance post of the labyrinth, tying it in the symbolic bridal knot exactly as she had shown him. He carried the ball of magical thread inside with him, unraveling it slowly as he walked the circuitous paths toward the hideous beast.

At the center of the labyrinth, Theseus met the Minotaur and defeated him in honorable hand-to-hand combat, shielded by Ariadne's love and delivering the final blow with the magical weapon that she had provided. His task complete, the hero retraced his steps out of the labyrinth by following Ariadne's thread, thus arriving safely at the entrance of the labyrinth and into the embrace of his newly beloved. Carrying off his princess, Theseus freed the remaining thirteen Athenian children and returned to their ship as the liberator of his people and the great slayer of the god-beast.

They sailed until arriving on the island of Dia, where they stopped for a night of celebration and to gather provisions for their return to Athens. Sadly, their joy was cut short when the wine-crazed god, Dionysus, appeared on Dia to claim his bride. Ariadne was his by the right of human and divine law, he said, betrothed by her royal father and with no will of her own to resist. Theseus resisted the god at first, claiming that Ariadne was his by her own choice and that it was his intention to make her the queen of Athens. Dionysus countered by reminding Theseus that he could make Ariadne immortal through her marriage to a god, and that if the Athenian truly loved her, he would release her to a more divine destiny. The argument lasted into the night, with the god Dionysus relentless in his attack on Theseus.

It was a terrible choice for the young Athenian prince, who was no match for the clever and determined god. In the end, Theseus believed that if he resisted Dionysus, the god would likely take Ariadne by force and inflict harm upon him and the remainder of the Athenians. And so it was that with a heavy heart, Theseus abandoned his Ariadne to the will of Dionysus and sailed away from Dia without his newfound beloved.

Ariadne was distraught at the loss of Theseus, and in despair at the prospect of becoming the consort to the hedonist god who had taken her by force of guile. But it was through the sacred strength of love that a miraculous change occurred in the god Dionysus. So enamored was he of the beautiful and pure Ariadne that he could not bear to see her in such anguish. He did not take her by force. Instead, he agreed that he would have her only when she agreed to be his wife of her own accord. Dionysus began to shower her with gifts and celebrate her beauty, even vowing to change his decadent ways to indicate the truth of his love for her. When Ariadne saw the extent of the god's devotion, and how it had transformed him, her heart softened. Through her prayers to Aphrodite, the embodiment of all love, Ariadne came to the understanding that Theseus would have fought for her if he had truly felt in his heart that she was his only beloved. That he did not was an indication that she must let him go.

For love that is not requited in equal measure is not love at all; it is not sacred. And holding on to the ideal of such love can keep us from finding the one that is true.

The day came when Ariadne agreed to be the wife of Dionysus, and they lived in a state of bliss into eternity as true and equal partners in the hieros-gamos. Here it was that Ariadne found the love that is real—with the beloved who had, indeed, fought for her.

Theseus, for his part, was left to mourn the loss of Ariadne and regretted until the end of his days the weakness that had led to his terrible decision to abandon her. In honor of she who was now a goddess, he created a temple in her name on the isle of Amathus. Taking the statue of Aphrodite which Ariadne had once carried with her upon leaving Crete, he erected a structure which he called the Temple of Love, *and dedicated it to "Ariadne-Aphrodite." Within the temple, he built a labyrinth which became the symbol of love and liberation, and a rhythmic dance that represented the celebration of divine union was established for the annual feast in Ariadne's honor, the feast of the Lady of the Labyrinth who defeated the darkness with her love. The new labyrinth was created as a place of joy, with one sacred, spiral path that led into the center and out again. No more would the labyrinth be a place where human souls were lost. Forevermore, it would be a place where the human spirit could be found: a place to celebrate what is both human and divine in us all, once we learn to slay the minotaurs that lie within ourselves through our necessary belief in the power of love.*

Theseus became the greatest of heroes, establishing democracy and justice in Athens, where he is still recognized as the wise and compassionate founder of that city, which gave learning to the world. It is without doubt that his deep understanding of the nature of love and loss was the element that made him a great leader.

For those with ears to hear, let them hear it.

THE LEGEND OF ARIADNE, THE LADY OF THE LABYRINTH,
AS PRESERVED IN THE LIBRO ROSSO

Isobel recounted the legend of the labyrinth as she had many times before, telling it as it had been preserved in their most sacred writings, as a cornerstone of the Libro Rosso, the Red Book. She tailored the story to the child's age, eliminating the overt sexual references and certainly halting before Matilda's professed "bad part" where everything goes awry for the young lovers and Ariadne is abandoned to Dionysus. For the child Matilda, the legend of the labyrinth ended happily ever after, with Theseus slaying the beast, saving the children of Athens, and carrying off his beautiful princess into the sunset.

There would be time enough for her to learn that most love stories were far from simplistic and did not end so neatly. Indeed, it was one of the great lessons of the labyrinth legend that the needs of women and the power of love were often not heeded in matters of human history. Ariadne's desire was never a factor in the argument between Theseus and Dionysus, although both men professed love for her and wanted to claim her. She was given no choice in her own destiny, a fate which had been sealed earlier by her father when he sold his own child to earn the goodwill and alliance of Dionysus. And this foreshadowed the time when humans truly fell historically—when women became pawns in the affairs of men, with no right to choose in their own future. They became property, game pieces on a political chessboard for the use of their male relatives: devalued and diminished, even dehumanized. As marriages became arranged political affairs where women were traded like cattle by their families and had no rights, what had once been the most sacred center of union became a place where rape was made legal by the state. The Fall of Man was complete.

Isobel knew that Matilda would eventually need to master all the complex lessons of love and power within Ariadne's story. But she would also have to teach Matilda that the union between a man and a woman was meant to be more than what it had become: a dehumanizing and often brutal transaction.

Isobel's duties as Matilda's nurse encompassed the child's spiritual and intellectual welfare, as well as her physical protection. Matilda was an exceptional child by birth, and her guardian had been selected most specifically. Isobel's task was to raise the girl within the highly secretive and protected traditions that had been in practice in Lucca since the first century. While Bonifacio was too preoccupied with conquest and territory expansion to bother himself with religion or spirituality, he held it in reverence as a tribute to his great-grandfather, the legendary Tuscan leader Siegfried of Lucca. It was appropriate that his daughter become educated and indoctrinated into those sacred traditions. Thus it was that Bonifacio and Beatrice had chosen the lovely Isobel from one of the grand houses in Tuscany. Indeed, Isobel was a cousin and a noblewoman, related to Bonifacio through the line of Siegfried himself.

While Matilda's mother, the lady Beatrice, was also descended from the exalted bloodline family of Lorraine, their spiritual traditions were centuries more remote and did not thrive immediately under the surface as they had in the wilds of Tuscany. Beatrice was well aware of her heretical heritage, yet she maintained traditional Catholic practices in her own household. This was necessary as she was a member of the German royal family who owed allegiance to the Catholic Church and the related, complicated political structure that determined power in Europe. Beatrice was pious and obedient, a graceful and strong woman in her own way, but happily subservient to her legendary husband. Beatrice had, in fact, been unusually fortunate for a woman in her time in that she found real love and contentment in her arranged marriage. That Beatrice was a renowned beauty with raven hair and slanting dark eyes was the delicious gravy on Bonifacio's full plate.

Matilda was not the first of their children. Sadly, they had lost the eldest two who preceded her to the influenza that swept through Europe earlier in the same year. One was Bonifacio's son and heir, who died in his teens, leaving a great wound in his father's heart. The second was another daughter lost in early childhood. The tragedy of losing two of her children so quickly had taken its toll on Beatrice, who was often weak and ill with the sadness and had little energy left for her surviving daughter. So while Beatrice was Matilda's mother by birth and lineage, Isobel was the only real maternal force that she knew.

"When you are older, child, I shall tell you a different story of the labyrinth," Isobel said. "One that involves wise King Solomon and the very exotic and glorious Queen of Sheba."

"Tell me now!"

"No, I cannot. You are not yet of an age to understand all that this story entails. I shall tell you following your sixteenth birthday, as appropriate."

Matilda's tone turned conspiratorial as she whispered, "Is it in . . . the Libro Rosso?" There was awe in her voice when she spoke of the magical red book.

Isobel winked at her, nodding. "It is indeed. And there is much in that book which you will have to grow into. Now, to bed. Here, let me braid your hair." With graceful fingers, Isobel began the nightly process of taming Matilda's copper-gold hair, which fell in heavy waves to the middle of her back.

A sleepy Matilda gave in to the idea of bed, rubbing her aquamarine eyes and yawning with the ferocity of a lion cub. "Will you sing me the song, please?" she pleaded. "The one from your mother's country?"

The Lady Isobel tucked the woolen coverlet under the child's chin and perched on the side of her bed. Her sweet, clear voice sang softly in French:

Il est longtemps que je t'aime,
Jamais je ne t'oublierai . . .

Matilda, who spoke her native Tuscan and her mother's German fluently, had only just begun to study French. When she repeated the verse in an answering melody, it was in her own native tongue.

I have loved thee a long time,
Forever, I will not forget thee . . .

And then Isobel finished with the ancient poem that was sacred in the La Beauce region of France, whence her mother had come before marrying into the sanctified lineage of Lucca. It came from a piece of poetry written a millennium before by a very great man about his love for a blessed woman and her children.

Je t'ai aimé dans le passé,
Je t'aime aujourd'hui,
T'aimerais encore dans l'avenir.
Le temps revient.

She kissed Matilda on her forehead, as the child reached over to the small altar table at the side of her bed. A little statue of Saint Modesta, carved meticulously from wood, graced the altar. It was a gift from the French side of Isobel's family, given in celebration of the little countess's blessed birth six years ago. In this depiction, the saint held one hand up in benediction, while the other clutched a book, colored in red with gilded accents. Matilda loved the statue, painted as it was to depict Modesta's hair in the same extraordinary color as her own.

Matilda ran her hand over the statue of Modesta, before whispering back the translation, which was part of her nightly ritual and a cornerstone of their tradition:

I have loved you before,
I love you today,
And I will love you again.
The time returns.

"Indeed it does." Isobel sighed as she gazed down upon this brilliant and complicated little being whom she loved as her own child. It appeared that God had chosen not to give Isobel children from her own womb. Certainly, with her sworn commitment to Matilda, she would never have the time or opportunity to marry and have children of her own despite the fact that she was only in her twenties. So be it. She understood that it was her destiny to raise this one above all others, and it was at times a daunting task that would require her sole focus.

Thy will be done. Isobel repeated it many times in her daily devotions from the Book of Love. It was the second of the six sacred teachings of the Pater Noster, the Lord's Prayer, which was the foundation of their practice. Obedience to God. Surrender to his will. And it was without doubt his will that Isobel devote her life to the raising of this child.

Matilda would one day prove that "the time returns" just as the greatest prophetess of their line, the blessed Sarah-Tamar, had decreed so long ago. It was her destiny. She would leave her mark on history, this child. But not tonight.

"Good night, *ma petite.* May your dreams be sweet."

"Good night, my Issy," she whispered sleepily, nestling into her coverlet, with a final yawn. "Love you."

❀

Matilda was manic, running through the castle and shrieking with excitement, unbound hair flying behind her in an unruly red-gold curtain.

"Luuuuuucca! Luuuucca! Are we really going to Lucca tomorrow, Isobel? Really? With Papa?"

"Yes, little one. We are finally going to Lucca."

Matilda repeated the name of her birthplace once more, this time stopping to whisper it in dreamy imitation of Isobel, who sighed often for her homeland and spoke of it in hushed tones, as if it were the dwelling place of all angels on earth. The child became suddenly, deeply serious as she turned her full attention to her nurse.

"I don't remember anything about how Lucca looks, Issy."

"I shouldn't think so, Tilda. You were an infant when we came here to Mantua. And yet the first breath in your body came from the sacred air of that place, and it will bring its special blessing to you as long as you live."

"Is it really so beautiful? And full of saints and angels?"

"Lucca is magnificent in a way that is special above all other places on God's earth. Come, I will tell you a new story tonight, one that is a part of our special heritage, and . . ." Isobel did not complete the sentence. Matilda, for all her precocious brilliance, was still far too young to understand everything that the complex legacy of their people entailed. Best to teach her in the tried-and-true way of storytelling until she was older.

"Now, I want you to go all the way back to the stories I have told you about our Lord," Isobel began in the more formal tone that indicated a lesson as well as a story was to come.

Matilda nodded solemnly, tucking her legs underneath her and settling in anticipation of the tale.

"Our Lord had a wonderful friend who was called Nicodemus. Nic-o-de-mus. Can you say his name for me?"

The child repeated the name obediently to praise from her nurse.

"Nicodemus was one of only two men who were with him when he died. Do you remember who else was with him?"

Matilda was an apt pupil with extraordinary talent for perfect recollection. She loved the story of the Passion and committed every telling of it to memory. She never shied away from the more graphic depictions of Jesus' sacrifice on the cross as taught by her mother's confessor, a dour cleric from Lorraine called Fra Gilbert. Fra Gilbert seemed to glory in the violent details of Christ's final hours on earth and recounted them in particularly graphic description when he was trying to make a point about penance, which was often. This approach horrified Isobel, who revered her Lord for his words and his work rather than for the means of his death. This philosophy was in keeping with the Way of Love as practiced by her people for a thousand years. Isobel discreetly disappeared when Fra Gilbert was present. But Matilda was enraptured by all versions of the greatest story ever told, even the most horrific. In that regard, she had proven to be Bonifacio's child from a very early stage—fearless and unflinching in the face of the harsher versions of reality.

But it was Isobel's version that truly captivated Matilda. For while the child felt deep devotion to her Lord and was moved by the telling of his sacrifice, it was another aspect of this history that kept her spellbound in the telling: the legend of the women in Jesus' life, and one woman in particular.

Matilda sat up respectfully and gave her answer. "The other man was Joseph of Ara . . ."

"Arimathea," Isobel helped her, and Matilda continued enthusiastically.

"His mother was with him, the Great Maria, and his most beloved, Maria Magdalena. And all the other Marias who followed him as disciples and taught his words and work forevermore." She lowered her voice to the childlike version of her conspiratorial whisper. "But we are not allowed to call Maria Magdalena his 'most beloved' in front of Fra Gilbert, right?"

"No, we most assuredly are not."

"But why, Issy? If Jesus loved her, why can we not speak of it and love her as he did? Why must we have so many secrets?"

Isobel sighed as she stroked one hand over Matilda's unruly hair, whose coppery color was but one sign that this petite countess was born of the most immaculate bloodlines in Europe, born of *her* bloodlines. It was said that Maria Magdalena had hair of this same color, even when she died as an old woman. Both of Matilda's parents were descended from the union between Jesus and his beloved Maria—her mother through the lineage of Charlemagne, her father through the secret Italian sects that had taken root in Tuscany during Rome's persecutions of the earliest Christians.

Matilda's question was difficult for the most learned adult to answer; she was not ready to understand. Isobel moved away from the question with the skill of a master storyteller.

"This friend of Jesus, Nicodemus, was a very special man with a great talent that is important to us today. Would you like to know what that was? He was an artist. A sculptor. He could take the visions given to him by God and create them by carving wood."

"Like Frederick?"

Frederick was her father's oldest servant, another trusted member of the circle from Lucca that surrounded the noble family. Frederick often entertained Matilda by carving trinkets for her out of wood. Her favorite doll, an exquisite carving of the legendary Ariadne, was a masterwork that the old man had created for her at Christmastide. He had even carved a replica of the labyrinth on the doll's back, that Matilda might begin to understand the complex pattern that was so intrinsic to their tradition.

"Yes, very much like our Frederick. But because Nicodemus was present when our Lord died on the cross, he could not get such a holy image out of his mind. So he decided to carve it in wood, that the world would have a memory of this great sacrifice for many centuries to come. It took him a year to complete his task, but when it was finished, Nicodemus had created the very first piece of art that shows us what our Lord looked like. It is called the *Volto Santo*, the Holy Face, because it is one of only two pieces of art in the world that were created by men who looked into the face of Jesus during both his life and death. One is in Rome, a painting that was created by holy Luke the Evangelist and is in the keeping of the pope. But the *Volto Santo* is the only one that I have seen, and it is most magnificent."

Matilda's eyes grew wide. "You have seen this carving?"

"Yes, and so will you."

Matilda began her customary squirming again. "But when? How?"

Isobel interrupted her. "Patience, my sweet. Let me tell you more of the story. When Nicodemus died, the carving disappeared. The earliest Christians took it away to hide it from the Romans so it would not be lost or destroyed. It was hidden in the Holy Land for seven hundred years. And then, when the prophets decreed that it was time, the *Volto Santo*, which had once held the most sacred treasure of our people, was brought from its hiding place and prepared for a voyage."

"Sacred treasure?" Matilda's eyes were wide with the idea of a great secret.

"Yes, love. For you see, while carving the *Volto Santo*, Nicodemus had left an opening in the back of the sculpture, a secret opening in which to store the most holy of items."

"The Libro Rosso?"

Isobel nodded. "Yes, the Libro Rosso. And it was the most sacred of treasures because it contained the teachings of the Way of Love as written by our Lord himself, and later the prophecies of his holy daughter. But you shall learn more of that when we arrive in Lucca. For it is there that you will view the Libro Rosso in person. It is time, my angel, for you to begin your proper training in earnest."

Matilda was speechless, which was entirely uncustomary, causing Isobel to laugh out loud. It was a beautiful, ringing sound. "What's wrong, little one? Are you so surprised that your time has come? You have just turned six, and that is a magic number. It is the number of

Venus, the number of love. The year when the training begins, particularly for an Expected One. And do not worry, I will be with you every step of the way.

"Now, I must prepare you to meet the great teacher. You will refer to him as the Master, and nothing else."

"Doesn't he have a name?"

"I am sure he does, but we do not use it. We call him the Master as a sign of respect, for he is from a very long line of chosen leaders for the Order, all of whom have been called the same thing. He is a very holy man.

"And I must warn you. He has a scar on his face, Matilda. A very ugly scar. But you must not be afraid of him. It will be a first lesson for you in learning not to judge a man by his physical appearance, but rather to wait and see what his disposition tells you about the true human within. The Master is a great man, a gentle man, and he will teach you as he taught me and many others."

Matilda wanted to cry with the weight of this news, but she would not allow herself to do so. But this fearsome Master with the scarred face, the training to begin in mysterious Lucca . . . it was all so much! Perhaps going to Lucca was not such a wonderful present. Staying here in Mantua, where she had never known anything but security, might be better. She bit her lower lip and would not allow it to tremble.

"Don't be afraid, *ma petite*." Isobel hugged Matilda tightly. She had the heart of a lioness, this child, but she was still just a little girl. "It is your destiny, and a beautiful one at that. Just remember who you are at all times, by the grace of God."

Matilda nodded solemnly. She was the countess of Canossa, and the heir of the great Bonifacio. She was a daughter of both Lucca and Mantua; she was the child of the prophecy. She was The Expected One.

She was *Matilda, by the Grace of God Who Is.*

The truth will take root in the area of marshes,
and here it will flourish in secret
by those with the strength to hold it there.
A great shrine for the holy writ and the holy face
will be made and remade as The Time Returns.
Many will doubt, but the truth will endure here
for the children of the future,
those with eyes to see and ears to hear.

The truth must be preserved in stone,
and built into a Valley of Gold.
The new Shepherdess, The Expected One,
shall see to its perfection
and encase the Word of the Father and Mother
and the legacy of their children within sacred spaces.
This becomes her legacy.
This, and to know a very Great Love.

For those with ears to hear, let them hear it.

THE SECOND PROPHECY OF *L'ATTENDUE*, THE EXPECTED ONE,
FROM THE WRITINGS OF SARAH-TAMAR,
AS PRESERVED IN THE LIBRO ROSSO

CHAPTER FIVE

Lucca
1052

*T*he city of Lucca was sacred by its very nature, one of earth's blessed power places that had been recognized as possessing a special aura for as far back as human history endures. There were scraps of paleolithic settlements that gave a glimpse into the truly ancient nature of this place, yet it owed its early endurance to the ancient Etruscans and the Ligurian Celts. It was generally believed that the origins of its name came from a Celtic word, *luks*, which meant "area of marshes." By the third century BCE, the Romans recognized Lucca as a special locale.

But for early Christians, it was the first and second century that formed the heart and soul of the city they considered sacred above many others. While the Romans continued to build superlatively, surrounding Lucca with important roads, enclosing it in its first set of walls and creating a spectacular amphitheater, it was the quiet settlement of the Christian underground that formed the backbone of the culture that would endure here within the hearts of the Lucchesi.

While traditional Catholicism flourished on the surface, Lucca had another Christian culture at its foundation, one that lived in harmony with the more traditional Catholic converts. For it was taught that the children of the original apostles and their followers settled here, where legend says they were joined by members of the holy family. These Christians claimed that their teachings came directly from Jesus Christ himself through the legacy of his children, and they had in their possession a sacred book from which they taught their descendants.

At the time of Matilda's arrival in Lucca, the power of orthodoxy in the Church through ascetic monasticism was growing in a way that required those who practiced the "old ways" of Christianity to be very discreet. Certainly, the new reforms concerned those who were devoted to the Way of Love. The whispers of heresy were beginning to grow in Italy and had already spread to other areas of Europe. Isobel's people were like many in Lucca who publicly attended and supported the Catholic Church but maintained their secret traditions behind the closed doors of their homes. But Isobel, as a descendant of Siegfried of Lucca's family, had been raised with the innermost teachings of the old traditions. She was a member of the Order of the Holy Sepulcher, the secret society created on the original Easter by Luke the Evangelist along with the holy Nicodemus and Joseph of Arimathea. The Order had branches in Jerusalem, the southern Italian region of Calabria, Rome, and throughout Tuscany. It was an order that not only accepted women as members but recognized them as leaders. This was in honor of Maria Magdalena, whom the Order was formed to protect, and her daughter, the prophetess Sarah-Tamar. They were the recognized successors of Jesus in their tradition, the holy women by whom Christianity endured and flourished in Europe.

The name by which the children of Lucca chose to be known, the *Lucchesi*, was a clever play on words. It defined them as inhabitants of Lucca but also as children of Luca the Evangelist, the founder who brought the sacred Order of the Holy Sepulcher to Italy.

The entourage entered through the San Frediano gate at the north, and Matilda was delighted to see that they were to be received with great festivity. She was wearing a golden dress of finest brocade and perched with her father upon his enormous black charger. Bonifacio was equally bedecked; his riding cape was trimmed in ermine and encrusted with jewels; there were thick and solid golden cuffs at his wrists that gleamed in the Tuscan sunlight. The people of Lucca had come out in throngs to catch a glimpse of this legendary little countess with the shining tresses and the extraordinary blue-green eyes. Isobel had braided her hair and woven flowers through the plaits that morning. Her refusal to cover the child's hair with a veil had caused some consternation in Bonifacio, who thought it unseemly for his daughter to be seen in public this way. But Isobel had a way with Matilda's father; she knew how to play to his familial sympathies and soften him. That Isobel was as lovely and graceful as she was did not hurt when she needed to make a point with the acutely male Tuscan warrior prince, albeit she never used her charms inappropriately.

The child countess of Canossa would need the support of the people in Tuscany as she grew older. She was now the only living heir of a great fortune, a fortune that law decreed could not be inherited by a woman. In order for Matilda to retain her claim as Bonifacio's heiress, she would need, among other blessings, to be beloved by the people of Tuscany. Isobel had explained this patiently to Bonifacio. Matilda's entrance into Lucca must be memorable. She must become the cherished child of the Tuscan people in order to ensure any hope of her inheritance when she was older.

But Isobel was also well aware of the growing strength of Matilda's living legend, even at this young age. The indoctrinated in Lucca were well versed in the enigmatic prophecies left by Sarah-Tamar and they had known that Matilda could be The Expected One since the propitious day of her equinox birth here. If this were the case, she was to be revered as the new Shepherdess, the woman who would lead them spiritually in the teachings and preservation of the Way of Love. Matilda had arrived at a time when the ancient Lucchesi people needed the symbol of hope that she represented for them. All of these factors must be considered as Matilda made her triumphant return to her birthplace.

Bonifacio relented, and the savvy Isobel had prepared the prophesied princess for her debut into the public eye. Matilda, for her part, behaved beautifully, laughing and waving and looking every bit like the petite, mythical creature she was believed by many to be. This came naturally to her, but today her excitement bubbled over and into the streets. She was with her heroic father, wearing a beautiful new dress, and people were shouting her name in the streets! She would remember it as one of the shining moments of her life.

✳

"Has she had the dreams yet, Isobel?"

The enigmatic wise man, known to his students only as the Master, stood over the sleeping figure of the exhausted little countess. It had been a busy day of parades and banquets, of being doted upon by her father and adored by his people. Matilda's official meeting with the Master would occur on the morrow, once she was rested. But the wise man wanted to have a first glimpse of her, and to speak to her guardian in preparation. He was an imposing presence, tall and weathered, with an appearance made deceptively fearsome by the long jagged scar that crossed the left side of his face.

"Yes, but she does not understand what they are or what they mean."

"And she has dreamt of Golgotha?"

"Not specifically, but she has dreamed of Good Friday, of that I am certain."

The Master nodded, deep in thought. He was satisfied. It was enough to fulfill the prophecy, even at this early age. For the prophetess had decreed that The Expected One would have visions of "the black day of the skull." While this had been interpreted to mean specific visions of the crucifixion, for a child so young and of otherwise promising birth to be dreaming of Good Friday was a strong omen.

"I believe she is what they say she is," the Master decreed. "Bring her to me immediately after breaking her fast. We have much work to do. And Isobel . . ."

"Yes, Master?"

"You have done well with her. She is a credit to your love."

Isobel smiled at her adored teacher, eyes welling with tears.

"No, Master. She is a credit to God."

The Lord challenged Solomon to build a tabernacle, a place where access to God's will might be attained by the faithful. In his wisdom and obedience to his Lord, Solomon constructed the Temple, and it is holy above all.

And within the sanctity of the bridal chamber, Solomon and Sheba created the labyrinth with its eleven paths in and out as a new tabernacle, where fully realized men and women may find there is no separation between themselves and God. It is a place where the Aeon, which is to say the Temple Space, can be simulated and experienced for those who cannot reach the Temple otherwise.

In the center of the labyrinth, the children of God will open their eyes. For most souls live in this world in a state of slumber. They must awaken in this life, in these bodies where everything they are on earth exists. Their bodies are their own sacred temple spaces, and yet they do not see this. They believe that the kingdom awaits them only in the afterlife, and so they miss the most important teaching: that we are to live on earth as it is in heaven, and create heaven where it does not exist on earth. The kingdom of God is for us, here and now, on earth and in our earthly bodies of flesh if we will only claim it. This is done through love and love alone.

In the labyrinth, one reaches the Temple Space, where one speaks directly to God. It is a gift to the children that they may become anthropos, fully realized humans, and fully awake. That they may find their authentic selves, their unique being, and simply become who they are meant to be on earth.

Pray in the manner I have shown you, at the center of the labyrinth and at the center of your life. Use the prayer as a rose and marvel at the beauty of its six petals, for it contains all you need to find the kingdom of heaven on earth. The central circle is love perfected.

The children of the world must open their eyes to see God all around them. Then they can live as love expressed. It is in doing this that they fulfill their destinies, and likewise their promises to and from eternity. They must awaken. And they must awaken now.

Love Conquers All.

For those with ears to hear, let them hear it.

From the Book of Love, as preserved in the Libro Rosso

Lucca
1052

His scar was horrible. She couldn't take her eyes off it.

"Come, little one. Let us get this out of the way. I want you to put your hand on my face and touch the scar for yourself. You will see that it is just old flesh, and nothing to fear. Come now."

Matilda looked over at Isobel, who nodded at her with a smile. She allowed the Master to take her tiny hand in his and hold it up to his ravaged face. Matilda ran her index and middle fingers along the jagged edge. Now curiosity was overcoming fear. She mustered the courage to ask, "How did you get this scar, Master?"

Isobel breathed a silent sigh of relief. Matilda had remembered her manners. *Praise God.*

"Ah, a fair question, and one that requires a story. Come and sit beside the fire and I shall tell you."

As promised, Isobel and Matilda had come early this morning to the settlement of ancient stone buildings known simply as the Order. Here the Master lived and worked, instructing students from the oldest local families in the teachings of the Way. The chamber where they sat was one of the study rooms, furnished with a long table with ink and parchment and a large wooden box containing scrolls of instruction. There was a massive stone fireplace for mornings such as this when the Tuscan spring was yet young enough to contain a chill. The Master spoke often of his aged bones and how he felt that cold deep within them.

Matilda and Isobel sat on the bench that was adjacent to the fireplace. The Master sat opposite them on a wooden stool and began his explanation.

"Long ago, child, one of the earliest leaders of our Order was injured in a great war. It was an epic battle between the forces of light and the forces of darkness. While it was feared for a very long time that he had lost this battle, in truth he did not. He won, through the power of love and faith, and through what evolved as his unshakable belief in an all-powerful and loving God. But he was left scarred from his ordeal, with a jagged mark across his face. He was easy to identify, to be sure, with such a mark. In the centuries since, those of us who would follow in his path have taken the same scar in his honor, a mark to show that we are dedicated only to the teachings left behind in the Order. It is self-inflicted as part of our vow. I know it is hard to understand why a man would take such a scar upon himself. But it is a sign of our devotion to what is inside, and not what is out."

Matilda's hands flew up to her porcelain face, causing the Master to laugh out loud.

"No fear, my little one. Such a thing would never be asked of you. I see that your beauty will be one of your greatest weapons as a warrior for the Way. But always remember that God has graced you with it to be used wisely."

Matilda nodded solemnly before asking in a small voice, "Did it hurt?"

The Master shrugged. "Honestly, I do not remember. It was so long ago. If it did hurt, all I know is that it did not hurt as much as what our Lord suffered through in his own final sacrifice. And now if we have sufficiently covered the history of my face, I would like to begin your instruction. Is that acceptable to you, my lady?"

Matilda nodded again and then replied politely, prompted by Isobel's clearing of the throat, "Yes, the Master."

He laughed in appreciation of her desire to show good manners. "Good. Then I shall start by giving you a flower. A very special flower for a very special young lady. It is a rose with six petals."

The Master opened the creaking hinge of the wooden casket that rested on the table and removed one of the scrolls. This one was tied with a scarlet silk ribbon embroidered with golden diamonds. Matilda's eyes lit up with the beauty of the gift as the teacher handed it to her.

"You may open it. And keep the ribbon." He winked at her, and suddenly his scarred face took on an animation that was kindly rather than fearsome. Isobel was right, of course. It was important not to judge a man solely by his appearance. The day would come when Matilda would remember this as the most beautiful face she had ever seen.

Matilda unrolled the scroll to see that it was a rough ink drawing of a flower. Six large, rounded petals surrounded a central circle.

"This six-petaled rose is the symbol of the Book of Love, Matilda. And with it, you shall learn the secrets of the Pater Noster." He turned to Isobel. "She knows it, of course?"

"She knows our version in Tuscan and the traditional in German and Latin. And I am teaching her French, so she will have it in four, Master."

"And how is her reading and writing?"

"She is a quick pupil in such things. Remarkable, in fact. I believe she will read and write in all these languages with great skill if her father determines that she will be allowed to continue with her education. And I have no reason to believe that he will not."

"We must see to it that he understands the importance of her education," the Master said with emphasis, before returning to Matilda. "Recite it for me, please. In any language you choose."

Matilda cleared her throat and sat up very straight before choosing to recite the prayer in Tuscan:

To Our Father Who is Benevolent and Reigns in Heaven,
Your names are hallowed and sacred.
Your kingdom comes to us through obedience to your will.
Thy will be done
on earth as it is in heaven.
Give us each day our bread, the manna,
and forgive us for our errors and debts
as we forgive ourselves and all others.

*Keep me on the path of righteousness and
deliver me from the temptations of evil.*

"Brava, child. Well done. But until you learn what every line of that means and how it will change your life and the entire world around you, that prayer is meaningless. With consciousness, those words contain everything that any human being needs to know to find the kingdom of heaven on earth. Without consciousness, they are lost words, mumbled by rote. You will never again say that prayer as an absent bundle of words, do you understand? Now, we must get to work in earnest. Let me show you how this prayer relates to the rose petals . . ."

And the man known only as the Master began the work of instructing Matilda in the most hallowed teachings of the Book of Love, the good news left behind for all humanity by the Prince of Peace.

Matilda spent the late afternoon visiting the sacred sites in Lucca, of which there were many, joining her father for a tour of the great church of San Frediano. Their guide was a gentle and learned young priest called Anselmo, who was a native of Lucca and extremely well versed in the history of his town. His uncle, also called Anselmo di Baggio, was the reigning bishop of Lucca and a very powerful man in Bonifacio's world. No doubt this young nephew was being groomed for a position of great importance in the Lucca community, as he came from such an influential family. The di Baggios were all very savvy and discreet members of the Order of the Holy Sepulcher who had learned wisely to integrate into the traditional Catholic power structures.

Anselmo the Younger explained that this church was named for a sixth-century bishop who built the first structure here with his own hands.

"We call him Frediano, in Tuscan, but his name was Finnian in his own country. He was from a place called Irlanda. Do you know where that is, Matilda?"

Matilda shook her head, listening in wonder. Irlanda sounded like one of the magical places from Isobel's stories.

"It is a misty green island, very mysterious and ancient, beyond the lands of the Normans and Saxons. But it is also a very learned and holy place. Finnian ventured here as a pilgrim because he had heard of the sacred origins of Lucca from the teachings of a blessed man called Patrick, and he wanted to live in a place where the lessons of Jesus were their most pure."

Matilda tried not to squirm through the solemn tour of the baptistery with its great stone font. But in truth, San Frediano held little excitement for her once the initial mystery of the foreign legend was over. Her real anticipation was for the church they were to visit next, for the Church of San Martino was the resting place of the *Volto Santo*, the Holy Face as carved by Nicodemus.

Anselmo recounted the colorful history of the arrival of this image in Lucca to Matilda and Bonifacio as they walked through the narrow streets toward San Martino.

"When the *Volto Santo* left the Holy Land, it arrived on the shores of Tuscany after many months at sea. Here it was unloaded with great care and then hitched to a cart pulled by two snow white oxen. The oxen were untamed, and they were left to follow their own instincts. It was believed by the custodians of the Holy Face that the hand of the Lord would guide the cart and deliver it to the place where divine will would choose for it to rest. A great many miracles were reported along the path that this holy item traveled. The oxen pulled for three days and nights, never stopping until they had arrived here, in the center of Lucca. We believe that the *Volto Santo* chose to come to Lucca because it was following the path taken by the Book of Love."

Anselmo turned comically conspiratorial again, to amuse Matilda. "The initiated, our people of the Order, know that the *Volto Santo* wanted to be where the true teachings were, and these were happening only within the congregation that celebrated here at San Martino."

They had arrived at the façade of San Martino's, which had been dedicated in the name of Saint Martin of Tours since it was first constructed, also by the Irish bishop Finnian, in the sixth century. What was left of it was unimpressive. And crumbling. Matilda did not think it looked at all suitable as a shrine for the very first piece of Christian art, carved by a man who looked into the face of our Lord after removing him from the cross! She pulled on her father's sleeve.

"Papa?"

"Yes, my sweet?"

"We are very rich, are we not? Can we not give our people of Lucca enough money to build a very grand church for the Holy Face?"

Bonifacio roared with laughter as he scooped up his daughter. "Yes, we are very rich. And I would hope to stay that way by not giving away all our wealth, and certainly not to the Church!"

Matilda, who wasn't a bit satisfied with this answer, squirmed out of her father's arms and raced toward the entrance door.

The interior of San Martino's was cramped and dark, and Matilda had to blink her eyes very quickly to adjust to the dim candlelight within. Without waiting for her father or Anselmo, she ran ahead to the main altar, not stopping until she was close enough to touch the most sacred image in all of Christendom.

She stood before it, transfixed. The image was life-sized, elegantly crafted by a sculptor of extraordinary skill. Nicodemus had coaxed the Lebanese cedar wood into graceful waves to form a robe that draped across both extended arms and down to the feet of the crucified Christ. His facial details, hair, and beard had been carefully stained to show his coloring. Our Lord was dark and beautiful. Waves of black hair fell to his shoulders, matched by a long, neatly groomed beard that forked slightly. He had long and slender fingers. But it was his eyes that arrested her: huge and black and heavy-lidded, they were eyes of great kindness and compassion, even as depicted in their final moments of suffering. Matilda had never seen anything more beautiful than the man who was before her on the cross. She looked into those great eyes and was certain that he was looking back at her.

"You are my daughter, in whom I am well pleased."

Matilda gasped. The Holy Face had spoken to her. She closed her eyes very tight and tried to listen, but there was nothing more to hear. She turned to see that her father and Anselmo were behind her by a number of paces. Anselmo was whispering to Bonifacio, no doubt in further explanation of the artwork and its history. Matilda did not hear them. She heard only the statue of her Lord Jesus Christ, and it had spoken. He was pleased with her.

She was not sure what she had done to please her Lord, but she was most determined to do something now. Thinking quickly, she remembered the golden baubles that Isobel had woven into her hair this morning. There were two of them, intricately worked in gold and given to her from the house of Lorraine upon her birth. They were extremely valuable. Surreptitiously, so that her father would not see, she began to wriggle the baubles from their resting place in her copper curls until she had them both in her hands.

Matilda smiled at the image who was well pleased and whispered back, "One day, I will build you a fine church for your Holy Face. I promise."

She curtsied to the image, walking backwards so as not to turn her back in disrespect. When she reached the place where her father and Anselmo waited, she smiled at them sweetly. "It is very beautiful," she said simply. She was not ready to share her experience of this place, not yet. And when she did, it would be first with Isobel. Issy would know why the Lord was pleased with her.

Bonifacio strode out of the church quickly. He had had enough religion for one day and was anxious to get back to his meetings with the men who were responsible for keeping this area of Tuscany secure. Following that, he had arranged a great hunting expedition as a reward to his most loyal soldiers, something he was very much looking forward to. Matilda walked slowly behind, hoping to get the young priest Anselmo alone. He had a nice face and a sweet smile. She liked him with the immediate instinct for human nature that is possessed by clever children. When her father was well ahead of them, she put her tiny hand against his palm.

"What is this, little princess?" Anselmo asked her kindly, looking down at the treasure she had placed in his hand.

"Shhh," Matilda whispered. "This is my promise to the Holy Face, that I will one day build him a proper church. Take this gold and keep it for that day when I can bring you more."

Anselmo looked at her carefully. She was, indeed, a most unusual child to give up such beautiful treasure for the glory of God. He placed his hand on her head. "Matilda of Canossa, you are a generous donor. I hope to one day guide the building of a greater church by the grace of your generosity."

Matilda smiled at him, satisfied that she now had a worthy conspirator for her grand plan. "Good. Then we shall do it together. When I am older and can give my money freely as I wish."

And turning to curtsy one final time to the Holy Face the six-year-old countess ran out the door and into the afternoon sun, yelling demands after her father to take her to Isobel immediately. The fierce Bonifacio, a man whose very name caused hardened warriors to quiver with their fear of him, stopped in his tracks before turning to laugh uproariously at the only human being alive from whom he would take orders.

Following the terrible time of crucifixion, it became unsafe for the family of our Lord to remain in Israel. His uncle, the blessed Joseph of Arimathea, worked quickly to find safety for Maria Magdalena, who was heavily pregnant with the savior's heir, as well as the other children and some of their close followers.

The fair city of Alexandria was known for its learning and tolerance, a flourishing society where many beliefs and cultures lived together in harmony. It was close enough to be a quick and temporary solution, far enough to be safe. Madonna Magdalena needed to be in a comfortable location for the pending birth of her blessed child.

Joseph of Arimathea knew exceptional prosperity through his success as a tin trader, and it was under cover of his trading ships that he was able to transport the remainder of the holy family out of danger and into Egypt. It would be the second time that a Great Maria was forced to flee her homeland to protect the blessed child in her womb, the second Flight into Egypt.

During her confinement, Magdalena called for her trusted friend, the learned apostle known as Philip, to come attend her in Alexandria. He heeded her call, and during those months our lady read to him from the Book of Love that he might transcribe it perfectly under her guidance and direction. It was thus that a nearly perfect copy of the original words of our Lord was made by these two great disciples and teachers. Maria Magdalena would always keep the original Book of Love in her possession as long as she lived. But it was her desire that a copy be sent to James, the brother of Jesus, who remained in Jerusalem. The emerging Jerusalem church was in need of the teachings in their purest form that the Way might continue there.

James received the copy from Alexandria and held it safely in Jerusalem where it was contained within the sacred vessel carved by Nicodemus.

Philip left for his own fate in Sumeria, where he preached the Way for the rest of his own blessed life, teaching from the Book of Love as he had once transcribed it.

THE STORY OF PHILIP AND THE BOOK OF LOVE,
AS TOLD IN THE LIBRO ROSSO

❁

The subterranean stone chamber that served as the chapel of the Order of the Holy Sepulcher was nearly a thousand years old. It had been built by the first Christians, who practiced their faith here in secret, away from the prying eyes of the Romans. Matilda climbed gingerly down the steep stairs, holding tightly to Isobel, who walked ahead of her. The Master led them with an oil lamp, but the chamber proper had been prepared for their arrival by some of the novices, who had placed beeswax candles in the iron wall sconces. Shadows flickered all around. The stone walls of the chapel were blackened by candle smoke, and the heady fragrance of frankincense infused the thickened air with a dense sanctity.

Matilda's experience with the *Volto Santo* today had rattled the Master, which was no easy task. While he knew that this child was special, he had not been prepared for her to have an authentic and waking visionary experience so young. And he was certain it was authentic. There was a light in her eyes when she repeated the story, first to Isobel and then to him. There was a grace there, a certainty. This was not a fancy created by a silly girl in search of attention. This was a mystical experience of a child selected by God for a special destiny. He had learned to recognize the difference in his long years as a teacher and mentor.

As such, the Master determined that Matilda must be brought immediately into the presence of the Libro Rosso.

The tiny chapel possessed a simple stone altar, original to the hallowed structure that contained it. Despite the fact that this was a consecrated chapel, there were no crucifixes or crosses depicted anywhere in the structure. Perched upon the rich velvet altar cloth was a wooden ark, a magnificent casket with carvings of scenes from the life of our Lord and Lady that had been guided by the hand of Saint Luke. The container was nearly as sacred as the contents and was known to the Order as the Ark of the New Covenant. The border of the ark was trimmed with a pattern of diamond shapes, the symbol of sacred union, while the *X* symbol of Gnostic enlightenment was carved deeply into each of the corners and highlighted with gilded paint. The Master led Isobel and Matilda to the ark and indicated that they should kneel before it. They complied and remained on their knees while he recited a prayer of thanks to the Lord for the gift of this sacred testament. He approached the altar and struggled momentarily with the heavy lid of the ark before removing it and placing it on the ground. He reached into the ark and lifted the elaborate volume that waited within.

Matilda raised her head as the Master removed the Libro Rosso. It was an enormous volume, bound in the deepest red leather, which was visible on the heavy spine. The front cover of the book was overlaid in gold and set with five large jewels that formed an *X* shape, rather than a cross. The Master brought the book to his lips and kissed the central jewel, a ruby that glowed in the candlelight.

"The Word of the Lord. For those with ears to hear."

He held the book out to Isobel, who kissed it accordingly and repeated, "The Word of the Lord" before holding it down to a very solemn and wide-eyed Matilda. She imitated Isobel's actions perfectly.

They followed the Master as he carried the Libro Rosso and placed it on a table in front of the altar. He smiled at Matilda. "You may touch it, child."

Hesitantly, her little fingers reached out to run lightly along the gilded cover. She jumped as if burned, letting out a little squeal, which caused the Master and Isobel to exchange glances. But when she returned her fingertips to the book a second time, she did not jump.

"Behold, the Libro Rosso. This is the most sacred book of our people, for, among other things, it contains the words written by the savior of the world. Within these pages, Matilda, is the complete gospel as written by Jesus Christ, the good news known to us as the Book of Love. This is the holy copy that was made by the apostle Philip in the presence of the original and given to Nicodemus to be preserved in the *Volto Santo*. It contains within it the seal of Maria Magdalena to indicate her approval of the copy. You will have seen this pattern before. It is used on the most secret documents of the order and worn by our highest initiates."

The Master opened the book with great care and turned a weathered but heavy page with gentle fingers. On the bottom of the second page was a Greek signature:

μαγδαλεν.

Magdalen.

Beneath the signature was an emblem that Matilda had indeed seen before. It was the pattern on Isobel's copper ring, the disk-shaped one that got caught in Matilda's hair sometimes when Issy was braiding it. It was a pattern of nine circles dancing around a central sphere. It was an image of heaven, worn by the Order as a reminder that they were never separate from God. On earth as it is in heaven. Matilda had not known that this symbol was the seal of Maria Magdalena. It was one of the secrets of the Order.

"You too shall have a ring with this, the Magdalena's seal, when you come of age into the mysteries," Isobel whispered to her. Matilda squirmed with the excitement of it, stopping as the Master continued.

"As you grow, you will be instructed directly from the teachings in the Book of Love. You will also be instructed in the prophecies of Sarah-Tamar. You will memorize them and you will learn to interpret them. Some of these are specific to your birth and you must understand them fully.

"Finally, you will study the histories that are contained within the Libro Rosso. These are the hidden Acts of the Apostles, the stories of disciples who sacrificed everything for the true teachings of the Way of Love. We do this in emulation of the book written by one of our founders, the most blessed Saint Luke. It is in honoring the memory and sacrifice of our martyrs that we honor God while praying for a time when these teachings will be welcomed in peace by all people and there will be no more martyrs.

"This is your first lesson, Matilda. Understanding of the three segments of the Libro Rosso: first among these is the text of the Book of Love, which is the one true word; second are the collected prophecies of Sarah-Tamar, which are sacred to the future; and the third are Acts of the Apostles, which have been accumulated by our people since the earliest days of Christianity. For tonight, this is all that you need to know."

❀

Matilda was thriving under the tutelage of the Master. But as much as she loved the lessons, her favorite thing of all was the wondrous labyrinth that was laid out in stone in the expansive garden of the Order. She had squealed with absolute delight when she saw it for the first time. Although she had seen drawings of the labyrinth and a small version was carved on her doll, Ariadne, to see one built into the ground of such enormous size—as many as twenty adults could walk its pathways at one time—was quite an amazing thing!

The Master had walked her through it the very first time, holding her hand as he guided her along the winding pathways that led to the center.

"There is only one way in, Matilda. Although the pathways make many turns, if you stay true to your path, you will never get lost. This is the first lesson of the labyrinth. Walk with purpose toward the center, for you know that God awaits you there. And even when the winding paths feel as if they are taking you far away from the center, you must always have faith that the path will take you back again. This is like life. It is this faith that will bring you to your destination of finding God every time and without fail.

"Most of what I will teach you about the labyrinth is really very simple. For the truth is always simple, Matilda."

He walked with her in silence for a few moments before continuing the lesson.

"Now, child, sometimes the Lord speaks to our slumbering souls in different ways. In dreams, for example. That is one way. I know that you sometimes have dreams that you do not yet understand. This is God's way of speaking to us, because our minds are open when we sleep and we can allow his messages to come through to us without interference. Another way that God speaks to us is through numbers. Numbers are a language unto themselves, with deep layers of meaning that most humans do not allow themselves to grasp. But the construction of this labyrinth is based on very specific numbers. There are eleven cycles that lead to the center, and eleven cycles that lead out of it. In the sacred language of numbers that came out of the Holy Land in the time of the wise King Solomon, eleven represented the path of initiation. When you add those cycles together, they become twenty-two. Twenty-two is the master number, the number of the completion of the initiation. This labyrinth that we are walking was created by Solomon himself, in partnership with his beloved, the Queen of Sheba. I know there is much for you to grasp and I do not expect you to hold it all in your mind or your heart at this time. Just allow yourself to listen as your feet follow the path of the labyrinth."

Matilda was listening and trying to understand, but there was a rhythm in her feet as she walked this sacred path that she could not deny. She was restraining herself and attempting to walk very solemnly, and yet she wanted nothing more than to dance and run through this magical maze where no one ever got lost and everyone found God at the center. There was joy in the labyrinth, and a type of freedom. Even at the tender age of six, Matilda was very much aware that the labyrinth was a special spiritual place. It filled her with light and love and the joy of learning in such a rarified environment. Eventually, she could no longer contain herself and she finished the circuit at a run. Upon reaching the center, she danced under the golden sunlight of her beloved Tuscany.

Let him kiss me with the kisses of his mouth!

Your love is more delightful than wine.
Delicate is the fragrance of your perfume.
Your name is an oil poured out
And that is why the maidens love you.
Draw me in your footsteps, let us run.
The King has brought me into his chamber.
You will be our joy and our gladness.
We shall praise your love above wine.
How right it is to love you.

THE SONG OF SONGS, 1:2–4

This, the first verse of the most sacred song of love, was inspired by the divine coming together of the great King Solomon and the Queen of Sheba. For as they were locked in the sacred union of beloveds in the light of trust and consciousness, they discovered that their greatest loves, through each other, were for God and for the World that God loves so.

You will be our joy and our gladness.
We shall praise you above wine.
How right it is to love you.

These words are praise for the Lord from the beloveds, as they have found God in the bridal chamber. Through the sacred union of their love, they have come to a full understanding of the blessings of life that God has granted us to express in our bodies of flesh.

All love is God and God is all love.

When we are united with our beloved, we are living that love expressed and God is truly present in the bridal chamber.

The song begins with a kiss, for this is the most sacred form of expression between the beloveds. In our holiest tradition that comes from Solomon and Sheba, the word is nashakh, *and it means more than simply to kiss; it means to breathe in harmony in a way that combines the spirits of two into one, to share the same breath, to blend the life forces in a single coming together.*

It is with the harmonious breath of the kiss that we are fertilized to become anthropos, *which is to say fully realized humans. Through the kiss we are born again. We give birth to each other, through the sharing of the love that is within us, blending God with the self.*

Through the sanctity of the kiss, two souls come together to merge as one. It is the prelude to the sacred union of beloveds.

For those with ears to hear, let them hear it.

THE SONG OF SOLOMON AND SHEBA,
FROM THE BOOK OF LOVE, AS PRESERVED IN THE LIBRO ROSSO

Lucca
1052

"She is perfect. Everything you said she was. I have absolute faith that she will lead us into a new era of the Way. There is no doubt that she is The Expected One. My uncle will agree when he hears all that has transpired. The time returns, Isobel. Just as we always knew it must in our lifetime."

Anselmo had listened carefully to Isobel as she recounted the most recent, miraculous events of Matilda's young life. Now he had a more complete picture of why the girl had given her gold to him. The *Volto Santo* had spoken to her in San Martino's. It was a beautiful omen.

Isobel smiled at him, her deep dimples showing in a most fetching way. He returned the expression, adding, "We are all so proud of the work you have done with her. But no one more than I, my love."

Anselmo moved to close the space that had separated them. The door was closed and there was little enough chance that they would be disturbed at this time of night. Besides, they were within the territory of the Order, a place that held the sacred union of beloveds to be the highest sacrament. It was a most important part of their teaching and it was emphasized in the Book of Love and therefore took precedence over any laws created by men. Within these walls, the vows he had taken for public scrutiny at the behest of his uncle the bishop, so that he might one day inherit a Church position of high rank, could be placed aside. Here he could be himself and celebrate the love that brought infinite joy to his soul, the love that God gave to all mankind as his greatest gift, so that they might find divinity within each other.

Isobel came to him then, slipping into the warmth of Anselmo's welcoming embrace, the touch she had missed so much since taking her position as Matilda's nurse. The two of them had been together since they were children in Lucca, and their love for each other was surpassed only by their love for the Order and the teachings of the Master, the teachings of the Libro Rosso, which they were both sworn to preserve.

She whispered the first lines of the sacred song, inflecting it with the softest sensuality as her lips approached his.

"Let him kiss me with the kisses of his mouth. Your love is more delightful than wine."

He should have whispered the reply, but he was already too lost in her to speak. They joined together through the slow, sweet sanctity of their kiss, blending souls in the prelude to blending bodies.

The sacred union of beloveds would assuredly find its most passionate expression on this night.

It had been far too long in the waiting.

❀

Matilda was screaming.

Isobel ran down the short hallway where she had been asleep on a novice's pallet. Matilda had stayed awake very late, working in the chapel with the Master, who had decided she should spend the night here in the simplicity of the Order's dormitory. Isobel's first thought was that the child had awakened in a room that she did not recognize. She chided herself for leaving the girl alone. She should have stayed with Matilda herself but had rationalized fairly that the child had been so tired, it seemed entirely unlikely she would awaken before sunrise.

Matilda was sitting straight up in her little bed, sobbing now.

"What is it, *ma petite*?" Isobel wrapped her arms around the girl and rocked her gently as she cried, until her sobs began to calm in the warmth and safety of her surrogate mother's embrace.

"Papa." Matilda tried to get the words out through her hiccups, but she was still crying too hard.

"Were you dreaming?"

She nodded. "Papa. Something terrible happened to Papa in the dream, Issy. God is angry with him."

"Nonsense. God is loving and just; he is not an angry and vengeful God. He would not hurt your papa."

"Fra Gilbert says that God punishes the unrighteous, and he says that Papa is unrighteous."

"Matilda, I am surprised at you. You have just spent an evening in the presence of our most sacred treasure, which is called the Book of *Love* for a reason. It is a celebration of God's love for his children."

Isobel was usually quite careful to respect the beliefs of orthodox Catholics, but at times they truly tried her patience—particularly when she had to undo the damage that preaching did to her precious child. Besides, it was late, she was tired, and she made no personal claims to sainthood. She snapped, "Fra Gilbert is a harsh man who knows little enough about the nature of God, or about your father or, I dare say, about love."

Matilda giggled in spite of herself. Isobel embodied the Way of Love very nearly all the time. As such, she was rarely angry; thus it was interesting to behold her when she was.

"But Issy, my father does not want to give money to build a church for the Holy Face."

Isobel nodded. "Your father is generous in his own way, Matilda. I know it is hard for you to understand, but there are a lot of adult reasons why he cannot give money to the building of a church at the moment." Isobel did not want to explain to a six-year-old that Bonifacio was well aware that any funding he provided to expand San Martino would likely go first into a number of clerical coffers that were not of his choosing and would have nothing to do with erecting a new church. But in her childish innocence, all Matilda could see was her father's refusal to help her Lord.

"In my dream, God was angry that Papa wouldn't build a new church and . . . something terrible happened. I need to see Papa. I need to tell him we will build a new church and then God will not be angry."

Isobel sighed. There would be no reasoning with her like this, not when she was still in the emotional throes of the nightmare. And Isobel was secretly concerned. Matilda's dreams had turned out to be prophetic more than once, which was to be expected given the circumstances of her birth. She kissed Matilda on the forehead for reassurance and prayed silently that this dream was simply the manifestation of a little girl's fear, and not a prophecy.

"Your father left this evening to go on his hunting expedition. But I promise you, as soon as he returns, we will discuss the rebuilding of San Martino with him. Will that do?"

Matilda nodded, then snuggled back into her bed, exhausted now by the whole ordeal.

"Stay with me, Issy," she commanded.

"Of course I will, my sweet," Isobel reassured her, and she sang the child softly back to sleep with the song that always calmed her down, the one in French, about eternal love.

※

The news came first to Mantua, where Matilda's mother, Beatrice of Lorraine, had stayed behind to run the household. The castle was thrown into immediate chaos, and the lady Beatrice had to be attended by a team of physicians after she collapsed in a hysterical heap. This was too much. God had taken far more from her than any woman should endure in one lifetime. Why would he punish her so? Fra Gilbert was surely correct. God took his vengeance on the unrighteous.

"Where is Matilda?" she shrieked through her tears. "Bring my daughter to me!"

Beatrice was reminded that Matilda was still in Lucca, but a retinue would be sent immediately, along with a double guard of heavy horse, to return her to her childhood home in Mantua. She must be home for the funeral.

As impossible as it seemed, the great Bonifacio, Count of Canossa, Marchese of Mantua, and Grand Duke of Tuscany, was dead. He had been killed suspiciously by a stray arrow that struck him squarely in the throat during his hunting expedition, the morning after Matilda's prophetic dream.

The time returns.

Many are called.
Those chosen take their vows.
They promise to God,
They promise to each other
that the Love never dies.
The prophets come again.
They must, because the truth is eternal
Just as the Love is eternal.
That all men and women of good heart
Will know and live the truth
And become fully realized beings
While here in their bodies
On earth as it is in heaven.
This is why
The time returns.

For those with ears to hear, let them hear it.

FROM THE PROPHECIES OF SARAH-TAMAR,
AS PRESERVED IN THE LIBRO ROSSO

Chapter Six

Rome
present day

"Wow."

Maureen's legs were tucked underneath her as she sat on the bed, staring out the window at the Pantheon. It was full dark now, and the floodlights had come on, illuminating the magnificent monument to its grandest expression. Her single word of exclamation was in appreciation both of the ancient sight before her and of the story that Peter had just related.

"Do you realize," Maureen began thoughtfully, "that when Matilda came to Rome, the Pantheon would have looked exactly like it does today? That it's possible she would have stood somewhere in this square and admired it in precisely the way that I am doing right now?"

"That's why they call it the Eternal City," Peter responded. "It's a great credit to the Italians, really, how carefully they preserve what remains." Peter had walked every inch of Rome in his time here and had certain routes that he cherished because they took him past the often awesome ruins of ancient civilizations. Rome was a marvel on foot. Around every corner there was a chunk of history by the roadside just waiting to be observed.

She returned her attention to Peter. "Are you exhausted?"

"Hungry. Shall we go to Alfredo's for dinner? It's right across the square."

"Can't do it." Maureen sighed dramatically. "Alas, I hear from Lara at the front desk that they have the best saltimbocca in all of Rome."

"And that's a problem because . . . ?"

"Because I'll hate myself if I eat veal. So lead me not into temptation. But I could be convinced to go after Florentine cuisine at Il Foro. Porcini mushrooms? A great Brunello? A worthy reward for all of this work. And it only seems right that we should eat Tuscan food in Matilda's honor."

"Twist my arm. You know I love that place."

Maureen had a lot of questions about what she had just heard. She knew that Peter would be far more inclined to answer them if he was well fed and able to relax for a bit. He was a master at language, but this type of translation was definitely taxing. Besides, the walk to the restaurant would be good for both of them. They stopped at the front desk to be sure that they didn't need a reservation, then walked the short distance, past Peter's church of Ignatius Loyola, and down the picturesque alley with its antique shops to the trattoria.

The staff knew Peter and welcomed him by name, leading them to one of the small, quiet tables in the rear room, against the window. Once the rich, red wine from Tuscany had been poured, Maureen began her questions.

"So, help me to be clear on this. The Book of Love and the Libro Rosso are not the same thing?"

Peter nodded. "Correct. Sort of. The Libro Rosso *contains* the Book of Love, or at least a copy of it. It seems to me that it was structured rather like the New Testament is in our traditional canon. For example, we have the four gospels: Matthew, Mark, Luke, and John. But then we also have the Acts of the Apostles as written by Luke, and then we have the epistles of Paul and assorted other letters, then finally the Book of Revelation. Those put together form what we call the New Testament. With me so far, right?"

Maureen nodded.

"So now let's compare. In terms of the book that Matilda's Master has in his possession, this is my understanding so far. Here we have a copy of the gospel of Jesus, which is called the Book of Love . . ."

Maureen was scribbling notes. She interrupted him for clarification. "A copy. This is the copy made by the apostle Philip. Because the original, written in the hand of Jesus, is still in France at this time, as far as we know."

"Also correct. Then the Book of Love is followed by the collected prophecies of his daughter, Sarah-Tamar. Certainly, the corroboration of The Expected One prophecy here is fascinating. How do you feel about it?"

Maureen took a sip of her wine and thought for a moment before answering. "Hmm. I feel strangely close to Matilda. We are similar in appearance, or at least in coloring and body type, we have the same birth date within a day or so of the equinox, and we both lived with the scrutiny and pressure of this crazy prophecy hanging over our heads. And Bonifacio's death made me cry. The parallels are interesting, at the very least."

"Given what you've been through, I'm going to say they're more than interesting."

"And what do you think they are?"

"I don't know yet. But I do believe that it is all part of some divine plan, Maureen. I really do."

" 'The time returns'? And what do you think that means, exactly?"

Peter shook his head. "Let me work on that awhile longer before I speculate."

She knew he was holding back. "No good, Pete. I want to hear what your first impression is. Just think out loud for a minute. Humor me."

He shrugged. "Okay. You know, my first thought if I'm just thinking out loud . . . well, it's about the prophets. Remember that in the time of Christ it was believed that John the Baptist was the second coming of the prophet Elijah? Jesus says, while speaking of John the Baptist, 'And if ye will receive it, this is Elijah who was for to come.' Which is a reference to a prophecy that Elijah will return to herald the coming of the

Lord. And then later, after John is executed, Jesus says, 'I say unto you that Elijah has come already and they knew him not.' So we see that there is a biblical tradition of certain prophets coming back to fulfill prophecy."

"So is it a reincarnation thing? Is John the Baptist the reincarnation of Elijah the prophet? Is Jesus actually Adam come back to earth? Do they share the same soul, or simply the same destiny?"

The more conservative aspects of Peter's religious training rebelled at the mention of anything resembling past lives. "I would certainly shy away from calling it reincarnation or putting an Eastern or a New Age label on it. But there is definitely biblical tradition that backs up this idea that the prophets come back when they are needed to do the jobs laid out for them by God. In the Gospel of Luke, when John's coming is foretold to his father Zacharias, it says, 'He shall go before them in the spirit and power of Elijah.' So I think that's where we have to look, perhaps. *In the spirit and power* of one prophet comes another to finish the job. Now to your point, the interpretation of the word *spirit* can take us in several directions. It could be literal—as in, they are actually the same spirit. Which forces us to look at the reincarnation question. But I am personally inclined to interpret *spirit* in a broader form."

Maureen knew they weren't grasping it yet. "The time returns. In my dream, Easa told me it was the one thing I needed to remember. And it's in the Libro Rosso, and it's part of Matilda's nightly prayer ritual. This concept had extraordinary meaning to these people on a daily, living basis. I'm not discounting what you're saying, I'm just suggesting that there's more."

"I'll get more translations finished over the next twenty-four hours. We'll just have to keep reading and hope that our redheaded countess gives us some more valuable information."

Maureen raised her glass. "To Matilda."

Peter met it with his own. "The time returns."

Back in his study, Peter reflected on his own set of concerns and areas of fascination in terms of what they had read in Matilda's manuscript. The theological implications within the Libro Rosso were astonishing.

The idea that the apostle Philip made a copy of the Book of Love was highly significant. Philip would eventually author his own gospel, a later copy of which was found in the cache of Gnostic discoveries in the Egyptian town of Nag Hammadi in 1945, and it was from Philip's gospel that Jesus was quoting in Maureen's most recent dream when he said, "You must awaken while in this body." Or was he? Could it be that Jesus was quoting from his own gospel, from the Book of Love, and that later his words were attributed to Philip?

Could Philip's early work on the translation of the Book of Love have inspired the majority of teachings from his own gospel? Could it be possible that his gospel was really an attempt to recall the Book of Love teachings? This was an important question, as it could mean that since 1945 the human race has had a decent copy of the original teachings of Jesus via the Gospel of Philip. But could this also mean that, if found, the Book of Love was going to have explosive repercussions about the sexuality of Jesus?

Philip's gospel was keenly focused on the physical aspects of sacred union and the sanctity of the bridal chamber—and on Mary Magdalene's importance as the beloved of Jesus. It was by no means a casual relationship according to Philip; it was committed, it was sexual, and it was holy.

This was highly problematic. Whereas the Gnostic material was authenticated and translated by many noted scholars, there was still great controversy about any passage that could be interpreted to indicate that Jesus was a healthy, sexual male. This was simply a concept that many Christians were not prepared to consider. Peter was surrounded every day by men who would die rather than accept this as a possibility. He knew that for certain, as it had been exclaimed outright by several of the members of the committee to authenticate the Arques Gospel of Mary Magdalene.

Over the next few sleepless hours, Peter made the decision to narrow his search for information by focusing on the history of the labyrinth. Clearly, this was a tool of extraordinary importance in the world of the "heretic" cultures, and he was fascinated by the multiple references to it within Matilda's story. In scouring the literally unequaled reference library at his disposal, Peter began working feverishly on a series of time lines to help him organize what he uncovered.

He was certainly aware of the numerous church labyrinths that could be found within Gothic structures. There were several that he knew of in France, and a few smaller maze patterns in Italy. As far as Peter was concerned, no one had ever offered a credible explanation for the presence of this pagan symbol within emphatically Catholic edifices. Now, with Matilda's manuscript, he was aware that there was much more to this ancient symbol than he had ever imagined.

Peter knew there was a very large labyrinth built in stone across the floor of Chartres Cathedral in France, a Gothic masterpiece located about fifty miles outside Paris. It covered the majority of the expansive nave, yet he hadn't actually seen it during his visits there. For reasons that he could never really understand, the powers in the Church who administer Chartres made the decision nearly two hundred years ago to conceal the labyrinth by covering it with rows of movable chairs.

Was there another reason that the Catholic Church wanted to keep the labyrinth covered and out of public view? Certainly, it was an architectural masterpiece, and just the fact that it was eight hundred years old and built to perfect mathematical precision at the height of the Gothic period should make it worthy of display, if not protection. And yet the portable chairs had scratched, chipped, and damaged the ancient stone of the labyrinth over the years and no one in the Church seemed to care a bit about it. At best, such treatment seemed negligent. At worst, it seemed like a deliberate act of vandalism by his brother priests who were physically responsible for the presence of the chairs and the systematic damage that they caused to the labyrinth. Was that damage intentional?

Further, Chartres Cathedral was enormous and easily held several thousand people. It was said that a full-sized soccer stadium could be placed within it, and it was twelve stories high in terms of the vaulting. Those extra rows of chairs could not be needed for seating purposes, except perhaps on the most extreme special occasions or the largest holy days, like Easter and Christmas. Peter began to feel more and more as though he were seeing a deliberate act of obscuring the labyrinth, a literal cover-up that had begun in the early nineteenth century and continued to this day.

Peter's stomach started to turn as he thought about this. As a priest, it was painful for him to come face-to-face with actions in the Church that were entirely counter to what Jesus may have actually stood for. But in the last two years, he had seen more and more of this evidence. It was, in fact, becoming his daily challenge. And while he wasn't quite ready yet to make a case for the sanctity of the labyrinths in terms of Christ's teachings, he felt that they at least needed to be respected as works of sacred art that were carefully installed in places of worship by master builders and craftsmen from the golden age of architecture.

Peter moved through the notes he had made, dividing them into categories for further research: church labyrinths, France, Italy, biblical connections. What of the King Solomon connection that had been mentioned by the Master? This was certainly worthy of exploration. There were a number of reasons why Solomon could have been associated with the construction of a labyrinth; the most obvious of course was that he was credited with building the Temple in Jerusalem. So the architectural applications were obvious. And certainly, as a son of the Davidic line—David was Solomon's father—Jesus might have been heir to the plans for the Temple, as well as other architectural devices. In fact, it was entirely likely that there would be secret wisdom teachings found in a family of such legendary blood and wisdom. Did Jesus possess blueprints for the Temple and for other structures that were preserved in his family? Was Solomon's specific eleven-circuit labyrinth one of these teachings? What else did Solomon pass down to his most holy descendant? And did Jesus use any or all of these things in the Book of Love?

Peter's hands began to shake when he found the references to a perfectly constructed labyrinth that was chiseled into the exterior wall of the west portico of the Church of San Martino in Lucca in the year 1200, the very church that housed Matilda's Holy Face. Built at eye level, it was a "finger labyrinth," a small version only two feet across—as opposed to the Chartres version, which covered a gargantuan forty-two feet of floor space. This Lucchesi labyrinth was unique in that it allowed the faithful to run their fingers along the pathways prior to entering the shrine of the church. These small labyrinths were convenient for two reasons that Peter could ascertain. The first and most obvious was that they provided the sacred symbol where there might not otherwise be space for one in the floor. The second was that labyrinths inscribed on the walls could not be covered up with chairs.

Unique to San Martino in Lucca was the legend inscribed in a vertical column along the length of the labyrinth, a pagan legend that on the surface had no business on the exterior of a Catholic cathedral and defied explanation. In three hexameters, it reads in translation from Latin,

HERE IS THE LABYRINTH THAT DAEDALUS THE CRETAN BUILT
AND WHICH NO ONE CAN EXIT ONCE INSIDE.
ONLY THESEUS WAS ABLE TO DO SO,
THANKS TO ARIADNE'S THREAD.

Peter discovered in one source another very interesting allegation regarding Lucca. One obscure Italian reference claimed that the center of the labyrinth, now destroyed along with an image of Theseus, once contained the continuation of the legend, representing the moral of the fable:

AND ALL FOR LOVE.

That there was a perfect eleven-circuit labyrinth in Lucca couldn't be a coincidence. That it was so similar to the Chartres labyrinth in terms of geometry and the design of their rounded paths couldn't be either. Specifically, Chartres and Lucca were connected in a more intimate way than the other labyrinths, almost as if the same person designed both.

The labyrinth had associations to sacred union as a result of the powerful and enduring Ariadne legend for several thousand years; Matilda's manuscript indicated that this legend may even have been recognized by Jesus. However, evidence from the Middle Ages indicated that the monks who transcribed the Grecian labyrinth legends for posterity made a deliberate decision to change their focus. Rather than preserving the elaborate and powerful nuances of love and loss, the transcribing brothers rewrote the legends—inexplicably—as treatises of architecture. The presence of Ariadne was eradicated in total. This couldn't be a coincidence. *Ariadne was erased from her own story.* By many accounts, including archaeological evidence, the legend originally existed for the purpose of showcasing the importance of Ariadne as the Lady of the Labyrinth who protects her man and the innocent people with her love. Yet her presence was completely, and quite possibly deliberately, eradicated in later versions.

In much the same way, Mary Magdalene was diminished and sometimes removed from the accepted chronicles of Jesus' life, also by men of the Church. Peter began to work through a radical theory: Ariadne became an allegorical symbol for Mary Magdalene for the "heretics" who would not let her importance die. Theseus' survival—his reemergence from the labyrinth after facing death—was a metaphor for resurrection. Ariadne, who protected him with her love, was the first to witness his glory as the savior of his people, just as Magdalene, who anointed Jesus, was the first to witness the glory of his resurrection as the Savior of his people. The union of Theseus and Ariadne could represent the love of Jesus and Mary Magdalene; their story would allow the heretics to depict their teachings in plain sight. Ariadne's thread was symbolic of Mary Magdalene's devotion, how she brought the Book of Love to Europe and dedicated her life to its preservation. By following this thread of truth, like Theseus, we can emerge from the darkness of the Minotaur's lair and find the light of freedom.

The following morning, after very little restless sleep, Peter resumed his search and found a reference to another church in Italy that struck him hard. San Michele Maggiore in the northern Italian city of Pavia was built in Matilda's time and would have been in her territories. A labyrinth was installed in the chancel there at some point in the twelfth or thirteenth century, now mostly destroyed. But drawings existed of the original structure when it was intact, and he was able to pull them out of the Biblioteca Apostolica in the Vatican. It was a perfect eleven-circuit labyrinth, as at Chartres and Lucca. In the center was the legend, "Theseus went in and killed the hybrid monster." Here the monster was specifically not the Minotaur but a centaur—a creature who was half horse and half man. There appeared to be a trend in the labyrinth designs of the Middle Ages, lasting into the Renaissance, which replaced the Minotaur with the centaur. Was this deliberate? Was it a reference to slaying some other kind of beast?

Could the "hybrid monster" be the Church that was beginning its persecution of the "pure" Christians in the Middle Ages? Peter contemplated this idea for a moment. Over the last two years, this was precisely what his Church had become for him. It was a hybrid of beauty and pain, truth and lies. It was an institution that he still believed in with a great passion half the time, and was completely in despair over the other half.

Mantua
1052

"It was no accident, Isobel. I am ashamed to say that I am related to that wicked wretch who wears the crown of Germany." Beatrice raged as she paced her chambers in agitation.

Bonifacio's suspicious death on May 6, 1052, caused grave consternation in Tuscany. Many whispered that the German emperor, Henry III, was behind it. The "hunting accident" was looking more like an assassination by a greedy monarch who had been eaten alive with envy of the great Bonifacio for many years. And yet while the obstacle of Bonifacio had been removed, Henry, who was Beatrice's cousin, had perhaps not considered his plan quite as carefully as he should have.

"But I have my satisfaction. The pope is also my kinsman and he has taken action to protect Matilda and me. Henry will not dare to confiscate Bonifacio's wealth now, as the risks of repercussions are too great. The Tuscan vassals will rise up against him. And"—Beatrice lowered her voice to ensure that no one but Isobel would hear her—"we have devised a plan that cannot fail."

"I pray it is so, my lady." Isobel was secretly terrified for Matilda and had to trust that Beatrice would do the right thing to protect her.

Beatrice continued, a smile of satisfaction curling her lips as she explained her strategy. "Pope Leo has arranged for me to become immediately engaged to Godfrey of Lorraine."

Isobel gasped. She had not expected this. The idea was controversial for many reasons, not the least of which was Godfrey's open hatred of the emperor. He had been publicly rebellious to the corrupt monarch, so it was deeply insulting to Henry for the pope to bestow Bonifacio's property on Godfrey of Lorraine in the guise of protecting Beatrice and her child. But there was a thornier issue to be addressed.

"But my lady, Godfrey of Lorraine is your first cousin. This is a violation of Church law."

Beatrice had already thought this through. She was proving to be far shrewder than Isobel had ever believed. "We have agreed to take vows of celibacy before consecrating the marriage in any Church. That is fine with me, as no man will ever touch me again now that my Bonifacio is gone." She softened for a moment, looking like a sincerely grieving widow. "You of all people must understand that, Isobel."

Isobel did understand. For while Beatrice didn't practice the sacred laws of hieros-gamos as they did in the Order, she was well aware of them. Bonifacio had been her beloved in the most sanctified sense, and she would mourn him for the rest of her life.

"This is strictly an issue of convenience." The noble mask of strength had returned. "Matilda needs a powerful defender to protect her territories. As a woman, she cannot inherit on her own. But I have called you in here to tell you one more thing, Isobel."

Isobel and Beatrice had never had a close relationship. Indeed, Matilda's mother was deeply jealous of her daughter's greater affections for her nurse. So while Isobel suspected that Beatrice held some motive for informing her of her plan, she had certainly not expected what came next.

"To ensure the protection of my daughter, the pope has determined that Matilda should be engaged to Godfrey's son, the future duke of Lorraine, to which I have agreed."

Isobel knew that she was powerless to affect this decision, but it made her heart sink deeply and she was forced to stifle the tears. To surrender a female child to an arranged marriage was blasphemous within the teachings of the Order, for whom the power of true love was the highest sacrament. Didn't Beatrice realize that she had just delivered a life sentence of misery on her special, magical little girl?

But by the time Beatrice broke the news to Isobel, it had all been irrevocably arranged. The exquisite little child-countess of Canossa was betrothed to the young man who was already known by the unfortunate nickname of Godfrey the Hunchback.

❁

When Beatrice's cousin, Pope Leo IX, died unexpectedly in the spring of 1054, the fortunes of Matilda and her mother shifted once again, this time with severe repercussions. Henry III stepped in immediately like the vulture that he was to lay claim to "his" massive feudal estates in Italy. Beatrice's new husband, Duke Godfrey, abandoned her to protect his own holdings in Lorraine, which were threatened simultaneously in a clever piece of strategy implemented by Henry. With absolutely no means of protection, Beatrice and her daughter were taken into custody by the German king, who had crowned himself the Holy Roman Emperor.

Henry III transported Beatrice and Matilda in heavy custody; Matilda was no longer an heiress. In one imperial declaration, she had lost everything her father's family had built over four generations. The emperor announced that Beatrice and Matilda would live by his charity and command at the German court of Bodsfeld unless or until he decreed otherwise. They were prisoners, abducted by a greedy and narcissistic monarch who held all the advantages.

Although she was still a little girl, the injustice of such oppressive tyranny would not be lost on the nine-year-old Matilda.

It was all too much. Matilda had not only lost her beloved father, her inheritance, and her home, but she was now exiled from the most consistent parental love she had ever known. Isobel, who was not allowed any access to her young charge once she had been abducted, returned to Lucca to pray for the safe deliverance of her beloved child.

Bodsfeld, Germany
1054

MATILDA AWOKE with a start. She blinked at the first signs of gray morning light that were filtering in through the windows. Germany was cold and dark in late October. There was no golden sunshine, no Tuscan warmth to relieve any of the pain of loss that she had suffered in her year and a half of captivity thus far. She hated Germany, and she hated the man who brought her here, hated that he had killed her father and stolen her inheritance, hated that he had humiliated her mother and reduced her to the status of a beggar. Most of all, she hated his child, the evil little troll who was her six-year-old cousin and the eventual heir to the throne of Germany. That one little boy could inflict such terror and misery was almost beyond understanding, but this *infans terribilis*, also called Henry, was capable of anything and got away with everything. His otherwise stern and self-righteous French mother doted upon him with an obsession that bordered on idiocy.

As Matilda raised her head, she was reminded of just how wicked her younger cousin could be. She felt the stickiness first on the back of her neck. Not again. Raising her hands to her hair, she felt with a sickening thud of her heart that her once-beautiful copper curls were matted down with a thick, gummy substance. She brought her fingers to her face to smell the offending goo that had been poured into her hair. Honey. Mixed with something else, something black and oily that would no doubt harden and destroy her curls.

"Mama!"

The only positive thing that had come from Matilda's captivity was her enforced closeness with her mother, Beatrice. Each was all the other now had. Matilda had come to learn that her mother was far stronger and more educated than she had ever suspected, and she realized that Beatrice's subservience to her father had been an issue of respect and choice, rather than weakness. Throughout their captivity, Beatrice shared possible political options with her daughter, advising her that they still had allies throughout Europe. Despite Godfrey of Lorraine's apparent abandonment of them, he was a strong and clever man, and he knew if Beatrice and Matilda were free, he would be restored to his own holdings in northern Italy. Indeed, he had spies from Lorraine in the castle and had smuggled notes of encouragement to Beatrice. He was working to create a strategy for their release. It was slow, but it was under way; they were down, but they were not defeated.

In turn, Beatrice came to realize just how gifted and strong her single surviving child was, which gave her even greater hope for the future. Matilda was every bit the worthy heir of Bonifacio's territories. Perhaps the time in captivity had even been good for her, hardening her into more of a warrior for justice and giving her a harsh but necessary education in politics.

Upon hearing her daughter cry out, Beatrice came quickly from the adjoining room where she had been immersed in her embroidery. They were imprisoned, but they were captive in a palace where they were not treated poorly. Matilda's mother found refuge in working with her hands here, as the task helped to quiet her mind and allowed her to think. She had attempted to school Matilda in the finer points of needlework, but her daughter had no interest in women's domestic craft. It felt like surrender to her, and she was not ever going to surrender, not in this place. Ever.

"That horrid Henry has poured honey in my hair again!"

Matilda didn't cry. She wouldn't give her cousin the satisfaction of seeing her weep as a result of his cruel pranks. Besides, he had done this before. This time she was more concerned. The last time, the honey had washed out and her glorious hair had remained intact and unharmed. This time Henry had mixed the honey with some other substance to make the concoction more destructive, something she could not identify. But it felt like it was beginning to harden in her hair, and she was panicked.

"Hurry, Mother. We have to try to wash it out before it hardens more. I don't want to give him the satisfaction of making me cut my hair."

Beatrice was still very capable of garnering compliance from servants, even in captivity. She called for a tub of warmed water and some of the heavy soap made from the roots of plants that were cut in the Ardennes forest by the locals. This soap was the detergent used to clean clothing, but it would be necessary to try something of this strength if she was going to save her daughter's legendary hair.

"I have never done anything to him." Matilda seethed. "Why does he hate me so?"

"Because he is jealous of you, and because he is the wicked spawn of an evil father and a dullard mother," Beatrice responded acidly. "God help Germany when and if he ever becomes king. He isn't even clever enough to lead the pigs to trough, much less govern Europe. And if he is this malevolent at six, the good Lord alone can imagine what he will be like when he is old enough to fully abuse his power and appreciate bribery. Or worse."

Since the day of their arrival in Germany, the heir to the throne, the imperious young Henry, had been terrorizing Matilda with relentless fervor. He spent the days concocting ways to make her miserable, and he spent the nights putting those plots into action. Many of his activities involved damaging her hair, which he had a particular obsession with. Sometimes he would follow her around and taunt her with a toy bow and arrow, screaming, "Look, I'm Bonifacio, the dead duke of Tuscany." Then he would pretend to be shot in the throat and fall to the ground in dramatic, twitching death throes.

Matilda, who had been raised to believe in the power of love, prayed every night in despair: *Dear God, please forgive me for how much I despise him. I know you tell me to love my enemies, but this is too much.* She tried to work through her anger within the Pater Noster each night before going to sleep, as she had been taught by the Master. The lesson of the fifth petal, forgive us for our errors and debts as we forgive all others, was always going to be her toughest. Henry the Terrible gave her plenty of opportunity to work through that lesson.

His verbal abuse was nonstop and consisted of phrases that were usually variations of "Father says you are half barbarian and don't deserve to be kept in such luxury, but he doesn't dare throw you out into the street because you will attempt to rally your pagan hordes against his holy imperial person."

Henry also said horrible things about Beatrice, things that he could not possibly understand at the age of six, about her unnatural and twisted marriage to her first cousin, Godfrey of Lorraine, and how that made her monstrous in the sight of God. Matilda had been locked up in a room by herself for over a week after she subsequently punched Henry in the face, doing serious damage to his delicate nose. It was the only thing on his vile, chinless, pudgy body that was delicate, and Matilda had made the mistake of saying exactly this to the queen when she came to her precious boy's rescue. Agnes of Aquitaine nearly fainted from Matilda's audacity and demanded the barbarian child with the unsightly flame-colored hair be locked out of her sight until further notice. Surely hair that color was unnatural, as was everything about this wicked, wild creature who tormented her precious lamb.

Beatrice washed the stickiness out of Matilda's hair carefully, working through the strands with the heavy detergent from the soap. She breathed a quick sigh of relief: the honey was coming out and would not harden into a substance that would have to be cut. There was some discoloration from whatever mixture Henry had devised, but time would restore the glorious red-gold color soon enough.

Once the hair debacle was resolved, Beatrice called for some reading material to be brought to them, along with her confessor, Fra Gilbert, who had been allowed to accompany them into exile as he was seen to be a loyal German subject. She requested the writings of Saint Augustine be brought in and presented to Matilda to read. If nothing else, she would see to it that her daughter's education continued. She wanted her to have every possible advantage in politics when this particular nightmare ended, which Beatrice was certain would happen eventually.

Matilda sat down to study before her little statue of Saint Modesta, the one given by Isobel's family to celebrate Matilda's birth. Modesta was recognized as a saint within the Order and by the people of La Beauce in France, because she dedicated her life fearlessly to the teachings of the Book of Love. The statue was the only possession Matilda had been allowed to bring with her from Tuscany, and most of the time it was her only comfort.

❦

That evening, Matilda and Beatrice were left to dine alone in a small, bare antechamber of the palace that was particularly chilly. Something was wrong, but they were not yet certain what it was. The family had not been seen all day, and Henry had not come by to gloat about his stealth mission to destroy Matilda's hair. This was highly unusual, for the little wretch desired nothing more than attention for his misdeeds.

The following morning, news came that caused Matilda to know happiness for the first time in eighteen months. The German emperor and murdering thief, Henry III, had died very unexpectedly of a fever in the night. The fortunes of his family were highly uncertain, as Germany and the surrounding territories were instantly in chaos. Queen Agnes was given no time to mourn her husband, as immediate action was necessary. She was declared regent and sole guardian to her son, who would henceforth be known as Henry IV.

Matilda and Beatrice were in limbo for several days, with no news being brought to them and no sign of Agnes or her child. On the fourth day, Godfrey of Lorraine, who had been plotting for just such an opportunity during the long captivity of Beatrice and Matilda, announced himself at the gates of Bodsfeld and presented an opportunity to the queen regent. He agreed that he would swear an oath of loyalty to her and to her son, as would the wealthiest vassals in Lorraine, thus unifying that region and creating some stability in their otherwise shaky kingdom. In return, Agnes would recognize Godfrey's marriage to Beatrice as legitimate and restore Bonifacio's property to them.

Trapped and confused, Queen Agnes agreed to do this. She was well over her head in terms of political strategy and had little time to seek advice in the rapidly escalating crisis of her son's future. She was desperate to at least attempt to secure Lorraine and Saxony for her child in the chaos that would surely follow the death of her husband, an unpopular and unjust monarch who had ruled by fear. Her first priority had to be the protection of Germany and the immediate territories. Italy was the least of her worries at this stage, and Godfrey was savvy enough to seize upon that opportunity. In the mercurial world of European politics, timing was everything.

Matilda and Beatrice departed Germany for Florence in 1057 to begin their lives as the family of Duke Godfrey of Lorraine. Matilda refused to look back as she left Germany behind her, determined never to set foot in that godforsaken frozen land again, unless it proved absolutely necessary to the will of her Lord.

❀

Tuscany was in tatters.

What four generations of Matilda's family had worked to build—a land of prosperity where the people thrived and the natural resources were harvested with utmost care—had been completely undone by the

German king in less than two years. Henry had raped this land and stripped it of its wealth, leaving these proud people to live as little more than beggars. Piracy, with all the murder and thievery that went with it, had returned to the waterways, but this time it was sanctioned by an emperor's crown.

As they made their way across Tuscany, the young Matilda was both sickened and terrified by what she witnessed. Gone were the vibrant, thriving towns and villages of her earlier childhood, places she had toured with her father, who had been hailed as a prince. In their stead were dingy structures where the inhabitants hovered nervously in the shadows, fearing the sound of hoofbeats on the roads. Horses brought conquerors and thieves, from which there was no protection, or mercy.

It was in one of these villages on the outskirts of her family stronghold of Canossa that the family stopped one evening for food and shelter. Matilda was exhausted physically by the journey across the Alps, but far more by the emotional toll of what she had been confronted with along the way. She did not, at first, understand what was happening as they entered the village. As one who had known captivity and abuse, she initially feared that the assembled crowd was a danger to her. But as their cortege drew nearer, she was able to make out the chanting of the villagers.

"Ma-til-da. Ma-til-da!"

A group of children carrying flowers ran to her and laid them at her feet. Their parents followed, hailing the return of their beloved countess. That evening, in the faded warmth of what had once been the grand banquet hall of a local lord, Matilda met with the inhabitants of the village. Many came to tell their shocking stories of loss and tragedy at the hands of a ruthless and greedy foreign monarch. At eleven years old, Matilda listened to each and every tale while sitting beside her mother and stepfather. The accounts of injustice against these beautiful people, her people, struck in the deepest places of her heart and spirit. She missed nothing and stored everything. She vowed silently that when they were settled into their new life, she would find a way to compensate each of these people for their loss.

The villagers came to plead to Duke Godfrey, who was now their feudal lord, to restore their holdings and aid them in rebuilding, while providing them with troops for protection. But most of all they came to see their legendary little countess, for she was Tuscan born and the child of a great prophecy. It was Matilda who represented the gleam of hope for the people of northern Italy. It was Matilda who would restore Tuscany to its former, glorious state of peace and prosperity.

The people were certain of it, and so was Matilda.

There exist forms of union higher than any that can be spoken,
stronger than the greatest forces with the power that is their destiny.

Those who live this are no longer separated.
They are one, beyond bodily distinction.

Those who recognize each other know the unequaled joy
of living together in this fullness.

The time returns.

When the Families of Spirit come together on earth, there is great rejoicing in the house of El and Asherah. Those who recognize each other in this life live in a fullness that is unknowable to those who do not have this blessing.

The only joy greater than union . . . is reunion. There is an awakening that must happen here. You must awaken while in this body, for everything exists within it, and only through this awakening will you have eyes to see and ears to hear. Only through this awakening will you recognize and remember those with whom it is your destiny to reunite.

For those with ears to hear, let them hear it.

FROM THE BOOK OF LOVE,
AS PRESERVED IN THE LIBRO ROSSO

CHAPTER SEVEN

Duke Godfrey chose Florence for their new home as he much preferred it to Mantua, where it was hard to compete with the local people's memory of Bonifacio. From Florence, he could operate in a more cosmopolitan and politicized environment. Mantua, Modena, and Canossa were more provincial in comparison. He expanded and renovated an aging palace that existed in the center of the city, near the stunning octagonal Baptistery that dominated Florence.

Matilda settled into life in Florence, heralded by an emotional reunion with her beloved Isobel. Beatrice, who was now working hard to run the Tuscan holdings in her daughter's name, was far too busy once again to indulge in maternal matters. While their time in Germany had brought mother and daughter closer than they ever had been, Matilda would always need and crave the nurturing that came from Issy.

Isobel was concerned about the edge that Matilda had developed while in captivity in Germany. She had lost a portion of her innocence and would be slow to trust anyone new who entered her life. And she had become restless and combative in her newfound passion for justice. Isobel and the Master realized that they would have to work hard to emphasize that the desire for justice must not be colored by revenge.

For while one was the work of the light, the other was the work of the darkness. As a leader, Matilda must learn to come from the place of love whenever possible. Love conquers all.

More to the Order's purposes, Matilda had also not had any real spiritual education for almost two years, critical years in a child's development. During her captivity, her only religious training had been the harshly orthodox scriptural interpretations that were the daily bread of the German royal family. Working to undo that damage was in itself going to be a challenge. As a result, the inner circle of the Order of the Holy Sepulcher in Lucca had come to the conclusion that emergency measures must be taken. The Master would relocate to Florence, where the Order had a base, a monastery at the edge of the river Arno which had been named for the Holy Trinity, Santa Trinità. A secretive and somewhat mysterious community of monks with ties to the Order had built a monastery there in the tenth century, under the patronage of Siegfried of Lucca, Matilda's legendary great-great-grandfather. The monks were not only sympathetic to the origins of the Order, some of them were descended from the most powerful bloodline families themselves and were sworn members.

Here at Santa Trinità, Isobel and the Master would resume Matilda's training in earnest. They would reclaim their child, their precious Expected One, and bring her back into the fold of the Way of Love. They would ensure that she was given every opportunity to fulfill her destiny. They would teach her that God had given her this trial of imprisonment and injustice for a reason, so that she would know and understand the pain of such treatment. She should use this learning to color her own decisions as a leader, to remember the humanity of each and every one of her vassals, to remember that the Book of Love taught that all human spirits were equal, with no man or woman having more value than another. Some might have destinies that appeared more exalted, but that was in human perspective. In the eyes of God, all souls were equal in value.

While Matilda's lessons had been harsh for someone so young, the Master would emphasize that they were clearly a part of God's plan for

147

Matilda's destiny. They would shape her into the greatest and most benevolent of leaders.

Another cause for concern was that Matilda's experience with the young Henry had tarnished her relationships with other children her age, particularly boys. The future would depend on her diplomatic abilities, usually with men, so this was an issue that had to be addressed. The Master decided to begin instructing Matilda in the presence of other children, starting with an orphaned boy who had been sent up from Calabria for training owing to his exceptionally quick mind and displays of leadership. He was of a similar age, and the Master believed the boy would be a worthy companion to their little countess. His name was Patricio, and at nine he was already proving to be intellectually and spiritually gifted. Patricio was a lovely child, blessed with a sunny disposition and yet also a strong will. He would be able to keep up with Matilda and even to challenge her; they were enough alike to get along but also to push each other. It was a perfect solution that could prove tremendously healing for Matilda.

Florence
1059

"MOTHER, I wish to be trained as a warrior."

Beatrice set aside the accounts she had been examining as her daughter, now thirteen and exceptionally beautiful, addressed her from the doorway.

"Come in and speak to me properly, Matilda. I cannot have you shouting such things from the hall where the entire household can hear our business." Beatrice smiled at her to indicate that she wasn't really displeased by her daughter's typically impetuous behavior. She not only expected it, she found it charming. "Sit down, my dear. Now, what is this fancy of yours and whence does it come?"

"I have been studying the law of inheritance." Matilda sat opposite her mother on a bench at a wooden table made of rough-hewn beams.

It was a dining table, but Beatrice preferred to work here as there was plenty of room for her to view all of the accounts in one place. She had become, by necessity, a shrewd and effective business manager for both her husband's and daughter's interests.

Beatrice gave Matilda her full attention. She was clearly intent on pursuing this subject, and when Matilda was serious, she would not be denied. By anyone.

Matilda continued with customary passion. "And while the law says that a woman cannot inherit such properties as we hold, it is specific as to why. It says that a woman cannot perform military service, and that the lords who control property must be capable of military service in defense of those lands. So . . . I would take up the sword and prove that I can lead an army. If I am capable of military service—and I intend to be as capable as any male warrior or more—then there is nothing I can see in the law to block my inheritance. I am already more skilled on a horse than any man in Tuscany, and Godfrey says that my understanding of strategy is greater than that of many of his advisers. I just need the skills in weaponry to become a complete warrior with the capability of defending my own lands."

Beatrice nodded thoughtfully. If Matilda had been born male, there was no doubt that she would already have been well on her way to being the most accomplished military hero of her time. A genius at strategy, she had delighted her stepfather Godfrey with her skill in chess and in the military games that he devised for her on paper. He even allowed her to sit in on his meetings when the regional Tuscan chiefs came to Florence to give their reports. While the duke of Lorraine was generally considered to be a hard man, he had learned to love both of these extraordinary women in his life and treated them like the family they had become. With Beatrice, he had discovered a solid and worthy partner in the complex ruling of an extensive kingdom. While their marriage was necessarily unconsummated, they had established a fondness for each other that was based first on respect but later on warmth and emotion. In several legal documents pertaining to her life, Beatrice referred to Godfrey fondly as "my man."

The duke had developed a special weakness for Matilda's strength and intelligence and had come to treat her like his own child, and with no small degree of respect. Beatrice considered this now and replied, "Your stepfather is indulgent of you, but he may not allow this. Lorraine is a far more conservative place than Tuscany. He must think of his reputation in both locations."

"He will allow this. He must. And with both of us insisting on it, he will have little choice but to give in. We are the two most convincing women in Europe, doesn't he say so himself?"

"I do dare say. You have thought this through, I see, and no surprise. Tell me, does Isobel know that you intend to train as a warrior?"

Matilda nodded. She had discussed her strategy with both Issy and the Master. "They do not object to anything that could ensure my inheritance and protect our ways. My strength is their strength. They know that I will use it to preserve the traditions along with my rights. And they feel that God will grant me special protection in battle."

Beatrice nodded. Nothing from this child of the two greatest families in Europe would ever surprise her again. While she was not herself a follower of the prophecies revered in Lucca, she was more certain each day that her daughter had been born for a special destiny. Perhaps she was indeed the child of the prophecies of which the Tuscan people had whispered since her propitious birth. She was certainly unique in her strength, beauty, and flourishing wisdom. Beatrice was proud of her and was certain that Godfrey would be impressed by Matilda's astute grasp of the law. No doubt he had given her the legal documents to review himself and wouldn't be terribly surprised at her savvy interpretation.

"So be it. I will raise a warrior daughter if that is what you wish. And I will speak to Godfrey tonight when he returns. He will need to find you an appropriate weapons master, and sparring partners who—"

Matilda cut her off. "Who will what? Go easy on me? I think not, Mother. What good to train in weapons if it is only against weak boys who have been told to be gentle with me? I want the best men in Tuscany, and the most hardened. Nothing less."

"Of course you do." Her mother was justifiably nervous that

Matilda's bravado might get her into trouble. But she was equally certain that the girl would have her way in this, as she did in everything. "And that is what you shall have, if Godfrey consents to it."

"Thank you." Matilda rose, curtsying gracefully and with respect. "And Mother, it is for you that I do this as well. Never again will anyone take anything that belongs to us. And never again will a German king ravage Tuscany, steal our resources, and terrorize our people. Never."

Beatrice looked at the strikingly beautiful girl who stood before her. The set of her daughter's jaw—pure Tuscan warrior—put her so much in mind of Bonifacio that it brought tears to her eyes.

"He would be proud of you, Matilda."

Matilda's own eyes welled up immediately. Not a day went by when she did not miss her father. Indeed, she spoke to him every night when she said her prayers. "He sees me, Mother. I know he does. And I will make him proud."

It would be a mistake for any man in Europe to assume that this petite and fine-boned female could not and would not defend what was rightfully hers. Godfrey of Lorraine would not make that mistake. He agreed to Matilda's request with surprising readiness, and personally oversaw the selection of her primary military instructor. He knew just the right man.

❋

The knife hit the target squarely in the center, and with such force that it shook the tree. The fearsome warlord who had hurled the weapon turned to face Godfrey of Lorraine with the full force of his wrath.

"Do I look like a whimpering nursemaid to you?"

At the moment, Conn of the Hundred Battles could not have looked any less like a nursemaid, whimpering or otherwise. He stalked toward the target to withdraw his knife, moving with an uncommon grace for such a gigantic man. It was the hottest time of the day and his broad chest was bare and dripping sweat. His long hair, an extraordinary ginger color that matched his beard, was tied back with a leather thong, giving Conn the look of a Celtic god from ancient legend. This giant did, in fact, hail from the magical and misty lands of the Celts and had come to Florence several years prior, for reasons he chose not to reveal, in search of a mercenary command.

"Not a bit, Conn," Godfrey replied with no small degree of amusement. Here was a man whom he counted as one of his most loyal warriors and a trusted friend. During their first interview, Conn had been guarded about his personal history. But Godfrey was an astute judge of a warrior's character, and he could see that there was intelligence and something else behind the pure brute force that confronted him. Over the three years that they had been allied, the duke had discovered extraordinary layers in the man who fought beside him with such strength and loyalty. He also knew that on the surface, Conn was too proud, arrogant, and harsh to consent immediately to instructing Matilda, and certainly not within earshot of his men, as he was now. This would be a bit of a struggle, but one Godfrey was certain to win. Because he knew something else about Conn. The Celtic giant had a soft spot for the girl and often commented on her extraordinary skills as an equestrian and how mythical she looked perched upon a horse and riding like the wind.

There was nothing soft about the glare that Conn turned in Godfrey's direction as he wrenched his weapon from the target. He lowered his voice as he addressed the duke.

"You will make me a laughingstock with the other men. I won't do it."

"You can handle the other men, methinks." But then Godfrey nodded, looking more serious. "I understand your concerns, Conn. But I need you. You are the best warrior and strategist in Tuscany. This is not a fancy for Matilda. She is deadly serious about her training. It is of the utmost importance that she be as prepared as possible in terms of real war. I cannot lose her on the battlefield because she is ill-equipped to survive. It would destroy her mother, it would imperil the future of Tuscany . . . and it would kill me as well."

Conn grunted, shoving the knife into his belt as he did so. Godfrey placed a friendly hand on the warrior's shoulder.

"Incidentally, this is a high-paid commission. And if that is not enough to sway you, think of it this way." Godfrey was fully prepared to use all his wits to garner Conn's acquiescence, in this case playing to the love of his Celtic heritage. "When Matilda is the most legendary warrior queen who ever lived, you will be remembered as the great man who trained her."

He had him. The promise of both wealth and legendary honor was too much for a man of such heritage. Godfrey could see in the big Celt's eyes that he was actually relishing the idea. He closed the deal.

"Besides, it takes one wild, red-haired creature to understand another. And when Matilda is older, the two of you will look like a ferocious brother and sister as you ride out to do battle together. Your enemies will cower at the very sight of you and the chroniclers will write about your adventures in perpetuity."

With a final grunt, Conn continued his show of disdain and pushed past the duke, determined not to reveal to anyone that he was secretly delighted by this task. He shouted his parting line for the benefit of the other men who may have been eavesdropping.

"Fine, but your version of high-paid and mine had best be the same."

❊

"Come in, little Boudicca."

While Conn sat on a stool with his back to the door, he had the acute hearing and highly tuned senses of the most experienced warlord. Knowing who came up behind him was a skill that determined life over death on the battlefield.

Matilda swallowed as she stepped into the soldier's chamber, a weapons room that adjoined the stables. Swords and pikes hung from the walls, while axes and smaller knives were displayed on a rough table. She glanced at them as she approached the man who would be her new weapons master. While she was secretly thrilled that Godfrey had taken her seriously enough to entrust her training to his most hardened warlord, this huge man's reputation for fearlessness in battle was daunting. Matilda was not sure what to expect from him, but she was determined not to be intimidated.

Conn gestured to the table where he sat, staring at a chessboard. He still had not looked up at her. "What move would you make here, if you were I? This one?" He indicated the black knight. "Or that one?" Pointing to the black bishop.

Matilda contemplated the board for a moment before responding. "Neither."

Conn looked up now for the first time, coming face-to-face with the teenage girl who would be his protégée, and caught his breath. He had seen her from a distance when she rode with Godfrey, but up this close he was completely taken aback. Even in her rough training garments, she was as utterly gorgeous as if she were gowned in silks and jewels. Perhaps that would be to her benefit in battle, as men would be disarmed by her appearance. He would need to find as many angles as possible to give her advantages in war, as her petite stature was going to be problematic.

"What do you mean, neither? Both are good moves."

Matilda nodded, getting closer to the board. "Yes, but both are obvious and provide only immediate relief. If you look ahead by three or four moves, you will see that neither is of any benefit to you in the long run. I would go after the rook, here. It will take longer, but it will bring you that much closer to taking the white king. Check in six. If your opponent is unskilled, checkmate."

The Celt's face split into a grin. "You do not disappoint me, girl. And you have passed your first test. Now sit down, and we shall play a proper game."

Matilda hesitated. "What do you mean, sit down?"

Conn shrugged. "Does *sit down* have another meaning that I am not aware of?"

Matilda snapped back at his sarcasm, "No, but I am not here to play chess. I can do that with the old men in the castle. I am here to train in weaponry."

Conn stunned her by leaping to his feet as fast and unexpectedly as a flash of lightning, knocking the stool across the room as he did so. He grabbed her wrist roughly and twisted it sharply behind her back until she cried out in pain. He kept it there to make his point. Matilda held her breath, but she didn't struggle as he delivered his first lecture to the fledgling student.

"Now, little girl. I could have just snapped your wrist in half. You are small and fine-boned, and the average opponent you face in battle will be built far more like me than like you. He will be a hardened soldier and a man who won't care that you are female and won't treat you any differently from the other men he is determined to slaughter. Or worse, he *will* care that you're female, which means he'll keep you alive long enough for you to wish that he hadn't. The point, little sister, is that in light of your size and your sex, you cannot fight with men on a level battlefield if you are, by chance, unhorsed. This means you will have to be smarter and faster in hand-to-hand combat than anyone you face."

Conn released her, gently now. "So, before we begin with your weapons training, I would see how your mind works."

He gestured to the chessboard, bowing theatrically. "After you, my lady."

Matilda beat him. But she had to admit that it was not the usual routing she was used to giving her other opponents across a chessboard. Conn was the rare mental match for her; it was an auspicious start to a relationship that must necessarily be based on respect. Matilda would learn over her training that there was as much to admire in Conn's intellect as there was in his weaponry skills. While he was completely mute when asked any questions about his past, he was clearly a citizen of the world, and an educated one.

Following the game, Conn chose one of the small, lightweight swords and tossed it to her without warning, to observe how she caught it. He was impressed by her speed and grace in reflex action. The first lesson would be in the basic handling of a weapon, and those qualities would determine her success. Matilda had indicated that she wanted to one day carry Bonifacio's sword into battle, but at the moment it was as tall as she was. That was a weapon she would have to grow into. As they walked toward the practice field in the growing heat of a Tuscan afternoon, Matilda asked him, "Who is Boudicca?"

"Boudicca?"

"Yes. When I entered the weapons room, you said, 'Come in, little Boudicca.'"

"Ah. You don't know who Boudicca is? Well, I suppose you wouldn't. But you should. Come listen then, as the history of great military leaders will be critical to your education."

Conn gestured to a bench at the edge of the practice ground that had been cut from a fallen tree. He began to reveal the legend of Boudicca, and the natural storyteller embedded within his genetics emerged from his soul as he did so.

"First, you must know about the great people who were and are the Celts. There was a time, little sister, when the Celtic tribes covered most of Europe. They were called the Keltoi then, and sometimes the Galli, which is where the land of Gaul gets its name. And here in Italy, you are aware, I hope, that the Ligurian Celts settled in Tuscany, establishing, among other things, your sacred city of Lucca. The Celts had a great passion for the gifts of nature as found in the land, and they were able to feel the presence of God in the earth. It was in this way that they chose where to settle and where to build places of worship. Lucca is one such place. There is another in France, a place called Chartres, which is so sacred that it became the center for all ceremonial spiritual initiations for the Celtic tribes in Europe." His eyes glassed over slightly for the briefest moment. "Chartres. It is a place of unequaled beauty and power."

Matilda sat up with the mention of Chartres. "Isobel has told me of Chartres. Her mother came from there, from a place called La Beauce."

Conn nodded. "La Beauce is the region, Chartres is the town at the heart of the region."

"There is a great school there." Matilda hesitated. She didn't know this enigmatic giant of a man well enough to speak openly about her personally held spiritual beliefs, particularly as they were now considered dangerously heretical by the orthodox Church. But Isobel had told her that the school of Chartres taught from the Book of Love. She waited to see if he would volunteer any knowledge of her heretical brethren in France.

She was disappointed. Conn was not a nut easily cracked, and he simply nodded, noncommittal. "There is."

She tried one more thing. "Have you been there?"

He turned the full force of his focus on his student now and took control of the conversation. "I have. And that is another story for a different day. The first lesson for any warrior is not to lose focus on the issue at hand. And our issue is the history of the Celts and the legend of Boudicca, so let us return to it."

Matilda nodded mutely and allowed him to continue without further questions. But he had revealed something to her in this brief encounter about Chartres, something she was determined to understand more about in the future.

"The Celtic tribes encountered great resistance by many opponents, but none as dangerous to their survival as the Romans. And while this was true throughout Europe, it was specifically the case in the islands. And it was there that Boudicca was a warrior queen of the first century, a woman of the Iceni tribe of Celts. After the Romans invaded her lands, she fought back and led an army against the Roman legions herself. While she was victorious in her first battle, the Roman factions chose to punish her for her audacity by kidnapping the girls of her tribe, including Boudicca's two daughters, and throwing them to the whims of the most hardened legionnaires."

Conn paused for a moment, remembering he was in the company of a teenage girl who was still a maid. He did not need to give her the graphic details of the mass rape afflicted upon Boudicca's daughters and the other Iceni girls.

"Suffice it to say that they were most violently abused and many were murdered. As their mother and queen, Boudicca became bent on having justice, gathered a Celtic army the like and size of which had never been seen before, and attacked the Romans. She decimated the legions who had invaded East Anglia but did not stop there. So inflamed was she by the pain and injustice that had been inflicted upon her people, she descended upon the great city of Londinium itself. Her siege of this sophisticated Roman stronghold was one of the most brutal in history, but it was also an example of superior strategy, which we will examine in later lessons. But here is what you must know most of all about Boudicca, other than that she is painted by artists as having hair the same color as our own." He winked at her then, pulling on one of her plaits to emphasize the physical anomaly that marked their spiritual kinship.

Matilda was listening with rapt attention. She loved nothing more than a magnificent story that was told with passion.

"As she attempted to rally support, Boudicca learned that the Iceni tribe were viewed as barbarians by the Romans. As a result, some of the allies she required were hesitant to join with her. You see, the Celts did not believe in committing their sacred teachings or their histories to writing, or to sharing them with outsiders, which made them a dangerous mystery to many. The Romans, on the other hand, used writing to expert effect and created advantage in war through the art of propaganda. And they had done exactly this in their war against Boudicca, by referring to the Iceni and other Celtic tribes as uncivilized monsters who sacrificed children to their pagan gods. Of course, this was not true, as the Celts revered all life in their sacred teachings. But in making the people believe that they were ridding the world of a monstrous race of animals, the Romans made it somehow acceptable to massacre as many Celts as they chose.

"So Boudicca, in her outrage, decided that she would go to war with the Romans on their own battlefield. In addition to her military might, she would hire scribes to tell the tale of what the legionnaires had done to the girls of the Iceni, to show who the true barbarians in this war were. At this time she adopted a battle cry which she would use for the rest of her life."

He paused to see how closely Matilda was listening. He was not disappointed. She hung on every word and could not wait to hear what the brave, avenging Boudicca's cry in battle had been. When Conn didn't continue immediately, she prodded him.

"Well? What was it?"

He grinned at her. "Something I think you will appreciate. Boudicca carried a banner into battle that read, THE TRUTH AGAINST THE WORLD."

He left it there, hanging in the air. *The Truth Against the World.* Matilda was speechless. It was the most beautiful thing she had ever heard. A warrior queen fighting for justice against a gargantuan opponent, carrying a banner for truth. When she finally spoke, it was with great resolve.

"Conn, you must train me in all of Boudicca's strategies."

The ginger-haired giant jumped to his feet with the grace of a panther. "Well, come on then, little sister. Boudicca didn't defeat the Romans by sitting on a log."

Thus began Matilda's training in arms, with a weapons master who would become her fiercest defender and protector but also one of her greatest teachers on and off the battlefield. As with everything else that she set her mind to, Matilda rapidly became capable to the point of deadly when handling a weapon. What she lacked in size and muscle she made up for with the grace of natural athleticism and superior cunning on the battlefield, much to the credit of Conn's expert training and careful understanding of his protégée's character.

By the time she was sixteen, the countess of Canossa was entirely capable of leading an army. She was, in fact, rather looking forward to it.

❄

Matilda was considered by those around her to be bold and fearless through most of her life, but the truth was that she had a tremendous fear of the dark, and of being alone in it. This was the result of the dreams and nightmares she had experienced as far back as she could remember. Her dreams had always been vivid, and often bizarre and disturbing. Now that she was older, she also understood that she was dreaming of the time of Jesus. This was part of the prophecy: that The Expected One would have dreams and visions of the last days of the savior's life, but specifically of his crucifixion. As she prepared for bed on the eve of her sixteenth birthday, she had thus far been spared the specific vision of our Lord on the cross. When she awoke the following morning, on the advent of the vernal equinox, she would not be able to say the same thing.

❋

Matilda was in the middle of a mob and all around her was chaos. People were screaming, shoving. The omnipresent sun of early afternoon beat down upon them, mixing sweat with dirt on the angry and distressed faces around her. She was at the edge of a narrow road, and the crowd just ahead began to jostle more emphatically. A natural gap was evolving, and a small group moved slowly along that path. The mob appeared to be following this huddled mass of humanity that began to move toward her. It was then that Matilda saw the woman clearly for the first time.

She was a solitary and still island in the center of the madness, one of the few women in the crowd. But that was not what made her different. It was her bearing, a regal demeanor that marked her as a queen despite the layer of dirt covering her hands and feet. She was slightly disheveled, lustrous auburn hair tucked partially beneath a crimson veil. Matilda knew that she had to reach this woman, to touch her, to speak to her. She knew all too well just who this was. But the writhing crowd held her back and she couldn't get to her.

"My lady!" Matilda was screaming in the dream, reaching out to the woman, who reached back, staring at her with a face of aching beauty. She was fine-boned, with exquisite, delicate features. But it was her eyes that would haunt Matilda long after the dream was over. Huge and bright with unshed tears, they fell somewhere in the color spectrum between amber and sage, an extraordinary light hazel that reflected infinite wisdom

and unbearable sadness. The extraordinary eyes conveyed a plea of utter desperation to Matilda.

You must help me.

The moment was broken when the woman looked down suddenly at a young girl who tugged urgently on her hand. Matilda gasped: she had experienced this part of the dream before, years ago when she was very young. She saw this little girl tugging at her mother's hand, and she knew what came next. Behind the little girl stood an older boy, her brother. The mob surged again and the older boy grabbed for his sister, to keep her from being swept up in the crowd. The little girl screamed in terror, and then Matilda could not see the children anymore.

It was starting to rain, and in the strange, nonlinear continuum of the dreamscape, Matilda was now out of the crowd, but she could see her lady, Maria Magdalena, ahead of her in her red veil. Lightning ripped through the unnaturally dark sky as she stumbled up the hill with Matilda behind her. It was a strange sensation of both participating and observing. Matilda could not tell if she was experiencing her own feelings or Magdalena's feelings, as they were all blending together in the experience.

She was oblivious to the cuts and scrapes—hers, Magdalena's, it no long mattered. She had only one goal, and that was to reach him.

The sound of a hammer striking a nail, metal pounding metal, rang with a sickening finality through the air. As she—or they—reached the foot of the cross, the rain escalated into a downpour. She looked up at him, and drops of his blood splashed down on her distraught face, blending with the relentless rain.

Matilda looked around, removed from Magdalena now and once again an observer. She could see her lady at the foot of the cross, supporting the figure of the mother of the Lord, who appeared to be nearly unconscious with her grief. There were other women wearing the red veils around them, huddled together, supporting each other. One younger woman dressed in white in the midst of them caught Matilda's attention. Strangely, there was a Roman centurion standing next to the women, but he appeared to be protecting them rather than terrorizing them. There was something kind in his face, and he appeared to be as tormented as the suffering family. In a brief flash, she noticed that this centurion had the most extraordinary ice blue eyes. No doubt the tears that filled them magnified their transparent appearance.

The children were nowhere to be seen, Matilda noticed with some relief. Somewhere in her consciousness she remembered Isobel telling her that the children had been taken to safety before the terrible event that would change the world.

Another Roman stood nearer the cross with his back to the mourning family. Matilda could not see his face, but something in this man's stature made her shudder. He snapped orders at the other Roman soldiers in the retinue near the cross. Matilda could not hear his words, but there was a cold arrogance to his voice that was unmistakably dangerous.

In her desire to take in as much of the scene as possible, she noticed that there were only two men in attendance with the women. One was older, dignified in his grief. He had his arm around a younger man, who appeared near to collapse. Matilda could hear Isobel in her lessons from ten years earlier:

"Our Lord had a wonderful friend who was called Nicodemus. Nic-o-de-mus. Nicodemus was one of only two men who were with him when he died."

Matilda gasped. This younger man must be Nicodemus, the great sculptor of the Volto Santo. *It was then that she realized she had not yet allowed herself to look upon the face of her Lord. Lifting her head slowly, she took in the holy and terrifying sight that was immediately ahead of her. The rain flowed down the planes of the most beautiful face she had ever seen. Even in his agony, he radiated a light and goodness that was impossible to define. His hair was indeed black as Nicodemus had sculpted it, long to his shoulders and also with a forked beard. But it was his eyes that were the real tribute to the talent of the artist who would celebrate his likeness later in wood. They were huge and dark and heavy-lidded, and full of kindness, just as Nicodemus had depicted them. Jesus looked at her then, for a brief moment that lasted into eternity. He held her gaze and she heard him say, although his lips did not move,*

"You are my daughter, in whom I am well pleased."

Matilda was crying now, sobbing, her tears and grief blending with those of the family huddled at the foot of the cross. She was part of them. She was separate from them. But somehow, they were all one.

A scream shattered the scene, a wail of absolute human despair that came from the lips of Maria Magdalena. As Matilda looked up at her Lord on the cross, she saw immediately what had happened. The dark centurion, the arrogant and dangerous one close to Jesus, had shoved his lance into her Lord's side until blood and water flowed from the wound.

The sound of Madonna Magdalena's sobs blended with the harsh laughter of the evil Roman, as Matilda awoke to the first light of a Tuscan dawn, a millennium later across the world.

❁

"The *Volto Santo* is a wonderful likeness of our Lord."

The Master, Isobel, and Patricio froze as Matilda entered the room with this unexpected announcement. She looked disheveled and obviously sleepless, but her statement was strong and she did not appear to be disturbed.

"What has happened, Matilda?" It was Isobel who asked.

Matilda told them all about the dream, describing in detail what and whom she had seen and how they all appeared. She described Maria Magdalena in detail, how beautiful and heartbreaking she was, then Nicodemus and even the Roman soldiers.

The Master stopped her here. "Did you see the faces of any of the centurions?" he asked.

When Matilda nodded, the Master was very still, waiting for her answer.

"One of them had the most extraordinary light blue eyes," she said.

"That would be Praetorus." He nodded. "The Libro Rosso describes him as a blue-eyed Roman very specifically." The Master was quite satisfied with this. Matilda had not yet studied Praetorus and Veronica, as their story was part of the lessons that were to come when she was of age, which was officially today. The lessons about sacred union of beloveds were not taught until after an initiate's sixteenth birthday. That Matilda saw Praetorus and was able to identify his unusual eye color, when she could not possibly have known about it otherwise, was a powerful omen that her vision was authentic. The Master had no doubt that it was, but this was blessed confirmation.

"Did you see the face of the other centurion?"

She shook her head. "The dark one, the one who pierced our Lord?"

"Longinus Gaius," the Master answered. "Someday I shall tell you more about him. But not today."

"No, I did not see his face. But . . ." She stopped for a moment, starting to choke up. The Master was nodding at her knowingly. He knew that this was a hard thing to have witnessed for one so young and emotional. But her answer was important.

"I saw what he did. And I think that I will never forget it, nor will I ever forget the sound of his laughter as it happened, not for as long as I shall live."

The Master looked very sad for a long moment before answering. "No, Matilda. And you should not forget it, for you have been blessed by a divine vision. And every part of it is sacred and should be cherished, even those moments that are very hard to endure. Continue, my child. What else did you see?"

Her voice caught in her throat as she attempted at first to recount her moment with Jesus on the cross.

"He was . . . so beautiful. And kind. And I could only think of how much his beautiful dark hair and eyes resembled that of the *Volto Santo*. It truly is a Holy Face because it is his face."

The four of them talked about the dream for quite a while. Patricio had many questions about all the characters present. For him, this was a grand adventure, a view into the past that made it all come to life in a most extraordinary way. And as a member of the Order who was also coming of age, he was greatly interested in information about their founders, Joseph of Arimathea and Nicodemus. Matilda told him all that she remembered—about the older man's dignity and his support of the younger man in his grief, and the fact that she was absolutely certain that there were no other men present.

Isobel wanted a complete description of Maria Magdalena. The two women cried together as Matilda recounted the extraordinary courage and pain she had witnessed in the face of such horror.

"Matilda, we have a gift for you."

The Master left the room for a moment, and when he returned it was with a wooden box that had been carved with the sacred elongated diamond symbol across the hinged lid.

"We had planned to give this to you today as your coming-of-age gift, and now it would seem that it is all the more appropriate. So in the name of our Lady, Maria Magdalena, and in the name of the Order of the Holy Sepulcher, which was created by Nicodemus and Joseph of Arimathea and the blessed Luke to honor her name and memory, we present this to you with great love."

She hadn't cried this much since Bonifacio passed. But the Master's verbal dedication was worth more to her than any physical gift, and her heart was touched deeply. She opened the box and removed the ring. It was identical to Isobel's in shape and size—the circular pattern of stars dancing around the single circle in the center. It was the official seal of Maria Magdalena as preserved in the Libro Rosso. But whereas Isobel's was bronze, Matilda's was made of gold. It was a beautiful gift, worthy of a Tuscan countess.

She slipped it on the fourth finger of her right hand, the finger that is believed to connect directly to the heart, where it rested perfectly. "I shall never take it off. Never."

She thanked them all profusely and spent the rest of the day crying through her lessons. She was surely the most blessed woman in Tuscany to have such friends. She asked that they end the afternoon with all of them walking in the labyrinth together and joining in the center to say the Pater Noster in the special way that was sacred to the Order, within each of the six petals. Once inside the center, she also reaffirmed her promise to build a greater shrine for the Holy Face, this time in thanks for the divine vision she had been given.

It was without a doubt one of the most beautiful days of a very memorable life.

And so it was that on the darkest day of our Lord's sacrifice upon the cross, he was tormented in his final hour by a Roman centurion known as Longinus Gaius. This man had served Pontius Pilate in the scourging of our Lord Jesus Christ and had taken pleasure in inflicting pain upon the son of God. If this were not crime enough for one man, it was this same centurion who pierced the side of our Lord with his deadly spear at his hour of death.

The sky turned black at his moment of passing from our world into the next and it is said that within that moment the Father in Heaven spoke directly to the centurion thus:

"Longinus Gaius, you have most offended me and all people of good heart with your vile deeds on this day. Your punishment shall be one of eternal damnation, but it will be an earthly damnation. You shall wander the earth without benefit of death so that each night when you lie down to sleep, your dreams will be haunted by the horrors of your own actions and the pain they have caused. Know that you will experience this torment until the end of time, or until you serve a suitable penance to redeem your tarnished soul in the name of my son Jesus Christ."

Longinus was blind to the truth at this time in his life, a man of sadistic cruelty beyond redemption, or so it would seem. But it came to pass that he was driven mad by the pronouncement of his eternal sentence to wander in an earthly hell. Therefore he sought out our lady Magdalena in Gaul to beg her forgiveness for his misdeeds. In her unlimited kindness and compassion she forgave him and instructed him in the teachings of the Way, just as she would any new follower, and without judgment.

What became of Longinus Gaius is uncertain. He disappeared from the writings of Rome and from those of the early followers. It is unknown if he ever truly repented and found release from his sentence by a just God, or if he wanders the earth still, lost in his eternal damnation.

For those with ears to hear, let them hear it.

THE LEGEND OF LONGINUS THE CENTURION,
AS PRESERVED IN THE LIBRO ROSSO

CHAPTER EIGHT

*M*aureen grabbed Peter's arm to steady herself as they entered one of the huge entrance doors to St. Peter's Basilica. There was a time in her life when she would not have been able to force herself to enter such a place, so deep was her resentment of the harsh dogmatic aspects of Catholicism. But discovering Mary's gospel had changed that, had changed her. While Maureen still had grave reservations about the politics of both the modern and historical Church, she tried to live the doctrine of forgiveness as preached by this woman who was an icon of nonjudgment and compassion.

And yet St. Peter's Basilica as the seat of the bishop of Rome was, by definition and design, monumental and daunting. Maureen took a deep breath and entered, allowing Peter to steer her to the right of the basilica immediately upon entering.

Maureen had come to the Vatican to see Father Girolamo de Pazzi, as he had requested a meeting with her. Peter was determined to be present for the introductions and to help his cousin negotiate the often daunting security measures within the world's smallest and most insular nation—Vatican City. Prior to the meeting, they had decided to go in search of their Tuscan countess.

"First, you must see the genius." Peter was leading her to the first niche on the right, where flashbulbs and tourists were a sure sign of an artistic icon on public display. As they drew closer, Maureen found herself gasping unexpectedly at the sheer beauty that confronted her. Michelangelo's masterpiece of sculpture, the *Pietà*, seemed to glow from within. The serene majesty of the Virgin Mary's face, as she held the body of her son, was sublime and awesome at the same time. Maureen waited for the crowd to thin before moving closer to study the sculpture, which had been encased in glass since the 1980s, when a nutcase attempted to destroy it with a sledgehammer.

Maureen made an observation to Peter. "She looks very young, doesn't she? Is it strange that this Mary looks younger than the man on her lap who is supposed to be her son? Do you think it's possible that this is another Mary? Our Mary?"

Peter smiled at her and shook his head. "No. There's no conspiracy here, Maureen. Michelangelo explained it himself in his lifetime, that the purity of the Virgin was such that she would have looked eternally youthful."

Maureen accepted this with a nod, although she wasn't necessarily convinced by this explanation. Whichever Mary this was meant to depict, she was astonishingly beautiful. "But what about the parchment that Bérenger received, the one with the family tree that ends with Michelangelo? The card that accompanied it said, 'Art will save the world.' The card was sent to Bérenger by the same person who also sent my parchment. The two are connected."

"And whoever sent your parchment also had you robbed at gunpoint."

"We don't know that for sure."

"Then who else? Come on." Peter turned Maureen around to move her just a few yards down the aisle. "I will introduce you to the enigmatic countess of Canossa."

Maureen drew up short, stunned by the massive marble monument before her. "Here? In such a prominent place? And forgive me for noticing, but so very close to Michelangelo? Could that be a coincidence?"

Matilda's tomb was in the second niche along the nave, just below Michelangelo's masterwork. The majestic Bernini sculpture that graced Matilda's resting place was a larger-than-life image of an extraordinary woman. She was depicted as a warrior goddess in the classical style, toga and all, with a baton in her right hand, ostensibly to symbolize her accomplishments as a soldier and strategist. She clutched the papal tiara to her body on the left, and in that same hand she held firmly to the key of Saint Peter.

"How strange a depiction for a woman in the Vatican, holding the key to the Church itself." Maureen was thinking out loud before turning to Peter. "What do you make of it?"

Peter translated the inscription over Matilda's tomb in response. "The Holy Pontiff, Urban VIII, transferred the bones from the Monastery of San Benedetto Mantua, of the Countess Matilda, a woman with a noble soul and champion of the Apostolic See, known for her piety, celebrated for her generosity. With eternal gratitude and deserved praise in the year 1635."

"Fascinating, but it still doesn't tell us why she is holding the symbols of the papacy in her hands."

"No, it most certainly does not." Peter flashed a sly smile at her.

"But you know something you're not telling me, don't you?"

"Shhh." Peter looked around surreptitiously. This was one place where the walls truly had ears. "Yes, I finished a large chunk of translations last night. We'll go through them this afternoon."

"You're killing me."

"I know, but it can't be helped. In the meantime, let me show you the other Bernini sculptures here. They're magnificent, and the art lover in you will appreciate them."

He took Maureen to the focal point of the basilica, Bernini's outlandish baldachino, the bronze centerpiece beneath the dome that was his attempt to blend art, architecture, sculpture, and spirituality. He created an enormous canopy cast in bronze, supported by elaborately carved twisted columns that he claimed came from a design drawn by Solomon himself for the first Temple. The baldachino was created to mark the tomb of Saint Peter at the center of the basilica, commissioned by the now enigmatic Pope Urban VIII.

In niches surrounding the baldachino were larger-than-life statues of first-century figures. Maureen instantly recognized Saint Veronica with her veil but puzzled over the enormous figure that appeared to be a Roman centurion with a spear.

"Who is this?"

"Longinus Gaius. The centurion who pierced the side of Jesus at the crucifixion."

Maureen shuddered. The character of Longinus had been clearly drawn in Mary Magdalene's gospel account of Good Friday. This was a hardened and cruel man, most infamous for adding to the suffering of Jesus on the cross. Wasn't it strange that Bernini had created such a beautiful and majestic image of him in the heart of the Vatican?

Peter answered Maureen's query. "It is believed that Bernini created statues that corresponded to the holy relics that were to be housed here. Urban the Eighth, it seems, was something of a relic hound. For example, Veronica's veil was to be kept under her sculpture. The Spear of Destiny, which is what the weapon of Longinus was called, was to be kept here with him. The Vatican only claims to have a piece of the spear, however. A museum in Austria claims another piece, and the rest of it disappeared centuries ago. It was, like the Ark of the Covenant, said to have magical powers and was one of the most coveted relics in history."

"The spear of destiny?" Maureen repeated.

Peter nodded, then checked his watch and called an end to her tour of the basilica. It was time for her meeting in the confraternity offices.

✦

Maureen wasn't sure what she expected, but it wasn't this. Father Girolamo was incredibly sharp and animated for his advanced years, but that wasn't the surprise. The surprise was that he was charming, warm, and apparently genuinely interested in making her comfortable. He had tea brought into his office, and Maureen sipped it, grateful that it was the strong Irish brew that she favored, and curious as to why a Tuscan priest kept tea from County Cork in his pantry.

Peter had left them alone so they could talk privately. He had prepared Maureen for the meeting earlier in the day, filling her in on the elder priest's expertise, but also on his warnings. Father Girolamo de Pazzi had been correct. Someone was using Maureen, and they needed to try to understand who that might be.

"You think whoever sent the parchments to me and to my friends and the gunmen who robbed us are one and the same?" Maureen asked him.

He nodded. "Yes, I do. If you don't mind, please describe what they took, exactly."

Maureen explained how the red book had been given to her by the little girl and then taken by the gunman. She did not elaborate after that. Maureen and Peter had not told anyone in the Vatican as of this moment about Matilda's autobiography. They had learned their lesson about turning over original documents and were keeping this one to themselves.

The old priest continued his questioning. "You never saw what the book contained?"

"No. It was locked, and one of the gunman took it before I could get a good look at it."

"And what do you think it was?"

"I really don't know. I'm sorry. It all happened so fast."

Father Girolamo changed the subject. "Are you willing to discuss your dreams and visions with me? I ask out of a passion for the subject more than anything else. But of course if I can offer you any counsel, I am pleased to do so. It is important for you to know that you can trust me. Most of all, I want to protect you from whoever is attempting to use you for his own purposes."

Maureen felt that she should tell him something, given that she had been so deliberately obtuse regarding the red book.

"Of course. What would you like to know?"

"You have visions of Mary. Waking visions as well as dreams."

"Yes. But it is not your Mary."

"You have never seen the mother of the Lord? She has never appeared to you?"

"No." Maureen wasn't being deliberately short, but she was uncomfortable with men of the Church at the best of times and wasn't inclined to give too much away to them. Old habits die hard, and he hadn't given her enough reason to trust him yet. Girolamo continued to probe gently.

"Your cousin tells me that you have dreams where our Lord speaks to you."

In an attempt to be diplomatic, Maureen provided an abbreviated description of her recent recurring dreams that featured Jesus and the Book of Love.

"And this book that he appears to be writing," the priest interrupted, animated by something she said, "did the pages, by chance, have blue light surrounding them?"

Maureen very nearly spit out her tea. "Yes. How did you know that?"

"Because I have heard this before."

"From whom?"

He shook his head. "It was a confidential consultation, my dear, so I cannot reveal the source. Just as I will tell no one what you reveal to me here. Do you know why the words on the page are alive with blue light?"

When Maureen said she didn't know, he explained, "Because all of the gospels are written for those with eyes to see and ears to hear. Even the canon as we know it today has layers within it that not everyone can readily read or interpret. If our Lord did write a gospel in his own hand, it is possible that he would have written it in such a way that not all the teachings were available to just anyone who would try to read it."

"But why would Jesus write a book that not everyone can read?"

"Because he did not write it at a time when there were printing presses and mass distribution with the understanding that billions of people would one day be able to read such words. That would not have been his intention—to have everyone read it. He wrote it at a time when it would be a teaching tool in the hands of a trained apostle, someone who would know how to interpret what he wanted us to know in a very specific way."

Maureen nodded. "And would it be a safety precaution? So if the book ended up in the wrong hands, it could not be used against him or his followers as blasphemous?"

"Very possible. We cannot know for sure. But you see? I was able to shine some light on your dreams, even though you were reluctant to come here. You will not find anyone in the world with more experience in understanding visions. I hope you will feel free to come to me at any time if you need to discuss this further. And please, for your own safety, inform us immediately if you receive further contact from any outside source."

Maureen thanked him politely for the tea and the conversation, and accepted his invitation to attend the confraternity's forthcoming pre- sentations on the appearance of our Lady at Knock. She knew it would mean a lot to Peter that she was trying not to hold judgment against all men of the Church. Hadn't Tómas DeCaro proven to be an absolute gem during her search for Mary Magdalene? And Father Girolamo had been quite lovely today. Perhaps there was some real hope that these men of the Church would come around and consider allowing the truth into their hearts after all. It was a secret wish that she held close as she made her way back across the Tiber to her hotel.

✿

The scent of the lilies hit her before she even opened the door. The room was filled with them. She smiled, certain this time that she knew who was responsible for the gesture. While Bérenger Sinclair had been persistent in his phone calls since the Orval incident, Maureen had not had the opportunity to speak to him. They had traded messages a few times but had yet to connect. She knew he was worried about her, and she longed for the comfort and safety that she felt in his presence. She didn't relish the idea of having to broker a truce between Bérenger and Peter, but clearly she couldn't ignore their rift much longer.

Bérenger was not a man to be ignored or denied. The card that accompanied his flowers read,

I'm in the suite upstairs, 4th floor. Dinner at 8:00?

Maureen laughed. Well, at least he gave her some notice. She had three hours to shower and get dressed.

Walking over to the picture window of her own suite, Maureen threw it open to take in the magic of the piazza. The fountain gurgled around the granite obelisk as tourists sat on the marble steps, snapping photos and eating panini. One of the tourists caught Maureen's eye, causing her to draw a quick breath. Sitting on the steps beside the fountain and looking directly into her room was a man she had seen before—a man wearing a dark hooded sweatshirt and large sunglasses.

Rome
present day

Useless.

Their nonproductive meeting was over and the leader of the hooded men was left alone to strategize in silence. He removed the midnight blue covering from his head and threw it in disgust. The younger recruits were big on passion but short on common sense. They enjoyed carrying guns and playing cloak-and-dagger games, but God forbid that you needed one of them to think. And he was getting too old to carry so much of this burden without competent help. Even the short trip to Belgium had worn him out.

That idiot actually allowed himself to be seen in the piazza today. Now they would have to assign the detail of following the Paschal woman to someone new. It was exhausting.

Nor did it surprise him that they had thus far been unsuccessful in their hunt for Destino. He was elusive, as he had always been. Always.

Destino, with many places to hide across the continent, could be anywhere. Likely he was in Italy or France, but he had been known to take refuge in Switzerland, Belgium, and the Netherlands. And he had so many aliases, had been known by so many names over so many years, that it was impossible to track him down when he didn't want to be found.

And it was clear that, at the moment, Destino didn't want to be found.

There are three promises made at the dawn of time, each of them sacred.

The First Promise is to God, your Mother and Father in Heaven. It represents your most divine mission, what you have come to accomplish in the image of your Creators. It is the reason for incarnation, the purest intention of your soul.

The Second Promise is to the Family of Spirit within which you were created and will belong through eternity. It represents your relationship to each of the souls in your family and how you have agreed to assist them in their mission and they in yours.

The Third Promise is to yourself. It represents how you desire to learn and grow and love within the context of incarnation.

Align yourself with these promises you have made, for they are sacred above all else. Remember them and cherish them, and you will know the greatest joy available to humankind. Do nothing that you know to be against your sacred promises, for that is the definition of sin.

For those with ears to hear, let them hear it.

From the Book of Love,
as preserved in the Libro Rosso

MATILDA WAS HAPPY to the core of her being, if exhausted. The emotional toll of the prophetic dream of the night before and her eventful day with the Order was catching up with her. Still, her sixteenth birthday was not over, as Beatrice and Godfrey were hosting a lavish banquet in her honor. Looking around the banqueting hall, she said a quick prayer of thanks to her Lord. She was most blessed to be surrounded by so many people who loved her, once again. The Book of Love stressed gratitude as a daily practice, and she was certainly thankful this evening.

After the dessert of chestnut cake, her stepfather rose from his place to make an announcement.

"My dearest Matilda, in honor of your coming of age, we have commissioned a special gift for you."

Conn came forward carrying a large wooden crate. He was dressed and groomed for the occasion, and Matilda realized that she had never seen him like this before. With his thick red-ginger hair smoothed and clean and wearing the rich garments of a gentleman, he was a strikingly handsome man. Later she would notice that many of the women in the room were paying very special attention to the virile Celt. No doubt he would have his choice of the single women in attendance tonight—and perhaps a few of the married ones, if he was discreet, given that they were looking at him like hungry wolves—should he choose not to spend the rest of the evening alone. But at the moment, his sole focus was on Matilda.

"For you, little sister."

He removed the lid with a flourish. Matilda reached into the box and gasped. Sparkling in the light of the thick beeswax candles was a sea of copper and bronze, undulating within the box. Reaching in to remove it, she was taken aback by how heavy the serpentine chains were. Conn helped her, as she held a full suit of armor, handmade with individual links of chain mail, against her body. But this was not the rough mail of an average warrior. The mail had been dipped in copper and polished to a high shine, so that it was the perfect complement to the color of Matilda's hair. The heavy bronze collar that matched was made to protect her delicate throat, but it was crafted to rival the beauty of Cleopatra's own, inlaid as it was with aquamarines to match the color of its wearer's eyes.

Matilda was overwhelmed by the beauty and thoughtfulness of the gift. She would discover later that while Godfrey and Beatrice had commissioned the armor and made the payments for such a costly present, it was Conn who had seen to the crafting of it. He had overseen every single detail of the design and fashioning. Conn ensured that it was created for her maximum protection but also emphasized that it must be a costume that would inspire the people of Tuscany to rally and support her when she rode out with her troops. The Celtic storyteller in him demanded nothing less than a suit of armor fit for a legendary warrior queen who would follow in the steps of Boudicca.

What she would also discover, many years later, was that during the fashioning of the garment, Conn had prayed over it every day. He had poured holy water over it, a special and blessed water that was taken from the ancient well at Chartres. He invoked God and the angels for their divine protection of his little sister in spirit, the magical warrior countess whom he had been sworn to protect. It was a promise he had made a very long time ago, a promise to God, and one he intended to keep at all costs.

❋

The fortunes of the papacy continued to wax and wane, and the great houses of Europe waged a prolonged and bloody battle for the soul of Rome, the city that would see nearly twenty popes come and go during Matilda's lifetime. It was in this climate that a young archdeacon from an influential Roman family, Ildebrando Pierleoni, arrived in Florence to meet with the duke of Lorraine and his advisers.

Known as Brando to his intimate friends, this Roman politician from the wealthiest family in that region was politically accomplished and savvy well beyond his years. He was a handsome and dynamic man, with chiseled features and intelligent eyes that were a striking light gray in color, highly unusual for a Roman. But it was not just his eyes that set him apart. Brando Pierleoni had a rare charisma that radiated from him as he entered the meeting hall in the duke's Florentine palace.

Godfrey of Lorraine greeted him warmly. "We are honored by your company, and offer our condolences on the loss of your friend and our most beloved Holy Father."

Brando accepted the greeting with equal warmth. There was sincere sadness in his expression as he discussed the recently deceased Pope Nicholas. "He was a great man, and I will miss him for the rest of my life. He was one of my finest teachers."

"And you have had your share of fine mentors." Godfrey wanted Brando to be aware that he was well informed on the young man's illustrious history in papal politics. "Your uncle was also a great man."

Brando Pierleoni was the nephew of the late Pope Gregory VI, a pontiff who had been sent into exile by Henry III, the same wicked emperor who imprisoned Matilda and Beatrice while confiscating their land. The diplomatic Brando had accompanied his beleaguered uncle into Germany, acted as the liaison for his family during the difficult period of exile, and made a name for himself as an intelligent and worthy counselor on issues of Roman politics.

He used his days in Germany well and wisely, approaching them as a fact-finding mission to garner understanding of the king's motives and to further his education in the fine institutions in Cologne. Most of all, he developed a burning sense of right and justice, becoming dedicated to the understanding that the interference of a secular ruler— particularly such a greedy and ruthless one—into the affairs of the Church was quite simply unacceptable. Secretly, in those dark days and long nights of German winter, he took a vow to dedicate himself to reforming the laws of the Church so that it would be immune from secular influence and no king could control papal succession. Brando disdained the hypocrisy that he saw all around him, and he swore to work toward an environment in which all churchmen were held to the same standards of integrity. He would demand that all priests and bishops stand for something other than the security of their position and the wealth they gained for themselves and their families. He would be bold enough to realign the very power structure of Europe if need be, to ensure that spiritual matters were administered by the papacy alone in perpetuity. Only then would Rome be sufficiently strong and worthy of the apostle Peter for which it was meant to stand. This was the vow he had taken, and he repeated it on a daily basis with absolute fervor.

When Nicholas II had ascended the throne of Saint Peter, his first action was to declare the savvy Brando Pierleoni his archdeacon in charge of fiscal operations, despite the fact that Brando was not a priest. He remained a secular politician, yet he was known to have a deeply held spirituality and was considered extraordinary in his piety among the citizens of Rome. Still, no one had ever before achieved so high a position in the Church without taking vows. It was just the beginning of what would become known as the infamous Pierleoni daring.

Within a few short months Brando had drafted an audacious election decree that stunned Europe. This decree stated that Roman families and the German king would no longer be able to influence papal elections. A select group of cardinals, called the College of Cardinals, would determine the papacy from this day forward. Brando was taking no chances. He was creating a process by which neither the German royal family nor the Roman aristocracy could ever again establish a puppet pope for their own purposes.

It was this election decree that brought Brando to Florence to meet with the duke of Lorraine and his faction. With the death of his mentor Pope Nicholas, a new pope would be elected for the first time utilizing Brando's invention, the College of Cardinals.

"Brando, I will speak to you plainly. We would like to put forward the bishop of Lucca, Anselmo di Baggio, as the successor to the Holy Father. He is, as you know, a strong reformer as you are. He is also opposed to German involvement in Roman affairs, which I know is a cause that is dear to you."

Brando nodded. Godfrey marveled at the young man's confidence as he considered the proposal. While the archdeacon was unerringly polite, he was clearly in control of the current situation. And his intelligence was a marvel to behold; Godfrey could watch him calculating, processing, and thinking throughout their meeting. When he replied, it was with a crisp understanding of the current circumstances and the history that led to them.

"Anselmo is a good man and a wise choice for many reasons, but he is also a liability. He once led an open rebellion against Henry, so it will be seen as an act of aggression against Germany if we install him on the papal throne."

Godfrey countered, "Yes, but the Germans will view any election by this so-called College of Cardinals you have installed as an act of aggression. Better to have a pope who will deal firmly with all threats, both to the papacy and to our Italian lords."

The two men discussed the merits of the bishop of Lucca well into the afternoon, ultimately coming to an agreement that forged a new and mighty bond between the house of Tuscany and Brando Pierleoni, a bond that would stretch into history.

✤

Within two weeks, Anselmo di Baggio, the former bishop of Lucca, became Pope Alexander II as the result of the first legal election under the new decree. The institution that would select the pope over a thousand years into the future, the College of Cardinals, had been inaugurated.

The Germanic bishops and northern aristocracy were infuriated by this selection of a man with overt and vocal anti-German sentiments. They demanded that their queen regent, Agnes of Aquitaine, oppose this pope in the name of their young king Henry IV. Agnes was never trained for the blood sport of papal politics and found herself at a loss to accomplish any of the tasks that were laid out for her. When she remained silent and took no action, the bishop of Cologne, an ambitious man called Anno, instigated a diabolical plot. Anno kidnapped his own sovereign, holding young Henry as an unreachable prisoner on his yacht. Bishop Anno demanded that Agnes surrender her regency and return to France, leaving the boy in the hands of the bishops who would raise him to be a true king to the German people.

At eleven years old, Henry IV had grown further into his arrogant, imperious, and petulant personality. He berated his captors for ripping him from the security of his mother and causing him untold trauma. In return, his abductors, who were the highest-ranking church officials in Germany, pandered to him outrageously in an effort to assuage their guilt. They spoiled him with more efficacy and corruption than his dull mother ever could have, turning him into a most lascivious creature. They created a monster. By the time he came of legal age to rule at fifteen, Henry IV had a proclivity for extravagance and sexual excesses that included prostitutes, orgies, and what would become legendary perversions. By most accounts, the bishops who procured the means for Henry to indulge in his sins participated with equal relish.

Henry's own mother, back in Aquitaine, now became his bitter enemy. Hearing of her son's growing depravity, the pious noblewoman disowned him and sided with her own people, against the German crown. The final desertion of his mother caused the troubled Henry's mind to snap beyond redemption. His utter lack of female influence after the age of eleven further distorted his psyche, and the young king evolved into a raging and sadistic misogynist. Had he been anything other than a king, it would have been discovered early that he was a dangerous psychopath. There were terrible rumors about the bodies of young women who had to be disposed of surreptitiously after Henry went on his periodic lust-filled rampages. No doubt the corrupt churchmen who surrounded him fueled his perspective that women existed for the most base satisfaction of his desires, and for absolutely no other reason. Certainly, the betrayal and weakness of his mother had proven that females were of no use politically and could not be trusted with any power. In fact, they could not be trusted at all and deserved the fate that he chose to mete out to them.

✺

The same northern bishops who controlled Henry's power and fortunes made the military decision to send an armed retinue of mercenaries to Rome, to place their own man on the papal throne by force. When it was determined that a troop from Tuscany would ride to Rome to defend the position of Pope Alexander, Matilda, now eighteen, insisted on joining the retinue. For her, this was a most important stand to take. Alexander was her pope, a proud and strong citizen of Lucca and a secret defender of the Order. She would fight for him to the death if need be.

Matilda entered Rome at the side of Conn, leading an impressive band of Tuscan warriors and wearing her polished armor, which glittered in the sunlight. The people of Rome were both scandalized and thrilled by this shining young warrior countess who rode to the defense of her pontiff.

Conn was careful to keep Matilda out of the thick of the fighting, but at the end of the day he had to admit that she had fought with both valor and wisdom. The unfortunate result for the Tuscan forces, however, was a bloody battle with heavy losses on both sides and no one able to claim victory. Brando Pierleoni escorted his new pope, Alexander II, back to the safety of Lucca, under the protection of the Tuscan guard. Matilda rode ahead with Conn to report back to Florence, but not before Brando had himself caught a glimpse of the extraordinary young woman who was already becoming the stuff of legend. His last view of her was from behind, a vision of copper light, reflecting the sun off the Tiber. Then suddenly, a ray of sun struck the river in such a way as to send a beam of light across his vision, blinding him momentarily with its white-hot intensity.

In a momentary flash of prescience, Brando knew that their paths would cross again.

Henry IV was also present in Rome when Matilda rode into the city in her spectacle of glory. It was a sight that burned his eyes and added to his simmering psychosis. Now his bitch of a cousin was causing trouble for him with her open rebellion, flaunting her wealth and her unseemly heretical ways. The people of Tuscany would pay for supporting something as wicked as a female warlord—he would see to that without a doubt. And he would deal with her eventually, and deal with her most personally. Henry still dreamed about her at night, dreamed of how it felt to have his hands in her unholy red hair all those years ago. He still had a lock of it that he had cut from her head when she was sleeping. The day would come when he would rule her, and he had no shortage of delicate torments that he would subject her to when the time came. Her captivity at Bodsfeld would look very different the next time around. Hadn't he lain awake at night for years imagining such things in elaborate, graphic detail? It was one of the most deeply held obsessions in a twisted mind full of unhealthy fixations.

The Germans were ultimately forced, by Tuscan might and cunning, to relinquish the papacy to the reformer from Lucca, who was officially and without contest invested as Pope Alexander II. Henry blamed Matilda for her part in his great failure. His hatred of her was now at full boil.

For the Order of the Holy Sepulcher, the positioning of a Lucchesi pope was the realization of a dream. It was perhaps the first time that a heretic from an ancient bloodline family was pope, but it would most assuredly not be the last.

The news of Alexander's confirmation gave Matilda cause for great celebration. Now, with the help of Pope Alexander and his nephew Anselmo, who would eventually become the new bishop of Lucca in his place, Matilda could finally keep her childhood promise. She would see to it that a worthy shrine was constructed as a home for the *Volto Santo*. The ancient and crumbling church of San Martino became a proper cathedral, rebuilt from the ancient foundations under her enthusiastic sponsorship. Matilda, as the countess of Canossa, attended the dedication ceremony along with the Lucca faction, at the side of their blessed Holy Father, Pope Alexander II.

The Holy Face now rested in a grand church, one worthy of Nicodemus and his masterpiece. Matilda had finally done something which she believed was deserving of her Lord's being well pleased with her.

It was only the beginning.

Florence
1069

"SIT DOWN, MATILDA."

Beatrice groaned in exasperation. She felt as if she had spent half her life uttering that phrase to a restless daughter who rarely stopped moving. That daughter, now twenty-three years old, shockingly beautiful, and intensely confident, was a powerful political force to be dealt with in Tuscany and beyond. Governing her with any kind of maternal authority was becoming an increasingly difficult prospect for the matriarchal Beatrice.

With Conn at her side, Matilda had led armies from the Apennines to the Alps to protect her beloved Pope Alexander from the schismatic forces who had been bribed to support Henry's antipope. In 1066, she rode at the right arm of her stepfather in the final battle that decimated the remaining supporters of the antipope, and when it was over, she was hailed as the victor, surrounded by men who shouted the battle cry that would follow her throughout her military career: "For Matilda and Saint Peter!"

By all accounts, Matilda fought with the same ferocity and valor as her male compatriots. Further, the men adored her and followed her without question or complaint. Conn had observed with no small degree of initial astonishment that their adulation was not in spite of the fact that she was a woman, but because she was a woman. He was to credit for this, in part, as he openly admired her and praised her worthiness as a military leader. The Celtic giant, who understood the power of myth and propaganda, added fuel to the men's sentiments by comparing Matilda often to the legendary women of history. The soldiers listened intently as Conn wove his magical tales around the campfire, stories of the Amazon Queen Penthiselea, who cut off one of her own breasts because it interfered with her accuracy in holding a bow as she fought against the Greeks in defense of Troy; the Egyptian Cleopatra, who defied the might of Rome; the Assyrian Zenobia, who ruled the largest kingdom of the ancient world, all the while drawing comparisons to their Matilda and emphasizing her superiority. He whispered to them of the prophecy of The Expected One when Matilda was not in earshot, explaining that she had been chosen by God to lead them. The soldiers saw themselves as part of a new mythology, as the men who would form a great warrior band around a woman who would be remembered in perpetuity for fulfilling her extraordinary destiny. They would all become the stuff of legend. And to be remembered by history, Conn reminded them, was a special type of immortality.

But the men were not merely blind followers of this canny strategy. The troops recognized and followed greatness, and they saw it in both the strength and strategy of Conn and the spirit of Matilda. They also followed nobility, which was as natural a trait of their petite warrior countess as was her legendary hair. Her very nature inspired them to feats of great bravery.

And it was through this combination of courage and valor, heart and spirit and powerful mythology, that Matilda of Canossa had become a legend of nearly epic proportions in Italy by the time she was twenty-three. She was called "Matilda the Maid" by the people who came out of the villages to watch her ride past in her copper mail and to take up the cheer for her:

"For Matilda and Saint Peter!"

At the moment, the legend incarnate was pacing her mother's interior chamber in obvious agitation.

She snapped back at Beatrice, "I do not wish to sit, Mother."

"As you will. You may take this news standing or sitting, it is all the same to me. But you will take it, Matilda. You have successfully managed to escape the terms of your betrothal for seven years. Godfrey has allowed this avoidance and so have I, for different reasons. Godfrey, to his credit, does not feel that you will find much to love in his son and he would shield you from this fate if he could."

Godfrey's only son from his first marriage was heir to the fortunes of Lorraine, and Matilda had been betrothed to him since the death of her father made such a legal bonding necessary. That the younger duke was known as "Godfrey the Hunchback" did not make him the most desirable husband for a sensual young woman who had been raised with an exalted view of love. A man more famous for his physical deformity than any other trait was hardly appealing to a woman who had studied the sanctity of the bridal chamber and dreamed about the sacred union of beloveds in its most romantic form. She fantasized about finding the exalted passion of Solomon and Sheba and Veronica and Praetorus as she had learned about it in the Order. This fulfillment did not seem likely under the circumstances that fate was attempting to enforce upon her in the currently intractable guise of her mother. Besides, her stepfather did not speak of his son often, which was further indication that he must be an unsavory character.

"I am never going back to Germany, and you of all people should understand that. You cannot ask me to leave Tuscany. It is part of my soul. My blood runs through this place and I will die if you force me from it. My father would never have done such a thing to me."

Beatrice sighed, shifting in her seat. She had expected this, and dreaded it. "It is Lorraine that you will go to, and Lorraine is part of your heritage. It is my heritage, Matilda, and as it is the legacy of no less than Charlemagne, it is good enough even for you. It is time that you claimed that part of yourself and found the honor in it. And incidentally the palace at Verdun is very grand and elegant. Most people would think they were in heaven to live in such a place."

"Then it will be a grand and elegant prison, but a prison I will not see. Because I will not go there, and I will not marry the hunchback."

"Matilda, there is something you do not know."

"Nothing you tell me will change my mind."

"Your stepfather is dying."

Matilda stopped pacing. She turned slowly to look at her mother, who clearly knew that her verbal arrow had struck its mark. Matilda loved Godfrey. He had been so kind to them and made them into a real family over the nearly fifteen years of their lives together. He had been a true father to her, and more. The duke had been a wise and patient mentor, teaching her how to administer and defend the Tuscan properties. She owed him so much. Now she was suddenly at risk of losing him, of suffering the nearly incalculable loss of another father.

"How do you know?" Matilda swallowed hard. In her heart, she knew that Godfrey had been deteriorating. In the two to three years following the schismatic wars, she had watched as his vitality had diminished. He no longer could sit a horse and he was forced to take to his room for long periods of rest. In the last years, she had been the one to hear the local councils, riding out to Mantua and Canossa to meet with their vassals and mediate in civic disputes. Matilda had been so enthralled with this assumption of power that she had not allowed herself to contemplate the reasons behind it. She tried to rationalize that Godfrey was merely allowing her to step into her inheritance, rather than accept that he was no longer physically capable of running Tuscany himself.

"You have been away much of this last year and have not watched him as I have. The gout has overcome him. He knows it, I know it. Travel across the Alps will be difficult, indeed the strain of it may bring death to him sooner, but he wishes to die at home in Lorraine. Further, he wishes to see you safely married to his son before he does leave us. It is necessary, Matilda. It will secure your inheritance with the power of Lorraine as well as through legal means that must be accepted by everyone. Do you not know that your wicked cousin will jump at the chance to steal your property on the day that Godfrey dies if you do not secure your titles through marriage?"

Matilda tossed her head with disdain at the mention of Henry IV. In her mind, he was still the creature who tormented her as a child, not worthy to be thought of as a king.

"He will never steal anything from me again. I will lead armies against him myself. Let him try to take what is rightfully ours."

"No, Matilda. I will not let him try to take what is rightfully ours, not as long as there is breath in my body. Further, it is your stepfather's dying wish to see you married. We leave for Verdun immediately, as Godfrey must cross the Alps before the winter, and we would see you wed by Christmas. I'm sorry, Matilda. If there was another way, I would support it. But there is not."

Matilda felt the strength begin to drain from her heart and her will. She finally allowed herself to sit down in one of the hand-carved chairs painted with the red and white fleur-de-lis shield of Lorraine. It seemed a symbolic gesture of surrender.

"I must go and notify Isobel so that she can prepare."

Now it was Beatrice's turn to stand. She knew that what would come next would be poorly received by her emotional and headstrong daughter. What was to come was perhaps even more dire for her than the previous decree that they were leaving for Lorraine to arrange her wedding.

"Isobel cannot accompany you to Verdun, my daughter. You are now a woman grown, going to a noble husband and with no further need of a nurse. It would not be seemly."

There, it was done. Both Beatrice and Godfrey knew that as long as the Lucca faction remained attached to Matilda, she would never concede to her fate as the duchess of Lorraine and the wife of Godfrey the Hunchback. They had to forcibly separate her from their influence. And while Beatrice was loath to admit her jealousy of Isobel's unwavering attachment to Matilda, it was a very real factor in her determination.

Beatrice could not look at her daughter. It had taken a heavy toll on her maternal soul to hurt her child in this manner, the child she had grown to love more than anything on God's earth, and yet it was for her own good. Matilda had lived in a strange fantasy world of believing she could command her own destiny for a little too long. It was time for her to face the reality that women did not control their fates in this world, even a woman who had already become something of a legend in her own time and place. It was a harsh lesson that Beatrice wished she did not have to deliver, but it was a necessary one.

She went to the window to look out at the fading Tuscan summer sunlight, waiting in the heavy silence that followed. The explosion that Beatrice expected did not come. Finally, Matilda said softly behind her, "I will go with you to Verdun, if only to give Godfrey some peace at the end of his life. I love him, I owe him, and I will give him that. Our Lord said to honor my father and mother, and I will do so."

She rose suddenly and strode toward the door, anxious to be out of this room and into what was left of the fading Florentine sun, a sun she would be forced to leave behind all too soon. She delivered her final words to her mother over her shoulder.

"For now, you win. But I promise you . . . only for now."

Matilda waited until she was in the safety of Isobel's presence in Santa Trinità to allow herself to show the extremity of her despair.

"How will I bear it, Issy? How will I let such a horrible man touch me? And how will I live without you, and the Master and Conn . . . and Tuscany?"

Isobel held Matilda and stroked her hair, allowing her to cry for a while before speaking in the strong yet gentle manner that had always calmed her charge.

"There are things in life that must be borne, Matilda. And when they occur, we must surrender to them as God's will. Our prayer says '*thy* will be done' and not '*my* will be done' for a reason. What have I taught you about such things?"

Matilda wiped her hands over her face. She would be deeply challenged in her spirituality now to find the sense in this current situation. "That the day will come when I will see the wisdom in God's plan, even though I cannot dream of seeing it today."

Isobel nodded. "Correct. For when you accept that you are here for the express purpose of carrying out God's plan, you will never know a day of pain. Surrender to it, Matilda. He is the great architect. We are merely the builders who carry out his plans, and we must do it by laying one stone at a time, just as he directs us. When we do this, we ultimately see that we are building something beautiful and enduring, just as the master architect in Lucca did while reconstructing San Martino. Clearly, God wants you to go to Lorraine as part of your destiny. Who knows what it is that you will find there?"

"It will not be the sacred union of the beloveds with a hunchback, I can tell you that."

"I know, Tilda. And I'm so sorry that your first experience with a man will not be one of true love. But I promise you that one day you will find that kind of love and it will be all that you have dreamed of and worthy of any wait."

"How do you know that, Issy? What hope is there, when at twenty-three I shall be married to a hunchback? I will be an old woman by the time that I am rid of him. If I am ever rid of him. May God forgive me."

"I can promise you this because the prophecy says it specifically." Isobel grew stern with her. "You either believe in the prophecies or you do not. But you cannot have it both ways, Matilda. You either are The Expected One, or you are not. And if you are, then you will fulfill your destiny according to the words of our prophetess: you will build important shrines for the Way to preserve our legacy, and you will know a very great love. Take comfort in that and find your faith, child. It will save you, when the times are bleakest.

"But for now, you must accept this trial, just as our Lord accepted his own trials. Surely, in comparison, being asked to wed a duke and live in luxury cannot be so bad."

When put in that context, it was hard to despair of one's fate and not feel terribly selfish. The Master was fond of asking Matilda, when she was feeling sorry for herself for one reason or another, "Is anyone approaching you or your loved ones with a large cross and iron nails? Because if that is not the case, you have little enough to complain about."

The Master had lectured her often on the sacrifices not only of the Lord but also of his mother and his wife, who had to endure the pain of witnessing his final ordeal. They had debated well into the night, more than once, just which of those fates was more noble— the lot of the sacrificial lamb, or those who were left behind to carry the memory of his ordeal into the future. It was a question that had no answer but that never failed to inspire worthy discussion among people of spirit.

Isobel had an idea. "Come tomorrow morning, just after sunrise, to the Oltrarno. I will see to it that the Master is there, and we will work through this."

On the other side of the river, called the Oltrarno, the Order possessed property in a more secluded area that was blissfully not under the immediate scrutiny of all eyes in Florence. Someone as recognizable and popular as Matilda could not simply walk unnoticed through a city such as this. When they were within the walls of the property at Santa Trinitá, they had privacy. But for other things, they had to get out of the city.

So it was for her that the Order built a labyrinth out of stone and brick across the river, which the Master had used for Matilda's education over the years. It had become her greatest refuge.

"You need to walk this through in the labyrinth, Tilda. *Solvitur Ambulando.*"

Matilda nodded. *Solvitur ambulando* meant "it is solved by walking," and it was an integral part of their teachings from the labyrinth. For Matilda had been taught that the labyrinth was a perfectly constructed device. It was created through the combined wisdom of Solomon and Sheba, a sublime indication of how beloveds can manifest great miracles through shared spirit. It was given to man as a means of accessing God most directly through inner listening. Walking the labyrinth gave the prayerful person ears to hear, so that upon reaching the center, the messages of God could be heard and understood most clearly. It was a walking prayer, a dance of meditation that brought the mind, body, and spirit together in a singularly powerful understanding. It was through the labyrinth that Solomon gained his legendary wisdom.

Perhaps Matilda would find her strength in the morning, once she listened to God in the center of the labyrinth. It had never failed her before. The six-petaled flower at the center of this labyrinth was her favorite place on earth, the safest, sweetest location ever created. To-morrow she would go there in search of herself, her future, and God's otherwise indiscernible will.

The summer sunrise over the Arno was a sweet play of golden light. Matilda paused to take it in, breathing in the beauty of her beloved Tuscany and allowing the tears to slide down her face as she did so. The rivers of this region—the Arno, the Po, the Serchio—they truly did run through her veins. To be deprived of them for any period of time, much less the years she would no doubt be required to live in Lorraine, was a hellish sentence. Perhaps it was even worse than being forced to marry a hunchback. She could almost stand that particular horror if she could at least do so while living in Tuscany.

But that was not to be. For whatever divine reasons, God had de-creed that Matilda would both marry the hunchback and be separated from her homeland. Now she would try to understand why and, within that understanding, surrender to that will.

Isobel was waiting for her at the gate that separated the Order's property from the main road. A copse of trees further shielded the sa-cred space from prying eyes, and they walked through the path, which Matilda could traverse with her eyes closed, so well did she know it and so much did she love it. The path ended at a clearing, where the enor-mous labyrinth had been carefully constructed utilizing Solomon and

Sheba's principles, with brick and stone inlayed into the dirt to create the eleven circuitous pathways into the center. While Solomon's original labyrinth contained a perfectly round center, this version had been carefully constructed to culminate in a six-petaled rose, the symbol of the Book of Love as designed by the messiah himself. The labyrinth was now a miraculous hybrid of the wisdom teachings of Solomon the Great combined with the central prayer of his descendant, Jesus Christ.

The Master was in the center upon Matilda's arrival, on his knees and deep in prayer. Fra Patricio, the young Calabrian protégé, smiled at Matilda from the entrance. She greeted him quietly, not wanting to disturb the Master in his meditation but happy to see Patricio. They had been raised together in the secrets of the Order, sitting side by side at the foot of the Master. They had quizzed each other and studied together, played memorization games that allowed each of them to commit the Book of Love and the prophecies of the Libro Rosso to memory. Together they studied Solomon's intricate and divinely inspired architectural drawings for creating temple spaces as they had been handed down for inclusion in the Book of Love. These were the most intense and difficult lessons, and studying this with a partner made processing the information easier. Both children proved so adept at the temple drawings that the Master commented on many occasions that either of these children could become most memorable architects.

They competed good-naturedly for the attention and praise of the Master, and sometimes not so good-naturedly as they learned to submerge their egos in the learning. Patricio had become the brother that Matilda had lost as an infant. The Master teased them that they were two halves of the same mind. Leaving Patricio would be wrenching to her soul.

The Master walked the eleven circuits out, bowing deeply to the labyrinth when he reached the exit-entrance. He walked the extra paces toward them, kneeling to touch the iron ring that was embedded in the dirt. With closed eyes, he thanked the Lady of the Labyrinth for her gifts and moved to embrace Matilda.

"Welcome, my daughter." He kissed her on both cheeks. "This is indeed a glorious morning, for the will of God makes itself known to us. I shall reserve my understandings until you have first found your own. *Solvitur ambulando*, child. Go and speak to your Creator." He gestured broadly to the labyrinth. Isobel, Patricio, and the Master stepped away from it at a discreet distance to allow Matilda sole use of the space. There were times when they all walked it together, when it was a beautiful dance of camaraderie and sharing. But this morning was for her alone. She thanked them all and then approached the iron ring in the ground. She got on her knees to give thanks to the Lady of the Labyrinth. Through time, the Lady had many guises, for she was the divine feminine, the essence of love and compassion, the female beloved who completes the male through their union of love and spirit, trust and consciousness. She was Ariadne, she was Sheba, she was Magdalena, she was Asherah.

In honor of Ariadne, Matilda plucked a long strand of copper hair out of her head and tied it in a bridal knot on the iron ring in imitation of the thread that saved Theseus.

As she approached the entrance of the great space, she remembered what the Master had said to her all those years ago when she first entered. "There is no right way to walk a labyrinth, and there is no wrong way. There is only your way. Go at the pace that your soul dictates, and stay true to your path."

Taking several deep breaths to clear her mind, Matilda entered the labyrinth. She walked slowly today, deliberately, watching her feet as they traveled the circuits, willing herself to let go of all the noise that filled her brain from the waking, conscious world. For her, the kinesthetic aspects of the labyrinth were the greatest balm to her mind. She was not skilled at sitting still in prayer or meditation for long periods of contemplation; she was far too restless a spirit for such quietude. Most humans are. But in the labyrinth, she could move, and think and feel, all at the same time. It was the most glorious form of prayer imaginable.

Breathing, purging, walking, following the winding paths; letting go of all the dross, telling God that she wanted nothing more than to hear his voice clearly and know his will so that she could follow it. As she reached the sanctified center, the holy of holies, the place of the temple and tabernacle, she fell to her knees and asked God to speak to her. There were days when she came here to work through the Pater Noster and the six primary teachings of the Lord's Prayer, in each of the petals. But this morning she did not do this. She had chosen to walk with a purpose, and that purpose was to understand her destiny.

God did not make her wait long. A vision awaited her in the center of the labyrinth.

Matilda was riding through a lush and verdant forest. In spite of herself, she had to acknowledge the beauty of the place. Patricio was by her side, had ridden out with her when she needed to get away from Verdun. They had ridden hard, as being on horseback was one of the few places where Matilda could find refuge here. And as there was no labyrinth, riding was her only means of escape, an opportunity to move and think at the same time.

They stopped when they came upon a small pond fed by a stream, so that they might water the horses and take some of the bread and cheese that Matilda had packed for their lunch. Patricio led the horses to the stream. Something compelled Matilda to walk on, toward what appeared to be a clearing up ahead. Something drew her that she could not explain at first. And then she heard it: the sound of a young girl's voice. She couldn't make out the words, but she knew it was a child. Was the child speaking to her? Calling out to her? She heard the girl giggle as she came closer to the clearing.

Beams of late afternoon sun glittered through the trees, bouncing off what appeared to be a pool of water just ahead. Enticed, she moved toward it. It was a well, or a cistern, wide enough for several men to bathe in at once. Leaning over to gaze into the water, Matilda was struck by the feeling of fathomless depths, that this well was sacred and ran deep into the earth.

The water was quite still, and then the tiniest ripple broke the surface. A wave of golden light began to suffuse the well and the area surrounding it. As she looked into the water, an image began to take shape. The scene was a beautiful valley, lush and green with trees and flowers. She watched as if looking into a scrying mirror, as a rain of golden drops fell from the sky, gilding everything in the vision. Soon the valley was flowing with rivers of gold, and the trees were covered with it. Everything glittered all around her with the rich warm light of liquid ore.

In the distance she heard the girlish voice, the one that had brought her here.

"Welcome to the Vale of Gold."

Matilda gasped. The Valley of Gold was mentioned in the prophecy. Her prophecy. And as if to assure her that she was correct, the childlike voice rang through the forest sweet and clear, reciting the words of their young prophetess, spoken a thousand years ago:

"The truth must be preserved, in stone and on parchment and built into a Valley of Gold. The new Shepherdess, The Expected One, shall see to its perfection and encase the Word of the Father and Mother and the legacy of their children within the sacred spaces. This becomes her legacy. This, and to know a very great love."

✵

Matilda rose from the center of the labyrinth, still reeling from the vision that she was certain had been given to her by the little prophetess herself. As she began to walk out the eleven circuits, she reviewed the vision and its images. There was no doubt in her mind that the Valley of Gold was in Lorraine. This is why God was sending her there, because she was to build a shrine to the Way of Love in that region. What form that would take she was unsure of, but she was also certain that the Master would know exactly what to do. Had he not said that God had made his will known this morning?

But the true joy came from the vision of Patricio in the labyrinth. God wanted her to have a friend in Lorraine, a friend who would truly understand her in a world of foreign ways and an unwanted husband. Perhaps she would find the strength to endure this with grace after all.

Thy will be done, she repeated to herself several times as she walked her way out of the sacred pathways. When she reached the exit, she bent her knee in benediction at the iron ring and said her thanks to the Lady of the Labyrinth, this time in the guise of Sarah-Tamar.

The Master had not seen Matilda's vision. That was for her alone, a gift from the prophetess so that she would not lose faith. But he had seen a vision of her building a great structure in Lorraine, one that would become the repository of not only all their teachings but the history of their people and the holy families. Matilda was being charged to build a library and a school to preserve all that was sacred to the Order of the Holy Sepulcher, and she would do so in the guise of a monastery. Once the location was found, this Valley of Gold that she had seen in the vision, she would work with Patricio to begin the building. The Master would select monks from Calabria who had proven themselves in their dedication as historians and scribes to begin the task of building the library. Patricio would become their abbot.

This task would be the greatest of honors for both Matilda and Patricio. For the Master had seen one more very important element in his vision. He had seen the Libro Rosso travel across the Alps in its gilded ark, carried carefully by Patricio on a cart pulled by oxen, just as the *Volto Santo* had been three centuries prior. Matilda must take the Libro Rosso with her, so that the contents could be copied exactly and installed with great honor into the new monastery in this Valley of Gold. Once the task was finished, they would return the Libro Rosso to Tuscany, where it was destined to reside in perpetuity.

The teachings of the Way of Love were going to find a new home in Lorraine, restored to the land of Charlemagne. It was Matilda's destiny to see that this happened. In spite of her trepidations about her pending nuptials, this promise gave her a great task to focus on, something positive in her future that was of tremendous importance. She would carry out this duty with honor and with grace.

She would fulfill her destiny and obligation as The Expected One and try very hard not to complain about marrying a hunchback and living in a palace.

And so it was that the beautiful Nazarene girl who was given the name Berenice at her birth was later to become known as Veronica. She was a friend of Madonna Magdalena as a child and a student of the Way, and was educated as a priestess at the feet of our Lord in the same way as her Nazarene sisters. Veronica was younger, and at the time of our Lord's passion, she was not yet a Mary. She did not yet wear the red veil. Her own was white.

It is told of the lovely Veronica's act of courage on the Day of Sorrows that when the Savior carried his burden to the hill on the Black Day of the Skull, his vision was obscured with the blood and grime that ran into his eyes from the wounds inflicted by his crown of thorns. Veronica moved bravely through the crowd that surrounded her master and pulled the white veil from her head. She brought it to him that he might wipe his face and find some comfort in his vision.

Later, it would be seen that the image of our Lord's face was impressed upon the white silk for all eternity.

Veronica attended Magdalena and the other Marys at the foot of the cross, a sister in love and grief. Here they were protected by the blue-eyed Roman soldier, called Praetorus, who had been in the private service of Pontius Pilate. This centurion had been healed of a broken hand by our Lord, and he was finding the light of conversion during the Holy Week when things of such terrible greatness transpired.

Praetorus would evolve into a different kind of soldier following our Lord's passion. He was destined to become a warrior for the Way, one of the earliest converts to our community, and certainly one of the most dedicated.

On the day of our Lord's resurrection, Praetorus ran to the sepulcher after hearing of the miracle. It was there that he first spoke with our Nazarene sister, Veronica. She told him of our Lord's great teachings, of the Way of Love, and how these would change the world if we would only allow their truth into our hearts.

From that holy Easter day, Veronica and Praetorus were never separated. Such a love that was found in the shadow of the Holy Sepulcher could only be blessed by God throughout eternity. Veronica began to guide him through the Nazarene teachings. And when our Lady came to Gaul to begin her mission, they followed her and continued their training, under her guidance, directly from the Book of Love as written by our Lord.

Thus they became the very first couple to teach the sacred union of beloveds on European soil and those traditions flourished as a tribute to the sanctity of their love and coupling. Where these teachings are held, there can be no darkness.

Love Conquers All.

As the time returns, Veronica and Praetorus will find each other and teach again. For it is their eternal destiny, and the model for countless others who have made the same promise from the dawn of time, to find each other and to live and teach the Way of Love. Together.

For those with ears to hear, let them hear it.

THE LEGEND OF VERONICA AND PRAETORUS
AND THE TEACHINGS OF LOVE AND SACRED UNION,
AS PRESERVED IN THE LIBRO ROSSO

Rome
present day

FATHER PETER HEALY paced the floor of his office, palms sweating. This was highly unexpected and somewhat awkward, but there was no escaping it. Bérenger Sinclair was on his way up to see him. Maggie had gone down to help him navigate Vatican security. It gave Peter just a few minutes to gather his thoughts, but there was little he could do to prepare. It would all depend on what Sinclair's purpose was for coming, and what approach he took. Peter was truly at a loss to guess, as Maureen refused to speak to him about any of her friends at Blue Apples. She merely avoided the subject completely, which could mean anything.

The door opened and Maggie ushered Bérenger Sinclair into Peter's office, looking somewhat put out when the aristocratic Scot refused any kind of refreshment. Bérenger waited until the housekeeper had closed the door before approaching Peter with his hand out.

"Father Healy. Thank you for seeing me on such short notice."

Peter took the proffered hand, relieved that the initial approach seemed cordial.

"Of course, Lord Sinclair. My pleasure. What brings you to Rome?"

Peter gestured to the armchair across the desk from his own. Sinclair sat as he replied, very simply, "Maureen."

Peter nodded. "I suspected as much. Does she know you're here?"

"Yes, but I haven't seen her yet. I wanted to see you first."

"Why?"

Sinclair settled, shifting his large frame in the chair. "Because I know she is concerned about how it will make you feel. So I was hoping to take care of that first, so it is one less thing that she has to worry about."

Peter remained quiet, cautious. There had been no personal contact between him and Bérenger Sinclair after he left the château that night with the Arques Gospel, but he had heard enough about how Sinclair felt about him and his actions.

"Peter, I have had a lot of time to think about the events of the past two years, and I need to tell you that I realize I have been unfair and harsh with you. I want you to know that I bear you no ill will for what happened that night. And I mean that. I understand what you did and why you did it. And on some strange metaphysical level that I cannot claim to understand quite yet, I think you did exactly what you had to do. You fulfilled your role in this great drama that we all find ourselves in."

Peter's response was wry. "Like Judas?"

Sinclair shrugged. "Perhaps. But as you are well aware, the Arques Gospel says that Judas was noble and loyal. He didn't betray Jesus, rather he obeyed him. He did what was necessary in order for all of them to fulfill their destiny. So in that regard, yes. I'd say that the similarities are great and remind you that our Magdalene referred to Judas as the one she mourned above all others, except one."

Peter nodded. That Judas was the most dependable and solid of the apostles was one of the more explosive revelations in Mary Magdalene's gospel. It completely altered the perception of this most reviled character in the first century. There was some comfort in that revelation for Peter.

"Thank you. I appreciate your coming, more than you can possibly know. Tell me, if you don't mind my asking, how was your reunion with Maureen? I'm afraid she doesn't talk to me about such things, given our history."

Bérenger smiled slightly in reply. "Having a relationship with Maureen is like waking up to discover there is a unicorn in your garden."

"Well, that's very poetic," Peter responded. "But what does it mean?"

Bérenger gathered his thoughts about it for a moment before explaining. "It's a completely unique circumstance and something of a shock. You've never encountered anything quite like it. Suddenly, standing there in the middle of your life, is something that proves the presence of magic in the universe. You always believed that the magic was real, but now you can actually see it—and almost touch it. Almost, but not quite. Because first you have to get closer, and yet how do you approach such a skittish, exotic creature? Do you even dare? And are you worthy? There is no frame of reference for such an encounter, no one who can tell you how to go about it.

"Then there is the issue of that very sharp horn. As lovely and gentle as the unicorn appears to be, you have a strong sense that it could also inflict serious injury, even mortal wounds, intentionally or not. Magic cuts both ways. So while it is beautiful and enchanting and you know that you have been somehow blessed by its presence in your garden, it's more than a little dangerous—and also highly disconcerting for the average mortal. Which is what I happen to be."

Peter joined in the allegory. "And gaining its trust, if you want to keep that unicorn in your garden, will require a lot of patience. And a hefty degree of courage."

Sinclair nodded his agreement. "Yes, and you also know this: if you scare it away, it will break your heart and the magic will drain from your life, never to return. Then your landscape will appear very, very empty for the loss. How could your world ever look the same again? For while you may encounter other things of beauty over the course of your life, there is really only one unicorn, isn't there?"

Peter leaned back in his chair and smiled at Bérenger, a sincere and warm smile. There was a time when he was highly suspicious of this man, but he could see now that those days were of the past. He would learn to appreciate him and to understand that he had a specific integrity. Most of all, he believed that the Scotsman truly loved Maureen and understood her in a way that few others ever could. And Peter was certain that Bérenger would do his utmost to keep her safe.

"I think you've come at the right time. Maureen needs you. The attack in Orval scared her. It scared all of us. You have an opportunity to approach her carefully, with the understanding that she needs. Remember the ending of the legend of the unicorn? Ultimately, the only thing that tames it and keeps it in the garden is unconditional love."

"I'm fully prepared to give her that, if she'll allow me to get that close to her."

"I believe you. How can I help you, Bérenger?"

Sinclair shook his head. "I wish it were that easy. But this is a unicorn I must win over by my own merits. Although you can help simply by not opposing me. If Maureen feels that you are supportive of my role in her life, then that is more than enough."

"You have my word. And just know that I do support that. When the chips were really down . . . you were more there for her than I was. I'll never forgive myself for what happened that night, and what my part in all this has been. I'm sorry. Truly sorry, and I hope you will convey that to Tammy and Roland. They deserved better than what I did to them."

Peter was choked up by the end of the speech. The depth of the emotion took him by surprise, but he did not try to hold it back.

Sinclair's reply was kind. "What's done is done, Peter. We have all learned from it and hopefully will grow from it. Forgiveness is the Way of Love and we all try very hard to practice what she preached. What *they* preached. Now, we have a new task ahead of us which may be even greater than the last. This is what we have to focus on above anything else."

They talked about the most recent developments and the strange clues, theorized over who could be behind the hostilities and what their next steps should be. Peter proposed they get together, all three of them, after Bérenger had the opportunity to spend some time with Maureen alone. They vowed to work together toward a higher purpose; it was long past time to do so. At the end of their meeting they embraced warmly, both men feeling relieved and strangely buoyant after the conversation. There is no greater healing than that which comes with forgiveness and reconciliation.

As Sinclair moved to leave, Peter called after him, "And, Bérenger, just know that this one thing is certain. I have chosen my master. And you can be sure that I have chosen wisely this time."

He pounded his fist on the desk for emphasis. "Come what may, I will never be on the wrong side again."

CHAPTER NINE

Palace of Verdun, city of Stenay
region of Lorraine
October 1069

*H*e was certainly unattractive and technically deformed, but he wasn't quite as monstrous as she had anticipated.

Until he opened his mouth.

Matilda faced the man she was to marry across the enormous and ornate dining hall at Verdun. She had dressed carefully, doing her best to look entirely feminine and every inch a duchess. She was gowned in an exquisite sea-foam silk shot through with golden thread, and matching gold baubles that were a gift from her stepfather. Her glorious hair was loose, flowing to her waist with fine golden chains braided into the strands at the temples.

They had been left alone to dine together and to begin the process of getting acquainted. The younger Godfrey had enough resemblance to his father that if she squinted a bit, she could almost make him tolerable to look at. Although the elder Godfrey was tall and lean, the younger was large and fleshy. He wasn't obese, exactly, but his deformity no doubt left it impossible for him to find much exercise. And it was equally unfortunate that the intelligence and wit that informed the senior Godfrey's face was missing from his son's. The features of this man were set in a perpetual scowl. Matilda was not yet sure if this was a part of his legendary deformity or if years of bitterness had simply twisted his face.

The hunched back whence his nickname derived was a congenital defect. Her stepfather had explained that his son had been born with an unfortunate disability that left him bent over, rather severely. The resulting insecurities it had created in him as a child were exacerbated by the cruelties that were inflicted upon him as a result of his appearance. It had turned him into a quarrelsome and difficult human being. Further, because he had little control over his physical body, he had become obsessed with everything that he could control, including his holdings in Lorraine, what he now relished as his future holdings in Tuscany, and his betrothed wife. Still, her stepfather assured her that the younger Godfrey was not a cruel man, even if he wasn't the most pleasant, and that Matilda was clever enough to learn to handle her future husband in such a way that ultimately he might learn to treat her with benign respect.

At the moment, he wasn't feeling the least bit benign. He jumped immediately into a litany of all the things he would not tolerate from her.

"I am told that you are headstrong and often behave in a way that is unseemly for a woman. While such behavior may be acceptable in the untamed wilds of Tuscany, it is most certainly inappropriate in a place as civilized as Lorraine. Not in my lands, and not from my wife. You will not leave this house unless properly dressed in a wimple and veil that covers your unnatural hair at all times. I will not have men looking at you with lust as a result of your wanton appearance. It is understood here that women with such red hair are possessed of loose morals and belong only in brothels. They are believed to be consorts of the devil. No proper man in Lorraine takes a red-haired woman to wife as a result, and I am alarmed that your own hair is so . . . lurid. While I was forewarned of your appearance, it was not described to me in quite so vivid terms. You should know that women have lost their lives here for simply looking the way that you do at this moment. The wimple is for your own good as well as my protection against any proclivities you may show toward such wanton behavior. Should you disobey me in this, I will have your head shaved and kept under a veil.

"Further, you must understand that I will be the new duke of Tuscany once we are married, and I will handle all administration of those lands. That my father has allowed you to do so is a disgrace, and proof of his deteriorated state and weakness. Clearly, this is also why he did not send you to me at sixteen as I was promised. Had I suspected any of this weakness, I would have come to Tuscany years ago to set things right."

The hunchback's current assertion that he would be running Tuscany—her Tuscany—was sticking in Matilda's craw at the moment, making it impossible for her to touch the food on her plate. She wanted to throw her knife at him but managed to keep her hands placidly in her lap. Matilda remained quiet rather than risk opening her mouth, not sure she could trust what might come out of it. But her betrothed wasn't nearly finished with his list of requirements.

"I am told that you have brought a confessor with you, a Fra Patricio from Lucca. I would speak to him to be certain that he is acceptable in my household, as I understand that you are connected to unseemly heresies that come from Tuscany. You will behave as a proper Catholic in my household at all times, do you understand this?"

What she didn't understand was which was more offensive: that he was giving her orders, that he was tremendously misinformed, or that he spoke to her like she was the village idiot. Matilda was seething, but she wouldn't let him see it. She was smarter than he was. Infinitely smarter. She would treat this entire encounter as a game of strategy that must be played out. This was war, and it would be filled with battles that she would be required to win in order to maintain her freedom and her properties. Only in this case, the battlefield would be the dining table and the bedroom.

She opened her aquamarine eyes very wide and explained with grave innocence, "But sir, my confessor is not from Lucca. He is from the pious lands of Calabria, deep in the south, and has no connection whatsoever to the heresies of Tuscany. You will know instantly by his accent and his dark skin that he is Calabrian. He was, in fact, chosen to prepare me to become a good and worthy Catholic wife for you."

Godfrey looked at her for a moment before grunting what appeared to be his approval and ripping into his chicken with gluttonous gusto. His table manners were disgusting, but at least when his mouth was full he wasn't talking.

The rest of the meal passed in relative silence, other than the sounds of the hunchback devouring his food. His final words to her before excusing himself were even more charming than his introductory sentences had been.

"I want to have many children, and I will expect to get sons on you immediately. I only hope that at twenty-three you are not too old to give me what I require. Had you been given to me at sixteen, we would have a house full of boys by this time. If it turns out that you are too old, then I will take a younger wife. And I will keep your holdings. Regardless of what is considered customary in the barbaric regions of Tuscany, that is most certainly the right of a gentleman in Lorraine."

Matilda bit her tongue until it bled. If this is what passed as a gentleman in Lorraine, she would gladly call herself a barbarian.

Matilda had prayed her way across the Alps, working with Patricio to approach her fate in the Way of Love, by finding good in all God's children. She had taken a vow to live by that principle and she intended to adhere to her vow to the best of her ability, keeping in mind at all times that she wasn't a saint and didn't plan to become one. God bless Patricio's patience, which she had no doubt stretched to its limits on the long trek from Tuscany. But by the time they arrived in Verdun, Matilda had been fully prepared to approach the hunchback in a loving manner. She had sincerely hoped that perhaps they could find some form of friendship with each other. And if the younger Godfrey was a good man, a worthy conversationalist, and a decent chess partner, she might even learn to love him. Sadly, this was not to be. While she had yet to face off against him on a chessboard, she was certain that he did not possess the first two qualities.

In essence, what the hunchback was doing was no better than what Henry would attempt if she were unmarried—which was to lay claim to her holdings and call them his own while completely eradicating all her rights and imprisoning her here in the frigid north. Was there really a difference? She didn't see one. At least she wouldn't have to sleep with Henry. Or dine with him. So, how was this situation better?

She called her mother and stepfather together to present these questions to them. While Godfrey's health was in a rapid state of deterioration, he was still the duke of Lorraine, a man who had brokered papacies and ruled over kingdoms. And he dearly loved Matilda and cared about her happiness and security.

Matilda presented her case with such efficient logic that neither her mother nor Godfrey the elder could immediately respond with a solid reason why she should go through with the marriage. This situation was rapidly escalating into a crisis and clearly taking its toll on her ailing stepfather. Godfrey requested that Matilda give him a few days to consider a solution, and to have serious words with his son.

Matilda had one more issue to address. "Why do the servants look at me as if I have two heads? Is it my coloring that terrifies them so?"

Godfrey explained to Matilda that it was understood that only women of the bloodline had her physical characteristics, therefore all women with such coloring were heretics. In previous generations, the accusation of heresy escalated into that of witchcraft, a crime that carried a mandatory death sentence.

"When I was a young boy, a number of women who were guilty of no crime other than their red hair were tortured, mutilated, and burned in the town square after suffering the humiliation of 'parading,' a spectacle that has since been thankfully outlawed in civilized Lorraine."

Matilda wasn't sure she wanted to know but asked anyway. "Parading?"

Godfrey elaborated. "A red-haired woman was shackled at the

wrists, feet, and neck and made to walk naked as the villagers pelted her with stones and rotten vegetables. She was exposed for all to see that the mark of her coloring was present in the most private and shameful places of her body. This was deemed proof of witchcraft, as it was decreed that the only cause of such an unnatural physical characteristic was . . . oral congress with the devil himself."

Matilda shuddered at the ignorance. What had once been a genetic disposition that indicated a woman was descended from the exalted lineage of Jesus and Magdalena had become a dangerous curse. It evolved from the sacred mark of a healer and prophetess to the condemning mark of a witch.

"Sadly, the peasant classes are still highly superstitious, and therefore the servants are extremely curious and more than a little afraid of you. I should have warned you, perhaps, but I have been long away and had hoped to see more progress here in my own home."

Godfrey sighed but then took control by rapidly changing the subject. "I will speak to my son and make everything right."

He then encouraged Matilda to explore the verdant lands in Lorraine before the winter hit and it became too cold to ride, knowing that getting her out and on a horse would improve her mood. And while it wasn't Tuscany, she might discover that there was much beauty to love in his part of the world.

Matilda left her parents and sought out Patricio. She told him to be ready in the morning, as they were going riding, off on an adventure to find her Valley of Gold. That is what she came here for, after all, wasn't it?

❁

Matilda was happiest on horseback. She rode through a lush forest, her hair blowing behind her without the restraint of the horrid wimple that she had torn off without ceremony as soon as she was out of sight of Verdun. In spite of herself, she had to acknowledge the beauty of the place. It was cold, to be sure, and it certainly wasn't Tuscany, but it had its own natural magic. Patricio was by her side, racing with her, taunting her, and losing. Matilda was impossible to beat on a horse. She was fearless to the point of recklessness, but she was also highly skilled. The one thing she could say in favor of the hunchback was that he had fine taste in horseflesh. Their mounts were beautiful and spirited, with tremendous endurance. They had ridden hard, determined to cover as much of the forest as possible in search of the Vale of Gold, the place Matilda had seen in her vision. So far, there was an abundance of verdant landscape, but she had not yet found the water source.

By the afternoon, Matilda started to feel shivery. It was a strange sensation, nearly indescribable, so she slowed her mount and allowed herself the experience. It was as if she was positioned at the crossroads of time: she had a surreal sense of past, present, and future coming together all at once. It made her a little dizzy, yet it was also exhilarating.

When the feeling waned, she pushed her horse forward again. Patricio followed, and as they rounded a bend in the forest, a small pond came into view.

It was there, just as she had seen it in the vision. A pond that was fed by a stream so that they might water the horses. They dismounted and Patricio offered to lead the horses to the stream, agreeing that Matilda needed to walk on her own toward the clearing up ahead. So far, it was all as she had seen in the vision. A single white swan glided past, looking back over its shoulder as if to say, *Follow me.* And then Matilda heard it: the sound of the young girl's voice in the distance. She heard her giggle as she came closer to the clearing.

There were the beams of afternoon sun glittering through the trees and catching the surface of water just ahead. Matilda moved toward it, already knowing it was a well. Leaning over to gaze into the water, Matilda was convinced of the fathomless depths, that this well was indeed sacred and ran deep into the earth. There was a kind of magic here in this place. The forest itself was ancient, primeval, a place of deep and natural power. It would be a fine location to build their monument to love and wisdom.

Dipping her hands gently into the dark and frigid water, Matilda did not feel her cherished gold ring, the seal of Maria Magdalena, loosen at first. It slid off her finger so quickly that all she could do was watch in horror as her treasure drifted into the depths of the well.

Matilda screamed.

Kneeling down at the stone edge of the well, Matilda searched the water to see if she could catch a glimpse of the ring, but it was hopeless. Rising slowly to her feet in resignation, she caught a sudden glimmer of something flashing in the water. Splash! An enormous fish, a type of trout glittering with golden scales, leaped from the water in the well, then back into the depths. She waited to see if the remarkable fish would return. Another splash split the water, and the trout leaped in the air again, this time seeming to move in slow motion. Protruding from the fish's mouth was her precious ring.

Matilda gasped as the fish released the ring and sent it sailing toward her. As she held out her hand, the ring dropped safely in her open palm. She closed her hand tightly around it and clutched it to her heart, grateful that it had been retrieved by the magical fish, which subsequently retreated into the depths of the well. The water went still once again; the magic was gone.

Returning the ring to her right hand, Matilda carefully peered into the well one final time to see if there were any more miracles to be had in this extraordinary place. The water was quite still, and then the tiniest ripple broke the surface. A wave of golden light began to suffuse the well and the area surrounding it. The sunlight appeared to flow as if liquid gold poured from the sky, gilding everything in Matilda's vision. Soon the valley was flowing with rivers of gold, and the trees were covered with it. Everything glittered all around her with the rich warm light of liquid ore.

In the distance she heard the girlish voice, the one that she knew belonged to their little prophetess, Sarah-Tamar.

"Welcome to the Vale of Gold."

Matilda heard a gasp behind her. She turned to see Patricio approaching, rapt with the same vision of a magical golden valley. It lasted as long as a vision lasts. Seconds? Minutes? It was impossible to know. But the golden light faded ultimately, as it must, and the two of them were left standing in the great green forest once again.

There was comfort in sharing such a vision with a trusted friend. Patricio was now as much a part of the prophecy as Matilda was. They shared a fraternal embrace, the warm and innocent exchange that occurs between two people who love each other in the most simple way. Truly, they could have been brother and sister in blood. Together they vowed to build the greatest abbey in Europe in this place: a shrine, a library, and a school, all dedicated to the Way of Love. They would install it with the richest treasure in all humanity.

And they would call it Orval. For this truly would become a Valley of Gold.

✳

Matilda returned to Verdun in the evening, exhilarated. She even remembered to restore the hated wimple to her head, covering her hair, which was more scandalous than usual after a day of hard riding. An urgent summons from her mother and stepfather awaited her; she was to come to their chambers upon her return. Her heart dropped. She prayed that Godfrey's health had not taken a bad turn while she was out. After cleansing the smell of horses from her and changing into more appropriate attire, she hurried down the long hall to her stepfather's quarters.

"Come in, my dear. Come in."

She breathed an immediate sigh of relief. While Godfrey was drawn and pale, he was sitting at his desk and looked better than she had seen him in weeks. Perhaps the last two days of negotiating with his son had brought some of his old politician's spirit back.

Beatrice spoke next. "Your stepfather has been working hard to come to an agreement that would benefit everyone involved. It will save Tuscany for you and save face for Godfrey the Younger. It will also protect you from the more outlandish and unlawful outcomes that Godfrey has threatened you with."

The elder Godfrey continued. "My son has agreed to sign a document that indicates he has rights in Tuscany only as long as he is married to you. If he chooses to put you aside for any reason, he loses all those rights. Further, you have the right to leave him and return to Tuscany if he is ever physically cruel to you in any manner, and for specific legal reasons which will be carefully laid out in the document. You also retain the right to visit Tuscany annually and to carry out the administration of your lands while you do so."

Matilda was stunned. Such an agreement was unheard of, but Godfrey knew the law well and had no doubt researched the legalities of it. It was certainly a better option than going to war against both Henry and the hunchback in order to preserve her inheritance.

"Would this be acceptable to you, daughter?"

Nodding slowly, Matilda considered the position she was in strategically. It was quite a strong one. She decided to push it one step further.

"Today I had a vision while in the forest. I wish to build a great abbey here and dedicate it to the glory of Our Lady, the mother of God, with Patricio as its abbot. I would ask that the younger Godfrey provide the resources to build such a monument as his wedding gift to me."

While neither Godfrey senior nor Beatrice was fooled in terms of whom the abbey would be truly devoted to and what its ultimate purpose was to be, neither saw fit to argue the point. If building an abbey in the forest for the Order would help to resign Matilda to her fate of marrying a hunchback and staying in Lorraine, so be it. Perhaps becoming the patroness of a great abbey would also aid in Matilda's reputation locally. There were already slanderous whisperings about her, but surely a duchess who was so devoted to the Lord and his holy mother that she spent all her waking hours building a monument to them could not be a witch.

Her stepfather smiled at her, with some of his old vitality. "I'm sure my son will be more than willing to provide the funding for such a worthy project, and equally overjoyed that his wife is such a pious woman and a fine Catholic."

Curtsying deeply, Matilda thanked her parents for their generosity and left their chambers. It wasn't a perfect scenario by any means, but she could learn to live with it. And most of all, she was in a position to begin immediate construction of the community she would christen the Abbey of Our Lady of Orval. She would fulfill her obligation as The Expected One, just as she had kept her promise to the Holy Face. Nothing was more important than that.

"Thy will be done," Matilda whispered as she walked back through the cold corridors of Verdun, eyes raised to the sky. She was in search of Patricio, to tell him the good news of his official new commission to become the abbot of Orval.

Patricio supervised the initial design and construction of the abbey, with the help of the elder Godfrey's Benedictine advisers. Matilda, of course, was consulted on all major matters. Messengers were sent to the Order in Lucca to advise Isobel and the Master that they had successfully found the Valley of Gold, and that the monks from Calabria who would begin the task of transcribing the Libro Rosso and other histories should be prepared to come north by the summer of 1070.

Matilda kept a carved ivory casket in her chambers; it had been a gift from her father on her sixth birthday. It was her prized possession, as it was inlaid with the crest of the Lucchesi side of the family, Siegfried's crest, in semiprecious stones. Within the casket she kept another of her cherished personal items. It was the scroll tied with a red satin ribbon that contained the drawing of the six-petaled rose as made by the Master. Removing the scroll from the box, Matilda carried it to the meeting hall where Patricio was conversing with the architects.

"I wish to create a window with this pattern," she announced, unrolling the scroll to display the symbol. "I want the light of day to shine through the petals of the rose and illuminate the floor beyond it. On the floor there shall be a labyrinth. Patricio has the design for it."

Solomon's drawing of the labyrinth and the specifications for building its eleven circuitous pathways toward the center were contained within the Libro Rosso. It would be a great challenge for the masons, as she wanted a labyrinth both within the walls as well as in the garden. But Matilda wasn't finished giving them difficult tasks.

"I have had a dream about how the nave shall look. It shall be the most exalted building in Lorraine, truly worthy of the treasure it will contain. While I am not so skilled as an artist, I have seen it in my vision and I shall try to draw it for you."

Matilda took the pen from the chief architect and began to illustrate as Patricio smirked at her false modesty. Matilda was brilliant at architectural drawing and had usually completed her lessons on Solomon's Temple faster and with greater attention to detail than he had.

She explained to the architect, "I would have these great pointed arches, as high as we can build them, supported by columns made of golden marble. There will be a long nave, with many columns and many arches. This will be a monument to the glory of God and of what can be created in the name of love. It must be accordingly grand."

The architect nodded at the future duchess of Lorraine with more than a little awe. This woman was astonishingly skilled in her drawing, and her understanding of architectural principles was thorough. What she was proposing was an enormous challenge but one she had obviously thought through. By the time Matilda had finished, the architect was convinced that he understood her vision, her very expensive vision: that of building the grandest abbey in Northern Europe.

✦

She had prolonged the inevitable as long as she could. The elder Godfrey was failing, and it would be necessary for Matilda to take her vows with the abhorrent hunchback in three days' time. She found Patricio in the chapel.

"Patricio, help me. I know that I must do this, but I am terrified to let him touch me. What shall I do?"

Patricio had had the same education as Matilda and was well aware of the sanctity of the bridal chamber. He was equally aware that Matilda would not find the sacred union of their scriptures in this marriage to an odious man whom she despised. But he had little enough experience with such matters in terms of practicalities. While Matilda often teased him that she was searching the blond German beauties in her household to find him a suitable abbess to partner with, Patricio had yet to encounter this opportunity. He was at something of a loss, so he asked, "What advice did Isobel give you?"

Matilda took a breath and tried to recall her last conversation with Issy. "She told me not to kiss him."

Patricio nodded. This was understandable advice. The Book of Love and the Song of Songs spoke of the kiss as purely sacred. It was through the kiss that the souls were blended, that two spirits merged together in the shared breath. This, as much as—or perhaps more than—the ultimate intimacy of intercourse, was considered integral to divine union.

Isobel had said, "It is his right as your husband to beget children, Tilda. You will have to submit your body to him, to surrender from the hips down whenever he desires it. But you do not have to submit your soul. Everything from the heart up belongs to you. Allow him his legal duties as a husband, but reserve your own rights. Do not allow him to kiss you if you find him abhorrent. That is not a treasure you have to yield to anyone other than your most beloved."

Issy had then given Matilda cause to blush by instructing her in a select set of shocking distractions that would make a man forget all about kissing. Quickly. She had listened closely, somewhat appalled, but taken mental notes. Now, as the ominous event approached, she was glad she had paid such close attention.

Matilda was nothing if not a great student. When the vows were said in the chapel of Verdun three nights later, she was shaking, both with the cold and with fear of the wedding night. But she had determined to approach the marriage bed with strategy, as just another battlefield where she would have to fight to protect what was rightfully hers. In this case, she was protecting her soul.

When the hunchback approached her in the bridal chamber, she scandalized him by playing the wanton with utter conviction. She greeted him in the full glory of her absolute nakedness, a vision of wild, copper-crimson tresses, contrasted against flawless alabaster skin. That the legendary, wicked red hair did not stop at her head and softly covered her most female region was both tantalizing and shocking, and surely too much for any Christian man to bear. He was certain that this unnatural creature was every bit the witch she was believed to be. Here was the serpent Lilith, the demon temptress, the consort of the devil. But at that moment, he was willing to risk his immortal soul even if this were the case. The devil had won.

Godfrey was mesmerized by his new wife, while at the same time horrified by her. For her part, she lost no time in taking advantage of his stunned state. Utilizing the harlot's tricks that Isobel had taught her, Matilda ensured at once that her husband would have no interest in kissing her. Not surprisingly, it was over quickly. Godfrey the Hunchback rolled over almost immediately and began to snore, leaving Matilda's body a little worse for the wear but her soul intact.

The following day, when asked about the wedding night by a retinue of his men, the hunchback grunted, "It is all true, what they say about redheaded women."

The lascivious laughter that followed the comment was clear indication that everyone in Lorraine knew only too well what red hair wrought behind the closed doors of the bedchamber.

❄

The elder Godfrey, the duke of Lorraine, fell into a deep coma the following day. He died three days later on Christmas Eve of 1069. Matilda mourned him with the honor and sincerity she would have given to her natural father, which was more than she could say for her husband. Godfrey the Younger had been perched like a vulture, waiting for his father to die that he might inherit the totality of his properties in combination with Matilda's own.

The good that came out of the hunchback's greed was that he was now too busy to bother with her overmuch. Matilda did what she wanted, which was to spend time with Patricio in the supervision of Orval. Building would not begin in earnest until the springtime, but they had plenty to do in preparation. The Ark of the New Covenant that contained the Libro Rosso was kept in a private chapel that only Matilda and Patricio could access; this had been part of her prenuptial demands until Orval could be built and it could be transferred properly for copying. Of course, she had lied to the hunchback about what the ark contained, but he wasn't nearly observant enough to notice. Patricio spent most of his time in the private chapel now, painstakingly attempting to re-create the sketch of Solomon's Labyrinth that was contained within the Book of Love. They would need a blueprint of it to present to the master mason.

Matilda also visited with her mother for several hours a day. She was widowed now for the second time, and on both occasions she had lost men she truly loved. Beatrice carried her grief with the same grace and dignity with which she had lived the rest of her life, but Matilda could see that it was taking a toll. A thick streak of silver shone through her once pristine black hair, and her legendary beauty was beginning to fade with age and strain.

"When the snow thaws, I am returning to Mantua," Beatrice announced unexpectedly one evening at dinner.

Matilda was taken aback. Because Beatrice was from Lorraine, she had believed that her mother was happy to be here in her ancestral home.

Beatrice elaborated. "Tuscany became my home over our years there, Matilda. It is far more my home than Lorraine will ever be. But beyond that, I do not trust your husband as I trusted mine. He will be tied up with the affairs here in Lorraine, and I would return to our lands to see to their proper administration. It is for your protection as well as mine."

"I wish I could go with you," Matilda sighed.

Beatrice reached a hand out to pat her daughter's arm. "One day, my dear, one day. Do not despair. You are young and you will see Tuscany again."

And very unexpectedly, Matilda did something she rarely allowed herself the time to do. She cried. Putting her head in her hands, she wept: for her lost homeland, her dead fathers, her friends who were too far away, her repellent marriage, her spiritual responsibilities, and now for her departing mother. Beatrice, for her part, allowed Matilda to cry until she had exhausted herself, all the while stroking her hair in a rare display of maternal affection.

Pray in the manner in which I have instructed you, using the rose as the model for the Holy Spirit.

And working from the left to the right always, embrace the first petal of the holy rose, which is to say the petal of FAITH, and pray,

> *To Our Father Who is Benevolent and Reigns in Heaven,*
> *Your names are hallowed and sacred.*

Contemplate here your faith in the Lord your God and the grace of the Holy Spirit, while giving gratitude for the presence of both in your life and on earth.

Embrace the second petal, which is to say the petal of SURRENDER, and pray,

> *Your kingdom comes to us through obedience to your will.*
> *Thy will be done.*

Listen to the voice of your Father that you may hear his will and carry it out without fear or fail. Stay in this petal for as long as it takes you to submerge yourself and find the blessed release of surrender to his will rather than your own.

Embrace the third petal, which is to say the petal of SERVICE, and pray,

> *On earth as it is in heaven.*

Here you will reaffirm your promise, to God and to yourself, if you are fully anthropos and have remembered it. If you have not yet reached the state of realization, you will confirm your commitment to create heaven on earth by acting in accordance with the Way of Love, by loving the Lord thy God above all else, and by loving your brothers and sisters on earth as yourself, for they are a part of yourself. You will pray then for enlightenment, that through gnosis you will remember the nature of your own eternal promise.

Embrace now the fourth petal, which is to say the petal of ABUNDANCE, and pray,

Give us this day our daily bread, the manna.

Give thanks to the Lord for all he has provided you and know that when you live in harmony with his will, and honor your promise to his service, you will know the bounty of abundance and never have a day of want. There is nothing that you need or desire that will not be provided you when you live in the flow of God's grace, and when you have aligned yourself with God's will.

Embrace the fifth petal, which is to say the petal of FORGIVENESS, and pray,

And forgive us for our errors and debts
As we forgive ourselves and all others.

Here you must list those who have harmed you, who have given ill witness against you, or who have otherwise caused you pain. And you must forgive them, while praying that they will one day be fully anthropos and realize their own connection to God and remember their own promise. You must ask that anyone you have offended forgive you in the same way, and most of all you must forgive yourself for all the actions and thoughts that have brought shame upon you in your human weaknesses. For while all forgiveness is the balm of our compassionate Mother, self-forgiveness is needed most of all.

Embrace the sixth petal, which is to say the petal of STRENGTH, and pray,

Keep me on the path of righteousness and
Deliver me from the temptations of evil.

For temptation is that which keeps us from becoming fully realized beings. It prevents us from keeping our promise to God and to ourselves and to each other and is found through the temptations of avarice, hubris, sloth, lust, wrath, gluttony, and envy most of all. Contemplate these sins and pray for your release from any that tempt you from the path of the anthropos.

Pray in this manner that I have given you, and teach your brothers and sisters in spirit to do the same. It is through living this prayer that men and women will create heaven on earth. It is through this prayer that they will live as love expressed.

Love Conquers All.

For those with ears to hear, let them hear it.

THE PRAYER OF THE SIX-PETALED ROSE,
FROM THE BOOK OF LOVE,
AS PRESERVED IN THE LIBRO ROSSO

Palace of Verdun
spring 1071

MATILDA WAS PREGNANT.

She was certain of it. There had been two full cycles of the moon since she had last bled, and the way her stomach roiled in the morning made it impossible to eat even the plainest breads.

Here was a conundrum for her. If she admitted her pregnancy immediately, she could insist that the hunchback not touch her for fear of hurting the baby. This would be a most welcome reprieve from his grunting and rutting, which she detested like poison. Perhaps she could even insist on private quarters for the duration of her confinement. Unfortunately, her husband had been most highly aroused by her wanton performance on their wedding night, which she had not anticipated. His desire for her had become an instant obsession, an unholy addiction to his exotic wife and her unnatural body. He now came looking for it on an all too regular basis, desperate and demanding.

The bedroom performances made Matilda ill, but she had still somehow managed to prevent the hunchback from kissing her. That he showed little interest in doing so, preoccupied as he was with the other pleasures of her femininity, was the only thing that kept her sanity intact after the sun went down.

On the other hand, if she told him she was with child, he would insist that she stop riding. This would mean that she could not continue to oversee the building of Orval, which was the one true joy of her life. To be deprived of it was more than she could take. She had placed the first foundation stone herself on the vernal equinox of 1070, almost exactly a year ago, and had been involved in every single decision that was made in the building. Further, the word had come from the Order that Patricio's brother monks from Calabria who would copy the Libro Rosso were on their way north to her. While she could house them in the palace initially, as the work began in earnest on the translations, she would need to get them out of Verdun and away from the interrogations that were part of Godfrey's everyday behavior. She did not want to lose her freedom to attend the building any sooner than was necessary.

As it happened, Matilda's hand was forced on a night shortly after she ascertained her condition. The hunchback was out late, as he often was, given that their lands stretched over a broad expanse beyond Stenay. Normally, when he rode to the edge of their territory, he did not return to Verdun until the next day, much to her relief. Matilda had gone to bed on this particular night, exhausted from the daily running of the household, the building of the grandest abbey in Europe, and the new life growing in her body. Because the hour was so late, she was certain that her husband would be staying elsewhere this night.

She was wrong.

Matilda heard him before she saw him. And smelled him before he entered the chamber.

"Where is my woman?" He stumbled into their bedroom, reeking of ale and something worse that Matilda could not quite identify until he got closer. Vomit. He was filthy and disgusting, as if he had been rolling about in one of the seedier alehouses for many hours. The hunchback periodically indulged his wretched unhappiness in such ways. For all his physical defects, he was a man and a healthy one, and prior to his marriage he had sought release regularly in the brothels and alehouses. Since wedding the red witch, he found that he needed to escape into the safe familiarity of straw-haired Germanic girls now more than ever, in hope of breaking the spell his wicked wife had cast over him. Compounding his torment was the fact that she hated him, that he disgusted her, and that he knew it.

Previously when Godfrey had sought relief in too much ale and time at the brothels, he had passed out long before he could reach his wife. Tonight she would not be so lucky. The bland milkmaids at the alehouse had simply been no match for Matilda in his fevered brain. Even with two of the more buxom girls in the back room at one time, he had not been able to blot out the vision of the firebrand who awaited him in his own bed. By the time he returned to the palace, he was a man possessed by both his lust and his inner demons.

"Come to your man and husband, you wanton bitch," he slurred as he moved toward her, pulling roughly at his breeches.

Matilda was half asleep when he came into the room and was now trying to gather her bearings to deal with his unexpected arrival. Her normally quick reflexes were dulled by both sleeplessness and her condition. The unexpected speed with which he climbed upon her barely gave her time to turn her head as he attempted to bring his stinking mouth down upon the softness of her full lips. He caught only her cheek with a grunt, and his teeth left an imprint on her face as he did so. She desperately tried to distract him with her skilled hands, but tonight this normally effective strategy was not going to work.

Godfrey slapped her hard with the back of his hand. "Turn your head to me, woman."

He didn't wait for her to comply. Instead, he grabbed fistfuls of her hair in both hands and forced her lips against his. She struggled to keep her teeth together, but the hunchback overpowered her painfully and forced his slithery, probing tongue into her mouth. Desperate to get out from under him, Matilda used a battle technique that she had been taught by Conn, pushing her knee deep into his chest and rolling over in one quick, painful motion.

The hunchback fell to the floor with a thud and a grunt. He was momentarily still as he waited for his breath to come back. Then he began to rise slowly, menacingly. His hands were clenched in fists as he approached her.

"I will have my rights as a husband from you, when I want and how I want. Your precious legal document does not excuse you from that."

Matilda blurted out as quickly as she could, before he took another sloppy step, "Godfrey, stop. I am with child."

He blinked at her, as if he had not heard her clearly, which was likely in his severely intoxicated state. He slurred at her.

"What you say?"

"I said, I am carrying your child. And the midwife says that given my fine bones, if you touch me, I will be at great risk to lose the baby."

She lied, of course, but he was too ignorant to know such things, even when he was sober.

He took another deliberate step in her direction, reaching out with surprising agility to grab a handful of her hair and using it to yank her toward him. "Why should I believe a lying witch like you?" His lust and his drunkenness were a dangerous and unreasonable combination. And the hunchback was a big man. She had to make him understand. Fast.

"Because you have waited all these years for an heir, and if you touch me, you risk any chance you will ever have of gaining one."

He loosened his grip but did not release her. Matilda was exasperated now. She snapped the next sentence with more than a little of her warrior attitude returning.

"There are any number of serving wenches in this house who will be happy to relieve you for the price of a trinket. Must you endanger our child—the future duke of Lorraine—with your drunken lust?"

It worked. Intoxicated as he was, with ale and with her, Matilda was still able to reach some part of his brain that contained his ultimate ambition. The hunchback mumbled something about discussing this with her on the morrow, and he stumbled out of their bedroom without looking back.

Matilda felt pity, and more than a little guilt, for the poor servant girl who would be required to entertain her lord duke in his inflamed state this night. Later, she would find out from the other servants which of them had suffered the indignity and double the girl's pay. It was the least she could do.

But secretly, she was infinitely relieved that the hunchback's masculine pleasure would not be her duty for the next seven months, at the very least.

Matilda was a prisoner in the palace. Just as she feared, Godfrey had provided her with a list of what she was and was not allowed to do. Riding was at the top of the list of forbidden activities. She was under constant surveillance by one or another of the hunchback's employees: priests, doctors, midwives, all who interviewed her constantly and left her no peace whatsoever. Even the cook monitored every morsel she placed into her mouth and surreptitiously stationed servants in the room while she was dining to be sure she ate what was laid out for her.

Thankfully, her husband had avoided her like the plague itself since the night of his humiliation in their bedchamber. Matilda was certain that he didn't trust her and that he thought she would deliberately harm their child, which was the reason for the intense and omnipresent observation from his staff. It was horrible to know that all these people thought her capable of something as wicked as that. But it was equally hard to feel the quickening life in her body and know that it had not been conceived immaculately in the ways taught by the Order.

This poor babe, through no fault of its own, had not been created in a sacred environment. The Book of Love taught that all children born from the union of true beloveds are immaculately conceived in the eyes of God, but when a child is conceived outside of love, it does not have so great a blessing at its birth. This was taught not as a judgment upon the poor infants who have no choice, but as a warning to adults not to bear children outside the realm of love.

Dear God, why did you take me from Isobel and the Master at a time like this? Matilda needed spiritual guidance now, more than ever. She was starved for it, and she was miserable. Her only sanctuary was the private chapel, the sole place where she could escape and close the door to shut out all the hunchback's spies. She entered, touching first as she always did the little statue of Saint Modesta, which was now perched upon a gilded altar.

As a surprise for her equinox birthday, Patricio painted a six-petaled rose in the center of the floor. While she would not have a labyrinth in Lorraine until Orval was completed, he could create a sacred place for her to work through their most holy prayer. Perhaps this would provide her with the spiritual strength that she required to get through her current tribulations.

Matilda relished this place, and she entered the rose now to begin her prayer. She started in the first petal and made her gratitude known for all that she had been blessed with in her life before moving into the second petal.

Thy will be done, she whispered to herself over and over again. *Dear God, why do you want this from me? Why have I been removed from everyone I love and the only place I will ever call home? How can I better understand your will?*

Sometimes she heard his voice clearly, but this was most often in the labyrinth. At other times, she heard only the sound of the silence in her ears. Today she heard him with a force she had not anticipated.

"When the Vale of Gold is finished, you may return home, where you will find great love as reward for your obedience to your destiny and your promise."

There were puzzles in that answer, such as how, precisely, she would be allowed to return home, but she was comforted by what she heard. God's will was for her to build Orval, and that was what she was doing. The construction of it was proceeding at a rapid pace; a mild winter had allowed the builders to work well past the normal season. And the Calabrians were here, working in earnest to copy the Libro Rosso. It was all going perfectly to plan.

She completed her prayer in the six petals, spending ample time in the fifth, the petal of forgiveness. She prayed to find the strength to forgive Godfrey for his wretchedness by having compassion for his condition and the pain it had caused him. Matilda prayed to God to forgive her for despising her husband as she did, and for perhaps not behaving in a manner that was more loving toward him. When she was finished, she felt a sense of peace that had eluded her previously. And God rewarded her for her piety, because Patricio arrived unexpectedly from Orval the same afternoon.

He came to inform her of the quick progress on their beautiful abbey, and to share drawings of the structures as they had been raised to illustrate their beauty and majesty. She wished more than anything to see the great, six-petaled rose window, which had already been erected, its outline visible from the garden labyrinth just beginning construction. Patricio was very excited about the grandeur of the entire structure and tried to share that passion while at the same time not making her feel despair at her inability to ride out with him. He could see the wistful longing on her face.

"Oh Patricio, I wish I could be there with you."

"Time passes so quickly. You will be there before you know it. And by the time you are able to travel, we will be nearly finished with the first buildings and I will have a perfect labyrinth constructed for you in the garden."

"I look forward to it, more than you know."

❁

It was the early fall when Patricio came again to Verdun to see Matilda early one morning, full of the news that the labyrinth was finished. He was buoyant in his excitement as he had christened it himself with the very first walk in and out of the eleven circuits the evening prior. He wanted to share this success with her. Together, they had created a magnificent library and training ground for the teachings of the Way of Love, and it was something to be celebrated.

The Matilda who greeted him was not herself and was in no frame of mind for a celebration. She was well into the seventh month of her confinement, and the child was showing on her small frame. They were walking in the direction of the stables now, Matilda gazing longingly at the horses. "What I wouldn't give to walk that labyrinth now. Within the labyrinth is the only place I have ever found real peace, you know." She stopped suddenly, looking around. They had not been followed, that she could see. Patricio knew her well enough to sense what was in her head; there was a reason the Master said they shared the same brain.

"No, Matilda. Don't even think about it. It's too dangerous."

"Godfrey is gone for the next three days. If we leave now, we can be back here before it is too dark. I won't stay long, Patricio. Just long enough to view the new construction and walk my labyrinth just one time."

"Have you gone mad? You are in no condition to ride. And you cannot ride in what you are wearing, even if you were."

"Listen to me. Have you ever known anyone more comfortable on a horse than I am? It is no different than sitting in a chair. I will take one of the older and more stable mounts. It will cost me an extra hour in each direction, but if we leave immediately, it could work. And there are riding garments in the tack room. Men's garments, but all the better to disguise myself and my condition."

"Do not ask me to do this with you, Tilda. Please."

"Whom else can I ask, my brother?"

Her aquamarine eyes filled with tears as she pleaded with him. "Please. I have had no joy in my life these past six months. To see what we have created in Orval, to celebrate it as you have said, is something that will give me life again. It will see me through the rest of my confinement."

"God forgive me if anything happens to you or that child," Patricio grumbled, shaking his head. "Come quickly then, before we're seen."

✳

Once they were in the forest, Matilda forgot she was with child. She urged the horse into a canter and began to ride at her customary break-neck pace.

"Matilda, slow down!" Patricio was sweating, despite the early autumn chill in the air. He had had a sense of foreboding about this adventure from the moment he saw her face back at the stables. While he knew she would never intentionally hurt herself or the baby, she was behaving in a most reckless way.

Matilda pulled up on the reins and slowed the horse. "I'm sorry. It just feels so good to be out again." She breathed in the scented air of the great pines that surrounded them in the Ardennes. They were close now, and she was tingling with anticipation. As they passed the pond where the lone swan glided, Matilda gasped in awe.

Ahead of her were the pointed arches of the nave, golden marble columns gleaming in the sunlight. The sight was positively magnificent. "Oh Patricio, look what we've done."

She dismounted carefully with her friend's help and walked toward the magnificent building. It was all she had dreamed it would be, a remarkable monument to the Way of Love.

"Come, you must see this." Patricio was excited now that they had arrived safely, with Matilda looking no worse for the ride. In fact, she looked more alive than he had seen her since her confinement. He helped her step across the threshold and into the great chamber that held the six-petaled rose window.

Matilda stood before it and cried. When she finally spoke, it was in a whisper. "It's perfect. Just the way I dreamed it would look."

He took her to the scriptorium, where the three monks from Calabria, two elders and an apprentice, were at work on the Libro Rosso translations. Matilda hadn't seen them since the earliest days of their arrival in Lorraine and was happy for the reunion. While the brothers were clearly surprised to see her, they were warm in their greeting and invited her to rest while they provided a lunch of bread, watered ale, and cheese, all of which they made on the abbey premises. Orval was already on its way to becoming a thriving and self-supporting community. Matilda could not have been happier with the progress.

After her lunch and an update from the Calabrians on the state of the translations, which were much further along than she would have guessed, Matilda was anxious to see the pièce de résistance.

"Take me to our labyrinth," she commanded of Patricio, who humbly complied.

It was magnificent. Patricio had worked with master stonemasons for over a year to fashion hundreds of matched paving stones, which had been carefully laid into the ground one by one to create the outlines of the eleven circuits. At the center was a perfect rose, outlined in a lighter-colored rock for contrast. It was a masterpiece of stonework.

"Look here." Patricio led her toward the entrance, which faced perfectly to the west. He walked approximately ten paces away from the entrance before kneeling to show her where the iron ring had been embedded in the earth. "For Notre Dame, our Lady of the Labyrinth."

Matilda beamed at him as she pulled several strands from her plaited hair and tied them to the ring in the bridal knot. She kissed Patricio on the cheek and thanked him, before making the long-awaited walk into her very own labyrinth, where God awaited her at the center.

✸

Matilda's time in the labyrinth was beautiful, if puzzling. She saw a vision of herself in Tuscany with Conn and Bishop Anselmo and Isobel—and someone else, another man, strong and striking, whom she did not recognize. She thought it odd that she looked no older than she did today. Surely if Tuscany was in her future, it was in a more distant future. Godfrey would never allow her to travel once the child arrived. Flash to another vision of Lucca, and it was Christmastide. She was standing outside the Cathedral of San Martino. Her cathedral of the Holy Face. And she was happy in both visions, almost unbearably happy. Could such happiness be possible? What time in the future was she glimpsing? Perhaps this was just the dream of her soul that she was seeing, rather than a glimpse of a reality that awaited her. She was disconcerted that she saw no vision of her child, and yet she could feel the baby stirring in her womb. Perhaps God did not want her to see the child prior to its birth.

Patricio, waiting for Matilda outside the labyrinth, was becoming concerned. She had been in there a long time, and if she did not come out soon, there would be no way they could get back to Verdun before dark. He closed his eyes and willed her to come out, praying all the while that she would do so at once. But he waited a long time before she finally emerged, breathless with the visions.

"Tilda, there's no time. We have to get to the horses now. You can tell me on the way."

She nodded, looking at the sky and realizing with trepidation that it was far later than she had anticipated. Patricio helped her onto her horse and followed immediately behind her as they rode toward Verdun.

It was well into the autumn, and the days were getting shorter. Matilda had to make a choice: to ride faster and make the most of the daylight, or stay at a slow and steady pace but risk the darkness. She chose the former and kicked her horse into a canter.

"God help us both," Patricio muttered, as he tried to keep up with her.

Whether it was written in her destiny or the actions of her free will had caused it, Matilda would never know. But the diminishing light and the enforced speed upon the older horse were a deadly combination. The mount lost his footing and stumbled, midstride, in a full canter. A more balanced Matilda might have taken the fall with an athletic roll and endured a few bruises at worst. But her ungainly body at late pregnancy and her disrupted equilibrium were no match for the circumstances she found herself in. Matilda was thrown completely from the horse, landing hard on her side.

Patricio roared with fear and anguish as he watched it happen, following behind her. He jumped from his own mount and ran to Matilda, relieved that she was breathing, if not conscious. He checked her for blood but didn't see any immediate signs of external injuries that would be life-threatening. Removing the heavy woolen blanket from his horse, he covered his best friend with it and said the most fervent prayer of his life over her. Leaping bareback on his mount, he rode to the palace of Verdun for help, rode as if the devil himself were chasing him.

The pain that shot through her abdomen was like ten heated swords plunged into her from all sides. She was regaining consciousness, but if this was how it felt, she much preferred the delirium. Another searing pain, and then the warm gush of fluids covered her thighs. Her eyes were opened now and she could see that she was in her bedchamber, with two of Godfrey's spies on either side of her. Midwives. The younger one wasn't so bad. Her name was Greta, and she was the only member of Godfrey's staff who had ever made any real effort to be friendly with the new duchess. She wiped Matilda's face with a cool cloth now and cooed to her in German that it was all right, that she was home.

The elder woman was hardly as kind. She was giving orders sharply to others in the room and prodding at Matilda's womb all the while.

"Push," she commanded in clipped tones. "This baby must come now if there is any hope of saving it." Matilda could only imagine what the rest of the sentence contained, muttered inaudibly under the midwife's breath in angry German. No doubt it was a curse for the duchess of Lorraine's wickedness in endangering the duke's child.

Matilda pushed. She had no choice. The pressure on her abdomen was beyond bearing, and with a strange popping sound and another searing pain, she felt the child move through the birth canal and into the hands of the waiting midwife.

It was too early, and they all knew it. There could be no happy outcome in this birthing chamber. Matilda was in shock and exhausted with pain and fear, but she was aware enough to care. She waited in the silence that followed as the elder midwife wiped the blood from the baby.

"A girl." There was no emotion in the announcement. And then suddenly, unexpectedly, there was the slightest cooing sound in the chamber. Matilda sucked in her breath. Could it be? Did her child live? She tried to sit up, but the younger midwife held her back gently.

The elder, for all her coarseness with Matilda, was surprisingly delicate and tender with the newborn, massaging it gently and whispering to it all the while. She snapped at the younger woman, "Fetch the priest."

Placing the baby on a fresh blanket of virgin wool, the old woman brought Matilda's tiny daughter and placed her next to her mother in the bed.

"She lives," the woman said, the emotion gone again from her words and demeanor, "but not for long. She is too small, and breathing too hard. She will die before the night is through. Before her father ever gets to see her alive." This was a pointed condemnation. "You must give her a name so that the priest may baptize her and her soul does not get lost. A Christian name." The emphasis on *Christian* was clear. The midwife would not have this witch condemning the duke's child any further than she already had.

It took all her strength, but Matilda raised herself and lifted the tiny bundle into her arms. The baby was so small that she didn't look real. She was perfect, even in miniature. There was no sign of her father's congenital deformity. In fact, the one trait that Matilda recognized was her lovely mother's cleft chin. And while there was just the slightest amount of hair on the baby's head, she could see that it was a deep reddish color.

For an eternal moment, the child locked eyes with her, and Matilda was sure that the baby was really seeing her. It was brief, but there was an instant of intelligence and recognition, a glimpse of the soul of this child who had come here for such a brief period. In that one wrenching moment they were connected, mother and daughter, and Matilda was certain that her heart would break. She had caused this tragedy, brought it on her precious, innocent child. May God forgive her.

The priest arrived quickly, Godfrey's dour confessor who disapproved of Matilda at the best of times. He sprinkled holy water on the child with great haste, as if certain she would be dead within the next minute.

"Have you given her a Christian name?"

Matilda ran her finger over the baby's dimpled chin. She nodded slightly.

"I have. I would call her Beatrice Magdalena."

The priest looked disapproving but said nothing. He baptized the infant and gave her last rites in the same few breaths, a strange sacrament of life and death all at once. Then he left the room without a second look at Matilda.

Gathering her baby to her breast, Matilda rocked the infant against her body for the remainder of the little girl's short life. She knew no lullabies, so the baby took her last breaths listening to her mother weep, in between verses of the only song that had ever comforted her. The one in French, about love.

❁

Matilda was smothering. Something was over her face and she could not breathe. She struggled to get out from under it, but to no avail. Her assailant was stronger than she was, particularly in her current weakened condition. As she was on the verge of slipping into unconsciousness, she heard a man's voice raised in alarm. There was a struggle in the bedchamber and shouting in German. Then the cushion was removed from her face.

Gasping for air, Matilda tried to make sense of the room in her dizzy state and through her blurred vision. The hunchback stood over her with a cushion in his hands, the intended instrument of her demise. But he was not her assailant. Against all odds, it appeared that Godfrey was her rescuer. The murder attempt had come at the hands of the elder midwife, who was glaring at Matilda with hatred. The woman spat at her.

"Devil. Murdering witch. You killed that child just as surely as if you cut her throat."

"Enough!" Godfrey would have to deal with the midwife later. He could not allow murder in his own bedchamber, even if it was considered justifiable, and most of his household would agree that it was. As the older woman stormed out the door, Godfrey approached his wife's bed. Matilda attempted to speak, but the words would not come out.

The hunchback looked down at her, pitiless and full of hatred. "Do not thank me for saving you, woman. It was not for your damnable flesh that I did so. I will simply not endanger my own mortal soul for the sake of a female infant by permitting murder in my house.

"But you should know that if the child had been a boy . . . I would have allowed the midwife to kill you."

She had to get out of here, immediately. Matilda was certain that as long as she stayed in Verdun, her life was in danger. Everyone in the household was loyal to the hunchback, and they all believed her to be a murdering witch who had intentionally killed his child. She had found that the younger midwife, Greta, was something of an ally, as the girl came in to check that she was recovering and bring her some bread dipped in watered wine. Matilda coerced the girl into talking, through a combination of guilt and bribery.

Greta informed Matilda that the whisperings in the household were that it was just as well that the baby died, as it had the same unholy red hair as her mother. No doubt she would have been a witch and a curse on their good duke. The danger to the duchess was immediate, however. It had been mentioned, more than once, that if Matilda were to die in the next few days, it would be easy enough to say that it was from complications of childbirth. No one in the castle would argue the point, and Godfrey would inherit all her properties and be free to take a younger wife and start anew.

Matilda offered Greta a portion of her jewel chest if she would arrange a horse for her. As fate would have it, the girl's brother was one of the stable hands, and a ruby necklace fit for a queen was payment enough for him to prepare a horse for Matilda.

In the dead of night, Matilda left the palace through the rear servants' exit with only the clothes on her back and waited in the stable for the boy to come. Once the horse was prepared, she rode out into the night, praying that the moon was bright enough to light her way, and pacing herself so as not to repeat her fateful fall.

❂

"I need to stay here, Matilda. Everything we built is at risk. The hunchback will not hurt me. He wouldn't dare. I am a monk, and this is a house of God. Remember, he has no idea what you are really creating here, and neither does anyone else. To the rest of Lorraine, we are simply building the most beautiful monastery in Northern Europe. That is a feather in Godfrey's cap."

Matilda nodded, praying this was true. She wanted Patricio to stay here in Orval, to finish the work, to complete the construction on their grand vision, which was coming to life in such a magnificent way. She had long since transferred all the funds into the abbey's coffers, which Patricio controlled, so that Godfrey couldn't halt the flow of money or their progress. But she was concerned that her husband would attempt to harm Patricio in some other way, as retaliation for what he believed was compliance in her treachery.

"My greater concern is what happens now. You have to get out of Lorraine immediately, but you cannot ride across the Alps as a woman alone."

"No. But my mother has relations here, outside Stenay. A cousin. I will go to her and tell her what has happened. From there, I will send a messenger to Tuscany and ask that they send a guard to escort me home."

"Can you trust this relation of your mother's?"

"I have never met her, but she is a duchess in her own right and one who has had to defy Henry on more than one occasion. So we have much in common, I think. I hope. But the truth of the matter is, I have no other choice, do I?"

"No. Godspeed, sister. And contact me as soon as you can. From now on we will have to use the Sator Rotas code for our communication."

The Master had taught them a cryptic for encoded messages when they were children. The code had existed from the earliest days of Christianity in Rome, when certain violent death awaited anyone discovered to be a practicing Christian. It was through the cryptic that the earliest converts had been able to communicate in secret. For the young Matilda and Patricio, it had been like a great game, sending notes back and forth in the strange sequence of letters and numbers that occurred within the magic square. Now it would be employed once again in the serious business of preserving true Christianity and securing Matilda's safety.

"God takes care of his own."

The Master had said this to her on many occasions, and she had known it to be true throughout her life. When Matilda was in the direst need of divine assistance, it always arrived for her. On this occasion, the divine will manifested in the person of her mother's cousin, Giselda, who had been named for the queen who raised Beatrice when she was orphaned. It appeared that strength and grace followed this name within their family. An eccentric, educated woman, it happened that this Giselda was disgusted and outraged by both the licentious reputation and the acquisitive nature of Henry IV, who had encroached upon her own hereditary territories a few too many times. She was herself a direct descendant of Charlemagne who deserved better treatment than she was receiving at the hands of this decadent upstart, king or not.

Matilda's arrival on her doorstep was a godsend, and before long the two women had formed a conspirational bond. Matilda pledged support from Tuscany when and if it was needed to protect Giselda's territories, and the woman had, in turn, provided luxurious accommodation, competent doctors, and enjoyable company. She had also dispatched her most efficient messenger to Mantua.

It took weeks for the Tuscan retinue to arrive in Lorraine, giving Matilda much-needed time to heal. She tried, through prayer and spiritual practice, to work through the grief of her loss, the wrenching guilt, and the trauma of the hateful, nightmarish aftermath in Verdun. Giselda's sympathetic ear and the peace of safe solitude nourished Matilda's soul with new strength, while expert physicians helped her body to mend before she attempted crossing the Alps with winter approaching.

By the time the Tuscans were sighted, the sun shining off the ginger hair of the giant on horseback who had come to see her safely home, Matilda was ready for the journey.

A letter arrived from Patricio, carried by a messenger from a Benedictine monastery, the following day as Matilda and her Tuscan escort were preparing to depart for home. Written in the cryptic, it was a plea of desperation that required some deciphering. Matilda sat down and drew out the cryptic, determined to remember how precisely the letters were converted to numbers and then back again into letters to create a cohesive message:

My Dear Sister,
*   The hunchback has seized Orval and confiscated the Libro*
Rosso. While the completed copies are blessedly safe in the scripto-

rium, he has taken the original along with the Ark of the New Covenant. He does not know what they are, exactly, but he knows that they are valuable and important to you, and he would keep them to force your return. I am safe, as are the brothers. But I am in despair over our most holy scripture. I believe that they are in the palace at Verdun. Please advise me, your brother, on what my course of action should be. Know that I will carry out your will in this matter, as I know you are in harmony with what God wishes for our people. I pray for you regularly and wish only for your safety and happiness.
Yours in love,
Brother Patricio

Matilda was seething. She was also stunned. It had not occurred to her that Godfrey would want her back after what had transpired. She certainly hadn't anticipated his attempting to blackmail her in such a fashion. She requested parchment and ink from Giselda and began composing her replies, both to Patricio and to the hunchback. The advantage of having such an exemplary education and intellect was that Matilda never had to wait for a scribe. She wrote the majority of her own correspondence and took great pleasure in doing so, particularly when she was able to express herself as she was today.

The first letter provided the catharsis. She injected the words with her outrage.

To the duke Godfrey of Lorraine, from the countess Matilda of Canossa,
  In the name of the people of Tuscany and the noble family of Canossa, I demand the immediate return of our most sacred objects of worship that have been illegally confiscated by the House of Lorraine. Most specifically, the Libro Rosso, my most precious red book, must be returned immediately to the holy brothers of Orval for safekeeping in the haven which was built to house it.
  If the Libro Rosso is not returned in my name immediately,

the House of Tuscany will declare a just and holy war against the
House of Lorraine. I will lead the might of every warrior in north-
ern Italy to march upon Stenay and reclaim our holy objects by
force if necessary.

She signed the letter in the unabashed strokes of her boldest signature: Matilda, by the Grace of God Who Is, embedded in a cross and
followed by the glyphs of Pisces and Aries, which had become her sig-
natory emblems as the Christian daughter of the equinox prophecy.
She was no longer acting in a charade for the hunchback, or for anyone. She would stand in the full glory of her identity and take back
what was rightfully hers and under her protection. From that day forward, Matilda would use this radical statement of a signature to indicate that she was entitled to all she had by the grace of God, as his
chosen child. She required no further acknowledgment, neither from
husband nor from king, to claim and keep all that had been given her.

The second letter was to Patricio, advising him that Conn was going
to personally deliver the letter to Godfrey and negotiate terms on her
behalf. Failure was not an option in this mission, and she never allowed
the thought of it to enter her consciousness. She assured Patricio that
the ark and its most precious contents, the Libro Rosso, would be returned to his care immediately. She would then have it transferred to
her for its trip across the Alps, back home where it belonged, in Lucca.

⚜

Godfrey of Lorraine was highly intimidated by the Celtic giant who
threatened war under Matilda's signature, but to his credit, he refused
to show it. He demanded the return of his wife in exchange for the artifacts he had confiscated from Orval.

Conn laughed in his face, reminding the hunchback that his personally selected servant had attempted to assassinate a helpless Matilda
in her own bed after she had just suffered the greatest possible tragedy,
the loss of a child. He deliberately used the term *assassinate* rather

than *murder*, as the political connotations weakened Godfrey's legal position. The duke was trapped in a mire of his own making, and he knew it.

Conn delivered the remainder of the terms. Matilda wasn't entirely unreasonable in her demands, as at the moment she wanted to accomplish two primary goals above all: the return of the Order's most sacred possessions, and her secured and unmolested exit from Lorraine. Once she was safely back in Tuscany with her advisers, her mother chief among them, she would deal with her marital circumstances. She hoped that Godfrey would acquiesce quickly and quietly to what she was demanding now, as she was not proposing to divorce him—not yet, anyway, given that the prenuptial document gave her legal grounds to do so for cruelty. He would retain his titles in Tuscany, so long as he didn't interfere with the administration of her lands in any way that she found offensive. This included supporting Henry from any of her territories. She had even told Conn to insinuate to the hunchback that, given time to heal, she might be willing to consider returning to their marriage bed if he would show good faith at this trying time by returning her property.

Hell would freeze over and the Alps would crumble before she ever allowed Godfrey to touch her again, but she hoped he was too stupid to know that. His obsession was still her most valuable bargaining chip in the war with her husband, and it worked. Godfrey agreed to return her possessions, including some of her personal items that had been left behind. The most valued of these was the treasured ivory chest that had been a gift from Bonifacio and her statue of Modesta. In exchange, Godfrey would give Matilda six months to visit her lands and her mother, before demanding her return as his wife. Conn agreed to the terms, knowing full well that Matilda would find any number of strategies to avoid returning to her husband. He kept Matilda's irate demand letter in his own possession. Better not to leave anything as incriminating as the threat of war in the hands of the enemy, as such a thing could be used against her later. And there was the issue of that heretical signature. He would return it to Matilda.

Perhaps, he thought somewhat absently, the future might someday hold use for such a letter.

❄

Conn escorted the ark and its sacred contents back to Patricio for inspection, and he rested for a night at Orval. With the Calabrian scribes, Patricio verified that the copies were complete, including the drawings and diagrams, and that the original was intact and unharmed. After each man kissed the gilded and jeweled cover with reverence, the Libro Rosso was returned to the ark and placed in the protective keeping of Conn of the Hundred Battles, who swore a vow to protect it with an unexpected and extraordinary fervor.

The Celtic giant praised Patricio for the magnificent work as he toured the grounds of Orval. He had truly built a golden abbey, a place worthy of housing the most sacred scripture, the true word of the Lord and the prophecies of his holy daughter. The arches of the nave, as they had been sketched by Matilda's own hand, were of a height and majesty that he had never seen, soaring to heaven. The stonework throughout was meticulous and artistically brilliant. The entire structure was a masterpiece built by the power of love. Conn, most impressed by the enormous labyrinth that extended across the garden, asked for leave of privacy that he might walk it on his own.

After spending the day with Conn, Patricio was shocked and more than a little dumbfounded by Conn's intimate understanding of the contents of the Libro Rosso. To his knowledge, the big Celt had never been a member of the Order, and Patricio wondered how he knew so much about their traditions. Certainly, Matilda had not shared this information with him, as he knew she would never violate her vows of secrecy by speaking outside the initiated. He wondered now, did Matilda even know that Conn could quote extensively from the Book of Love? That he also knew exactly how and why to walk the labyrinth, with no prompting from Patricio?

Here was a mystery to be investigated, but the man himself wasn't giving away any clues to his history. Patricio considered sending a Sator Rotas letter to Matilda on this subject, but he couldn't take the risk that the Celt might know that code as well. Better not to offend him. He was clearly an ally who viewed himself as something of a holy defender of their precious Expected One. This man would die for Matilda, without a moment's hesitation. Patricio decided that Conn was likely one of God's chosen, and it was not for him to interfere with what he knew or how he knew it. The treasure of the Order of the Holy Sepulcher would be safe traveling under Conn's sword, and Matilda's. The Libro Rosso and the Ark of the New Covenant would find its way safely back to Italy, where it belonged. For now.

❁

Exactly six months later, Godfrey began to send messengers with letters to Mantua, demanding that his wife return to Verdun no later than June of 1072. Matilda ignored him. His letters came more frequently and softened in tone, which she also ignored. Over the course of eight months, Godfrey of Lorraine was eventually begging his wife to at least see him to discuss the future of their marriage. When she refused to even answer his letters, he marched into Tuscany to assert his rights as duke and to hold court in Mantua. Again, he pleaded with Matilda to join him, to sit at his side as his duchess and rule with him in Italy. She simply moved to her hilltop fortress in Canossa to avoid him.

Beatrice was left to apply salve to the wounds of the tormented Godfrey, imploring his patience and forgiveness for Matilda's refusal to see him. A placated Godfrey was a benign one, and Beatrice was determined to neutralize all potential dangers to Matilda's inheritance. She explained in hushed tones that her daughter had not been the same since she had lost her child, and that her husband merely needed to give her a little more time. This tactic worked for a while, but eventually the scorned and offended hunchback returned to Lorraine in a state of high agitation. Shortly thereafter, he took his woes to Henry IV, who was only too happy to uphold Godfrey's claim as the only acknowledged ruler of Tuscany—in exchange for the sworn allegiance and military might of the province of Lorraine. Henry declared Matilda in violation of the Salic laws that gave women no rights of inheritance, and stripped her of everything. With the king's support, Godfrey took a further step to infuriate his estranged wife: he named his nephew, Godfroi de Bouillon, as his sole heir to the fortunes of Lorraine. And Tuscany.

Matilda ignored this too, flagrantly. She answered to no master but God, and it was by God's grace that she held her lands. She thought less of Henry than she did of the hunchback and had long since determined that neither of them would ever steal from her again. Possession *was* the law in her eyes, and she possessed Tuscany: the land and the people. She continued to tour her kingdom with her mother, passing judgments and holding councils not only in her chief territories but also in the smallest hamlets. She was entirely visible as the leader of her people and completely adored by them. Her reputation for justice and compassion spread across Italy as the great Matilda continued to implement programs that brought relief to the needy and rebuilt those towns and villages that had been reduced to rubble during the schismatic conflicts. She funded architectural projects to rebuild and beautify the monasteries and churches for the glory of God and the spiritual benefit of his flock. Charity programs were administered from the monasteries and convents, where food was supplied to the poor on a regular basis.

Her base in Canossa was called "the New Rome" and it flourished as a center of thriving commerce and learning. She fortified and restored the monastery in San Benedetto Po outside her home in Mantua, built by her grandfather in the memory of her sainted grandmother. She had developed a true love of inspiring architecture, one that had begun with the rebuilding of San Martino in Lucca and had reached an apex in Orval. She missed Orval terribly, and Patricio, and all that they had created there. It was her sole regret about leaving the nightmare of the north. As a result, she set out to turn San Benedetto into the Italian Orval, and here she brought members of the Order to maintain her own studies from the Libro Rosso. The Master was firmly ensconced in the

Order's headquarters in Lucca and not inclined to travel, so Matilda did not see him as often as she would like. However, Anselmo visited frequently. While in residence, the bishop of Lucca spent his days studying with Matilda, and his nights with his beloved, Isobel.

Tuscany was thriving under her reign, as it had in the days of her father. A canny and charismatic young general from a noble Tuscan family with ties to the Order, one Arduino della Paluda, commanded her garrisons and implemented a series of strategies that eradicated piracy and made the price for robbery too high for anyone to commit such a crime in Matilda's lands. He ensured that taxes were collected from foreign merchants in exchange for the restored peace and safety of the trade routes. Bridges were built to enhance travel, some drawn and designed by Matilda herself, and commerce was thriving with even greater strength than it had when Bonifacio was alive.

Peace and prosperity returned to Tuscany under the countess, who was known to sit at table with the poorest of her vassals and break bread with any who invited her. These were her people and she loved them all and loved them equally. For this was the teaching of her most beautiful Lord, from both canonical scripture, as Matthew twenty-two, and from the Book of Love: to love thy neighbor as thyself. And Matilda understood that all her people were her neighbors, each and every one of them, and she taught this commandment through example. No feudal leader in memory had ever behaved in this fashion.

As a maturing leader, Matilda had developed her own strategy, one in keeping with her deeply held spiritual traditions. She not only selected loyal, strong, and intelligent advisers, she ensured that everyone within her intimate circle was someone she loved. She surrounded herself with those souls who she was certain were her "family of spirit" as defined in the Book of Love. They had made promises long ago, to each other, to themselves, and to God, to be here in this place and time. *The time returns.* Her friend Arduino captained the armies that kept the Tuscan people safe, while Conn, who was closer to her than a blood brother, retained control of her personal guard. Bishop Anselmo of Lucca maintained the soul of Tuscany, supporting all the reforms of his uncle, who was Pope Alexander II, while secretly protecting the Order and their goals. Isobel, her most trusted confidante, remained the mistress of her household, and Beatrice was her social and political mentor in matters of public importance.

The greatest concern of this extended feudal family was keeping Henry and Godfrey at bay. They had become a de facto Tuscan government essentially controlling the territories that extended from the Alps nearly all the way to Rome. Then, in April of 1073, their much-loved ally and leader, Pope Alexander II, died very suddenly.

CHAPTER TEN

Vatican City
present day

Father Peter Healy walked through St. Peter's Square, awed by the beauty of Gianlorenzo Bernini's masterpiece of architectural design. He didn't think he would ever be immune to the magnificence of this place. While his eyes had recently been opened to the ruthless politics of the Church he had dedicated his life to, he remained committed heart and soul to the vocation that caused him to take vows in the first place. For him, St. Peter's was still a holy place, the seat of the first apostle and his successors.

The spring sunshine warmed his dark hair, which was just beginning to gray at the temples. Funny, he hadn't had this much gray hair until he relocated to the Vatican. Reaching into his pocket, he pulled out the credentials that would be necessary to bypass the Swiss Guard and access Cardinal DeCaro's exalted office. He was dressed in full collar today and breezed through the security measures quickly and without incident.

There was a meeting of the Arques Gospel committee at the end of the week. Peter was here to discuss with his mentor how they would approach what promised to be something of an ordeal.

He hated the committee. It was the bane of his existence, and yet it was also his reason for being. Thus, his current life in the Vatican resembled the seventh level of Hell. The committee was created not only to authenticate the Arques Gospel of Mary Magdalene, discovered by Maureen in the south of France, but also to place the controversial issues contained in it within a Catholic perspective that could be easily digested by the faithful. This was proving to be an impossible task.

The committee of twelve had become a combative and difficult environment, populated as it was by elder, conservative clerics. Peter and Cardinal DeCaro were the only obvious supporters of the truth at any cost. There were a few members who appeared to be on the fence and engaged in internal struggles over the issues, but the others were clearly in favor of keeping this material out of the public eye forever. Peter was being challenged on a number of important points in his original translation, which he was going to have to defend at this week's gathering. In preparation for this particular battle, he had begun to make notes on the primary points of controversy that were found in the Arques Gospel of Mary Magdalene.

Peter was going to have to come up with strong and cogent arguments as to why all these points did not contradict the current traditions of Catholicism. Whether or not these were the truth was, sadly, not the point. Peter had learned over the last two years that the truth was highly subjective everywhere, but nowhere was this more true than in Rome. And the truth mattered far less than preserving the status quo. Peter often thought, while strolling through Vatican grounds, that they should hang banners from the porticos that read Tradition Over Truth. He was quite sure that some of the elder clerics on the committee had this motto tattooed over their hearts.

This was going to be an uphill battle, but one he would have to fight with as much vigor and commitment as he could muster. He had created this terrible dilemma, and now he would have to live within it. At least he was not alone.

"Come in, my boy." Cardinal Tómas Borgia DeCaro welcomed Peter into his office, which was as elegant and Italian as was the man himself. As his name implied, Cardinal DeCaro was related to one of the wealthiest and most aristocratic families in Rome. He moved with the grace that comes with privilege and noblesse oblige. It was precisely his powerful Italian heritage that allowed him to hold such an exalted position in Rome, despite the fact that his own theology was considered radical by the current conservative hierarchy.

"Thank you, Tómas." DeCaro was Peter's mentor and closest friend in a world where friends were as important as they were rare. While he was on a first-name basis with him in private, he would have never called him Tómas had he known they were not alone. Peter startled when he realized that there was another man in the room, as Cardinal Marcelo Barberini rounded the corner from the antechamber.

"Father Healy, a pleasure to see you." Cardinal Barberini held out his hand to Peter, who shook it warmly. Barberini was a leader on the committee, one of those few who maintained silence most of the time, a listener who appeared to be struggling with some of the larger issues. He was also a very high-ranking member of the papal inner circle. Peter was suddenly very nervous.

"Sit down, my friends, sit down." DeCaro closed the doors on both sides of the room, ensuring their privacy, before joining them in one of the soft leather armchairs that made up his meeting space. "Peter, for the moment what happens in this room has to be absolutely confidential. But I have brought Marcelo here to talk to you today about some recent activity in the Arques case."

DeCaro had been involved in the Arques Gospel case since the beginning, had even come to the château after the discovery to meet with Maureen and to provide support and counsel to her. He was completely convinced of the authenticity of the Magdalene Gospel. More than anyone, Tómas DeCaro had reason to understand the importance of these documents. With the authority of his rank, he had access to materials in the Vatican that most of the world could not even dream about.

"As you are more than aware," DeCaro continued, "there are members of the committee who are not aligned with the idea that this gospel could be authentic, regardless of the evidence that proves it to be so. While your presentations have been excellent and thorough, in many ways they served only to remind the more conservative members of our committee just how controversial and potentially dangerous this version of events may be."

Peter nodded but didn't comment. Best to see where this was heading before making any statements in front of Barberini, who was still an unknown quantity.

Barberini, a pudgy little man with a pleasant, ruddy face, sat forward in his seat. "Father Healy, I am very distressed at the current turn the proceedings are taking. There is far more focus on how best to shield this material from anyone outside the council than there is on authenticating it."

Peter spoke carefully. "And you mean by shielding it . . ."

DeCaro leaned toward Peter reassuringly. "You may speak freely here, son. Marcelo is . . . one of us."

Peter was grateful for the confirmation and continued his thought. "That they want to bury it."

Barberini nodded. "I'm afraid that's true. I am gravely concerned that this most important document may never see the light of day. Worse, I believe that there are those among us who may even be willing to destroy it completely and claim it never existed."

Peter ran his hands over his face in exasperation. This was his greatest fear come to life.

"Don't despair yet, Peter. This isn't over," Barberini said.

DeCaro continued the thought. "But the three of us have to determine, right here and right now, who our master is. Do we serve a council of fallible human beings who are allowing their earthly concerns to dominate their decisions, or do we serve our Lord Jesus Christ? And if we serve our Lord Jesus Christ, and his truth, do we not have an obligation, no matter what the odds, to fight for that truth? Any way we may have to?"

Cardinal Barberini surprised Peter as his speech became more impassioned. "These men whom we call our brothers cause me to weep for them. They wear the garments of their power and they stand for spiritual authority. But somewhere, for all that they are good men, they became lost. They claim their holiness, and yet embody none of the love, none of the understanding. I sometimes think to myself, when we are in committee, 'What would our Lord say to these men if he were in this room with us today?' And I have no answer. Only sorrow."

The three of them contemplated in silence for a moment. Each of them had felt this same growing sense of sadness over the last year. Peter broke the moment to ask a question that had been on his mind since his meeting at the Confraternity of the Holy Apparition. "Where is Girolamo de Pazzi in all this?"

"Well, as you know he isn't a part of the committee, nor would he want to be. He is an old man, Peter, and one with a very specific vocation, which is to celebrate the apparitions of our Lady. He can't be bothered with committee business, although I believe he is interested in Maureen because of her visions. That is his passion and his expertise."

"Do you trust him? Should I?"

DeCaro shrugged. "He has never given me a reason not to trust him, for all that he is a conservative. I believe him to be perfectly harmless. But that said . . . I'm not sure that I entirely trust anyone who isn't in this room."

"This may become the ultimate test of faith for all of us," Barberini said softly. "We will have to be very careful and canny about the steps we choose to take to protect the Arques Gospel. It may require us to participate in . . . guerrilla tactics."

Peter was shocked to hear such insurgency from this little man with the sweet face whom he had always viewed as quiet and unassuming. He said nothing but looked to DeCaro, who added, "We may be forced to take the originals out of the Vatican. And if we do, we will not be welcome here."

"For Tómas and myself," Barberini said with a sigh, "this life is all that we have ever known."

"And yet," DeCaro added, "in many ways we have always known that this day and time would come. We were prepared for this from the time we were boys. We just didn't know what course it would take. But we all chose our destinies, long ago when we made our promises to God. Now comes the time to remember, for all of us."

In Alexandria, Joseph brought the holy family to shelter in the home of a great man, a Roman who was called Maximinus. Joseph had known him many years from their shared business in the tin trade and trusted him. Maximinus was an exile from Rome, a refugee in his own way. He knew the dangers of Roman persecution all too well and had great compassion for those who had suffered from it.

Madonna Magdalena and her children arrived at his home exhausted by the journey and nearly overcome with distress. He welcomed them with kindness and ensured that the great lady knew only comfort in her days of confinement.

Maximinus had learned much from the mystery schools in Egypt, and he was a man hungry for learning, for wisdom, and for the truth. He developed a deep friendship and understanding with our Lady during this time, as the Nazarene Way of Love had many traditions that had come from this rich land. They had much to talk about and to learn from each other, and the bond that formed between Magdalena and Maximinus would become unique and enduring.

Maximinus had endured great tragedy and suffering in his life, as his own wife and baby had perished from childbed fever when they were forced to flee Rome and live in exile. Thus it was that he ensured that the finest midwife in Alexandria was brought in to care for Magdalena at the time of delivery. Sarai, the Egyptian priestess, delivered the holy infant, who would be known as Yeshua-David in safety and health and by the grace of God.

Both Joseph of Arimathea and the Roman Maximinus provided care for this infant, as well as for the other holy children. During their time in Alexandria, Maria Magdalena began to instruct Maximinus directly from the Book of Love, and he became the most devoted convert to the teachings of the Way.

When the time came for the holy family to leave Alexandria for their destiny in Gaul, Maximinus insisted on accompanying them. This he did, and he never left. For the remainder of Magdalena's long life, he was her protector and companion, a man of extraordinary devotion and an example of paternal love for her children. It is said that the love of Maximinus knew no limits, and yet it was by necessity purely of spirit.

Maximinus wrote poetry in praise of Our Lady's extraordinary grace, celebrating his love for her in a chaste and honorable form. The great poets in France whom are called troubadours are the heirs of this tradition, singing their songs of courtly love to the sanctified woman they can never touch because she has been promised in the hieros-gamos to another. But love for such a perfected woman lasts until death and beyond. It was thus that Maria Magdalena became the greatest artistic muse, and Maximinus the first troubadour poet.

For in the French, the word troubadour means "to find lost gold." It is in understanding the mysteries left to us through the teachings of the Book of Love that we will find this blessed treasure.

His greatest poem endured among the people, preserved in French by these troubadours, as it contained one of the treasured truths of our teachings, the truth about the return of love which is a gift from God:

je t'ai aimé dans le passé
je t'aime aujourd hui
t'aimerais encore dans l'avenir
Le temps revient.

I have loved you before
I love you today
and I will love you again.
The time returns.

Maximinus became a great leader of the Way in his time, giving the holy sacraments to Magdalena upon her earthly death. He asked to be buried at her feet when his own time came, and this was done. They rested together for many years in the region now named for this great and holy man, Saint Maximin.

For those with ears to hear, let them hear it.

THE STORY OF MAXIMINUS THE ROMAN AND
HOW HE BECAME THE BLESSED SAINT MAXIMIN,
AS PRESERVED IN THE LIBRO ROSSO

Rome
April 1073

OF THE SEVEN FABLED HILLS of Rome, the Esquiline was the highest. Below its western slope were seedy and overcrowded slums; to the east were the villas of prominent citizens, advisers to the Caesars. There were houses in between that belonged to mid-ranking Roman nobles and politicians. It was in these private homes that Christianity flourished in secret during the first century as key citizens were converted by no less than Saint Peter himself. By Matilda's time, these early centers of secret Christianity were recognized as the oldest churches in Rome.

The church of San Pietro in Vincola, Saint Peter in Chains, was one of these locales. It sat atop the steep hill, a holy monument for Christians in the center of the Eternal City. It was named for yet another relic of great import to early Christianity, one that was immortalized within the gospels, in the Acts of the Apostles. In Acts, chapter twelve, Saint Luke wrote of Herod's imprisonment of Peter in the Mamartine, following the execution of the apostle James the Less. Peter was kept in chains, shackled to the wall of this dankest dungeon, until a miracle occurred as specified in verse seven:

> *And behold, the angel of the Lord came upon him, and a light shined in the prison; and he smote Peter on the side and raised him up, saying, "Arise up quickly." And his chains fell off his hands.*

The angel who released the shackles then led Peter out of the prison and to freedom, completing the miracle. The chains that had bound Peter in his captivity were sent to Constantinople for protective keeping as holy relics and proof of the miracle, where they remained until the fifth century. It was then that the Empress Eudoxia sent one half of the set to her daughter in Rome and the other half to Pope Leo I. The pontiff chose this site of a former Christian residence, one where Peter was known to have conducted many secret baptisms, as the foundation for the grand church he built to enshrine the chains.

It seemed a likely place for miraculous events to occur.

It was here that the funeral mass was held for the deeply mourned Pope Alexander II, and here that an extraordinary incident occurred on the same day: the impromptu selection of a new leader for the Church by an emotional mob of churchmen and clerics, a man who wasn't even an ordained priest on the day he was selected to hold the highest and most sanctified office in all of Christendom.

It started slowly, quietly, as the bishops who came to mourn their pontiff whispered among themselves. They required strength under the papal tiara, a strong reformer who could continue to stand up against the tyranny of the German king. Among other outrages, Henry continued to practice simony and had purchased a number of bishoprics for his closest supporters, despite the strong laws passed against this corruption. Turning the Church back into a spiritual entity with no ties to a temporal monarch was going to require a leader of great wisdom, experience, and strength. It required someone bold and fearless to the point of outrageous. The bishops all agreed that only one man among them had the singular potential to fulfill that destiny: Ildebrando Pierleoni. On the cusp of his fiftieth year of age, Brando was significantly younger than many of the popes who had preceded him, giving him a further advantage through his virile and masculine persona. Even his physical appearance identified him as a strong and capable leader.

One of the Roman bishops stood first and made a short but impassioned speech regarding the need to support Brando as their new pontiff. The tide swelled quickly, and within minutes, the entire faction of mourners was chanting his name and insisting that he accept his election to the papacy, right there and right then. A chant of "God has decreed the new pope" began to build, first from within the church and then bursting throughout the streets of Rome. Brando, who was immensely popular with the people of his city, was confirmed overwhelmingly by both bishops and the populace as the only acceptable heir to the keys of Saint Peter.

Nobody seemed to remember that Ildebrando Pierleoni had never taken any kind of clerical vow, or that he had just been elected pope through an illegal and outmoded process, in violation of the very election decree that he himself had written and implemented under Pope Nicholas II.

❊

Every pope since Peter himself had taken a new name on his accession to the papal throne. Ildebrando Pierleoni knew immediately what his own name would be. In honor of his uncle, the deposed Pope Gregory VI, who had been his mentor and greatest teacher, he took the same name, the name that meant "one who cares for his flock." It was seen by savvy politicians for what it was: a powerful statement and an intentionally provocative choice, one that sent a message to Henry IV and alerted everyone else that the battle between the German crown and the might of Rome was far from over.

During the final days of June 1073, ceremonies were called to ordain the newly elected Brando to the priesthood and to invest him on the throne of Saint Peter under the name of Pope Gregory VII.

Matilda and Beatrice arrived in Rome with a full retinue to witness the new pope's investiture ceremony and to show their encouragement for this man who had been loyal to their people in Lucca and to the elder Godfrey during his lifetime. As Isobel adorned Matilda's hair in preparation for the ceremony, Beatrice briefed her daughter on the politics and protocol that this day would require.

"We will no doubt be in a highly visible position today, which is why you must take such care with your appearance. With us, we bring the support of almost half the Italian land mass. I expect to be seated in a place of honor as a result."

Matilda smoothed out the exquisite and costly silk of her skirts, laughing as she did so. Isobel smiled at the mischief she saw in Matilda's eyes.

"Romans have always looked askance at Tuscans; they have always felt themselves superior," Matilda said. "And what is worse, they do not allow women in positions of authority here. So I shall take great plea-sure in showing them just exactly what a Tuscan countess looks like! I hope they place us in the front row, so we can waltz past the Roman aristocrats and scandalize them all."

Matilda of Tuscany was now twenty-seven years old, outlandishly wealthy and extremely powerful. She was relishing the idea of causing a stir in conservative Rome by adding a splash of colorful Tuscan culture to the ceremony today, while at the same time reminding the stodgy Roman nobility that she was one of the wealthiest and most powerful rulers in Europe. Anything that elevated Tuscany in the eyes of the Ro-mans—and the pope—would benefit her and her people.

But there was great substance beneath her lavish style. Matilda held sway over tens of thousands of troops who could be mobilized at any time under her expert strategic command. Matilda's military support, combined with her control of the Apennine Pass, would be the deter-mining factor in a war with Germany.

Beatrice, who wasn't as amused as Isobel by Matilda's antics, re-turned the topic to their political influence.

"Your military might is, no doubt, going to be of far more interest to the new pope than anything else. So while our show of wealth is im-portant, you must remember what is at stake here and not get too caught up in the frivolity."

"Yes, of course, Mother." Beatrice still treated Matilda like she was a child, for all that she ruled half of Italy and led her own troops into battle. Matilda had learned long ago to nod obediently while in her mother's presence, and then go and do exactly what she wanted.

But in this case, she thought Beatrice might actually be right. This pope was, after all, a Roman nobleman. It was likely he would be as conservative and dreary as his countrymen.

�֎

The newly named Pope Gregory was receiving a similar briefing in his chambers prior to the formal investiture ceremony. His advisers went through the list of influential guests, providing details about each of them.

"Next is Matilda, Countess of Tuscany. No doubt you have heard of her, Your Grace. She is . . . controversial."

Gregory was definitely curious about this woman who was a legend in the northern territories. Everything about the countess was mythical: her wealth, her power, her appearance, and her behavior, which was decidedly outrageous for any feudal leader, but unimaginable for a woman.

"I cannot be bothered with her outrageous habits. What I am bothered with is her military might. And her territories, which are strategically critical. Be sure that she is seated in a place of honor. We need her to be well disposed toward us."

He had seen her once, some years ago when she was little more than a child. Now she was a married woman, although by all accounts something of a rebellious one who did not openly acknowledge the influence of her husband, the duke of Lorraine. This was one of the issues he wanted to address with her.

"Godfrey of Lorraine is Henry's lapdog, and therefore dangerous," Gregory mused aloud. "I must know where the countess stands in relation to her husband, and I must know today. Her support could mean everything in the event of war."

Gregory had opposed the German king virtually every day since Henry's coronation at fifteen years of age. The tensions between the sacred throne and the temporal throne, the Church versus the German crown, were about to rise to epic proportions. The new pope was determined to increase the separation of the papacy from monarchical influence, while Henry was determined to unify the two by calling himself Holy Roman Emperor. There would be no middle ground, no possibility for compromise, from either of them.

"In this case, it could be to our benefit that Countess Matilda is not one to behave as a good Christian wife. If her actions allow us to save our Church from Henry's grasp, I am sure that God will forgive her whatever transgressions she is guilty of. That glorious end would surely justify any method of achieving it."

✣

As Gregory VII climbed the altar to take his seat, he turned to look out upon the bishops, nobles, and supporters in attendance. He radiated strength and confidence on this, the most important day of his political career. Here was the culmination of everything he had worked for, the reward for the years of exile and hardship in defense of the papacy. He did not think that there was anything in the world that could equal this feeling of ascending these steps on the path to becoming the greatest spiritual leader in the world.

And then he looked down.

In a place of honor in the very front row was the most mesmerizing sight he had ever encountered. Matilda of Tuscany sat with her mother, a vision in azure silk. Strands of pearls were woven through her remarkable hair, which was only partially covered by a gossamer veil. Her coiffure was anchored by a gold and jeweled crown of fleurs-de-lis, a vivid reminder to all in attendance that Matilda and her mother were direct descendants of the holy and exalted emperor Charlemagne. Her slender throat dripped with a fortune in jewels; she was breathtaking to the point of distraction. So disconcerted was he that, as he accepted the key of Saint Peter as the symbol of his new position, Gregory VII had to turn his head away from the crowd in order to maintain his concentration.

The new pope was not the only disconcerted spirit in attendance that day. The Countess of Canossa, Duchess of Tuscany and Lorraine, sat perfectly still and entirely speechless throughout the ceremony. She could not take her eyes off the powerful and charismatic man who was inheriting the papal tiara. While he was certainly an arresting presence and an astoundingly handsome man, Matilda was most stunned by the realization that she had seen him before: she had seen him in a vision, at the center of the labyrinth, just before she departed from Orval on that terrible day.

✣

Beatrice of Lorraine was a wise woman and an experienced one. She also had eyes. She had not missed the heated, if silent, exchange between her daughter and the new pope during the investiture ceremony. Here was a relationship to be cultivated if ever there was one. The alliance of the Holy Roman Church with the might and wealth of Tuscany had the potential to be an unstoppable force. When the time came later in the afternoon for her to attend the papal audience with her daughter, she pleaded exhaustion and insisted that Matilda attend alone. She was a married woman and a countess in her own right; surely she did not require a chaperone in the presence of the Holy Father.

Matilda was escorted to the audience chambers, where she waited only for a moment before the door was opened to admit Gregory. She prayed that he could not hear her heart pounding in her chest, because it sounded like ten war drums in her own ears. He reached out his hand to her and she kissed the papal ring, dropping into a deep curtsy. She steadied her voice as she looked up at him, aquamarine eyes locking with steel gray.

"I have come to pledge the loyalty of Tuscany to the cause of Saint Peter. You may count on my support and that of my people in all things which are dear to preserving and protecting the teachings of our Lord as the focal point of our communities, and to enforcing your selection as God's chosen apostle to lead the Church."

Gregory thanked her for her fealty, impressed by the strong statement, and indicated that she should sit down. After pleasantries that included asking after her mother's health and giving regards to Bishop Anselmo, the pope stunned Matilda with an outrageous question.

"I understand that you are indoctrinated into the ancient heresies that are still held in Lucca. What am I to make of that?"

Matilda sat motionless, trapped. She had believed this man to be an ally because of his support of Alexander, but perhaps she had miscalculated. Matilda was thinking quickly, trying to conjure a safe response to buy more time. There was no need to. The pope continued almost immediately.

"It is not my intention to make you uncomfortable with the question. Rather, I would have you know from the outset of our relationship that I am aware of who you are and where you come from. I am the pope, elected by popular opinion of the clergy and the people because I am so well versed in the issues that face my Church. You cannot be surprised that I am familiar with the whispers of heresy that emanate from Tuscany."

Matilda nodded mutely but still said nothing. Gregory smiled at her broadly then, working hard now to allay her obvious concerns.

"You have nothing to fear from me, Matilda of Canossa. I was not born into the priesthood and I do not bring any of the prejudices that come with the narrow view of some who preceded me. I like to think of myself as a scholar, as a man who will learn entirely what it is to be a Christian, not from reiterating the popular teachings, but from studying all documents and traditions that are available to me. And my grandfather was a Jew, which broadens my religious perspective, and my desire for learning, even further. Some would applaud me for it, others would despise me for it. I am told that the traditions of Tuscany, though shocking to many, hold deep secrets and can be traced directly to the first Christians. Indeed, even to those who were contemporaries of our Lord Jesus Christ himself, including his own family. What manner of spiritual leader would I be if I did not examine those traditions and teachings in depth for myself? I have spent enough time in Lucca, with both Anselmos, the elder and younger, to understand that there are many layers to the way Christianity is expressed there. For those with eyes to see and ears to hear, no? And so, Matilda, we have many things to speak of. If you are so inclined to do so."

Matilda fought hard to find her voice. On completely uneven footing here, she asked softly, "Are you asking me to instruct you in the ways of the Order?"

"If you are so inclined."

She nodded at him then, in awe of the peculiar situation she had just found herself in. Was it possible that the pope himself was asking for her to instruct him in the ways of heresy?

His chaplain entered the room to advise them that the next appointment was waiting and their audience must come to an end. When the attendant priest took his leave, Gregory held out his hand to Matilda, this time taking her own and bringing it to his lips. As he did so, he noticed her ring, using it as an excuse to hold on to her hand longer than necessary.

"What does this symbolize?"

Matilda smiled at him coyly, feeling the return of control for the first time in the long and trying day. "I cannot tell you yet, but it will be a part of your . . . instruction."

"Ah, I see. Well then, I shall await it eagerly and we shall begin in all haste. Tomorrow?"

"Tomorrow."

Matilda made her exit with a final deep curtsy and a feminine swish of elegant silk. He watched her leave, surprised at his own extreme, breathless reaction to her. The man who was now known to the world as Pope Gregory VII, the pontiff who would successfully institute the laws of clerical celibacy as a primary reform, had just lost his heart—and perhaps a little of his mind—to the remarkable and alluring countess of Tuscany.

It was not like Matilda to gush.

Lady Isobel of Lucca stood transfixed and a little alarmed at the flood which poured forth from her foster daughter, following her second meeting with Gregory VII. The new pope had, impulsively and unexpectedly, summoned Matilda to a council meeting following the investiture banquet, to discuss issues of strategy in a critical matter that he had inherited from Pope Alexander II. The previous pontiff, immediately before his death, had excommunicated five of Henry's German bishops and censured the king for selling them their offices in the first place. Henry himself risked excommunication if he did not comply with this papal decree and acknowledge the censure to his bishops by deposing them immediately. It was an overt act of war, and one that

Gregory intended to uphold. He needed the assurance that Matilda would support him from her lands in Tuscany if it proved necessary.

Their meeting had been an intense, stimulating game of wit and banter, highly charged on both sides. It was tribute to the sharpness of both intellects that they were capable of having a keenly productive political conversation against the backdrop of their supernatural attraction to each other. They had both taken and given the opportunity to sum up the other's thought process and strategic approaches and had found that they were compatible in all areas, almost beyond explanation. It had been a successful and exhilarating meeting of two great spirits. When they were in the same room together, there occurred an undeniable merging of immense forces of nature, stars colliding to create an extreme burst of light.

Gregory had ended their meeting by reminding Matilda that she had promised to begin his education in the Way, as it had been taught uninterrupted in the Order since the first century, on the morrow. This was the source of Matilda's current consternation and uncharacteristic giddiness.

"Oh, Isobel, he is as wise as Solomon, and as magnificent. I felt like Makeda, the Queen of Sheba herself, in his presence. It was like all that you have taught me, yet all that I never thought I would know in my own heart. What shall I do? What he is asking is outrageous, and yet it is also a marvel. Can I teach him these things? Dare I teach him these things?"

"What does your heart tell you, child? And your spirit?"

"It tells me that I must trust this man, and more."

"And more?"

"I cannot explain it, Issy. But when I first saw him, I recognized him. I had seen him before, seen him in my vision, but it was more than that. I knew a moment of extreme joy. And then when he looked at me . . . it was as if a knife pierced my heart. There was a second in time, before the entire court and the Lateran council, when I felt it was only he and I in the room. How is that possible? But in that moment, I knew him. And I knew . . ."

She paused now, lost in the moment and breathless with the overwhelming infatuation that accompanied it. It was like a type of madness, this emotion. She had never felt anything like it. It was terrible and wonderful and completely paralyzing. Isobel had to prompt her to continue.

"Go on, Tilda."

"I knew that . . . I had loved him before. In that single moment I understood the teaching of our prophetess, and the poem of Maximinus, in a new way: 'I have loved you before, I love you today, and I will love you again.' It was something so strange and yet so eternal. And I believe that he feels the same. I saw it, in the way he looked at me. He knows it, just as I do. That there is destiny at work here. And he is not afraid of it, I think. But I am."

Matilda rose from her seat to pace the room as she spoke. She was unable to sit at the best of times, and certainly not when agitated at the level she was now. She pulled at her skirts as she continued. "Because it is terrifying, isn't it? This feeling. There is no control over it. I have been in battle and faced the fiercest men on the field, with the sharpest swords and the most evil intent, and yet I have never encountered the fear that I feel at this moment. I cannot breathe, Isobel. Help me."

Isobel sighed deeply before reaching over to hold Matilda's hand in hers. "Oh, my sweet. I cannot help you other than to tell you that what you are feeling, as hard and as powerful and as overwhelming as it is, is also God's greatest gift to us. I always knew that when it happened to you, it would be deeply meaningful, perhaps even a relationship that could change the world, much in the model of Veronica and Praetorus, or even as exalted as Solomon and Sheba. But I could not have foreseen . . ."

"Foreseen what?"

"That the man whom you were destined to find love with, the 'very great love' as foretold by the prophecy, would be the pope himself." Isobel paused for a moment to consider the wisest counsel she could give to her precious child at this critical moment in her life.

"Tilda, you will have to be terribly careful. Both of you have far too much to lose in the event of an indiscretion. But I think you have even more to lose if you do not pursue this and see where it takes you, for it appears to be ordained by God. I do not have to be a prophet to know that you will encounter great challenges and hard times as a result of this love, a love which by its very nature must be a secret from the world at all times. No one can know, and you can never let on, that you have shared any intimacy. Ever."

"But we have not."

"Yet, Tilda. Yet. But some things are inevitable, and this appears to be one of them. Remember that intimacy between you will be judged as wrong, even criminal, if you are discovered. You have powerful enemies who would seize on such a crime and use it to destroy you both. Do what you will, do what you must, but remember discretion at all costs. He is the pope and you are a married woman; those are undeniable and unchangeable facts."

"I can divorce Godfrey."

"Can you? Legally, perhaps, but divorce is opposed by the Church, and you cannot expect the pope to uphold that decision, and certainly not this pope, who was selected for his strength to uphold strict reforms. And such an action would only call attention to your relationship. You are both caught in your own trap, my sweet. But I have no doubt that you will find a way to make it work, if it is truly the great love of the prophecy. Love always finds a way, Matilda. It overcomes the laws of man because it is a law of God. The rite of sacred union, the *hieros-gamos* between true beloveds of the soul, is the highest law that transcends all others. And that is all you really need to know, isn't it? There is only one thing that you need to hold tight to in the days that will come, and it is the simplest teaching of our Way:

"Love conquers all."

CHAPTER ELEVEN

Mantua
October 1073

Matilda was miserable. She couldn't concentrate on any of the issues and activities that usually absorbed her intellect as well as her heart. Nor had she eaten or slept properly in weeks, and she had no one to share her torment with. Isobel was in Lucca on business for the Order, and to visit Anselmo and the Master. While Beatrice was a brilliant adviser and political strategist, she was not one for discussing emotional issues with her daughter.

It was in this state that Conn found Matilda wandering alone at the edge of the forest. She jumped when he came up behind her.

"You should be armed if you are going to walk in the woods unescorted."

"If I were armed, you'd be wounded and we'd be staunching the blood."

"And I would be pleased that I had done my job so well. Why are you out here alone and sulking?"

"I'm not sulking."

"I see that."

Matilda sighed dramatically. Lying to Conn was as useless as lying to Isobel. Both knew her mind and heart better than she did herself.

"I haven't heard a word from the Holy Father in six months."

"And you haven't heard from Gregory either."

"Make your point."

"It's not the pope that you miss, it's the man."

"And now you've made your point. I'm pathetic."

"You're not pathetic. You're in love. And the last time I checked, that was a sacrament within the Order."

"He's forgotten all about me, Conn. And it's killing me. Does anything else feel worse than this? How can something so beautiful also be so horrid?"

"Do you really think he's forgotten you? Or are you the one who is forgetting? He's the pope, Tilda. *The pope.* The spiritual leader of the world."

"Thank you for reminding me," she snapped. "Because of course I do not obsess about that fact every minute of every day all on my own."

Conn wanted to groan with annoyance but found his patience. "Would you like to hear my thoughts, or would you rather I leave you alone so you can be despondent and lovesick all by yourself?"

"As I know that you won't really leave me alone even if you say you will, I'll listen, assuming that you are going to tell me a story that makes me feel less wretched."

"You're in luck. I just happen to have the perfect story for you. So let's sit down and I will tell you the tale of Princess Niamh of the Golden Hair, and the poet prince known as Oisin."

He gave both names their heavy Irish pronunciations, which Matilda loved, *Neev* and *USH-een*. The Celtic language was so foreign and beautiful to her ears. Sometimes Conn recited devotional poetry about Easa to her in the lyrical, magical syllables.

"Princess Niamh was the lovely and gentle daughter of Mannanan Mac Lir, the sea god, and she lived on his most beautiful western island, called Tir n'Og, which means Land of the Young. Niamh's mother was a queen of the faery world, and as the daughter of two immortals, Niamh had not a drop of human blood in her. This is why her father kept her on the island and would not allow her access to the mortal world, for if Niamh were to fall in love with a human, it would have dire consequences.

"But the fair Niamh had heard so many stories of the legendary heroes and poets of Ireland that she was desperate to witness them for herself. She heard the tall tales of the Fianna, the warrior band who defended the innocent and protected the weak. And there was a prince among the Fianna, a youth called Oisin, who was legendary for his chivalry, his prowess in battle, and the skill of his poetry and music. Niamh had never seen such a creature on the island and was fascinated by the idea of human males who could be expert in both love and war. No such thing existed in the magical realms, where there was no war and therefore no reason for warriors. And so it was that after much nagging—as we know how relentless young girls can be when they want to get something, don't we?—the sea god gave in to his precious daughter. He allowed Niamh to take his magical white horse, a creature that could skim the waves and cross to the mainland, advising her that she must stay out of sight and have no contact with the humans. Niamh agreed, and her journey over the water commenced.

"Now, our Niamh was a good girl and she did not set out on this adventure to disobey her father. But as she rode through the hazelwood forest, she came upon a band of men. They were young and strong and vital, for these men were the legendary warriors known as the Fianna. Niamh watched them quietly from the trees, listening as they discussed their victory in the battle to save a village against a tyrant who was terrorizing the womenfolk. All the men were exemplary, but one stood out. He was beautiful as men go, with chestnut-colored curls and sapphire eyes, and Niamh was struck by him immediately. The youth carried a harp carved out of oak, and when the men quieted, he began to play. Like Orpheus, this bard had a magic with music and poetry, and Niamh realized that she was now watching the legendary Oisin. So enchanted was she by his playing that she swooned and fell from her horse. This startled the men, and being warriors, they rushed at her with weapons drawn. But it was the poet prince who reached her first; it was Oisin who rescued her, for that was his destiny.

"Now, you must remember that not only was Niamh painfully beautiful, with her golden hair sparkling with sunlight and eyes that flashed the colors of the sea, but she was immortal and likewise filled with magic. There was a glamour to her, a power, that no mortal man could resist once it was turned upon him. And so when Oisin's eyes met Niamh's, there was an instant bond between them that could not be broken. One would never forget the other, from that day into eternity. But alas, they were from different worlds, were they not? Oisin begged her to stay with him, but Niamh could not disappoint her father in such a way, nor could she deny the responsibilities that she had to her kingdom as their favored princess. Sadly, she said to him, 'Your world is not mine, and mine is not yours,' and moved toward the white horse that would carry her home.

" 'Take me with you!' Oisin begged, not wanting this magical creature to leave him behind. But Niamh could not, for she loved him too much. You see, if Oisin were to go with Niamh, he would never be able to return to the mortal world. Once a mortal ventures into the deepest places of magic and immortality, he can never return to a human life, and this is most certainly true if he kisses a woman from the magical realms.

"And so Niamh left him there in the forest with the Fianna, where he belonged with his comrades and his music. Her heart was heavy but she could not ask him to leave his exemplary life here for her, nor could she leave hers for him. But for the next year, Oisin pined for the princess and the glimpse of magic she had shown him. He dreamed of her each night and asked his brothers in arms what they would have done in his place. They all, to a man, told him they found the golden Niamh to be completely irresistible and advised Oisin to go after her.

" 'But I cannot,' he told them. 'For if I go after this woman, I know I will never be able to return to this, the land I know so well, where all is familiar and I am regarded as the chief poet and prince of my own people. I can never give that up. There is too much to risk here.'

"For a year, Oisin tried to forget his lady love, but to no avail. She haunted his dreams and his memory beyond all human bearing. And so on the anniversary of their meeting, he went to the seashore and wrote a song to call out to the great god Mannanan Mac Lir. When the sea lord replied, Oisin advised him that he wanted to marry his daughter and humbly requested permission to do so. Mannanan asked Oisin if he understood what sacrifices must occur for him to marry Niamh—that if he were to make the journey on the white horse across the waves to Tir n'Og, he would never see his home or his friends again. He must be willing to give up his old ways for new ones. Of course, Mannanan assured him, life on the island was joyous and peaceful and full of music and light. It was an existence like no other, one of pure magic and happiness, and most of all, love.

"But all the same, humans tend to hold on to the past and to what they know with tight hands, don't they? Would Oisin be able to let go and live in happiness with his immortal beloved? For he too would become immortal upon joining her in matrimony and physical union."

Conn stopped the story at this place to help Matilda see the comparisons.

"I'm flattered that you think I'm as beguiling as the legendary Niamh," she commented, her smile wry.

"Don't fool yourself, little sister. You are every bit as enchanting, and every bit as dangerous. Particularly to a man with as much to lose as the pontiff himself. So at the moment, Gregory is grappling with the understanding that if he takes that fateful trip on the white horse, if he experiences the immortal and mystical kiss of such a woman . . . he will never be able to return to the human world. And this is why you haven't heard from him, Matilda. Because he is wrestling with a mighty demon—the demon of his own mortality, and all that it entails."

She thought about it for a moment, realizing that, strangely, she did feel better. Conn's stories always had that effect on her. Finally she asked, "How does the tale end?"

Conn smiled. "Oisin rides to Tir n'Og, marries Niamh, and discovers that the magical world is wondrous beyond his expectations and his immortal woman is full of love and delightful surprises so that he never grows bored. He and Niamh have a son, called Oscar, who is the joy of their lives. Because Oscar is both human and immortal, he is able to travel between the worlds and have the best of both of them. And his parents can rejoice in this. So it is a happy ending, sister."

Conn neglected to tell her that the legend of Niamh and Oisin had two endings, depending upon the storyteller. The second ending was not nearly as golden, but he chose to reveal only the most blissful outcome to boost her spirits. The responsibilities of storytelling required such choices.

"There is a happy ending waiting for you here, if you will just have Niamh's patience—and dare I say it, her unselfishness—to leave Oisin to his own decision making. Because I am willing to wager all that I have ever possessed that the time will come when he craves your presence beyond reason and saddles the white horse to ride across the waves and claim you."

Within the hieros-gamos, the sacred union of beloveds, God is present in their chambers. For a union to be blessed by God, both **trust** *and* **consciousness** *must be expressed within the embrace.*

As the beloveds come together, they celebrate their love in the flesh: they are no longer two, but one. Outside the chamber, they will live as love expressed in the spirit.

In its sanctified form, love is present in six aspects of expression:

Agape—*a love that is filled with the joy of each other and for the world, a purest form of spiritual expression; here is the sacred embrace that contains consciousness;*

Philia—*a love that is first a friendship and full of respect; this is the sister-bride and brother-bridegroom, but also the love of blood siblings and true companions; here is the sacred embrace that contains trust;*

Charis—*a love that is defined by grace, devotion, and praise for God's presence in the chambers; this is where the love of our mother and father is found, on earth and in heaven;*

Eunoia—*a love that inspires deep compassion and a commitment to the service of the world and all God's people; this is where our love for charity and community lies;*

Storge—*a pure love that is full of tenderness, caring, and empathy; this is where the love of children is found;*

Eros—*a love that is a profound physical celebration in which the souls come together in the union of the bodies; this is the ultimate expression of beloveds which finds its most sanctified form in the hieros-gamos.*

There is no darkness that cannot be defeated by the light of love in one of these expressions. When all are present in harmony on earth, darkness cannot exist at all.

Love Conquers All.

For those with ears to hear, let them hear it.

FROM THE BOOK OF LOVE, AS PRESERVED IN THE LIBRO ROSSO

Fiano, north of Rome
June 1074

CONN WAS rarely wrong where Matilda was concerned.

It would be a full year before Matilda and Gregory had the opportunity to begin his education in the teachings of the Way of Love. The antagonistic political climate that they found themselves in immediately following his investiture demanded their focus as leaders and politicians, leaving no time for anything that would distract from the protection of the papacy. The German king Henry IV refused to censure his bishops and recognize their excommunication as instructed by Rome, causing the tensions between Germany and Rome to escalate. Matilda proved, conversely, to be utterly loyal to the pope in the name of her holdings, which served to further infuriate her husband. Godfrey continued to assert his rights as the duke of Tuscany while immersed in the service of Henry IV, and the battle between husband and wife turned deadlier than any other brewing in Europe. However, Matilda was in Tuscany and Godfrey was not. Matilda commanded the people of the Apennines, hearts and swords, and Godfrey did not. As always, she didn't care a whit for what her husband said or did and ignored his existence at all times. Outrageously, the pope supported her position, refusing to address any correspondence to her as a married woman and acknowledging her as a co-ruler of Tuscany with her serene mother. As far as Pope Gregory VII was concerned, Godfrey did not exist outside Lorraine.

Ultimately, the bloody nature of the Saxon rebellion in Henry's own territories forced Germany to seek a humiliating reconciliation with Rome. Henry's resources were depleted, and he had stretched his loyal nobles, including Godfrey, to their limits. In November of 1073, Henry took an oath of allegiance to Pope Gregory VII before an audience that included papal legates, in the city of Nuremberg. He apologized for his disobedience and swore to participate in the reforms of the Church as dictated by the pope from that day forward. While Gregory was hopeful that this truce would hold, he was too wise and experienced in Henry's ways to believe that this oath was not taken with the king's fingers crossed. It was lip service, but it had been a very public display which would at the very least force Henry's submission for a period of public decorum. As a result of the king's newfound loyalty to the pope, Godfrey too was forced to reduce his aggression. He left Matilda alone and focused on his own lands in Lorraine and the north.

After months of silence, the pope began to write to Matilda very suddenly and without cessation. The Tuscan countess and Pope Gregory VII engaged in frequent correspondence for the following six months. Their affection for each other was increasing, deepening despite the distance that separated them, or perhaps because of it. As such letters were by nature public, they were written in careful language, and yet both contained effusive sentiments of adoration within their proprietary cover. Matilda referred often to her "great and undying love for Saint Peter" and Gregory expressed his own heart to her in even more emphatic terms. He addressed his letters to her as "My daughter in Christ" but his expressions on paper, containing phrases such as "you must know the love I bear for you" were beyond the boundaries of the filial. Ultimately, he nearly begged her to return to him in Rome with a letter that read:

> *I am extremely anxious to have further interviews with you, desiring to have your advice in my affairs as a sister and daughter of Saint Peter. Please do not make me wait any longer.*

In answer to his plea, Matilda traveled to a private villa in Fiano, outside Rome. She was as anxious as he to have "further interviews." Beatrice accompanied her, as did Isobel, to play the role of chaperones for any and all who might find impropriety otherwise in such a private meeting place, away from the intense scrutiny of the papal court in Rome, away from all but the most intimate and trusted members of their mutual inner circles.

❈

The chambers Gregory had prepared for their interviews were magnificent. Opulently furnished and dripping with rich fabrics from the Orient, the rooms were worthy of the reunion of King Solomon and the Queen of Sheba. It was a clever and intentional piece of seduction. For while he was not thoroughly informed in the ways of Matilda's beloved Order, he was well aware that its followers believed all teachings began with the exotic king and queen of scripture and their legendary union.

Matilda was equally prepared for her role in the great pageant. Isobel, who was still a master at such presentation, spent hours dressing her until she was a vision of alluring, feminine mystery. The countess arrived in the pope's private chambers swathed in layers of turquoise silk over a deeply cut and jeweled bodice of Turkish damask. Gossamer veils covered her décolletage as well as her hair, giving the illusion of propriety but woven of a material so sheer as to be nearly nonexistent. Her rich copper tresses had been brushed to a high shine beneath the diaphanous veil and were completely unbound, which would have been scandalous in public. Aquamarines and pearls were woven on strands through the soft curls, while matching jewels hung from her ears. For the first time in her life, Matilda's skin was most thoroughly perfumed and oiled with an attar of roses mixed with frankincense, myrrh, and spikenard from the Holy Land. This costly and sacred preparation had been used since ancient times in accordance with the Song of Songs, to anoint the bride in anticipation of the *hieros-gamos*, the sacred marriage of true beloveds.

Gregory was speechless as she entered. His memory of this woman had haunted him to distraction for a year, and yet when confronted with her again, he realized that his mind had not done her justice. He kissed her hand, and she his ring, but otherwise they maintained an appropriate distance as they sat on cushioned benches, facing each other.

She began, as he knew she would, with the legend of Solomon and Sheba. There was no better place, for this was the beginning of the teachings regarding sacred union.

Gregory was certainly familiar with the passages in the First Book of Kings, chapter ten, that described Sheba's coming to Jerusalem. But the extended version as it was taught by the Order both astounded and fascinated him. The applications to their own situation—two great leaders of opposing gender coming together in a meeting of minds and spirits—were unavoidable.

He decided to challenge her immediately, to see how she would defend this cornerstone of their teachings. "Whence does this version of their story come? Surely, nothing in the scriptures indicates that Solomon and Sheba develop such a relationship."

Matilda had studied this material all her life, was committed to it, and knew it as well as any official teacher in the Order. Her answer was instantaneous.

"First Kings ten, verses two and three: 'And when she had come to Solomon, she communed all that was in her heart. And Solomon answered all her questions. There was not *anything* hid from the king, which he told her not.' The word *anything* is emphasized there in the scripture. This indicates that Solomon, despite the fact that he is the wisest and most important king in the world, hides nothing from this woman. It is an indication of deep intimacy, as is the language that she communes 'all that is in her heart.' No queen on a strictly political mission opens her heart to such a powerful man. Again, it implies a depth of intimacy and, I believe, passion."

The correlations hung heavy in the air between them, but they were both enjoying the titillating nature of the game far too much to approach it in any direct manner as yet.

"Perhaps. But it does not give us such a complete biography as you claim to have."

"Their story is preserved as such in the Libro Rosso, as the traditions of our people were passed down and transcribed. But there are also references to the coming together of Solomon and Sheba in the Book of Love, which we have in the hand of the apostle Philip himself."

"But it is not proof."

"I would not venture to lecture the pontiff himself on the essence of faith. But I will say that with all matters of spirit, the only proof is in our hearts. No ink or paper can provide truth. Only our hearts can tell us if what is on that page, whether it is your Bible or my Book, is the truth. And each man or woman must come to that choice of his or her own faith."

He conceded to her eloquence. "I will look forward to seeing this holy book and perhaps gaining a greater understanding of how it has come to give you such extraordinary faith."

"And I will look forward to showing it to you. You must make your way to Lucca in the near future, as your time permits, and perhaps we will have the opportunity to explore the Libro Rosso together."

She took him then through the Old Testament version of the Song of Songs, again giving it a new interpretation—which was in essence the oldest interpretation—through the eyes of the Order, via their holy book. That such an overtly erotic piece of poetry was an accepted and exalted piece of scripture was something that was often overlooked in biblical studies, even in an education as thorough as Gregory's. Church leaders emphasized the idea that the Song of Songs, allegedly written by Solomon, then transcribed again in the fifth century BC, was an allegory for the love of God for the people and his Church. Matilda claimed it as the ultimate proof that Solomon and Sheba were the prototype lovers for sacred union and as an epic poem containing the greatest mysteries of love within it, written originally by Solomon with Sheba as his muse. In fact, she pointed out, the complete first line of this segment of the Bible reads "The Song of Songs, which is Solomon's."

Gregory presented the traditional arguments against the Song as a paean to erotic love, insisting that the Church could only take the position that it was sacred poetry about God's love for the Church and its children, and only God's love. Matilda parried once again, as skillfully as any learned cleric he had ever met.

"Why does it have to be one or the other? The problem with many scriptural interpretations that are accepted by the Church is that they are narrowly exclusive. Either the Song of Songs is about God's love and a love of the Church, which is divine, or it is about human love, which is therefore profane. But this is not what Jesus tells us in the Book of Love. He tells us that both are true, and must be. That it is through our love together as humans that we find God. God is present in the bridal chamber when true beloveds are united. It is this essence that is found completely in the very first verse. 'How right it is to love you.' This is what the beloveds say when they find God as they come together. Why cannot such a thing be true when it is so beautiful?"

"Tell me then, Matilda. Did you find God in the bridal chamber?"

She was shocked into silence for a moment when Gregory shifted the direction of his questioning to make the inquiry so highly personal. He had never ventured into such territory before. She responded the only way she knew how. With honesty.

"I was forced into marriage with a man who was not and could never be my beloved. He could not even be my friend. Such is the bane of many women, never to know true love and to subsequently be denied this particular path to feeling and understanding God. I believe that such forced marriages are a high human crime against the teachings of love. There was never, at any time, trust or consciousness in my marital bed. And the teachings insist that both must be present for a union to be sacred. So the answer to your question is no, I have not found God in the bridal chamber."

He was watching her closely, testing her now, and she knew it. "So you have a conundrum, do you not? You have never known such union, and yet it is the ultimate sacrament of your people. You are not spiritually whole without this understanding of union, are you? But to search for such an experience outside matrimony is adultery, and a cardinal sin. How do you reconcile that in your spiritual well-being?"

She was ready for the question, had thought about this concept many, many times. "Adultery, as you define it, is a cardinal sin within the Catholic Church, that is true. But adultery is defined differently in the Book of Love. Our scripture states that any embrace that is against the will of another, or that otherwise violates the spirit of trust and consciousness, is adulterous. Therefore most arranged marriages, where women are forced to provide their bodies against their will, constitute real adultery. And yet they are sanctioned by the Church as well as by man-made laws.

"How can true love ever be adultery, if love is the greatest gift given us by our benevolent father in heaven? Solomon and Sheba were not married to each other, indeed he was married to others, and yet they have never been called adulterers. That is because their love was a higher law. How is it possible that two souls, joined by God in heaven at the dawn of eternity, could ever commit a sin by reuniting in the flesh on earth? Remember this: what God has joined together, let no man separate. I say to you that the law of love will always defy the law of man when and if it must. And that every time Godfrey touched me, that was adultery, despite the laws of man and the Church that claim him as my husband.

"But to embrace the other half of my soul, to merge with him completely through the joining of our bodies as an expression of pure union . . . this is a sacrament without sin, and I would stand by that in the face of God on the day of judgment."

She held his eyes with her own. When neither could find their voice in the immediate aftermath of such a speech, it was Matilda who continued, finding a safer place—if only momentarily—within continued scriptural discussion.

"The Song of Songs contains within it the teachings of the six aspects for expressing love, which Jesus later emphasizes individually in his gospel, *our* most holy scripture." She raised her chin with a touch of hauteur when she used the possessive pronoun. "And one of these aspects is Eros, which is intense and beautiful physical expression. Sacred union."

Gregory responded to the mental challenge with some degree of relief, back on level ground. "But you are making an assumption once again that the verses have intimate, physical connotations. The scholarly interpretations do not say so. They are adamant that this song is not about erotic love."

Matilda began to reply but held back for a moment. When she did respond, it was to lean forward, causing waves of soft copper hair to fall becomingly over her porcelain skin. Her blue-green eyes sparked as she began to recite from the Song of Songs, never once breaking eye contact as she intoned in a throaty whisper:

How delicious is your love, more delicious than wine!
Your lips, my promised one
Distill wild honey.
Honey and milk
Are under your tongue.

In the boldest move of a life defined by daring, she rose from her own bench and closed the distance between them. She came before him, kneeling at his feet, and continued to recite, slow and tortuous, as she gazed up at him. With slow, careful fingers, she removed the veils that covered her hair as she continued to hold his eyes.

I eat my honey and my honeycomb
I drink my wine and my milk

I sleep but my heart is awake
I hear my beloved knocking.
"Open to me, my love,
My dove, my perfect one."

The next veils to be removed, carefully, gracefully, were those that covered her full breasts. They floated to the floor, leaving her creamy flesh and delicate rose-colored nipples exposed to his gaze. He watched her, immobilized, as the poetry dripped from her lips and she leaned forward to graze his thighs lightly with her fingertips.

On my bed at night I sought him,
Whom my heart loves.
My beloved thrust his hand
Through the hole in the door;
I trembled to the core of my being,
Then I rose
To open to my Beloved.

She leaned in closer to him, still at his feet, resting her cheek on one thigh now, fingertips trailing along the other. She finished the Song, breathing against his hardness as she intoned,

Myrrh ran off my hands
Pure myrrh ran off my fingers
And I opened to my Beloved.

Matilda invoked the last line with delicate slowness. There was more than a touch of triumph in her slanted aquamarine eyes as she witnessed his discomfort, his fascination, and his passion. Never had scripture been so seductive.

"And so I ask you," she whispered, rising full on her knees to meet him now, face-to-face, increasing the pressure on his thighs with her fingertips. "Does that sound like a song written about the chastity of the Church to you?"

"I concede," he whispered, hoarse in his reply, his mouth against hers. They stayed there in that space for some time, breathing together and living in the moment of forbidden closeness. They would both come to savor every second that they were able to be alone and to touch in such a way, yet there was an exquisite torture in the waiting. When their lips did finally come together in full, it was a deeply sensual and exquisite prelude to the prolonged merging of their bodies. They spent the next hours intertwined, locked in the specific alchemical magic that occurs when hardened masculinity enters yielding feminine softness.

No more were they two, but of one flesh. And what God has put together, let no man separate.

Theirs was a union of trust and consciousness, a perfect expression of the *hieros-gamos*. The beloveds of scripture had found each other once more.

❁

In emulation of Solomon and Sheba, they remained together, very nearly undisturbed, for the better part of a week. In the sanctity of the chamber, Matilda introduced her beloved to the most intimate secrets of the *hieros-gamos* as preserved in the Order. These were highly protected and sacred teachings, passed down from woman to woman for thousands of years, for providing ecstasy in a way that was unimaginable to any but the indoctrinated. It was an approach that emphasized worshipping the body of the beloved, in full understanding that it was the sacred container of the soul. While Matilda had learned these lessons as part of her instruction, she could not have imagined what they would feel like in practice. Once experienced, they altered one's existence indelibly. This was as true for women as it was for men.

Isobel had laughed at first when passing the instruction on to Matilda, saying that she felt sympathy for those who would never know just how exquisite divine union could be.

"Do you know, Matilda," she explained, "that no man in the history of the Order has ever strayed from his beloved? This is because once the *hieros-gamos* is consummated within the secret teachings, there is nowhere else for him to go! He will never desire to couple with any other woman, knowing full well that the same levels of ecstasy can never be reached with another. It is an ecstasy that touches divinity. His desire for his beloved partner becomes so singular and intensified that his commitment to her is eternal and his fidelity assured. This in itself is a great gift from God."

Isobel turned serious then, indicating that it was truly a tragedy that this blessed understanding of pleasure had been lost to most. This specific path to finding God through sacred union was known now only to a few, and the changing times would continue to threaten these secrets until they were very nearly eliminated. Even the public and open teachings, as those within the Gospel of Matthew, chapter nineteen, "No more were they two, but of one flesh. And what God has put together, let no man separate," had been diluted in interpretation to eradicate the truly sensual nature of the beautiful gift that Jesus was attempting to impart.

Pope Gregory VII was not a shallow man. His attraction to Matilda was not limited to her beauty, her power, and all that she had to offer him as a result of those things in combination. He was deeply and wholly in love with a woman whom he believed had been created for him by God; he had come to understand the nature of *hieros-gamos* as a truly religious experience during his days and nights with the glorious countess. He had found God with this woman in a way that he had never dreamed possible through any of his studies. Further, he was now more than ever fascinated to the point of obsession with all these original teachings of early Christianity. He had become pope as a reformer, dedicated to returning the Church to a sacred and spiritual office, where the teachings of Christ were centric above all. That Matilda represented such an immense challenge to what that might mean in truth was both important and intriguing, nearly beyond measure.

"I did not become pope because I am a holy man, Tilda," he confided as they dined on their final evening at Fiano. "I became pope because I am a pragmatic man, and a savvy politician who cares about the fortunes of Rome and its Church. But I do mean it when I say that I hope to become a holy man as I hold this exalted place. And what is it that will make me holy as I sit on this throne of the apostle Peter? I would be holy by emulating Jesus Christ. And yet the more I read and study—and learn from you—the more I begin to question exactly what it means to emulate Christ.

"Is it possible, I wonder, to maintain a Church with the power and structure to influence a flock that covers all Europe and more, and yet is based entirely on these ideas of love that you have? This is quite a dilemma, because I do not think that such a thing is possible. Love knows no reason, Matilda. It knows no logic, no strategy, no law except its own. It is not something that can be controlled, administered, or passed into law. It cannot be taxed or profited from. Indeed, I have passed laws that forbid love within my own clergy, haven't I? I have forbidden priests to marry and have enforced laws of celibacy. And yet those same laws protect elements of the Church that require preservation, they protect the Church as an institution, which is something I am sworn to do. I must stand by those laws as necessary for the higher good.

"But what does it mean if this higher good that I am protecting is against the very nature of what our Lord wanted us to understand? These are the trials that we face, trials of faith and free will. I will need you at my side, as often as possible, to be my partner in navigating these uncharted waters. God has put us both in this place, and he has put us together. We have the opportunity to change history, to ensure that the Church remains strong and that our people keep Christ at the center of their lives. What form this takes may not be what you envision, it may not be possible to ever introduce this Way of yours to the world as we know it. But we will do what we can to protect the Way as it exists. And all the while, we will explore this idea of love."

Matilda challenged him, as she would every day of their lives together. "I dare say that as you become more familiar with the simple and awesome power that is the Way of Love, you will feel differently.

The Way is for everyone, Gregory, just as the kingdom of God is for everyone. Rich and poor, men and women, humble and noble. It is strong enough to endure anything. Strong enough to bring peace to the world."

Gregory considered this idea as the pragmatic politician struggled with the newly awakened poet within him. "Love. It is surprisingly complicated, particularly in matters of state. It is troubling. It is beautiful. But most of all, it is something I have no precedent for.

"And thus I must ask you before you depart for Tuscany in the morning: will you swear to stand by me, Matilda? To help me understand just how we are to preserve the Church in a way that will not weaken it against the great threats that we face each day, and yet preserve these traditions that you know to be true to the best of our ability?"

She took his hands across the table and held them in her own as she replied to him very simply, with the vow she would never break: "*Semper.* Always."

Rome
present day

Maureen and Bérenger strolled slowly through the church of San Pietro in Vincola, hand in hand. His arrival in Rome had surprised her. But once Maureen understood that he had gone first to reconcile with Peter, before even letting her know that he was here, she felt tremendous relief. It was the action of a real man—an action that revealed humility and accountability.

She had had dinner with him the previous night, and in the space of those two hours had filled him in on what she had discovered about Matilda thus far from her autobiographical documents. She also made him aware of the man in the hooded sweatshirt who had been watching her window.

"I ran up to your room, but you weren't in. By the time I was back in my own, he was gone."

Bérenger listened closely, concerned. "Well, you aren't going anywhere in Rome again without at least one of us with you at all times."

During the course of their meal, Maureen allowed herself to remember all the reasons that she adored him. Speaking to him was like a homecoming. He understood her, he was like her, and he made her feel as if she was home. And now he had decreed himself her official Rottweiler while in Rome. When Maureen wanted to visit locales that were important in Matilda's history, Bérenger was insistent on accompanying her. Maureen was enjoying his company immensely.

As they walked through the Church of Peter in Chains, Maureen repeated the story of Matilda and Gregory's first meeting to him.

"It was absolutely love at first sight, on both sides and by all accounts."

Bérenger nodded. "Was it? What causes love at first sight? Is it more accurate to say that it is love at . . . recognition? Do we fall for someone so quickly and so hard because we are recognizing that this person is someone we have loved before and are destined to love again? Do we feel instant connection or attraction to someone because on some level we know that they represent another piece of our own soul?"

Maureen thought about it as they walked through the expanse of the church, which was crowded with tourists, most of whom hovered around the horned statue of Moses created by Michelangelo. They dropped euro coins into the light box with a loud clink, so that the masterpiece in marble would be illuminated for a few minutes of enhanced viewing. This building had changed dramatically since the day of Gregory's impromptu election, having gone through a major renovation in the Renaissance and a number of other alterations throughout the centuries.

"Maybe. Perhaps this is another aspect of 'The time returns.' "

"Go on."

"Well, these couples of which they speak in the Order. Veronica and Praetorus, are they returning in the model of other great couples who were teachers? Easa and Magdalene? Are they the return of Solomon and Sheba in their own time? It appears that Matilda believed that she and Gregory were the return of Solomon and Sheba. Is that literal, or were they reliving an archetype? An archetype that is available to all who are lucky enough to find that kind of connection with another? I don't know, I'm struggling with this concept. With all of these concepts."

He considered her for a moment. Interesting, that so many humans would find this idea of eternal love unimaginable, and yet it seemed so natural and simple to him. And unspeakably beautiful. He said nothing, reserving his deeper thoughts for when she was ready. Patience was the virtue he needed to cultivate to keep this unicorn in the garden of her own free will.

They waited in a short line to view the relics for which the church was named, the large linked chains that were preserved in a gold and glass reliquary. Whether or not they were the actual chains that shackled Saint Peter was anybody's guess, but there was a strange aura to them, a mystical patina that can only occur on an object that has been revered for so many centuries.

They emerged from the church a few minutes later, into the amber sunlight of the fading Roman afternoon. As they climbed carefully down the marble stairs toward the street, it was Maureen who chose to reintroduce the subject as they walked. "What happens when it's one-sided?"

"What do you mean?"

"Well, in this case, we see that Matilda and Gregory both recognized the connection, they both knew it instantaneously. Does it always happen that way, in these cases of predestined love? Or is there sometimes a partner who figures it out first?"

Bérenger didn't need time to consider his answer. "I think that it often happens in such a way, where one person recognizes the connection before the other, maybe even long before. I think it becomes a matter of patience, perhaps even the greatest test of that love."

They walked slowly through the narrow streets of the *centro storico*, engrossed in the conversation and all that it meant to them. Maureen responded, "It must be so hard for the partner who recognizes it when the other is in the dark. It's as if one is awake, and the other is asleep."

"No doubt. Ignorance is bliss, as they say. And it truly is, if you think about it. When we are ignorant, we can go through life blithely believing that we control our own destiny. But when we become enlightened, when we understand that our destiny is to surrender to God's will, well then . . . it is not always so blissful, is it? And perhaps God's will is for us to be terribly patient with our sleeping beloved, so that we can gently awaken her. Or him."

Maureen stopped.

"What's wrong?" Bérenger was immediately concerned that he had gone too far, made an allusion that was too personal. But that wasn't what had stopped her. He breathed with relief as she began speaking in that excited way she had when elements of a puzzle began to come together for her.

"What you just said there. Gently awaken her. It's like the fairy tales, isn't it? Sleeping Beauty is awakened, Snow White is awakened, both from something called 'the sleeping death.' How are they awakened? How?"

"By a kiss."

"By *true love's kiss*. It is very specific in the oldest versions of these legends, that the princess is awakened by true love's kiss. Not just any kiss. A sacred one. Perhaps one that blends the life forces of the beloveds together, one that represents the coming together of the souls. And the 'sleeping death'? It represents the soul before it is enlightened."

Bérenger was equally excited by this line of thinking and joined in. "Therefore, allegory. A sacred teaching that had to be hidden in plain sight, yet taught with great power so as never to be lost."

Maureen nodded, considering before continuing. "And taught in a way that this most critical concept could be introduced to children. Do you think it's possible? You're the one who has taught me that the connections never stop, that there is no end to the places where we will find the truth hiding in plain sight if we open our eyes. Could it be that even our most beloved children's stories were created to contain the secrets of the Book of Love? That every time we tell one of these stories we are honoring the original teachings of Jesus? Perhaps even dating all the way back, thousands of years, to the coming together of Solomon and Sheba?"

"You are a genius, my dear. This is an aspect that has certainly never occurred to me. And yet we know that the Cathar cultures began instructing their children very early in their development. We have seen where Isobel taught Matilda important concepts this way. Perhaps that was the original purpose of bedtime stories. To educate our children as much as to inspire their imaginations. Bedtime stories can be digested in the sleep, processed through the subconscious mind in the dream state. It's really quite a fantastic concept."

Maureen wasn't finished with the train of thought. "And there are male versions of the legend, too. Like in the Frog Prince. The princess has faith that this is her beloved, despite the fact that he appears to be a wart-infested toad. She sees through the physical illusion, she *recognizes* him, and subsequently turns him physically into the prince that he has always had the potential to be. She transforms him into a real prince, with a kiss of true love. In Beauty and the Beast, Belle recognizes the prince beneath the monster and saves his life as he is dying for love—with her kiss. Of course."

"Of course." Bérenger was aching to tell her one of the great secrets that she was yet to discover. That there was a reason that the beloved was always a prince in these stories. But she was not ready to know everything yet. He was not going to rush her. He decided to lay the groundwork for future discussions.

"You're onto something else, I think."

"What's that?"

"That there is a male version of the story, just as there is a female version. There is always balance where there is truth. If there is a legend or a prophecy about a woman, there is an equivalent about a man.

That's alchemy. It's also physics. The coming together of opposites. For every action there is an equal and opposite reaction. It's as much Isaac Newton as it is Mary Magdalene. Cerebral and emotional, earth and water, masculine and feminine, conscious and subconscious."

"Prince and frog." She smiled at him now, in a way that he had seen very rarely—with an unguarded happiness and light, and perhaps something more. He was desperate to kiss her right there, in the middle of the Roman street, but restrained himself. They were coming to a new understanding regarding the sanctity of what had once been viewed as a simple action, a reflex meeting of the lips. There was no such thing as a basic kiss for them anymore. He would wait until the time was perfect, until they were both committed to what it would truly mean to find union in the sharing of life force and breath.

Until then, he would simply enjoy his time with her. He realized that, in spite of the emotional challenges that would confront them in their coming together, they were far more fortunate than many of the other preordained couples who preceded them in history.

At the very least, he wasn't the pope. And she wasn't married to a treacherous hunchback. It was, comparatively, a promising place to begin.

Vatican City
present day

FATHER GIROLAMO looked over the list. It was incomplete. He was missing a number of women who fit the criteria and he would have to go back through his notes. But he had to admit that his aging memory was beginning to fail him. There was a time when he could have rattled these off by rote, but with each day that was harder and harder to accomplish. It didn't matter; they would all be in the records with necessary details, including their true birthdates and the often tragic ways that these women, many of them celebrated as saints and martyrs, had met their deaths.

He had reached an impasse in his work and was extremely frustrated. He made this list off the top of his head, hoping that it would help him determine what the next step would be. They were in chronological order:

Sarah-Tamar—first century, year of birth and death unknown (cause of death unknown)

Margaret of Antioch—birth year unknown, died 304 (tortured and beheaded)

Lucia—born 284, died 304 (defiled in a brothel, eyes torn out, and beheaded)

Catherine of Alexandria—born 287, died 305 (tortured and beheaded)

Modesta—fourth century (beheaded, then thrown in the well in Chartres)

Barbara—born and died early fourth century (beheaded). Apocryphal?

Ursula—born and died in fourth century. Massacred along with a thousand virgins. Apocryphal?

Godelieve of Flanders—born 1046? died 1070 (strangled, then drowned in well)

Matilda of Tuscany—born 1046, died 1115 (of complications from gout)

Catherine of Siena—born 1347, died 1380 (of a stroke at age 33)

Jeanne d'Arc—born 1412, died 1431 (raped and burned alive)

Lucrezia Donati—born 1455? died? (of natural causes)

Giovanna Albizzi—born 1465? died 1489? (of complications from childbirth)

Teresa of Ávila—born 1515, died 1582 (of unknown illness)

Germaine of Pibrac—born 1579, died 1601 (poisoned)

Margherita Luti (La Fornarina)—sixteenth century, exact dates unknown (poisoned?)

Lucia Santos—born 1907, died 1995 (of natural causes)

Satisfied that it at least gave him a place to start, he added the final name. This most recent woman was special, in that she had accomplished what none of the others had been able to do, and he hoped to understand how and why.

Maureen Paschal

Perhaps the past wasn't the key after all. Maybe everything he needed was right here in Rome, right now.

CHAPTER TWELVE

*M*atilda was back in Rome, happier than she had ever been to be with her beloved. They had just completed the very successful second synod of Gregory's papacy, where his Dictates of the Pope were introduced to the world. The dictates were the result of their days and nights together, a passion project of two souls who were determined to reform the Church and protect both its structure and spirit from its most dangerous enemies.

The document was unlike anything that had ever been released from the throne of Saint Peter. It was radical, bold, and brilliantly constructed. Essentially, Pope Gregory VII dared to liberate the Church and all its faithful from allegiance to any monarch or secular leader anywhere in the Christian world. The Church was declared to be the sole arbiter of justice on earth, and within that justice all people were created equal under God. The dictates specified that this law of equality as affirmed by Jesus Christ applied to everyone, including women and slaves, and even the king. No person was better or worse than another; no person had more or less value under God. It was the first document of its kind to ever express human equality across gender and economic boundaries. It was absolutely revolutionary.

Matilda's influences within the dictates were blatantly obvious, for those with eyes to see.

In this new world of equality under God, feudalism, the social and economic structure that the entire European continent lived by, was essentially dead. The pope was now the sole authority of justice in the world. And to solidify the strength of the Church under its divinely selected defender, the dictates declared that the pope was infallible. Rome was the center of the civilized world and God was the only ruler. And in God's name, the pope would carry out all justice, as well as the dispensation of wealth and power that emanated from the Church.

It was outrageous. The Dictates of the Pope constituted a revolution unlike any that had been witnessed in history. It separated Rome, as the sole representative of God's will, from all secular influence and attempted to disempower the majority of European temporal rulers, Henry being chief among them. It put Rome and the papacy at the center of the universe as completely omnipotent.

But Gregory, who appeared to thrive on the controversy, wasn't finished. There had been whisperings about his relationship with the exquisite countess of Canossa, and indeed she was greatly disliked by the chief families in Rome, who viewed her as an outsider of dangerous influence. Gregory and Matilda's supporters condemned the rumors as political blackmail and jealousy, and for the moment this position was generally accepted by the Roman populace, who were still inclined to support the charismatic Gregory. However, the pope was determined to dispel these murmurings before they could develop into something more dangerous to him and his beloved. Utilizing the astute political perspective that the best defensive strategy is an offensive strategy, Gregory issued severe dictates concerning clerical sexuality as a supplement to original laws he had imposed under Nicholas II. He demanded that any priest who violated the laws of celibacy was to be immediately relieved of his duties, and he called upon his bishops to preach the necessity of celibacy and an unblemished body and soul for all members of the clergy. And he strengthened the laws that forbade any priest to find himself in a position that could even potentially leave him alone with a woman.

The issue of pristine behavior for priests was emphasized with such force that it became an impossibility for anyone to claim that the pope himself was anything but celibate. Surely no man was audacious enough to emphasize so strict a law with such zeal, and then violate it himself. All whisperings of inappropriate conduct with Matilda ceased abruptly under such dictates. Such a thing was simply not possible.

But what the people of Europe forgot in the face of these new laws was that Gregory VII was not just a man. Nor was he just any priest. He was the pope. And as such, he was no longer subject to any law except God's. He was, by rule of his own dictates—and those of the woman he loved and shared his bed with—infallible.

❀

"Henry's vows mean nothing! He is a king without honor, which is no king at all."

Matilda was pacing the halls of the Isola Tiberina, the fortified house and watchtower on the edge of the Tiber that had become her headquarters when she visited Gregory for prolonged periods in Rome. Her tirade was in response to word that Henry had proved traitorous in his sworn allegiance to Pope Gregory. He and his German troops, with no small amount of assistance from Lorraine, had defeated the Saxons on June 9, 1075, at the battle of Hohenberg, after years of war. The decisive victory and the subsequent support that the king was receiving in the northern territories emboldened his pride and ambition, and Henry took decisive action against Gregory. He had been seething for the three months since the papal dictates, as had his bishops in Germany and Lombardy. To their minds, this new pope was an upstart and a dangerous one. How dare any man claim supremacy over the king himself?

Henry had been forced to bide his time, but the winds of power were blowing back in the direction of Germany. To make his point, he reinstated the excommunicated bishops, who paid him huge tribute for doing so. Bishop Teobaldo, the most radically rebellious against Gregory's reforms, was now installed as the archbishop of Milan, positioning Lombardy in complete opposition to the papacy. These were flagrant acts by Henry, of both simony and lay investiture, intentional violations of everything that Gregory stood for. War had been officially declared.

Conn watched Matilda pace but held his seat. They would need to return to Tuscany immediately under this new threat. He needed her to see that. Leaving Rome and Gregory was never an easy thing for her, but it was necessary.

"Matilda, Henry is not our only problem. Godfrey has sent another letter, demanding his rights as the duke of Tuscany, not only to his lands but also to his marital rights as your husband. Henry has offered to back him with military might if needed, to take both you and Tuscany. Your recent actions in Montecatini have driven the hunchback to the brink, it seems. Along with the other usual things."

In the previous month, Matilda had deeded her prized property in Montecatini in the name of Anselmo of Lucca, as a gift to the Order. These were her lands, inherited from Bonifacio, and as far as she was concerned she was entitled to give them as freely as she pleased. However, in the eyes of the laws implemented by the German king, Godfrey had the sole right to administer the region of Tuscany. The pope, of course, had upheld Matilda's rights to dispense with her lands as she wished and refused to entertain Godfrey's protest.

Godfrey of Lorraine was not entirely stupid, for all his odious flaws. He was well aware of the rumors that surrounded his wife's extremely close relationship with Gregory, and was unutterably tormented by them. Indeed, while on the Saxon campaign, even the king made lascivious comments concerning the demonic red-haired temptress who had corrupted no less than the pope himself. The recent outrage of Montecatini caused Godfrey's sanity, always tightly stretched where his wife was concerned, to snap.

"I am not afraid of him, Conn. I shall take his letter to Gregory to-night and gain advice on how to handle him."

Conn was exasperated. "There's no time. We have to leave today. Now. If the hunchback arrives in Tuscany and you are not there to defend it, there is no telling what will happen."

"Arduino is there, as is my mother."

"They are not Tuscany. You are. Your people will need to see you among them as these rumors begin to spread."

"What rumors? The usual? No one believes those anymore. Gregory put an end to that."

The big man stood up now and took a deep breath. "Matilda, Godfrey and his evil spawn of a king are out to destroy you. You have to know that and understand it. They have begun a campaign against you and your reputation. I wished to spare you this, because I know you so well. And I know that in spite of all your apparent strength, such things wound you to your core."

Matilda stopped pacing, steeling herself for the rest. "Go on."

"There is a rumor out of Lorraine that you murdered your child. There are several, actually, as you know what occurs when rumors spread. They're all ridiculous, of course—superstitious babble from the ignorant. But they're also dangerous. One says that you sacrificed her on an altar to the devil in order to gain such extreme power and wealth. There's more where that one came from, but suffice it to say that it has something to do with you and the devil having an indecent relationship, in quite graphic detail, no less. The other is that you suffocated her at her birth in front of your husband to frighten him into submission to you, also with the help of the devil. I believe that is the one that Godfrey himself is supporting to garner sympathy. The people of Lorraine are crying for your blood as a witch."

She sat down slowly, sick with what she was hearing. Conn was right. Such hateful rumors did cut her to the core. She saw them for what they were, but they still hurt her terribly. Why had God given her such responsibility, even such skill as a warrior, but not more resistance to emotional pain? She would suffer in silence over these things all her life, long into the dark nights where sleep, more often than not, did not come for her.

Conn spoke with all his Celtic passion now, knowing how to rally her when she was feeling defeated—by taking the focus off her personal circumstances and causing her to embrace a greater cause of justice. "It is a war of propaganda, Matilda. And it has been the scourge of humanity for too long, to damage a woman's name in order to diminish her. A dirty war. Powerful women have always threatened weak-willed men. You must fight this as Boudicca did. You must take up her war cry."

Matilda looked up at him, not quite possessed of her usual energetic and fearless nature but struggling to get through what she had to do now. She stood up to join him and held out her hand to him. "The Truth Against the World?"

He took it, and embraced her. "That's my girl. The Truth Against the World. Come on then, little sister, we're off to Tuscany to hunt for hunchbacks and German vipers."

❁

On December 8, 1075, Pope Gregory VII fired a salvo at King Henry IV. In honor of the feast day of the Immaculate Conception, he was calling Henry out on his lies and his crimes, and demanding that he come clean in his behavior through apology and repentance, or risk immediate excommunication. No pope had ever excommunicated a sitting monarch, and it was an unprecedented threat in European politics.

Henry responded in the way he knew best: with violence. He enlisted the help of the Cenci family in Rome, old rivals of the Pierleoni who were easily turned by German gold. They hired mercenaries to infiltrate the holy Christmas Eve services at Santa Maria Maggiore in Rome. As they approached in the line to receive communion from the pontiff's own hand, the mercenaries broke ranks and bludgeoned the pope. They dragged a bleeding and unconscious Gregory out of the cathedral and locked him in a tower that belonged to the Cenci.

No one would ever know why Gregory was not immediately murdered by his would-be assassins. It was believed that in the haste to put such a diabolical abduction plot into play, the exact orders—what to do once they had the pope as hostage—had not been properly delineated. And no one involved wanted to have the blood of the Holy Father on his hands if that was not what the king had requested or paid for. As a result, they held him overnight until a decision could be made.

The people were outraged. The bloodshed on the altar against a pope who was still favored by the Roman populace caused a near riot on Christmas morning. The Cenci palace was stormed by a mob, led by the Pierleoni family, and Gregory was liberated while the Cenci were driven out of their city.

Pope Gregory VII returned to his primary home in the Lateran Palace. After being treated for the wounds to his head, he called for pen and ink and wrote immediately to his beloved so that she would not worry unnecessarily.

❁

Matilda rode with Conn at breakneck speed across Tuscany, toward Pisa. Her mother had taken seriously ill while handling administrative matters in Pisa, and Matilda was desperate to get to her. She prayed as she rode that her mother would be alive and conscious upon her arrival. She could not bear the thought of losing Beatrice at all, but losing her without having the opportunity to see her and speak to her again would be more than she could bear.

Matilda was relieved that Beatrice was alive, although unconscious, upon her arrival. She was told that her mother slipped in and out of consciousness based on the rise and fall of her fevers. At the moment, she was sleeping soundly, which gave Matilda time to consider the other matters that were weighing heavily on her heart.

She received the message from Gregory as she left for Pisa, the one that assured her of his safety but described in some detail his violent abduction. How desperately she wished she could go to him right now. She needed to see him and touch him, to be reassured that everything would be all right. But it wasn't possible with her mother in such a condition. She wrote him a letter, in her necessarily careful public way, expressing her love to him in terms that would not convict her if they were read by papal legates or, worse, by enemy interceptors.

> *My Most Beloved Holy Father,*
>
> *How distressed I am to hear of the pain caused to you, but how thankful I am to God for sparing his one true and chosen Apostle.*
>
> *Know that I would do anything to attend your needs in Rome, as your beloved daughter and servant, but I must remain at the side of my ailing mother. I beg you to intercede with God through your sanctified prayers on her behalf.*
>
> *Although I am separated from you by distance, know this: Neither tribulation nor anguish, hunger, peril, or persecution, nor swords nor death nor life, no principalities or virtues, nor anything of the present, will ever separate me from my love of Saint Peter.*
>
> *I remain eternally yours.*

Gregory would know exactly how to read between the lines, as the letter was couched in their personal code. She referred to herself as his beloved, and to him as hers, but in the careful phrasing that made such an open declaration safe. So while she was invoking the phrase in their Song of Songs, "My beloved is mine and I am his," the phrasing would not appear to be inappropriate to an outsider, who would see only a loving daughter of the Church sending her devotion to the Holy Father. Her fervid, final declaration of never being separated from her love of "Saint Peter" under any circumstances referred to a key teaching of the Book of Love: that true beloveds are never separated by anything of this world or time, because their souls are bound together for eternity.

Upon receiving Matilda's passionate letter, a morose and tormented

Gregory sent another of his own. Perhaps his recent head injury had caused him to be careless or perhaps he had simply tired of the pretense, but as he wrote to his beloved, he allowed himself in this one instance to forget that he was the pope and that she was married to the duke of Lorraine. He wrote a beautiful and passionate letter, one in which he indicated that he wished they could both abandon their current responsibilities and run away together to a place where they would not be under constant scrutiny. He closed the letter with the lines from the Song that would haunt them both over the next year, words that could condemn them both in the wrong hands:

I will wait in pain until I see you in the flesh, my perfect one, my dove, until you open to me again, knowing that it is all too fleeting. Until we can be together in eternity, where you will be forever at my side in the eyes of our Lord, I await you.

Pope Gregory VII was careful to screen his messengers, particularly those who carried his correspondence to Tuscany. What he could not know was that his most trusted messenger would ride into a trap laid by the duke of Lorraine, his innocent throat sliced for the price of a single slip of paper.

The pope's passionate letter to his eternal love would never reach her hands. It would, however, reach the hands of her husband.

Conn was certain, and Matilda agreed, that Godfrey had been instrumental in the attempt to assassinate the pope, if not the mastermind himself.

"Of course it was Godfrey. It was a failure, wasn't it?" Matilda spat her anger and frustration. "But thanks to God that it was a failure, Conn. What would I have done? To lose Gregory and my mother at one time? I would not survive such sorrow."

"But it did not happen that way, Matilda. Gregory is safe. God takes care of his own."

She nodded, too overwhelmed by the current circumstances to realize that Conn had just quoted from the teachings of the Order. Because in spite of Gregory's rescue and the obvious indicators that pointed to the king and his duke, Henry had not backed down. He did not have enough shame to beg forgiveness for attempted assassination. Instead, he declared that the royal court of Germany intended to put the pope on trial and prove to the rulers in Europe that Gregory must be deposed as a criminal. A trial date was set, for January 24, 1076, and nobles from all over Europe were invited to attend in the German city of Worms, where they were to have their revenge upon the upstart pope who would call himself the sole ruler of the world.

The Synod of Worms
Germany
January 24, 1076

THE BISHOPS of Germany had spoken.

Gregory VII was accused of multiple crimes against the people of Europe and their rightful king, and petitions had been hastily assembled and signed to give legal support to his guilt. They utilized Gregory's own law as the key piece of evidence against him. He had stolen the throne of Saint Peter in an illegal election; he had not been chosen by the College of Cardinals and had violated his own election decree. He was condemned for his arrogance in attempting to strip the bishops of their rights and influence and to consecrate himself as the sole holder of all sacred power.

In the middle of a heated presentation of evidence in the presence of the king, a red-faced, hunchbacked Godfrey, the duke of Lorraine, burst through the door, waving a document in his clenched fist.

"I wish to add another charge against this demon who would deceive all Europe and call himself the pope."

Henry IV was perched on his throne and feeling very full of himself. He enjoyed this kind of chaos and high drama, and he knew what Godfrey was about to introduce was going to be the sweetest and most succulent piece of evidence that any of them had thus far.

"Come forward, my good duke. You have a personal complaint against the papal usurper, I am told."

"I do, Your Grace."

"By all means, state your accusation before this council."

"I wish to accuse this man of adultery." The hunchback's tormented voice rose with his outrage, echoing off the stone walls of the council chamber. It reached a crescendo with his final, emphatic statement. "With my wife."

The council chamber burst into immediate chaos. While the rumors of Gregory's relationship with Matilda were known by all in attendance, no one had anticipated a formal charge of adultery brought against them by the woman's own husband.

"And what proof do you have of this terrible injustice against you, my lord Godfrey?"

Godfrey thrust the document forward. "This letter, written in the false pope's own hand, was sent to my wife on Saint Stephen's Day. It is filled with the most debased language and confirms their wicked and lustful alliance."

Henry licked his lips in anticipation as he gave the command. "Read it."

Godfrey squirmed with discomfort. It was one thing to admit to being cuckolded before all his peers; it was yet another to compound the humiliation by reading the correspondence of his wife's lover aloud to the court. "I would prefer to enter it into evidence and allow the council members to read it of their own accord."

The king reached out his hand to snatch the letter from the hunchback. "Then I will read it."

Henry took great pleasure in reading the private correspondence of Gregory and Matilda to the council. He stopped before one sentence, relishing it a bit before reading it with the most lecherous inflection,

" 'I will wait in pain until I see you in the flesh, my perfect one, my dove, until you open to me again.' "

There was silence in the chamber until the king broke it. "Well, my lord Godfrey. I am sorry that you have been confronted with the unfortunate truth that your wife is a whore, but most grateful that you have come forward with this piece of evidence for the benefit of all Europe. Is it agreed by all here that this letter, in combination with the accounts that many of us have been given of the unholy sexual liaisons between the false pope and this man's harlot of a wife, provide ample proof of criminal behavior? If there are no objections, I hereby put into the official decree that both Pope Gregory VII and Matilda, Countess of Canossa, are charged with adultery."

The formal decree that was delivered to Gregory read:

> Thou hast filled the whole Church with the odor of a most serious charge, that of too familiar living together with a woman, who is another man's wife.

Henry did not stop there. He had several scores to settle, and he drove his misogynistic point home with a condemnation of Gregory's esteem for women in general:

> It is our understanding, and our shame for you and the Church, that all your decrees have been set into motion by women, so that the entire Church is now administered by women.

That Gregory had frequently held meetings with not only Matilda but also her wise and experienced mother had been a source of ire for a number of churchmen who believed with grave intensity that the apostle Paul had never been more divinely inspired than when he wrote his first letter to Timothy, the one that reads, "I suffer not a woman to teach, nor to hold authority over a man, but to suffer in silence." Henry's estranged mother, now his bitterest enemy, had also become an adviser and ally to Gregory. Henry referred to these women as "Gregory's unholy trinity," and it was ultimately the introduction of this evidence, that the pope was constantly influenced by the advice of women, that swayed the remaining bishops into signing the decree of deposition. The counsel of women in matters of state was deemed far more scandalous and unforgivable than adultery.

Henry signed off on all the accusations, as well as the statement decreeing that Gregory had been deposed as pope and was required to step down with what would become an infamous signature:

> *I am Henry, king not by usurpation, but by the pious ordination of God, to Ildebrando Pierleoni, no longer pope but a false monk. I am Henry, king by the grace of God, and with all of my bishops, say to you, come down, come down, and be damned throughout the ages.*

✸

Ildebrando Pierleoni did not become the most powerful pope thus far in history by succumbing to the will of such men. He knew what was brewing in Worms but chose to ignore it until the German bishops made their formal presentation of the charges. They chose to do this at the third synod of his papacy, in February of 1076, which was attended by two hundred bishops and assorted nobles from all over France and Italy. None of the German bishops had the courage or audacity to attend and present such accusations in person. It fell upon an ill-equipped priest who had likely drawn the short straw to present the letter to the pope. He informed the council coarsely, "You are ordered by the king and bishops to leave this throne of which you are not worthy!"

Gregory, so experienced in the theater of the papacy, expressed his sympathy for the poor man who had obviously been terribly misinformed and carried the unfortunate fate of making such ludicrous pronouncements against the pope. He followed the accusations with an eloquent dissertation and graceful reading of scripture, making it clear to all in attendance that he was every bit the great leader that they believed him to be. By the end of Gregory's elegant performance, the messenger priest was reduced to a shivering heap in fear of the outrage that was turned upon him by the attendant bishops, who supported their pope without question. It was unanimously decided that there was no option except the excommunication of Henry IV, King of Germany.

The pope waited until February 22, 1076, so as to add the full weight of the date—the feast day of Saint Peter—to his proclamation:

> *I deprive King Henry, son of the emperor Henry, who has rebelled against the Church with unheard-of audacity, of the government of the kingdoms of Germany and Italy and I release all Christians from any allegiance they have sworn to him, and I further forbid anyone to serve him as king.*

For the first time in history, a formal sentence of anathema had been enforced upon a reigning and legally ordained monarch. It sent shock waves throughout the Christian world. Now it was a waiting game to see who had the greater power: the king who had deposed the pope, or the pope who had excommunicated the king. And there was an interesting and most critical factor in the deciding of the outcome: the land and territories that separated these two bitterest of enemies and would determine strategic military victory, while technically the holdings of Duke Godfrey of Lorraine, were entirely controlled by Matilda of Tuscany.

Pisa
February 1076

As with all outrages imposed upon her by Godfrey the Hunchback, Matilda ignored the charges of adultery that came out of the Synod of Worms. She knew that Gregory in his wisdom had made such an elaborate and dramatic show of Henry's excommunication for a number of reasons, chief among them to distract attention from the adultery charges against her. So for the moment he had bought her time, which she needed with her dying mother. Matilda was also focused on keeping her armies intact in the event that Henry attempted to cross the Alps into Italy and march through her lands to get to Rome. She would never allow that to happen, but the German army was in a swelled state and would be difficult to defeat if it came after her with all its might. She had sent messengers to her commander in chief Arduino, who was in Canossa, but was confident that he had the situation well in hand, as he always did.

In spite of her confidence and bravado, Matilda was worried and had stayed up for most of the night with Conn discussing strategy. There were rumblings that Godfrey was heading back to Lorraine to gather his troops and march on Tuscany, intent on reclaiming his titles with a vengeance. Because Matilda now faced a formal and evidenced adultery charge, brought against her by the king himself, her husband had the legal right to lock her in a convent at his pleasure. He would eliminate her influence as he allowed Henry's troops free access to the Apennine passes, on his way to capture Rome and install his own man on the throne of Saint Peter.

Matilda went out for a walk, hoping to clear her head in the chill winter air after spending the early morning with her mother. She had fed Beatrice with a few sips of broth and wiped her brow with a soft cloth in those few moments of moderate strength. But the efforts, small as they were, exhausted Beatrice, and she had gone back to sleep.

Matilda stopped when she saw Conn securing a pack to his horse, surrounded by a small retinue of men. Not just any men. These were nicknamed "the Incorrigibles" and were the most hardened of the guard, those with whom Matilda was most uncomfortable. She had strong codes of conduct for her armies and enforced them without compromise. She would not put up with pillaging or wholesale slaughter in any battle, and the rules of war were to be observed at all times. These men who surrounded Conn at the moment were some she had censured and even threatened to release for their excessively violent behavior. The Celtic giant had stopped her before she could alienate them. For all their flaws, they were loyal to her, just as their fathers had been loyal to Bonifacio. And sometimes, he explained patiently, it was necessary to have men this hard in an army. Every commander needed a few incorrigibles. Conn promised that he would be responsible for their conduct and would ensure that they never took pillage or ravaged innocents in any war circumstance or otherwise. Matilda had agreed, reluctantly. But she also knew that she had to give her friend free rein to do his duty and to reinforce her absolute trust in his judgment.

When she could stand it no longer, she approached him.

"Where are you going?"

His answer was clipped as he strapped a double-sided axe to his favored warhorse. This was clearly not a messenger's mission. "I have business to take care of."

"What kind of business?"

"My business."

He wouldn't budge. Neither would she. Finally Conn broke the stalemate. "How is your good mother this morning?"

She dropped a satirical curtsy. "The same, but many thanks to you for your kindness in asking after my mother's welfare, good sir." She snapped at him now. "Don't change the subject. I need to know, Conn."

"No, you don't. And please don't ask me again. If you do not ask me, I do not tell you. If I do not tell you, you do not know. Understand?"

"I understand the manner of men you are taking with you."

"I am taking loyal men who have nothing to lose and do not know what fear looks like."

She was exasperated so decided to play to his protective nature. "You're scaring me."

He didn't buy it. "Nothing scares you."

"You do, right now."

He turned to her and put his hands on her shoulders. "Tilda, I am the one person on earth you will never have to fear. My sole mission under God is to protect you, against all threats and against all harm. Do you trust me to do that?"

She nodded solemnly. "Of course."

"Then pray for my safe return, little sister. And stay out of trouble until I come back to you." He kissed the top of her head and ruffled her hair the way he had always done since she was a teenager.

Matilda watched him go, followed by the ragtag Incorrigibles, all of whom had multiple weapons hanging from their mounts. She shook her head with trepidation. These men were capable of anything.

Antwerp, Belgium
February 26, 1076

CONN'S MEN rode hard across the Alps, galloping north to reach Flanders in time to intercept the soldiers from Lorraine. Godfrey and his own troops were returning to the palace of Verdun on the heels of his victorious adultery accusation at Worms. The Incorrigibles shadowed them now, riding deeper in the forest so as not to be seen by Godfrey's entourage. When the Lorraine group had settled to make camp for the evening, Conn's warriors did the same, close by but well secluded by the density of the trees.

They had a plan to attack at first light, making it appear that the duke had been the unwitting victim of highway robbers. It was not exactly honorable combat, to ambush sleepy soldiers who were completely unprepared, Conn had to admit. But the stakes were so high where Tuscany was concerned, with Matilda's safety specifically at stake, that he had ruled out the necessity of playing fair. This was why he could not allow Matilda to know; she would have never allowed such a plan to be carried out. Assassination was not in her. For all her strength, she was more of a mystic than a warrior. He knew that battle made her ill for days afterwards and gave her nightmares, although it was a secret observed only by those in her immediate circle. She fought in real combat because she had to, not because she enjoyed it.

They were outnumbered by the Lorraine soldiers, and at a disadvantage in terms of territory: Godfrey's crew would know the region well, but the Tuscans were strangers. Further, it was February and bloody cold, which the warm-blooded Italians found very hard to take. Cold was akin to pain for them, and they did not fight as well with frozen fingers, whereas the Germans were used to this ungodly ice. Conn needed a plan that leveled the battlefield and reduced his risks. This is what he had come up with, and he prayed it would work.

It had not been difficult to convince any of the Incorrigibles to accompany Conn on this mission, particularly after he told them in some detail—much of it fabricated for dramatic effect—about the horrific and depraved sexual practices that the hunchback inflicted upon their divine and perfect countess against her will. The Incorrigibles had been horrified that Godfrey had ever dared to touch Matilda in that way and immediately agreed to seek their revenge on the monster.

Umberto, the eldest of the band, who had had his mercenary start as an orphaned teenager on Bonifacio's original campaign against piracy, was positioned to keep watch on the duke's camp during the frozen night. Umberto wasn't the most savory character, but he had in his own way a type of affection for Bonifacio's little girl, and like all these men held a peculiar code of honor. He hated the hunchback, as most of Matilda's men did, because of the threat he posed to their girl and because he regarded the people of Tuscany as little more than objects who existed for the whims of the German king. At the moment, he hated him even more for living in this godforsaken frozen hell that had turned his toes to ice in his boots.

It was in this state of agitation that Umberto the Incorrigible witnessed movement in the Lorraine camp. He grabbed his sword, the long, sharp one with the double blade, and he moved with the stealth of a forest creature to get a closer look.

He could not believe his eyes. Godfrey himself was moving toward him. Had the hunchback seen him? No. The man was clearly unarmed. What was he . . . ? Ah, of course. What other reason would any man risk freezing cold in the middle of the forest in the pitch dark? The call of nature. Godfrey had to relieve himself.

Umberto paused for a moment. He had learned many things from the great Bonifacio, but one of them was this: when you are outnumbered, you must take any advantage that is put in your path. Place survival above all, and the result will most often justify the method. He had also learned something else from Bonifacio: anyone who threatened his little girl had to be eliminated.

Fueled by Conn's stories of the hunchback's depravity, Umberto made the snap decision that this man did not deserve a noble end. He whispered "for Bonifacio and Matilda" as he charged the hunchback from behind, plunging his double edged sword into Godfrey of Lorraine's buttocks. The blade tore into the hunchback's intestines, giving him neither the time nor the ability to scream. Umberto withdrew his bloody sword and ran back to Conn with the signal to his men to break camp and ride. He would explain later what he had done. It had not been pretty, but it had eliminated their target without risking any of their own men in open combat.

The hunchback languished in excruciating pain for several days before dying. His horrific execution, unanticipated and unplanned as it was, had an interesting and beneficial side effect for Matilda. It sent a message throughout Europe: anyone who threatened Matilda of Tuscany would be dispatched by whatever means necessary. Even the protection of the king would not be enough to save her enemies from the wrath of her defenders. The men of Italy respected the show of strength, and their support for Matilda swelled to its greatest levels, visible in terms of military might and tribute sent in her name.

For Henry IV, this was a very bad omen.

Germany
Easter 1076

THE SENTENCE of excommunication arrived on King Henry's doorstep at the beginning of Holy Week in the year of our Lord 1076. It did not come as a surprise, and the Germans had been planning their formal response to the pretender pope. There could be no backing down now that war had been declared. It would be necessary to maintain the continued attack against Gregory based on the criminal findings from the Synod at Worms for many reasons, chief among them to keep the German feudal lords aligned with Henry's strategy. Many of them were distrustful of this king and his acquisitive, narcissistic nature, to say nothing of the whispered rumors that followed him everywhere regarding his darker personal proclivities. Finally, they were by nature a superstitious people, and deposing a pope who had already been saved by God from an angry mob was cause for grave concern among many of them.

Henry's closest "spiritual adviser," Bishop William, chose to launch the first line of defense from his seat in the cathedral at Utrecht on Easter Sunday. Following the service in celebration of the risen Christ, William preached a vitriolic condemnation of the pretender who would be pope. He emphasized that God had chosen Henry as king and that this is what the people needed to cling to in their faith. If Henry was God's anointed king, then surely this pope who would call himself the ruler of the world was an imposter who had to be removed.

It was a controversial sermon, and an ill-advised one on a day as holy as Easter. For many German citizens, such vitriol on the highest holy day was unthinkable. Shocked by the behavior of their bishop, the nobles of Utrecht agreed in secret to convene an emergency council meeting the following day to discuss this current state of affairs. The meeting never occurred. The next morning, the citizens of Utrecht awoke to find that their cathedral had burned to the ground on the holiest night of the year. The cause of the fire was never determined.

The event was deemed to be a portent, sent by God to the people of Germany to reveal that they were following the wrong path in condemning his chosen pontiff.

Bishop William did not back down. He continued his invective against the pope, with the king by his side. He blamed the destruction of the cathedral on papal sympathizers who were working to create just the kind of fear that was beginning to build in Germany. Three weeks after the catastrophic fire, the bishop gave yet another impassioned speech in an attempt to rally support from other clergy around Europe. He would never know what impact that speech would have. Bishop William, perfectly healthy and robust when he retired to bed that night, died in his sleep.

King Henry IV was instantly immersed in a serious crisis. The sudden death of his chief spiritual supporter within a month of the destruction of the cathedral was just too much for the majority of his citizens. They believed what Bishop William had said—that God had spoken—but he had spoken against their king and in favor of this pope.

And this pope, Gregory VII, was ever the astute politician with miraculous timing. Wasting not a single moment, he launched a full campaign against the king's reputation. Matilda came enthusiastically to his aid. She paid homage to her heroine, Queen Boudicca, by imitating the Celtic warrior queen's canny propaganda strategy that had helped her to defeat the might of Rome a thousand years prior. Pamphlets referring to Henry's tarnished character were circulated throughout Italy and Germany.

The pope's own writings regarding Henry IV were vague, referring only to "sinister deeds," "dishonorable acts," and "unheard-of wickedness" without providing specific evidence. Because rumors of Henry's depravity stretched across Germany and northern Italy, Gregory and Matilda's strategy allowed for unlimited speculation.

The ambiguity was ruthlessly effective.

The restless German lords and vassals were sufficiently spooked by recent events, and excited by Gregory and Matilda's ingenious propaganda, to demand that the king make amends with the pope. The excommunicated monarch had been given a year from the date of the anathema to repent his wickedness and swear renewed fealty to the Holy Father. Henry scrambled to gain support, but the macabre and gruesome murder of Godfrey the Hunchback was a shadow over the German feudal lords. No one else was going to risk such a hideous fate, and certainly not for a king who just might be a monstrosity against God after all.

Pisa
April 1076

"I WAS NEVER the mother to you that Isobel was."

Beatrice croaked the words through cracked lips. She was dying, as she had been for months, slowly and painfully. But it was clear to Matilda, and to her mother, that the end was approaching more rapidly now. Both had things to say before the inevitable.

"Do not say so, Mother," Matilda admonished, wiping her brow again with a cloth dipped in cool water. "You have been my best friend and my adviser. I could have done none of these things without you." She was crying now. She had tried so hard not to cry, but she could contain it no longer.

"Just know . . ." Beatrice was struggling now. "I love you so. And . . . I am sorry for the times . . . for the times I . . . for your unhappy marriage."

Matilda nodded. She knew what a toll that decision had taken on her mother, knew that her mother had lived many years to regret so much about that terrible period of time. Beatrice did not know about the hunchback's recent execution. Matilda had decided it was best not to tell her, lest she worry that blame for it would be placed at their door.

Beatrice wandered in and out of delirium for the rest of the day, sometimes babbling, other times lucid. Late in the afternoon she startled in her bed, grabbing Matilda's hand.

"I see him, Tilda."

"Who, Mother?"

"Your father. Oh, how I loved him and love him still." She paused for a moment, lost in what she was seeing. A slow smile crossed her face. "He is proud of you. Our daughter. He watches you from his place next to God. And . . . I am going with him now." Beatrice used what was left of the strength in her body to squeeze Matilda's hand. "He loves you, Matilda. And so do I. Love . . ."

Beatrice's voice faded away on that one simple word that defined all that had mattered most in her eventful lifetime, her feelings for her beloved and for their daughter, and what they had been together as a family. Her smile broadened before she closed her eyes for a final time. Beatrice of Lorraine was lost to this world now and on her way into the next, where her one true love waited to welcome her into the arms of God, where they would be together for eternity.

CHAPTER THIRTEEN

Rome
September 1076

*M*atilda paced the bedchamber of the Isola Tiberina, the fortified tower that was her haven in Rome. She moved to the window to peer at the sun, rising over the Tiber that ran like an artery through the city and the surrounding territories. Gregory was asleep in the bed behind her, or so she thought, until he startled her with an observation.

"You are so restless, my Matilda."

Matilda slept sparely, and fitfully, which Gregory was discovering as he spent rare and precious nights with her. When awake, she was always moving. Her essential nature would not allow her to rest and had not since she was a little girl; she had too much to accomplish, too many things to think about, and what often felt like infinite responsibilities to her people and their land.

Matilda turned from her place in the window and smiled at him, an expression that was surprisingly soft and sad. "God has given me many blessings in this life. Peace is not one of them."

He nodded his understanding. "What is bothering you so much this morning?"

"Godfroi. The hunchback's nephew and namesake in Bouillon. I have word that he would press his advantage since the killing of his uncle and claim his rights as the heir to my own lands. Is there no end to what these men think they can take from me?"

"Why didn't you tell me this earlier?"

"Because I haven't seen you in months, and I did not choose to waste our first night together in strategy discussions when we had more important matters to attend to."

Gregory rose on one elbow now, considering her from the bed. They had spent a magnificent night together, and he wasn't inclined to let it end just yet. He wasn't due back at the Lateran until evening. "Do not worry about it for another minute, my love. Henry is trapped and knows it. His dukes and bishops are demanding that he make peace with me. Godfroi will not dare make such a claim without the support of the king and his bishops, which he will not have. I will send word to the bishop of Verdun this very day that he is to take control of your affairs and protect your inheritance in Lorraine. Consider it done."

Henry was in a severely weakened political condition following a meeting at Tribur, where the German nobility had convened to reinforce support for the sentence of deposition against him and to decide upon a successor to the throne. The assembled men had been unable to come to an agreement in deciding on the new king, and Henry reigned another day. However, the Tribur contingent had insisted that the sitting king make peace with the pope immediately and pledge his absolute obedience. It was declared, by Henry's own dukes and bishops, that he would forfeit the throne if he had not made appropriate reparation to the pope by February 22, the anniversary of his sentence of excommunication.

Gregory was right. His countess had nothing to fear at the moment.

The flourishing Roman sun shone through the window, highlighting Matilda's unbound hair. Gregory thought, as he often did, that she was an utterly breathtaking sight. He raised the coverlet and invited her back into bed. "Come, my dove. I will endeavor to give you the peace that you long for."

She joined him then and allowed herself to be enfolded in the warmth of his love for the remainder of the morning, and well into the afternoon.

When it was time to leave Rome, Matilda was less distressed than usual; Gregory had made a commitment to her that thrilled her to her toes and gave her something beautiful to look forward to. He had agreed to spend Christmas with her. In her beloved Lucca.

Lucca
Christmas Eve 1076

THE ANCIENT, subterranean chapel that had served as the sanctified center of the Order for a thousand years glowed in the light of several dozen beeswax candles. Pine branches and winter flowers adorned the walls, draped from the sconces and tied with ribbons. Anselmo, the esteemed bishop of Lucca, was in attendance for the ceremony. He clasped Isobel's hand in his as they took their place on the side of the altar. Gregory and Matilda stood together in the central space facing each other, joined by outstretched hands, while the Master stood behind the altar, with the Libro Rosso open to a page from the Book of Love. He read from it, although he did not need to as he knew these words by heart and had for more years than he could remember.

Gregory had spent the week studying with the Master. At times it was just the two of them; at others, Matilda joined them in preparation for what was to occur today. Gregory had devoured the teachings of the Libro Rosso, hungry to know everything about the extraordinary red book and its history. He had studied to learn and understand the particular passage that had been given to him in preparation for this day. He repeated the poem of Maximinus with conviction and passion, while looking into the eyes of his own beloved.

I have loved you before,
I love you today,
And I will love you again.
The time returns.

Tears streamed down Matilda's face as she repeated these same words to Gregory, in a voice choked into a whisper. This poem was special and sacred to her. She had recited it from the moment she could talk: with Isobel, with her friends in the Order, and even with Bonifacio. For it applied to love in all its guises: parental, familial, fraternal, and romantic. But when the poetry was spoken directly to one's most beloved, it took on a meaning that was exceptional in its impact, and in this case overwhelming.

Once the vows were completed, the Master came forward holding a braided silk rope, called a *cordeliere*, which ended on either side in elegant tassels. He gently wound the length of the soft cord around the wrists of the beloveds, tying it gently in a knot to symbolize the joining of this pair as it had been ordained by God at the dawn of time. As the Master passed his own hands in blessing over the couple's, Isobel began to sing, in her sweet, melodic voice, the French song about love that Matilda revered.

I have loved thee a long time,
I will never forget thee . . .

When Isobel sang the final lyrics, the Master untied the *cordeliere* to release the couple. He then invited the two to exchange the traditional nuptial gifts, small gilded mirrors, while reciting one of their sacred teachings.

"In your reflection, you will find what you seek. As you two become One, you will find God reflected in the eyes of your beloved, and your beloved reflected in your own eyes."

The Master concluded the ceremony with the beautiful words from the Book of Love, those that are also included in the Gospel of Matthew. "For no longer are you two, but you are one in spirit and in flesh. And what God has put together, let no man separate."

He turned to Gregory. "The bridegroom may now gift the bride with the *nashakh*, the sacred kiss that blends together the spirits in union."

Gregory closed the distance between himself and his beloved, wrapping Matilda in his arms and pulling her tightly against him. There were tears in his own eyes now. In the sacred and hidden space of this ancient chamber where the true words of the Lord had been protected and revered since their earliest arrival on Italian shores, the pope had just been joined in a holy and secret matrimony to the woman he loved.

The most powerful woman in Europe, perhaps even the world, was now the wife of the pontiff, a secret that would never be known to any but those in this chamber: Anselmo, Isobel, the Master, the couple themselves, and the unborn child in Matilda's womb who had been conceived in trust and consciousness when his parents had come together in Rome three months prior.

Matilda would remember it as the most beautiful time of her life. For those two weeks in Lucca, she and Gregory lived as man and wife in the privacy of the Order's property and grounds. It was the first time they had ever been together when they did not have the constant shadow of pretense and propriety over them. Here, they were completely protected from the outside world and were able to celebrate the joy of the birth of Jesus together with their brothers and sisters in the Way. Here they were able to pretend, if only for a blissful few weeks, that they were an ordinary, newlywed couple who lived in a world of freedom.

Gregory continued to study, fascinated and enchanted by the teachings of love that the Order claimed came directly from the Lord. As a man of spirit, he was able to embrace these in total. As a scholar, he found them challenging but also surprisingly logical and acceptable.

There was very little here that should be considered heretical when examined against the canonical gospels. In truth, the "heresy" of these original teachings had nothing to do with scripture and everything to do with man-made traditions of the past thousand years—including those enforced recently by his own actions. As the pope, he was now confronted by the reality that much of what the Church currently stood for was contrary to the earliest teachings of Christianity. He was daunted by what this meant to his own legacy. Most of all, he was at something of a loss as to how the teachings of love would ever hold up in a structure by which the world could be governed financially and politically. He was not sure that such a thing was possible. And yet his time with Matilda had renewed his spirit, made him believe in love. Could he dismantle the current Church structure, wipe away the years of politics and tradition, and create a new model in which love could rule? Such an idea seemed as impossible as it was beautiful.

Matilda was undaunted, however, and worked with him daily. "*Solvitur ambulando,*" she said to him, and taught him the powerful tradition of aligning oneself with the will of God by meeting with the divine in the center of the labyrinth. She read to him the legend of the Minotaur from the Libro Rosso and they discussed at length the allegorical applications of that story to their own.

After one of their working sessions where Gregory had been particularly inspired, he asked Matilda to take him into the presence of the *Volto Santo*. Anselmo secured the Cathedral of San Martino for them so that they might have it to themselves and be completely undisturbed.

Kneeling before the graceful image sculpted by the hand of Nicodemus, Gregory took a vow to preserve the Church to the best of his ability in a manner that was harmonious with the true teachings of the Way. He knew it would be a challenge, but he was determined to do so—for his love and for his Lord. He understood that he had been put in this position of unequaled authority for this purpose, and he would find a way to make it happen. It would be a difficult time and he would face enemies at every turn, but his beloved renewed her own promise to him that she would be there every step of the way, to inspire him, to fight by his side, and to love him through it all. *Semper.* Always.

Matilda had taken her very first vow in this place, at the age of six. She had kept it, spectacularly, as she would keep every promise she ever made.

At sunrise on Saint Stephen's Day, Matilda and Gregory were escorted by Anselmo, Isobel, and the Master to the portico of the Cathedral of San Martino. There the newlyweds were surprised by a gift that had been given them by members of the Order. On the western pillar of the façade, a perfect eleven-circuit labyrinth had been painted in a deep crimson color. In vertical letters, the following edict was painted alongside the sacred symbol:

HERE IS THE LABYRINTH THAT DAEDALUS THE CRETAN BUILT
AND WHICH NO ONE CAN EXIT ONCE INSIDE.
ONLY THESEUS WAS ABLE TO DO SO
THANKS TO ARIADNE'S THREAD.

In the rounded center of the labyrinth were the final words of this fable:

AND ALL FOR LOVE.

Anselmo explained that he had devised the design and the motto, with the help of the Master and Isobel, to commemorate Gregory's vows to both Matilda and the Order during this most blessed holiday season in the presence of God and each other. It was a monument to Gregory's blessed remembering, to aligning himself with the promises he once made in heaven: to himself, to the others, and to God. The allegory of Theseus and Ariadne was used, hiding their truth in a place only for those with eyes to see and ears to hear. For here Gregory was Theseus, the hero who would escape the dark labyrinth of Church corruption and politics that had been created to entrap the innocent in a web of harsh dogma and untruths. With the help of the saving thread of truth that had been provided by Matilda/Ariadne, this reborn Theseus would find the light and save his people, proving once again that the time returns.

Just over a century later, in the year 1200, a sculptor in Lucca would chisel the fading paint from the façade of San Martino's into a permanent monument to the secret wedding of Gregory and Matilda, where it would remain in perpetuity.

And all for love.

❋

Matilda and Gregory's idyllic honeymoon was cut short when a messenger arrived in Lucca. Henry IV was crossing the Alps en route to Tuscany. He was ready to make restitution to the Holy Father and pledge his loyalty and obedience to the throne of Saint Peter.

It was determined that Matilda's stronghold in Canossa, owing to its impregnable and protected position, would be the safest location for Gregory to receive Henry. They rode through Florence, where a formidable Tuscan escort met them at Conn's insistence. The Tuscans were determined to protect both their pope and their countess and would take no chances of an ambush.

While it was unlikely given Henry's weakened position that he would attempt treachery, it was never out of the question where Matilda's volatile cousin was concerned.

IF KING HENRY IV arrived in Matilda's territories expecting to be treated as royalty and admitted immediately into the presence of the pontiff, he was bitterly disappointed. Gregory VII was determined to extend the power play and emphasize his own position of absolute authority. He flatly refused to have an audience with Henry and gave no immediate indication of when, or if, he would change his mind. The king had arrived with a retinue of royals and bishops who were hoping to regain the pope's favor by begging forgiveness for their own transgressions against him at the Synod of Worms. Gregory was aware of each and every man who had stood against him—and his Matilda—and had proclaimed harshly against them all. He was not inclined to be generous to any of them.

Henry arrived with a formidable ally who refused to be ignored. Hugh, abbot of Cluny, was a leader of the German entourage, having been named Henry's godfather when the king was an infant. Gregory was unmoved by this show of strength. He was the pope, after all, and despite the fact that Hugh reigned from the influential monastic settlement of Cluny, this man was still just an abbot. It was Matilda who offered to end the stalemate, and Matilda who volunteered to conduct the initial meeting with her cousin and Abbot Hugh. Arrangements were made for a first encounter to occur at her fortress in Bianello, outside Canossa.

The countess of Tuscany was a brilliant, bold, and accomplished woman. She also had enough experience with her cousin to know that he was not to be trusted. And yet when he came to her in the manner of a supplicant, pleading with her, as his "most beloved and generous cousin" to intervene on his behalf to Gregory, she softened. For all her military experience and genius, Matilda was a student of the Way of Love and believed in the power of those teachings, including forgiveness. It was this belief that led to her first substantial argument with Gregory.

"I cannot believe that you are taken in by his false supplication." Gregory stared out the window of their bedchamber at Canossa, over the jagged, snow-covered mountains. He was trying to keep his anger in check, but he was at a loss to understand how such a brilliant woman could have been so easily duped.

Matilda, pacing the chamber, was equally agitated. "I'm not an idiot, Gregory. No one knows what and who Henry is more clearly than I."

"Then perhaps your condition has impaired your wits," he snapped. "Perhaps this is why women do not rule."

Matilda froze in her tracks. At three months pregnant, her condition was still a secret easily concealed by the voluminous skirts that were the fashion. But Gregory was aware every minute of her state, which was a constant source of worry for him. There were massive responsibilities upon his broad shoulders as pope, as a leader, and as a man. The impact was taking its toll, clearly. As he watched the blood drain from Matilda's face, Gregory immediately regretted his outburst. He moved toward her and grabbed her hands.

"I'm sorry, Tilda. That was unfair. And untrue."

She did not pull away from him, but she did not embrace him either. There were tears welling, but she refused to shed them. Instead, she made her point with a calm she did not feel.

"Perhaps if women did rule, there would be less war, less death, less destruction. Did you not glean any of this from our teachings while in Lucca? That it is the loss of the female principle in leadership, and in spirituality, that has caused so much devastation all around us? The balance was destroyed with the Fall of Man, when women were disinherited and disempowered. When all that is pure and powerful about feminine wisdom was packed away and sent into exile so that mankind would be enslaved by a need for power with nothing to temper it. Even men like you—as great as you are in heart and spirit—more often than not cannot overcome their nature. And it is the male nature to desire power and wage war when opposed or threatened. Women, conversely, have a different nature. Ours is to collaborate and mediate, to seek peace over death. And yes, as I stand here before you with our child growing in my womb, I want him, or her, to be born into a world where there is peace and prosperity. And if that makes me weak, then so be it. God's will has decreed that I be in this condition at this time and place. And it makes me want to see an end to senseless suffering."

Gregory was in too agitated a state to listen closely to what felt like a chastisement. "I am trying to protect you, and our child—and perhaps all of Italy—from Henry. And after all he has done to you through your lifetime, I simply cannot believe that you will forgive him this readily."

All remnants of calm were leaving her now. "I refuse to be a hypocrite, Gregory. Jesus teaches us forgiveness, and that is the path of the Way as I have been taught, and as I follow it. Therefore if a man professes repentance and begs forgiveness, who am I to judge whether or not he is sincere? That is for God alone to do."

"I am the pope," he snapped. "It is my obligation to act as God's intermediary on earth. And as such, I have determined that Henry's apology is insincere and unacceptable. Tell him to return to Germany and let his own people deal with him as they will. I understand that Rudolf of Swabia has been prepared to take over the throne from him if I refuse pardon. And I do."

Matilda was torn. The fiery side of her nature wanted to storm out of the room and abandon him to his arrogance. But she loved him, above all else, and she knew that it was part of her mission as his partner to help him through these spiritual challenges. And hadn't she just emphasized that female rulers were most capable of diplomacy and mediation in times of war? She took a breath and addressed him with quiet strength. "What would you like me to do, my love? I have to give Abbot Hugh an answer, and I simply will not tell him to send Henry back to Germany. What would you have him do to prove his penance?"

Gregory thought about it for a moment. His first instinct was to snap back at her that there was nothing Henry could do and that his decision was final. But he softened somewhat as he looked at her. There were dark circles under her eyes, contrasting deeply against her otherwise alabaster skin. She looked terribly fragile. This was taking a toll on her too.

"Tell Abbot Hugh that I would see Henry make a very public display of his repentance, to be witnessed by all the citizens of Canossa. I would see him take the hair shirt and kneel before the gates here in the snow, abandoning all pretense of his royalty, and begging like the most humble pilgrim for admission into my presence. Ask that he arrive at the gates of Canossa in this way tomorrow, and I will consider hearing his petition."

Matilda accepted this concession from him. It wasn't ideal by any means, but at least he hadn't refused completely. She left Gregory in their chambers and went in search of her messenger to deliver the terms that had been provided by the pope. She did not return to him in their chambers that night, electing to sleep with Isobel.

✸

The following day dawned gray and frigid. Against a backdrop of threatening skies and freezing winds, Henry IV approached the formidable gates of Canossa, along with his retinue of penitents. They were led by Abbot Hugh of Cluny, who brought them to the gates and knocked, seeking admission for the king and his followers.

Hugh, carrying a crozier and intoning prayers of penance, led a procession up the long and tortuous mountain path to Matilda's stronghold. Immediately behind him was the humiliated king, dressed in the *cilicium*, the garment of repentance that was made of coarse fabric and goat's hair. It was designed to irritate the skin, to tear it and cause terrible itching as a mortification of the flesh. To further demonstrate the extent of his repentance, Henry walked the rocky and freezing path in his bare feet. An assemblage of once proud bishops and nobles, all of whom had attacked Gregory at the Synod of Worms and called for him to be deposed, followed their king in similar postures of penitence.

The people of Canossa and the surrounding areas who had come out to witness this spectacle lined the road to the fortress. Some jeered, throwing rotted vegetables at the tyrant who would call himself their sovereign. Others watched in silence, perhaps aware that history was happening all around them, perhaps simply in awe of this high drama between a pope and a king.

Upon arrival at the gates, the king stepped forward to knock and formally request admittance. His practiced speech rang out through the frozen air.

"I seek an audience with the Holy Father. I come as a penitent, to declare repentance of my sins against him and the church that he represents. I come in humility. I come as both a man and a king to seek his blessing and forgiveness."

A papal legate delivered the response in an announcement from the tower that faced the front of the fortress. "The Holy Father has rejected your petition. He does not feel that you have, as yet, shown that your penance is sincere."

There was stunned silence in reply. Was it possible that even following such a humiliation, the pope would not receive the king? Henry turned to Abbot Hugh for support. The bishop of Cluny replied, "The king has humbled himself before God and his blessed messenger here on earth. Do you now see how he bleeds to show his penance? Can the Holy Father not find it in his heart to at least hear a further plea of forgiveness and a vow of obedience?"

Henry's feet were torn from the rocky walk up the mountains, and trickles of blood ran over the rash that covered his arms from the terrible hair shirt. He was an impressively wretched sight. Clearly, he had suffered in this journey. But the legate merely repeated his original pronouncement as it had been given him by the pope and disappeared inside, leaving the most powerful king and abbot in Europe to stand at the locked gates as the snow began to fall once again.

❁

Matilda was beside herself with frustration. She could not believe that Gregory was so intractable. Henry, for all his odious behavior, had made a very dramatic and public show of penance. He had humiliated and humbled himself in a way that no king in history ever had, and yet Gregory still would not allow him into his presence. The pope was not listening to anyone, including his most beloved. She had ceased speaking with him as it only caused them to argue.

While Matilda had sought Isobel's counsel on this conflict as a woman, she decided that she needed a male perspective and went in search of Conn. She found him in the stables, where he was not pleased to see her.

"What are you doing out here? It's freezing."

"I need you."

"Come inside then, little sister. I know what this is about and I would tell you a story that I think you should hear."

He rushed her back into the warmth of the castle, in the antechamber near the kitchen. This room had the benefit of being close to the cooking fires, as well as possessing its own fireplace. Matilda's grandfather had built it specifically for the purpose of holding meetings in the wintertime, to combat the fierce cold of these mountains. Matilda warmed her hands over the fire and sat on the padded bench, with her back to the wall. She sighed heavily as she leaned against the hard stone.

"Oh Conn, what am I going to do with him? He is acting as a tyrant."

Conn shrugged. "Is he?"

Matilda was taken aback. She had fully expected him to agree with her. "Of course he is. After Henry's display of penance, he still will not admit him? It's outrageous."

"No, it isn't. It's strength. Respect it and leave him alone."

"You're not serious."

"I am serious."

"But—"

"There is no *but*. Gregory knows clearly what Henry is. And what Henry will always be. Matilda, that man is a monster in a crown. Do not ever underestimate what he is capable of. Now *I* am begging *you*. Whatever it is that has softened your heart toward your evil cousin, do not allow yourself to forget what you know of his past and his actions. He is a very dangerous man, and a more dangerous king. And he is more deadly to you than to anyone else. How can you not see that? And believe me, as angry as you are at Gregory, he is really protecting you more than himself."

Matilda considered this for a moment. While she did see it, she also wanted to believe that there was potential, given the strength of Henry's exhibition today, that there was sincerity in the penance. "So you do not believe that a wicked man can ever change his ways?"

"I do not believe that this particular wicked man can change his ways. And this brings me to the story I wanted to tell you."

Matilda nodded and settled in to listen to the great Celtic warrior weave his hereditary magic through storytelling.

"When I was a student at the school of Chartres . . ."

"Chartres?" Matilda jumped at the mention of the holy city, which Conn always refused to talk about. He scowled at her.

"Later. Don't interrupt me. The school of Chartres brought learned men from all over Europe, and I was once fortunate enough to spend time in the presence of a man from the east. A Sufi master. He told me this story which I am about to tell to you. It is the story of the scorpion and the toad.

"Toad was a kind and gentle creature who swam happily in his pond and had many friends, as he was liked by everybody. One day as he was bathing, he heard a voice calling him from the edge of the pond. 'Hey, Toadie,' the voice called. 'Come over here.'

"And so Toad swam to the shore, and there he saw that it was Scorpion who was calling to him. Now remember that Toad was by his nature a trusting creature, and a kind one, but he was not stupid. He knew that Scorpion was dangerous and known for his poisonous sting, which could strike at any time and often for no reason. Thus Toad kept his distance but replied politely, 'What can I do for you, Brother Scorpion?'

" 'I need to get across the pond,' Scorpion told him. 'Yet it would take me many days to walk. If you would carry me on your back and swim across, it would take me no time at all. I am told that you are kind and generous, and I hope that you will consider doing me this great favor which would help me so much and be very appreciated.'

"Now, Toadie had a conundrum. His nature was to help, but he was afraid of Scorpion's bad reputation. He decided to be honest. 'Brother Scorpion, I would like to help you, but you are known for your volatile nature, and for your deadly sting. If I put you on my back and swim into the pond, what if you decide to sting me? I would die then, and I do not wish to die.'

"Scorpion laughed at this. 'Ridiculous! Brother Toad, think about what you have just said! If I were to sting you while you were swimming, you would sink and we would both drown. I have no desire to destroy you, and certainly not myself, so why would I ever do such a thing? I simply need to get across the pond, and I need your help to do so. Please, brother.'

"And so the trusting toad allowed the scorpion to climb upon his back and began to swim. When they were midway into the pond, Toad felt a sharp and horrible pain. 'Ouch! What was that?' he cried. To which Scorpion replied, 'Oops. I stung you. Sorry.' Toad was incredulous, and as the poison seeped into his body and he began to sink, he asked the Scorpion, 'But why, brother? Why did you sting me when now we will both surely perish?'

"The Scorpion sighed, going down with the Toad, and explained very simply as they both prepared to die, 'I couldn't help it. It's just my nature.'"

Conn let the moral hang in the air for a few moments before continuing. "You see, Matilda, what is equally important as the ending of this fable is another understanding, and that is this: when the scorpion told the toad that he did not want to hurt him, he came across as sincere because he was sincere—at the time. At that moment, he really didn't want to sting him and he didn't want to do anything obviously self-destructive. But his nature overcame him, as it always had and always would, and he simply couldn't help himself."

Matilda sighed with the truth of it. "Henry is indeed a scorpion."

"He is. So whereas he may even believe himself that he is repentant, do not think for a moment that he has overcome his nature. And Matilda . . ."

"Yes?"

"The final lesson is that Toad is as much to blame for his own demise as Scorpion. He knew what Scorpion's nature was, and all his instincts told him not to trust. But he denied his own higher wisdom."

"So what exactly are you saying to me?"

"Don't be a toad, little sister. Don't be a toad."

❁

The German contingent camped at the base of the hill, outside the fortress. They repeated the spectacle of Henry's penance, and that of his noble retinue, for three days. At the dawn of the fourth day, the papal legate announced that Henry's penance had been accepted and that he would be admitted into the presence of the Holy Father.

What Henry, and history, would never know was just how instrumental Matilda had been in the ultimate acceptance of this king's repentance by Pope Gregory VII. The countess of Canossa, while not wishing to make the mistakes of the tragic toad in Conn's fable, was terrified that her cousin the king was actually going to freeze to death at the gates of her fortress. She could simply not allow such a thing to happen. It was inhumane and violated everything she stood for spiritually and personally. Further, it would not serve Gregory's agenda to strengthen the Church, and certainly not a church dedicated to love and compassion. She feared that Gregory's actions would ultimately be viewed as tyrannical, harsh, and unforgiving. Even her own people of Canossa, as loyal as they were to her, were beginning to stir with discomfort. They watched the daily spectacle of a king who was wasting away with fasting and cold. The shamed monarch begged for simple admission into the papal presence—in order to continue his pleading and further his humiliation. Gregory's resolve bordered on ruthlessness. It had to stop.

Before retiring to bed on the third night, Matilda presented Gregory with an ultimatum that represented the most difficult choice of her life. While she loved him beyond reason, her supreme duty was to her mission and to the promise she made to God in her role as his servant on earth. It was a promise to live by the teachings of a man they called the Prince of Peace. In light of this, Matilda could no longer stand by and allow the spectacle of humiliation to continue. Either Gregory admitted Henry into his presence, or she was leaving Canossa. She would no longer participate in any action that she felt to be against the will of God or the teachings of his son.

The pope was stunned by Matilda's extreme position, but he refused to be swayed by her ultimatum initially. It was not until he heard her giving orders to prepare for her departure that he realized she was indeed serious. Gregory finally concluded that he needed to relax his position in order to save everything that he held most dear.

The same extraordinary passion and intensity that brought Gregory and Matilda together would also serve to challenge them at this critical juncture in their relationship. Two minds and spirits of such strength cannot expect to live in the same place in total harmony at all times. It was a lesson that both of them needed to learn. It was one of many that were brought to light in Canossa during the winter of 1077.

King Henry IV was admitted into the presence of Pope Gregory VII, with Matilda standing by his side, late in the afternoon of January 28. He was a pathetic figure of chapped and torn flesh. To look upon him as he prostrated himself, near to tears, before the pope was to see a broken man in total surrender. Matilda felt pity as she watched him; Henry was, indeed, a victim of his own nature. His viciousness had caused him to be in this place now, half dead and completely demoralized, face down on the cold stone floor and begging for forgiveness from a man he hated.

Gregory agreed to forgive him, as a man if not as a king. The sentence of excommunication was lifted, and Henry was allowed to take communion inside the small chapel within the fortress. He was then welcomed into Canossa, where he was fed and given fine chambers to recover from his ordeal.

Henry stayed just long enough to observe his cousin and her style of leadership within her own domain. He sought audiences with her for hours each day. While Matilda would never trust him, she was generous with her time in her genuine hope for peace and reconciliation. Her cousin, who genuinely appeared to care about finally becoming a great king, spent several hours asking for her advice on methods for ruling Europe with justice. The people of northern Italy adored Matilda, and he explained that he would emulate her actions in the future in an effort to win back his own subjects. Perhaps, he proposed, as they were cousins who had known each other since early childhood, they could forget their differences and come together as great rulers to work in harmony.

And perhaps the scorpion would allow the toad to swim gently and happily across the pond.

Henry's time in Canossa was indeed a great turning point for his poisoned, imperial psyche, but not in the way Matilda had hoped. The humiliation he experienced at the hands of Gregory burned within Henry. It was a conflagration that destroyed any semblance of humanity that may have once existed in his twisted mind. Worst of all, he concluded that his whore of a cousin was obviously the force behind it all. She controlled the pope, clearly. It was obvious that such a witch could manipulate any man using her demonic feminine wiles. It could only have been Matilda who demanded that Henry remain in the snow for three days and nights. She would pay for what she did to him, just as the pretender pope would pay. But he would make Matilda pay most personally.

Nothing would hurt his cousin more than destroying her precious Tuscany and giving the Tuscan people an understanding of what loyalty to such an unnatural demon would cost them. He would start, perhaps, with Lucca. Or her childhood home of Mantua. These were the places she held most dear, and they were the places that would suffer.

As King Henry IV returned to his own lands across the Alps, he took careful stock of the regions he passed through and began to plan his retribution, the devastation of Matilda's beloved Tuscany. He paused in Lombardy to rejoin the schismatic nobles who opposed Gregory. Within mere days of his pardon, Henry had once again declared himself the bitter enemy of the pope—and the nemesis of the Tuscan countess.

It was, after all, his nature.

Hail, Mary.

It is a name of great sanctity. It comes from many sources and many traditions, and in all of them it is holy, as each of these contains the seed of knowledge and truth. It is known in forms all over the world, where it is Mary, Maria, Miriam, Maura, Miriamne.

From Egypt it is Meryam, and this was the name of the sister of Moses and Aaron. Here it comes from the root of the word mer, *for love, which becomes the name Mery, which is to say cherished. Or beloved. It was used for daughters who were determined to be special, chosen by the gods for a divine destiny in terms of their birth, family, or prophecies that surrounded them.*

It has been said that the form which is Miryam combines several words to create the meaning "myrrh of the sea," and some variations carry the meaning "mistress of the sea."

But there is yet another great secret of this perfected female name. It blends both the Hebrew and the Egyptian traditions within it: the Egyptian mer, *for love, and the Hebrew* Yam *which is a sacred abbreviation for Yahweh. Thus the name when the traditions are combined means "she who is the beloved of Yahweh."*

During the life of our Lord and beyond, the name was often given after the coming of age, as a title earned by a girl who had proven her worth and special nature.

To become a Mary was a blessed thing.

THE HISTORY OF THE SACRED NAME,
AS PRESERVED IN THE LIBRO ROSSO

Chapter Fourteen

Confraternity of the Holy Apparition
Vatican City, Rome
present day

*P*eter escorted Maureen and Bérenger into the Vatican City meeting hall where the monthly meeting of the Confraternity of the Holy Apparition was held.

Peter was here tonight in support of Father Girolamo as well as his housekeeper, Maggie Cusack. Maggie was a most dedicated member of this confraternity and had committed much of her spare time to the celebration and commemoration of Our Lady's miraculous appearances throughout Europe: at Fátima, La Salette, Medjugorje, Paris, Lourdes, and the Belgian apparitions of Beauraing and Banneaux. These meetings, which welcomed the public, featured a presentation highlighting a specific incident of Our Lady's apparition. Tonight the presentation featured Our Lady of Silence, the apparition that occurred in western Ireland in the nineteenth century, in the village of Knock. Maggie was giving the presentation and had been preparing it for weeks, often asking Peter for his opinion and perspective on the related history. Peter's family was from a neighboring county, and Knock was easy to visit from their home in Galway. He and Maureen had been to Knock on pilgrimage with his mother several times as kids, and they knew the village and its history well.

Bérenger Sinclair was fascinated by the idea of the confraternity and wanted to see it for himself. Yet if he was hoping to see any semblance of secret society activity, which the confraternities had been full of during the Middle Ages and Renaissance, he was to be disappointed. The twenty-first-century version was filled predominantly with Italian Catholic matrons who baked lovely biscotti, served coffee to the newcomers, and handed out leaflets with information on the confraternity and a prayer to Our Lady of Fátima. This was a friendly and open environment. There was nothing at all secretive or mysterious about it. A few priests filed in at various intervals, as did some local families who were no doubt connected to the biscotti makers. Peter noticed with more than a degree of surprise that Marcelo Barberini, the cardinal he served with on the committee, slipped in quietly and was standing at the rear of the room. Everyone took their seats as Father Girolamo came to the podium at the front and welcomed them to the meeting. He thanked Maggie Cusack for her hard work and introduced her to the group, who applauded politely as she took her place at the podium and began to tell the story of the miracle of Knock.

Knock, County Mayo, Ireland
August 21, 1879

IT WAS A TINY PLACE, unimportant even as most small villages go, located in the southeast corner of County Mayo. Even the name was unimaginative. Cnoc. It was quite simply the Irish word for "hill" in honor of the windswept location on which the town was perched. It wasn't even much of a hill, truth be told. Why Our Lady chose this place for her particular blessing was still a great mystery.

The only indication of grace in its history had occurred some 1,300 years prior to the apparition. Saint Patrick himself had seen a vision here and pronounced the location blessed. He announced that it would one day become a site of devotion and worship, that pilgrims would travel from all over the world to venerate the sanctity of the place. The "hill" was now holy.

In 1859, the newly completed but unremarkable church in Knock was consecrated to Saint John the Baptist. It was a difficult time for the people of Mayo, still recovering from the terrible famine that had ravaged Ireland with death and dispossession, killing an estimated one third of the native population. British landlords continued to use the enforced poverty of the famine to evict the destitute peasants and confiscate their property, land that had been in the care of Irish farmers since the dawn of the Celts. A number of families who could not pay their rent in County Mayo had been made homeless by wealthy English noblemen who had no conscience about leaving them to suffer the elements, abandoned to a fate of destitution or death.

In 1867, during this bleak period, a great and saintly man, one Father Cavanaugh by name, came to Knock. During the worst days of the Great Hunger, he had worked tirelessly to relieve the poor. He sold all his possessions, including a fine horse and a watch given to him by his father, in order to raise money to feed the children of his parish. But he convinced his parishioners that they were never poor, as long as they had their faith. Father Cavanaugh became the heart and the soul of Knock, and he was much beloved of the people from his own village and from the neighboring parishes as well.

Early in August of 1879, a terrible summer storm damaged the church, ripping a hole in the roof and destroying the two interior statues, one each of the Virgin Mary and Saint Joseph. Father Cavanaugh, in his patient and meticulous way, patched the roof and ordered replacement statues. But in a freak accident, both of these were smashed beyond repair while in transit to Knock from Dublin. Feeling that the forces of evil were, for some reason, taking vengeance on his little parish, the priest vowed not to be defeated and prayed more fervently than ever for the deliverance of Knock. He ordered two more statues, and these arrived intact and were installed in the church.

The following evening, there was another great storm. Father Cavanaugh's housekeeper, Miss Mary McLoughlin, left him in the presbytery to visit her friends, the Byrne family, who lived on the other side of the village. As she walked past the church, she noticed three strange statues outside that appeared to be illuminated through the rain. She stopped for a moment to consider them, confused. Had the good father ordered even more statues to replace the damaged ones? Strange, he never mentioned it, and he told her everything. They had talked of almost nothing else but the curse of the statues since the first set had been destroyed. And she had helped him install the new statues yesterday. What were these, and why were they outside in the rain?

The Byrne family were upstanding and devout parishioners who took great pride in their duties as caretakers for the church. When the priest's housekeeper reached the Byrnes' home, she was brought in to dry off and take tea in the sitting room. Here it was that a teenage daughter of the Byrne family, Margaret, told Mary that she had just come from locking up the church. Margaret had noticed a strange white light near the south gable of the church. It was unusual, but it could have been a trick caused by the rain. She noticed it again on the way out and stopped to look at it for a moment before returning home, somewhat puzzled by it.

Another parishioner, Mrs. Carty, came by the Byrne home shortly thereafter. She also had seen the statues and the light and wondered why Father Cavanaugh was adding to the new collection in the church. Wasn't this overkill? Given the hardships that so many were suffering in the area surrounding the village, there was surely better use of funds. Adding statues to the exterior of the church so soon after the famine and evictions seemed frivolous and irresponsible. And it didn't seem a bit in character for the humanitarian priest who gave so much to his flock. The priest's housekeeper reassured her that Father Cavanaugh would never behave in such a way.

Curious now that three of them in such a short time had noticed strange happenings, the two older women decided to investigate. They walked together in the inclement weather, slowing as they neared the church, where they could both see the strange statues outside in the rain.

Mrs. Carty asked, "When did Father Cavanaugh put those statues there?"

Mary McLoughlin replied, "He didn't. I'm quite certain he did not. This is what I don't understand." They continued to watch, squinting through the raindrops to see if they could determine which saints were depicted in the statuary.

Margaret Byrne jumped with a squeal. "They're moving! Those are not statues. Look!"

Watching quietly, they realized that indeed, these were not statues. On the far left was an older man with a gray beard, on the far right was a young man with long hair, and appearing in the center was a most luminous woman. The female figure was floating above the grass, surrounded by an incandescent white light. This central lady was identified by both women instantly as the Virgin Mary, and they reported later that they were quite certain the other figures were Saint Joseph and Saint John the Evangelist. When questioned, neither could say specifically why or how they identified the figures, other than by the ages of the males.

Margaret Byrne ran home, breathlessly informing her family that a miracle was occurring at the church. All of them followed her out to witness the apparition of the three holy figures in the rain. In the later official investigations by the Church, fourteen people testified to the vision: six women, three men, and five children, three of whom were teenage girls.

All attested to a magical light, golden at first and then changing to a bright white that illuminated the entire wall of the church. Each witness saw three figures, but the details varied. One woman claimed that she saw a young lamb on an altar, adamant that the lamb was facing west and that it was important that they know he was facing the west. She referred to this as the Paschal Lamb. Several others testified to seeing angels, flying and hovering over the site, or hovering over the lamb and a large cross.

Our Lady was dressed in a shimmering white robe that appeared to be made of liquid silver. On her head was a sparkling crown, and in its center was a bloodred rose. She held her hands out, as the witnesses said, "in the same position as the priest does when he says Mass." She looked up toward heaven, as if she were praying, while some even said that she appeared to be preaching. But unlike other Marian apparitions, Our Lady did not interact with the citizens of Knock. She did not speak to them and she did not offer any secrets.

All witnesses later described one male figure as Saint Joseph, because of his gray beard, and perhaps weight was added to this assumption because the statues in Knock were of Mary and Joseph. Joseph appeared on the left, and the young figure identified as Saint John the Evangelist was on the right. Strangely, the long-haired youth wore a bishop's miter and vestments, in contrast to the first-century robes worn by Our Lady and Saint Joseph. "John" held a very great book in his left hand and gestured, as if preaching, with his right. One of the children also emphasized that John was preaching and that this was important, but the child could not hear the words. The significance of the book, and its extraordinary size, was emphasized by a number of witnesses.

Mary McLoughlin hurried back in the rain to tell Father Cavanaugh, but he was unimpressed and advised her that they were probably all seeing a reflection of stained glass in the rain. He would regret that reaction and his ultimate decision not to view the images for the rest of his life, as Knock became a legendary site of Marian apparition.

And Patrick was correct, of course, as all great saints are. His vision was infallible. Pilgrims did come from all over the world to Knock, as this was one of the later Marian apparitions to be acknowledged as authentic. Pope John Paul II visited Knock in 1979 on the centennial anniversary of the apparition, and he presented the village with a golden rose in commemoration of the holy occurrence. The city built an international airport to accommodate the huge number of pilgrims who come to this place in honor of Our Lady's appearance.

Over a million people now visited Knock annually in celebration of this most Holy Apparition.

Following the presentation, Maureen was uncharacteristically quiet as she, Bérenger, and Peter walked through the streets that led away from St. Peter's. Bérenger noticed.

"What are you thinking about?"

Maureen shrugged. Maggie was so dear and sincere in her presentation, but the story she told didn't sit right with Maureen. In fact, even when she had visited Knock as a child, Maureen had found the place somewhat disturbing. It was commercialized, full of souvenir shops and plastic holy water bottles. She had always found this aspect decidedly unspiritual, but there was something else bothering her now.

"Well . . . there are a lot of assumptions, aren't there? I mean, the apparitions didn't exactly identify themselves. She didn't say, 'Hi there, I'm the Virgin Mary, and this is my friend John the Evangelist and my husband Saint Joseph.' I've had my share of visions, and that just doesn't happen. You make assumptions based on what you know to be true in your own life. The people of Knock, who were very traditional and conservative Catholics in rural Ireland in the nineteenth century, made an assumption that this is what they were seeing based on their frame of reference."

"So, what are you saying?" This was Peter's question.

Maureen considered another moment before continuing. "Could it be that they were seeing something other than what they assumed? What if all of these apparitions around Europe, where a beautiful woman appears to children and tells them secrets, are something other than what has always been assumed? A different Mary, perhaps? Some of the witnesses at Knock say she appears to be preaching, which is an integral part of the Magdalene legacy but is not part of the Virgin Mary's legacy. And the John figure is paramount, particularly because he holds this enormous book which is out of proportion to everything else, from which he also preaches. Yeah, I know, it's his gospel, thus the title Evangelist. But is he really John the Evangelist? Because if he is, then why is he dressed like a bishop and why doesn't the rest of his iconography match? Could it be because he is somebody else? Or representative of a different tradition? Are all three of these figures something completely different than what they've been assumed to be?"

Peter asked, "Where are you going with this?"

"I don't even know yet. But what I do know is that there is a truth about the origins of Christianity and its authentic teachings that has been deliberately obscured. And therefore I have to wonder if perhaps God has been creating miracles all this time to direct our attention to that truth. Or maybe I've just been immersed in this too long. It seems that I see everything as a conspiracy these days. I suppose I'm just asking the question: what if all these Marian apparitions aren't what we have been told they are?"

Peter was quiet, considering the question. Bérenger responded. "Fascinating idea, but it leads me to ask this question: to your point, the apparitions occurred in famine-torn rural Ireland in the late nineteenth century, when no one would have had any frame of reference for the scenario you just presented."

"So why bother?" Peter continued. "Based on your heretical theory, why would the apparitions attempt to show themselves in this way to a people who could not even begin to comprehend what they were trying to convey?"

Maureen stopped walking as an idea hit her. "Because they weren't conveying the message to them."

"What do you mean?" Peter wasn't following her line of thinking.

"Just maybe . . . they were conveying the message to us. In the future. In a time when we could reinterpret it."

It was Bérenger's turn to question. "But why?"

"You don't think that's arrogant?" Peter asked. "To say that these events happened all for our benefit?"

"I'm not saying that they happened for us specifically. I'm saying that they happened in order to leave clues for anyone who was motivated to find them and inspired to follow them. And we are. Our obligation is to not let those clues go undiscovered."

"For those with ears to hear and eyes to see," Peter mused.

Bérenger was struck by a thought. "Maggie mentioned Saint Patrick in the presentation, and that he had declared Knock a holy place. Think about it. What do we know about your patron saint?"

Peter responded first. He was passionate about Patrick's legacy in Ireland. "The miracle of Patrick is that he did not shed one drop of blood in his conversion of the Irish pagans to Christianity. He converted them through understanding and integration."

"And where do you think he learned that strategy?"

Maureen wasn't sure where he was going and listened as Bérenger continued.

"From the Prince of Peace, who was his ancestor. Saint Patrick was the grandnephew of Saint Martin of Tours, the French saint who shows up all over bloodline history. I've tracked his lineage and can almost definitively prove that he was the direct descendant of Sarah-Tamar."

"San Martino!" Maureen was excited by where the connections were taking her. "Matilda's church of the Holy Face in Lucca was named after Saint Martin of Tours."

Peter was grasping it too. "And built by an Irish saint Finnian, who was inspired by Patrick."

Peter was shaking his head in wonder. "Remember who Saint Patrick's true successor was? Saint Brigit. A woman. A very powerful woman. One of the greatest leaders in the early Church."

Maureen was speaking quickly now, putting it all together. "So Patrick is a direct descendant of Jesus and Mary Magdalene, and he declares that Knock will be a holy place after he sees this in a vision. His successor is a powerful woman, who is also a prophetess. Are we saying that the early Celtic church was founded by our people? By heretics?"

Bérenger nodded. "I think it deserves consideration. Perhaps there were others in Knock that night who also witnessed the apparitions— but who saw something very different, something that the Church would not have recorded in the eyewitness accounts for obvious reasons."

"A vision for those with eyes to see?" Peter asked. "You think there were heretics still living in County Mayo in the eighteen hundreds?"

"I don't think we can rule it out," Bérenger said.

Maureen nodded her agreement, her mind racing with the possibilities. They continued on their way across the Tiber, making their crossing on the monumental bridge that joins the edges of Vatican City to the rest of Rome. Bernini's majestic angel sculptures shone in the moonlight as they passed.

"One thing that has always fascinated me about these visions of Mary is that many of them happen to children." Maureen addressed her next question to Peter. "She appears to the very innocent, the very young, and the very poor. And she tells them secrets, right?"

Peter nodded now in agreement. "Usually, yes. She also tends to appear in times of great stress. Knock occurs when Ireland is recovering from the famine, the vision at La Salette occurs in France as that country is healing from the revolution, and Fátima has the backdrop of the First World War. In the midst of all this turmoil, secrets of faith are imparted to children by the Holy Mother. This is integral to the apparitions. Knock is unique in that it is one of the few Marian apparitions where there are no secrets and there is no contact, possibly because she is seen by adults as well as children. This is why she is called Our Lady of Silence."

"But Knock is also unique, correct me if I'm wrong, in that the Marian figure is not alone. She is accompanied by companions who are as important as she is herself."

Peter nodded. "That is true."

"So what do we know about the secrets that Mary gives to the children in her other apparitions?" Maureen asked. "Are they ever revealed?"

"Sometimes, like in Fátima, the secrets were revealed a little at a time over the years," Peter explained. "But some of the others were taken to the grave because the children refused to tell them."

"And why do you think that is? Could it be that Mary told them something they were too afraid to share? Something that could be deemed . . . heretical?"

Bérenger found that the more time he spent with Maureen, the more uncannily similar their thought processes became. He joined in.

"You think Mother Mary is appearing to tell the children, 'The true teachings of my son are not being honored'?"

"That's where this is leading me."

Peter shook his head. "We have no way of knowing, do we? I have to confess that I never really looked at it this way and I don't think I can now, either. I think these are beautiful, religious experiences that are had by pure believers during times when an increase of faith was vital to their communities. Children can see Our Lady because they are as pure as she is. I really don't think it's anything more than that."

Maureen was tired, and she wasn't even sure she wanted to make a case for the Marian apparitions being anything other than what they appeared to be. She just felt the need to voice these questions. It was interesting to her that Knock Shrine had become the focal point of the Catholic conservative movement in Ireland. Agenda-driven programs criticizing contraception, divorce, and homosexuality were born and nurtured around Knock. Wouldn't it be somewhat ironic if these apparitions that were used as a backdrop for intolerance were actually of a heretical nature? It was something to think about, but it was just one of many things that Maureen had to consider as the tortuous path of history continued to take her on a completely unpredictable journey.

The three of them had a late dinner in the Piazza della Rotonda, but Maureen rarely joined in the conversation. Finally she admitted that she just wanted to be alone for a few hours to contemplate all that was swirling through her consciousness. Something was nagging at the back of her brain, and she had to give in to it, to see where it would take her.

Back in her room, she flipped open her laptop and began trawling online to find out more about Marian apparitions. She wasn't certain what she was looking for or why these suddenly mattered to her quite so much. But she had learned not to ignore her instincts regarding such things. Maybe something would jump out at her, help her to understand why this was suddenly important.

Peter was right. With the exception of Knock, all the apparitions that Maureen found had similar characteristics: they were witnessed by very poor children who were also illiterate. These children were all told "secrets"—some to be kept in perpetuity by the chosen child, others to be shared at designated times with the world. Was the Church censoring these secrets? Fabricating them? Some of the eyewitness accounts were written in ornate and flowery language, utilizing phrasing that simply could not have come from the mouths of illiterate children.

One of the young visionaries from a French village near the Swiss border, La Salette, was a fifteen-year-old shepherdess. Mélanie Calvat was so poor that her parents had sent her out to beg in the street from the time she was three years old. Despite her lack of education, it was the perspective of history that she had given this verbatim report of her vision to the Church:

> *The clothing of the Most Holy Virgin was silver-white and quite brilliant. It was quite intangible. It was made up of light and glory, sparkling and dazzling. There is no expression nor comparison to be found on earth . . . She had a pinafore more brilliant than several suns put together. It was composed of glory, and the glory was scintillating and ravishingly beautiful. The crown of roses which she placed on her head was so beautiful, so brilliant, that it defies imagination. The Most Holy Virgin was tall and well proportioned. She seemed so light that a mere breath could have stirred her, yet she was motionless and perfectly balanced. Her face was majestic, imposing. The voice of the Beautiful Lady was soft. It was enchanting, ravishing, warming to the ears.*

Maureen thought about this for a moment. She didn't know any fifteen-year-old girls in the twenty-first century who used words like *scintillating* or *intangible*, much less spoke in this type of prose. It simply didn't seem possible that these words could have been spoken by an illiterate and terrified girl in 1851. This was the equivalent of a press release from the Vatican: an obvious marketing tool.

She noted one interesting sentence in Mélanie Calvat's testimony, one that invited deeper exploration. This was the sentence referring to the "second secret":

> *Then the Holy Virgin gave me the rule of a new religious order.*
> *When she had given me the rule of this new religious order, the*
> *Holy Virgin continued the speech in the same manner.*

As Maureen searched for further documents on Mélanie Calvat's statements, she found no further information on this "new religious order," nor did it appear that the Vatican had elaborated on it in any detail. Could the Virgin have been referring to the Order of the Holy Sepulcher? Was the "new" religious order in fact a reference to restoring the true teachings of her son—and his wife?

One more critical element that Maureen took note of: virtually every account of a secret revealed during an apparition had some discrepancy or objection around it. Either the child recanted later or claimed that he or she was misrepresented. Some refused ever to speak of the revelations that were entrusted to them by Mary.

And some were never allowed to speak.

Most famous of these was Lucia Santos, the oldest child to witness the multiple apparitions in the Portuguese hamlet outside Fátima. Lucia was a special child with a sunny disposition, and by the accounts of her relatives there was "something magical" about her. She took her first communion at six, years earlier than usual, because hers was such a spiritual nature that she was known to lecture other children on the nature of God. At the age of ten the little shepherdess, along with her two cousins, Jacinta and Francisco, witnessed an apparition of Our Lady while walking through the fields near their home. The date was May 13, 1917. Lucia would later describe her vision in terms similar to the apparition from the Book of Revelation, chapter twelve, "And a great portent appeared in heaven, a woman clothed with the sun." The apparition identified herself as Our Lady of the Rosary and emphasized the importance of reciting the rosary daily. The lady explained to the children that it was the key to personal salvation but also to world peace. From May to October of 1917, the Lady appeared on the thirteenth day of each month, at the same time.

More than 70,000 people witnessed the final apparition on October 13, 1917. Although it had dawned dark and rainy that day, by the time of the Lady's appearance the sun had burst through the sky in a show of light and color, and it appeared to be moving back and forth across the sky. This dazzling astronomical event became known in Portugal as the Miracle of the Sun, and it converted many skeptics into believers on that day. Of all the Marian apparitions, Fátima remained the most famous because this miracle, in which the sun was said to dance, was witnessed by so many.

Key to the Fátima apparitions were the three secrets that the Lady imparted to the children. These were not immediately revealed to the public. They were, in fact, kept as secrets between the children and their religious advisers for many years following the apparitions. Sadly, both of Lucia's cousins, Jacinta and Francisco, died shortly after the events at Fátima. It is believed that they were merely two of many children who were lost to a flu epidemic spreading through the Iberian Peninsula at the time.

Lucia Santos became the only surviving child to know the truth of the Lady's secrets. She was subsequently committed to a series of convents for the duration of her long life and took vows of silence as a Carmelite nun. Lucia's deep spirituality would indicate that her vows were voluntary and a part of her calling; however, Maureen wondered about the vows of silence, which appeared extreme. Lucia was not only under a traditional monastic vow of silence, she was under restrictions from the Vatican not to speak to anyone about the apparitions without express approval from the Holy See. As she grew older, these restrictions were tightened to the point of strangulation, as Lucia was forbidden to have any visitors who were not deemed acceptable by the

Church. Even her personal confessor of twenty years was ultimately denied the right to visit her. In the final years of her life, no one except Pope John Paul II and Cardinal Joseph Ratzinger were allowed to gain or grant access to Lucia Santos, who now lived in an imposed solitary confinement. Despite Church claims that Lucia was an esteemed and venerated member of their community, she died in 1995 from complications of an upper respiratory infection because the cell she lived in was damp and mildewed and her aged body could not recover from the multiple, prolonged infections she suffered.

Immediately upon her death, an edict was issued by Cardinal Ratzinger, who was the head of the Inquisition—now known by the politically correct term Congregation for the Doctrine of the Faith. The order called for Lucia's monastic cell to be sealed off as if it were a crime scene. It had been reported throughout her life that Lucia never stopped having visions, and that perhaps she never stopped writing about them. It appeared that the Church was taking no chances that this visionary may have been hiding accounts of her experiences somewhere within her cell. What they found was unknown to anyone except the pope, his congregational general, and the select council of clerics who were committed to the preservation of the holy apparitions. While a number of books claiming to be Lucia's personal memoirs were released during the course of her life, these came out under the direction of the Church. As Lucia was never allowed to discuss any aspect of Fátima freely, it was impossible to know if these Vatican-approved biographies truly represented her visions and experiences, despite the fact that they had her name on the cover. Not surprisingly, the Fátima secrets as they were ultimately revealed focused on the conversion of the world to Catholicism, beginning with Russia, and other issues very specific to Catholics and the preservation of the faith in its traditional and established form.

The screen of Maureen's laptop blurred as the tears began to stream down her face. This girl's story touched her deeply. There was something terribly wrong here, an injustice that screamed to be examined. Lucia Santos had witnessed one of history's most famous and accepted miracles, was by many accounts an exceptional mystic and visionary—perhaps the greatest of her time. And yet she had been imprisoned for seventy-eight years under an imposition of silence and often in terrible conditions by the very institution that claimed to revere her. As an elderly woman plagued by illness, she was not even allowed the comfort of a warm and dry place to sleep.

Maureen burned with Boudicca's battle cry of the Truth Against the World. There could only be one reason to keep such a woman from talking, one reason to deny her the comfort of friends, family, and even her personal confessor at the end of her life: someone was afraid of what she was going to say. That someone was the hierarchy of the Catholic Church. What was the Church so afraid of with regard to Lucia that her jailer was none other than the pope and his right-hand man, the right-hand man who succeeded Pope John Paul II to become Pope Benedict XVI? Would her truth contradict the carefully crafted history of the Fátima visions? Or was there something greater, something truly shocking and dangerous to the Church that had been revealed to this very special little girl?

And was it true that Lucia never stopped having visions?

The world would never know. Lucia Santos had been successfully silenced, and all that remained of her story was the sanitized official version, the version created by those who imprisoned her. The Church completely controlled the documented events to ensure that their agenda was served. Truth would not be allowed to get in the way of politics, power, and economics. Historically, it never had. Perhaps it never would, Maureen mused.

As Maureen prepared to close out her research, one final detail leaped from the page, something about Lucia's life that she had not noticed before. She caught her breath as she saw this one shocking fact in the girl's biography.

It was now obvious to her why the blessed Lucia Santos had been treated like a danger to the Church.

According to Portuguese documents, the recorded date of Lucia Santos's birth was March 22, 1907.

Lucia Santos was an Expected One.

"I NEED TO KNOW about Lucia Santos. Please."

Father Girolamo had been pleasantly surprised when he received the phone call first thing this morning advising him that Maureen Paschal was anxious to see him immediately. Peter made the arrangements.

"Ah. I see our presentation on Knock has inspired interest in the apparitions of Our Lady. But why do you come to ask about Lucia specifically?"

Maureen met his gaze squarely across the desk. "You tell me."

He smiled at her. "You have done a good deal of homework in a short period of time, my dear. I see that there will be no need for pretense, so let us agree to be completely honest with each other. I knew Lucia Santos."

Maureen was startled by this. While she knew that Father Girolamo was considered the expert on apparitions, she hadn't expected him to have had personal experience with the famous witness of Fátima.

"Do you remember when we discussed your dream? I was aware, before you told me, that the book that Our Lord appeared to be writing radiated with blue light, and you asked me how I knew this?"

Maureen nodded but said nothing, intent to see where he was taking this.

"I knew because Lucia had the same dreams."

Maureen gasped before catching herself. "So we are . . . connected. Beyond the birth date."

"Yes, you are. Lucia Santos was one of the most remarkable visionaries of all time. You should feel it an honor to be in her company."

Maureen felt the tears brimming, hot behind her eyes, as she nodded in acknowledgment of the honor.

"Then why?" she asked when she found her voice. "If you believe that she was so great a visionary . . . then why was she silenced for so long? And treated so poorly?"

"It was not as harsh as you believe it to be. Lucia was not like you, aside from the visions. You are, in fact, a rare case. Do you know that? Most women who had these experiences were not able to function in everyday life as you do. They entered convents voluntarily and for their own protection. Many of them became completely unable to lead lives outside their visionary experiences and had to be cared for. Lucia was one of these. She did not live in our world much of the time, and she needed solitude. She requested it. I assure you, she was very well provided for by all around her."

Maureen had a million questions, but knew she had to consider the next one carefully. "The secrets. Were any of them about the Book of Love?"

The old priest's reply was firm but not harsh. "You venture into territory that you must know I am not allowed to discuss with anyone. For now, I think it is enough that you know that Lucia had the same dream of our Lord as you have had. Perhaps you should pray about this. You have much in common with Lucia Santos, and she was a great help to the Church. She inspired many faithful then as she still does to this day. Perhaps you should change your focus. Turn your attention to all the good that has come from her legacy, and stop trying to find the ill. That is what Lucia would want from you, if she were here today. Of that I am certain."

❊

As Peter walked with Maureen back to her hotel, they discussed Father Girolamo's revelation. They were to meet Bérenger in his suite and finish reading through the final pages of Matilda's autobiography.

Maureen needed to duck back into her room to grab her laptop and her notebook for their meeting. She opened the small closet to retrieve the leather carry-on bag where she stored her writing materials.

The bag was gone, and so were her laptop and her notebook.

It was the last straw for Maureen's nerves, strung as taut as they were in the aftermath of the last weeks.

"What next?" She looked at Peter as she sat on the edge of the bed. "I'm not sure how much more I can take."

Peter put his hand on her shoulder. "Breathe, Maureen. Just breathe. It's terrible, but it isn't the worst thing that has happened. And you got through all that."

Maureen nodded. "I'm trying, Pete. But it's getting harder. What happened in Orval was really scary. And now this. I'm starting to feel very exposed. And I'm really struggling with the fact that I feel like I have no control over my own life."

"But you do. You have free will."

"I'm not sure that's true."

"Of course it is. Right now you're here in Rome, chasing the clues and trying to find the truth about the Book of Love, which I believe is exactly what God wants you to do. But that's your choice. Your free will. You can tell God right now to get another storyteller and grab your passport and get on the next flight back to L.A. You can walk away from this entire process at any moment that you want, simply by choosing to do so. That's what free will means."

Maureen snapped at him as her exhaustion got the better of her. "But what about *the time returns*? If this is my mission—to do this work—then I can't walk away from it, no matter how much I may want to."

Now it was Peter's turn to raise his voice. He could feel his own anger and frustration building within him. Those emotions had been churning for the better part of two years, and now they were finding expression.

"Why do you think there is even a need to say *the time returns*? It's because humans can't get it right. If we accomplished what we were put here to do in the first place, the *time* wouldn't have to *return*. But we can't do that. We can't be obedient and follow God's plan, as simple as it is, because all our human rubbish gets in the way when the going gets tough—our ego, our anger, our envy, our greed. That's what Jesus was trying to tell us. That was his real message: that this is all so simple. It's about love and faith and community. And that's *it*. Do you know what I consider the most important thing I have learned in all my years as a priest? The only piece of spiritual wisdom that really matters? It's this: you can throw away the entire Bible if you just keep what Jesus tells us in Matthew twenty-two, verses thirty-seven through forty. '*Love the Lord thy God with all thy heart and love thy neighbor as thyself. On these two commandments hang all the law of the prophets.*' Done. Finito. That's all you need to know. And they'd throw me out of the Vatican for saying this, but we can make Bible study courses three minutes long, because that's the entire teaching right there. Everything else just gets in the way and obscures the message."

He took a breath, but he was far from finished. "This is easy stuff, right? It should be—it was meant to be. But the human race has made a mess of it for two thousand years and wreaked the worst havoc and wrought the most horrific destruction, in our Lord's name, because we can't live by those two most basic commandments. So God has to keep sending souls to earth who he thinks might be right for the task of reminding us how to live in that simple love. But the free will factor does us in every time. *Every time.* And we can't create heaven on earth with just a few people having that intention. We need to get the whole world on board with these simple understandings. It's a ridiculous, daunting, insane task, but one that God clearly thinks can be done, which is why we have to keep trying. It's why we have to keep searching and why you have to keep writing, no matter what. It's your job and your mission—and, yes, it was apparently your promise. But it's still your free will to do it or not."

She was listening to him, as she always did, and he was making a lot of sense. But she was overtired and overwrought. What she really needed right now was someone like Tammy, a girlfriend who would let her cry and tell her that it wasn't her job to save the world. Because she just wasn't up to it. Not tonight.

"Sometimes, I just feel so . . . used."

"Really? How tragic for you. God has chosen you for a task so special that his own son speaks to you in dreams, and you feel used. Miracles happen all around you, things literally fall out of the sky to provide you with what you need, and you feel used. Your work changes lives, maybe even saves lives, and you can't be bothered to think that's a good thing because you're too busy being immersed in your own personal pity party. Knock it off, Maureen. I'm sorry this is upsetting for you, but you need to snap out of it. We have work to do."

Peter waited in the silence that followed. The last speech was a calculated risk. Sometimes that approach with her worked and she did, indeed, snap out of it. Sometimes, she just cried harder. At other times, she threw things at his head and didn't speak to him for weeks at a time.

He held his breath, but he didn't need to duck.

"Okay." Maureen sat up straighter and ran her hands through her hair, trying to pull herself together and focus on the work facing them. "So let's say that the time is returning and a group of us are here to fulfill a promise. So . . . what does that look like? When, exactly, did we make this promise? Easa mentioned the promise in my dream. He said: *'Follow the path that has been laid out for you, and you will find what you seek. Once you have found it, you must share it with the world and fulfill the promise that you made.'* Is this promise something we made in heaven? Is it a promise to God? A promise to each other? To ourselves? Do we all sit together in some great conference room in the sky and plan this out and say, 'Right, I'll see you down there, don't be late?' I just don't understand."

"I can't answer that, Maureen. This is a matter of faith at the moment, believing in something we can't see and don't understand. And maybe we need to find the Book of Love in order to fully grasp whatever *it* is."

He looked at her closely for a minute, beginning to feel guilty about berating her. There were dark circles under her eyes and she looked very fragile. This was quite a burden to carry for anyone, and most people would have snapped under this pressure a long time ago. Maybe he had gone too far. "How long has it been since you've had any sleep?"

Maureen stopped to think and shrugged. "Define sleep."

"Well, I know you better than to say an entire night, but how about at least a few hours at a time?"

She shook her head. "I don't remember. Not recently."

"Your brain needs to rest and to process all the information that you put into it, and it never gets a chance to do that. You need to get some sleep."

Maureen nodded. "I hate taking sleeping pills. They make me groggy and useless. They numb my brain, and I can't afford to do that."

"Have you tried praying?"

She smiled weakly at him. "Why didn't I think of that?"

"Given that you have a pretty direct line to those with ears to hear, I think you should really try it. Ask and you shall receive. In the meantime, I'm going home. And I am not coming back tomorrow unless you tell me in the morning that you at least tried to get some sleep and got yourself straight with the Lord your God. How's that for motivation?"

"It's not motivation, it's blackmail. But I'm too tired to argue with you. So, yeah, I promise."

True to her word, Maureen got on her knees at the side of the bed, just as she had done as a child. She asked Easa to help her, to give her some rest and some comfort in all of this. She knew she was acting in a manner that was ungrateful for all of the grace he had bestowed upon her, and she was most heartily sorry. But sometimes, this was hard. The responsibility was too great. She just needed to sleep a little better and to feel more protected in this process.

Then, she did something she hadn't done in years. She recited the Lord's Prayer, and tried to remember exactly how it fit within a six-petaled rose.

"Thy will be done," she whispered. "Really. I mean it. And I'm sorry."

She climbed into bed and allowed herself the release that can come only with crying alone, as long and as hard as one needs to. Tonight, it was for a very long time. There was a litany in her soul that she had to work through: the pain, the insecurity, the uncertainty, the risk, all the things that accompanied the supernatural experiences that were becoming a daily part of her life. All the emotions and fears she could not show to the world, even to those closest to her. Perhaps especially to those closest to her. They all needed her to be strong in this, depended on it. Like Matilda, she was The Expected One, and she was never allowed to doubt that, or to be anything less than that.

Hardest of all was the loneliness. It seemed crazy, to say that she was lonely, when there were so many people who cared about her. She did not suffer from a lack of love, and for that she was grateful. But the loneliness came from something she could not control, and that was the feeling that no one else on earth could really understand what she was going through. How could they? How could anyone know what it felt like to be in her skin? To have her responsibility and yet not be affected by it, not get so caught up in it as to become nonfunctional? Because most of the time she couldn't allow herself to think about the gravity of what she was trying to accomplish, or why it was even her mission in the first place. That way madness lies. Instead, she had to live one day at a time and simply do the work as it was given to her, and be strong enough to deal with what was put in her path.

And that was the true mental and emotional conundrum; the paradox of her life was that it required her to be sensitive and vulnerable and emotionally open in order to experience the visions, listen to them, believe in them. But to act upon them in a twenty-first-century world, which was hard and cynical and had long since given up on mysticism and faith, required tremendous strength. It was very difficult to have it both ways.

It wasn't that she truly felt sorry for herself; it was simply that she wished there was a single person in the world who could understand and with whom she could talk about the weight of it all. Perhaps that was why she was beginning to feel such emotional closeness to Matilda in the telling of this story. Here was another human being who had experienced this strange destiny that had the power to be both miraculous and malevolent. They were sisters across time and space. Unfortunately, Matilda had been dead for a thousand years and wasn't much for dialogue. Maureen hoped that in the continued unveiling of Matilda's life, she would find more comfort than questions.

When she had exhausted herself through introspection and more tears than she had shed in a long time, she felt better. And she felt tired. Maureen rolled over on her side and for the first time in years, she slept a dreamless, peaceful sleep until dawn broke over Rome and the first rays of light glittered off the marble of the Pantheon.

❊

Father Girolamo was disconcerted as she left his office. He had not anticipated the meeting with Maureen and had not expected her to come to these conclusions at all, much less so quickly. Either she was the most gifted visionary of all the women he had studied, or she was receiving extraordinary divine guidance on her journey. Both scenarios were of tremendous interest to him.

He took the key that he wore around his neck and unlocked the desk drawer. He removed the prophetic manuscript from his desk and began to page through it once again, all the while clutching his precious reliquary in one hand.

Canossa
January 1077

GREGORY AND MATILDA NEEDED time to find their love again and heal, following the stressful exhibition of Henry's penance. They would be granted this by the Lord himself, as the winter that approached was too severe to allow the pope's return to Rome. Gregory VII would, in fact, find a way to stretch this visit into a six-month period of respite in Tuscany at the side of his beloved, who was now heavy with his child.

The Benedictine monk Donizone would write later about Matilda and Gregory's time in Canossa: "As Martha who served Jesus, attentive and inviting, and like Mary who sat at the feet of Jesus, Matilda listened to every word uttered by this pope."

They lived together as man and wife in Canossa, as the stronghold was staffed only by Matilda's most trusted insiders, all of whom were members of the Order and sworn to keep this secret of the pope's wife and child. So it was that on the day that Matilda went into labor, she was surrounded by those who loved her most.

Unlike in her first experience with childbirth, she was safe and comfortable. Most of all, she was eternally in love with the man who had fathered this child, a baby who had been conceived "immaculately" as defined within the Book of Love, created through a union of trust and consciousness. And as Isobel was on hand to serve as midwife, Matilda knew that she and the infant would be cared for perfectly. Gregory remained in the chapel, visited often by Conn, praying for Matilda's safe delivery.

Her baby arrived quickly and without great effort to the mother. He was small but perfectly proportioned, with a hearty cry that indicated his strong lungs and general health. Matilda sobbed with relief as she held this newborn to her breast. She was infinitely grateful to God that this baby had been delivered safely, so much so that she could not, at this joyous moment, allow herself to think of the future. She would not allow herself to consider the sad reality that she would never be able to publicly acknowledge that this precious being was her child. The world must never know that Matilda of Canossa had given birth to this little boy. The world must certainly never know that this little boy was the child of Pope Gregory VII.

Matilda held the baby close to her face, and he looked at her with eyes that were wise beyond those of a newborn. She gasped, realizing that she had made eye contact with this same little being once before. Staring back at her were the eyes of her first child, the tragic infant she had named Beatrice Magdalena just minutes before the infant passed from this world to the next.

Was it possible that this was the same spirit, the same child returned to her in a different form? Matilda was certain that the eyes she was looking into were the same she had connected with so briefly once before. The eyes were truly the windows of the soul, and Matilda knew she had gazed into these. Her baby had come back to her in a time and place where its spirit would be safe and nurtured.

The time returns.

The baby, whom she and Gregory named Guidone, stayed with his mother and father until Gregory's return to Rome. Matilda kept him with her until the end of the summer, when it was time for her to join the pope at the Lateran palace to put into play the elaborate plan they had been constructing during their confinement. On the day before her departure to Rome, Matilda entrusted her son into the keeping of the brothers at San Benedetto de Po, brothers of the Order who would raise him in the sacred traditions of their people. If Matilda could not acknowledge this baby as her own, at the very least she would dedicate him to God.

Chapter Fifteen

Rome
October 1077

*K*ing Henry IV waited in Lombardy for months in an effort to gauge Gregory's position. He had his own set of problems, as the dukes who had demanded his surrender to the pope were appalled at Henry's ability to turn his coat so quickly. Realizing beyond doubt that there was no honor in such a king, the rebellious dukes of Germany elected Rudolf of Swabia as their new monarch. This election was supported by fully half the German territories, while the other half maintained loyalty to Henry. A bloody civil war loomed; however, it did not keep Henry from continuing his attacks on Gregory and Matilda.

In Canossa, the couple had spent their months together creating a strategy by which to protect Matilda's properties in the likely event that Henry decided to declare them forfeit under Salic law. Like his father before him, Henry could attempt to confiscate all Tuscany, as it was within the German king's feudal territories. He could also choose to give them to Godfroi of Bouillon, the hunchback's legal heir, in exchange for a pledge of fealty and a very large cut of the tribute that they would demand of the Tuscan people. Either possibility would push Italy and Germany into war. Either possibility would prove catastrophic to Matilda and the pope.

As Matilda and her retinue from Tuscany made the approach into Rome, Conn rode up beside her. He was uncertain how she would be received by the Roman populace, and he intended to stay near in case of a hostile reaction. Gregory's own position in Rome was now somewhat tenuous as his prolonged absence from the Lateran had been terribly unpopular with both the cardinals and the noble families who supported him. All of them blamed Matilda, and Conn was concerned about reprisals.

"Quiet so far," he commented.

She nodded. "Thanks be to God." They rode in silence for a few moments before Matilda spoke again. "Conn, we will get through this. With the declaration I am prepared to make, I believe we can win the allegiance of the Romans to our side once more."

Conn considered this for a moment. "Are you certain that you want to do this? It is . . . a great risk, Tilda."

Matilda swallowed hard. She was nervous about the decision she had made and the proclamation she would present in Rome the following day as a result. But she was equally determined to follow through with it. "It is a risk I am prepared to take, and one that I believe will save Gregory. As such, it is the only possible course of action for me. Gregory is more to me than life, more to me than even Tuscany. There is nothing I would not risk for him."

Conn nodded silently. He knew that to be true, whether he liked it or not.

It was against this backdrop of uncertainty that the countess of Tuscany rode into Rome, determined to save her inheritance, strengthen Gregory's position and that of the Church they intended to reform, and thwart the wicked Henry once and for all.

✵

Matilda of Canossa addressed the Lateran Palace, dressed for grandeur in a red velvet robe trimmed in ermine and wearing her golden crown of fleurs-de-lis over her heavy silk wimple. She looked as grand

and wealthy as any empress who ever reigned; her appearance on this day would be discussed and recorded for posterity by scribes and artists. With all the noble Roman families in attendance to witness her historic decree, she stood and read aloud the following proclamation:

> *I, Matilda, by the grace of God who is Countess of Tuscany, do bequeath for the good of my soul to Saint Peter through the intervention of Pope Gregory VII, all my goods and property and all that I possess through inheritance or that I own outright. I give all that once belonged to me to the Holy See in the name of my Lord, Jesus Christ.*

There was silence immediately following Matilda's proclamation as those in attendance wrestled with the reality of what they had just heard. Could it be possible? Was the countess of Tuscany, the most powerful woman in Europe, relinquishing all her worldly possessions to the Church? Had she just proclaimed that all her properties—which constituted nearly a third of Italy, and certainly the most wealthy and strategic territories—were now under the absolute control of Gregory VII?

It was shocking, it was unprecedented, and it was brilliant. In one stroke, Matilda had protected Tuscany, strengthened the papacy and indeed all Rome, while diminishing Henry's claim on Italian territories. The Roman families and the cardinals were overwhelmed by this tremendous display of loyalty and generosity, the likes of which had never been witnessed. Gregory must surely be a blessed and honorable man, more than worthy of the papal tiara, if he had secured such an enormous, unparalleled donation to the Church. Matilda was immediately celebrated as a savior in Rome, as the cry rose up through the Lateran:

"God bless the countess Matilda! May she live forever!"

Matilda moved her household to Rome to spend the next three years with her beloved Gregory and to sort out the administration of her territories through the Church. She made special stipulations for the monastery of San Benedetto de Po to be protected by the pope into perpetuity, as this was now a significant outpost of the Order as well as the dwelling place of her son. Matilda and the pope were inseparable during their time in Rome, and yet given her generosity to the Church, no one dared speak out about it. Her presence was accepted, if not always revered, as a result of her extraordinary donation. It was proof of her undying love for Saint Peter.

Donizone, writing later about Matilda and Gregory's days in Rome, said, "The wise countess kept the words of this blessed man in her heart just as the Queen of Sheba kept the holy words of Solomon."

For Matilda, the declaration to bequeath her property to the pope had been painless. He was, after all, her husband.

❁

Henry's response to Matilda and Gregory's outlandish plan to bequeath Tuscany to the throne of Saint Peter—his Tuscany—was to call once again for the pope to be deposed. The king went further than ever this time, nominating an antipope in Gregory's place. Guiberto, the archbishop of Ravenna who had served Henry's father before him, was elected pope by the schismatic German bishops.

Gregory responded by excommunicating Henry for the second time, and he excommunicated the antipope Guiberto, also for the second time. The battle lines were drawn, and Henry was poised for war. But it was now a highly personal conflict, and the king decided to twist the knife in his cousin's back by diminishing her hold on the most sanctified locale of her people: Lucca. Henry seized Lucca and harvested discord against the countess and the pope, expelling Bishop Anselmo and confiscating property that belonged to the Order. Thankfully, the Libro Rosso had been saved, as had the Master and the remaining elders of the Order, who had moved to San Benedetto Po, under Conn's armed escort. But Lucca seceded from the duchy of Tuscany, demanding independence from Matilda and embracing the antipope in collusion with the schismatic Lombardy lords who were loyal to Henry. Matilda was heartbroken by this loss but had little time to mourn it as Henry continued with more vicious attacks on both Tuscany and the papacy.

Matilda had cause for alarm. Her dramatic gift of property to the Church protected her from Henry—but only as long as the reigning pope was loyal to her and gave her continued free rein to administer the territories at her free will. If Gregory lost his footing and was replaced by Henry's antipope, she risked losing everything she and her family had ever fought to build and protect. And Henry was gaining strength as the northern Italian dukes, many of whom had been aligned with the schismatic contingents since the first days of Gregory's investiture, bonded together to support the antipope in hopes of avoiding invasion by German forces.

The vernal equinox of 1081 did not bring with it a celebration of Matilda's birth as it normally did. Instead it brought dangerous and troubling news. Henry IV had crossed the Alps and was riding for the Apennines, with an army of invasion at his back. He was coming to claim Tuscany.

Matilda and Gregory spent that night in her tower in Isola Tiberina, quietly discussing their options. There was no choice but for Matilda to ride back to Tuscany immediately and defend her territories. It was a harsh and sad time as they considered the dire nature of their circumstances. The German king was invading with great strength, and it would require all Matilda's forces to oppose him, forces which Henry had systematically decimated over the last four years.

"I don't know when I will see you again, my dove," Gregory said, pulling her into his arms to kiss her gently. He stroked her cheek with his long fingers and toyed absently with the strands of hair that surrounded her face as he spoke. He appeared to be memorizing every-thing about her. "This war is escalating. God is sending you to Tuscany while at the same time demanding that I stay and defend my position in Rome. We must surrender to his will, of course, but I cannot say that I understand it."

There were tears welling in her eyes as she clasped her hands over his own. "God's will is done, Gregory, as it always must be. Someday, somewhere we will understand it, even if that time is not today. Per-haps this is our greatest test as beloveds—the test of Solomon and Sheba, to know that we must be separated as duty demands, and yet know that we are never truly separated. For we are connected in our hearts and souls, as we have been since the dawn of eternity. And what God has put together . . ."

Gregory finished the sentence, "Let no man separate." And he took her in his arms and into their deepest embrace of trust and conscious-ness, where their spirits were intertwined once and for all in the pas-sionate union of their bodies.

❀

When Matilda returned to Tuscany, she arranged for the creation of a piece of art as a gift for Gregory. She had their son brought to Canossa. Guidone was now a bright and thriving five-year-old Tuscan boy with dark curls and gray eyes, the perfect image of his father. Matilda sat with him upon her lap, when she could stop his squirming, as their portrait was created by one of the monks from San Benedetto, who was a highly skilled illuminator. Because the painting was to be delivered to the pope in these troubled, warlike times, it was disguised as a typical madonna and child. Matilda wore the sumptuous azure silks that were her trademark in public and covered her hair with the traditional wim-ple and veil beneath the crown that identified her as a descendant of Charlemagne the Great. The golden tiara was capped with fleurs-de-lis, and the crown studded with the same five jewels that could be found on the cover of the Libro Rosso. The fortress of Canossa was painted at the very top of the parchment, and the perfected dove of their tradition hovered over the image of the mother and child.

To any unsuspecting eye, it was a devotional portrait of a regal madonna and child. For Pope Gregory VII, it was a beloved image of his wife and his son.

Destiny is the search. Destination is the finding.

Whoever searches must continue to search until they find, for to seek is the sacred task that drives all men and women who would become fully realized. What if we all stopped searching for God? The world would turn dark as we would have no means in which to understand the light.

But those who know they must seek have already found God.

In the finding there is disturbance, a knowing that all we have ever believed that is outside God's love is an illusion.

And finally, there is wonder. Wonder that the world created by Divine Will is more perfect and beautiful than we ever imagined.

From the Book of Love,
as preserved in the Libro Rosso

Rome
present day

"Guidone." Maureen was the first to comment on the name of Matilda's child, but Bérenger was already on the same page.

He retrieved the copies of the document which had been sent to the château, the family tree that began with a child called Guidone, born in Mantua in 1077. He displayed them for Peter and Maureen.

"Now I understand it," he explained. "When I first received this document, I did some research into how Michelangelo could have been related to all this. I found several references to the fact that he claimed openly during his life that he was a descendant of Matilda of Tuscany. He was ridiculed for this claim as all recorded history regarding Matilda asserts that she only had a daughter—the infant Beatrice who died the day she was born. Michelangelo refused to elaborate, other than to insist that he knew who he was and that he was Matilda's descendant."

"So he knew." This was Maureen. "He knew about Matilda and Gregory, and he knew about Guidone, because that is where his line of descent comes from."

Bérenger nodded. "Art will save the world? This opens up an entirely new investigation into the works of art that the great one was creating, doesn't it?"

Maureen jabbed Peter, who was sitting next to her, in the ribs. "Like the gorgeous young Pietà in Saint Peter's, who is clearly not a mother holding her son."

Peter nodded. "I may have to concede based on this. You realize, of course, that this gives us far more questions than answers?"

Maureen laughed. "Doesn't it always?"

But the questions of Michelangelo's contribution to preserving the truth would have to wait for further investigation. The Roman police had arrived to take a report regarding the theft in Maureen's room. While they were treating it as a routine robbery, Bérenger and Peter were both certain that whoever stole the computer and the notebooks was looking specifically for Maureen's journal entries.

Maureen wasn't sure what to think, other than that she was terribly frustrated by the loss and now had no formal means of keeping track of her thoughts or her dreams. Perhaps her sleep would be dreamless tonight.

❁

Exhausted from the events of the day, Maureen decided to turn in early. As she drifted to sleep, her last thought was of the shocking realization that she and Lucia Santos were sisters of the spirit. So much for dreamless sleep. The vision that came was more vivid than ever.

✺

She moved through the mists, the heavy silver-gray curtain that was specific to the Irish countryside so near to the western coast. It was midnight and the streets of Knock were deserted. The souvenir shops with their Connemara marble rosaries and lenticular postcards had long since closed their doors to pilgrims. Maureen walked alone, in the direction of the church dedicated to Saint John the Baptist with its extreme charcoal spire that pointed upward to heaven. The church glowed in the moonlight through the mists, and as she drew closer to the now famous south gable, an iridescent shimmer emerged from the left side of the wall.

The figures appeared one at a time, beginning on the left. The elder man emerged from the tangible, swirling silver-white light first. He was as the villagers described him 150 years ago: with graying hair and a beard. His presence was potent, however. There was a strength to him that was paternal rather than patriarchal. He gestured to the other side of the wall with both hands, as if creating a new image out of the radiance. This figure appeared on Maureen's right, as the light increased and the second character appeared. Here was the younger male, he whom the villagers had identified as John the Evangelist. In full animation, he was clearly a youth, depicted with the same long hair that medieval and Renaissance artists used to indicate a young man. He too was strong in his presence but with a very different aura than the elder man. The youth was dressed in vestments and was preaching. Maureen could not hear the words, but they were strong and heartfelt—and full of love. There was a grace to this young man that melted Maureen's heart as she watched him. The book he held came into clearer focus through the shimmering light: it was enormous, and yet the young man balanced it with one hand with no apparent effort as he read from it. The book was covered in what appeared to be deep red leather with gold bindings. Five golden baubles decorated the cover, crossing it in an X shape. As Maureen attempted to study the book's appearance, she was distracted by an intense burst of light at the center of the wall.

Both men, the elder and the younger, turned toward the center and gestured to the apparition that was emerging with infinite grace from the light. She was the most beautiful woman Maureen had ever seen, sublime, elegant, graceful. Her gown was liquid silver and she was crowned with a halo of glittering stars; white lilies and red roses were woven through her garments. She floated above the other figures, ethereal and angelic. Like the young man, the lady also appeared to be preaching. She stood in a position of absolute authority, the central figure of this tableau, conveying a silent message with great intensity. Maureen watched, transfixed, until the lady very suddenly looked down to lock eyes with her. She delivered one audible sentence, directly to Maureen.

"I am not who you think I am."

She smiled then, an expression full of the light of the moon and the stars, looking first at Maureen, then at the young man, and finally at the elder. The lady reached out, extending her hands to each of them. As the men came near her, the light grew brighter and the three figures merged perfectly into one bright and eternal burst of light.

It was still the middle of the night in Rome, and the floodlights on the Pantheon had long been put to sleep. Maureen wakened to a dark room in stark contrast to the visions of light that had been prevalent in her dream.

Her dream about Knock. Her dream about the apparitions. Her dream about an astonishingly beautiful female form who said only one thing to her.

Maureen switched on the bedside lamp and sat up, rubbing her hands over her eyes to help herself wake up. Instinctively, she reached for her notebook before remembering that it had been stolen. She climbed over the bed to the minibar and grabbed a bottle of San Pellegrino water on her way to the desk and the hotel notepad. She scribbled,

I am not who you think I am.

So . . . who was she?

Maureen crossed the room to throw open the window that faced the Piazza della Rotonda. The moon was waxing and near to full, shedding the only light into the square. The lovely fountain gurgled at all hours of the day and night, and it was this soothing sound of running water that Maureen was listening to as her gaze fell on the obelisk, a monument brought from Egypt to Rome at great expense and effort originally to grace a temple to Isis. Isis, who to Egyptians was the great lady of the mysteries; Isis, who was the mother of the gods. Isis, whom both the Romans and the Egyptians referred to as the Queen of Heaven.

The Queen of Heaven. This term had been used to define a number of great female spiritual entities: Isis, the Virgin Mary, numerous goddess forms from virtually all Near Eastern cultures, like the Sumerian Inanna and the Mesopotamian Ishtar, the Hebrew Asherah, and even Mary Magdalene by her heretical French followers.

If there was a queen of heaven, wouldn't this imply that there was a king? And would they be married? And equals?

Maureen thought carefully about the dream from which she had just awakened, reviewing each detail of the apparitions. The order in which the figures appeared had to be important. The first who showed himself in the dream was the elder man.

The Father.

The next apparition was of the younger man.

The Son.

And the final apparition, the ethereal feminine being of such light and radiance that even in the dream state her feet could not touch the ground.

The Holy Spirit.

Maureen knew then that the villagers in Ireland had, indeed, seen a most blessed and holy vision. But what they saw was not a vision of the Virgin Mary, her husband, and John the Evangelist. What the apparition at Knock represented was the Holy Trinity.

And within that trinity, the Holy Spirit was paramount. And female.

She rang Peter as early as she thought was civilized. Thankfully, he was up. And fascinated by her dream.

"Is the Holy Spirit ever considered feminine, Pete? For us it was always the 'Holy Ghost,' which is decidedly unfeminine, but was that a later evolution?"

Peter explained that there were traditions that believed that the Holy Spirit was indeed feminine, but they were considered "fringe elements" and therefore heretical. Or nuts.

"In Greek, the word used most often for spirit is *pneuma*, which is gender neutral. It is assumed to be male, of course. But there are those who argue the gender is different in other languages, specifically Hebrew and Aramaic, and I think Syriac."

"What about the dove?" Maureen asked. "The Holy Spirit is often depicted that way in art, right? And isn't the dove feminine?"

"Well, the dove depicts the Holy Spirit because it appears at the baptism of Jesus in the Jordan. But you're right, it does take on feminine symbolism at other times. The Gnostics believed that the Holy Spirit was female, in the guise of Sophia. Sophia is the entity that represents divine feminine wisdom, a goddess of sorts, but more exalted. She is sometimes depicted as a dove."

Maureen was thinking back on the Matilda material. "Like in the Song of Songs? My dove? My perfect one? Could there be a connection? Is the Song truly about the union of God and his counterpart— let's call her his wife for lack of a better term—as much as it is Solomon and Sheba?"

Peter's head was swimming, and it was only 7:30 in the morning. "Give me a few hours to pull up some translations and I'll be over by lunchtime."

True to his word, Peter was in Maureen's hotel room with several file folders in his hand by noon. They used the desk in her suite, as well as the bed, to spread out the paperwork that Peter had compiled for her examination. Before digging into the paperwork, Maureen asked Peter about the prayer known widely as the Hail Mary.

"I don't have to remind you of where that prayer originates, as you're the one who taught me."

"Luke. Chapter one."

"Uh-huh. So it is canonical, as is the Lord's Prayer. But only partially. Because what else did you teach me about Luke, chapter one? And what else do we know about our Luke?"

"Luke founded the Order of the Holy Sepulcher, so we're looking for what his original motivation may have been, right? Okay, I see where this is going. In the New Testament, Mary's name isn't used. That was added later. The prayer, as recited by the angel Gabriel, was 'Hail, full of Grace. The Lord is with thee, blessed art thou amongst women.'"

Maureen nodded again. "Certainly, this prayer is about the mother of Jesus in this context. But what I am saying is this: what if it isn't just all about her? What if she is just one of many women chosen to embody this aspect of God? This creative, fertile, maternal aspect that gives birth to new life. And what if her name wasn't used in the original greeting because Luke was showing us that this salutation is to all women of great faith and love who conceive, as Matilda tells us, with trust and consciousness? Which is to say, according to the Book of Love and the Gospel of Philip, the definition of an immaculate conception."

Needing to process the idea, Peter decided that the best approach was to go through the notes he had made earlier in the day and see what corroborated Maureen's burgeoning theory. "Let's start with the traditional canon, because I think that has the most immediate and powerful impact. I brought some examples of critical translation issues. Translation is everything," he told her, taking out two sheets of paper. "First, I want to show you a verse from the gospel of John which really illustrates this. Here is the most universally accepted translation into English from the Greek, the King James Version. This is John fourteen chapter twenty-six. It reads, *'But the Comforter, which is the Holy Ghost, whom the Father will send in my name, he shall teach you all things, and bring all things to your remembrance, whatsoever I have said unto you.' "*

Peter held out a sheet of paper where he had printed just that verse. Then he handed her another, with the same verse in a different translation. "Now take a look at this one. This is a translation from Aramaic, and it matches another in Syriac that was taken from scrolls found at the monastery of Saint Catherine of Alexandria in Mount Sinai—scrolls that predate the Greek texts. See what you think of this."

Maureen read the older translation out loud. " *'But She—the Spirit, the Paraclete—whom He will send to you, my Father in my name, She will teach you everything; She will remind you of that which I have told you.' "*

Maureen sat down hard on the bed. "Wow. That's pretty emphatically feminine." She let it sit for a moment, contemplating it. "And the word *paraclete*? How does that translate?"

"Traditionally it is translated as 'comforter' or even 'counselor.' But I think it is more accurately translated as 'one who intercedes.' So you could make the case here that the Paraclete intercedes between humans and their father in heaven."

"Which is a very female and maternal role, isn't it?"

"It also relates to an interesting Old Testament concept, that of 'the comforter.' Look at this passage, Isaiah, chapter sixty-six, which compares Yahweh with a mother comforting her children. Isaiah is loaded with references to God behaving as a mother—God as a woman in labor, God as a mother who gives birth to and protects Israel. In Hebrew, the word equivalent of Holy Spirit is *ruach*, which can be either masculine or feminine, dependant on usage. It is similar in Aramaic, where the word is *ruacha*. But there it is definitively feminine."

Peter picked up another sheet with two translations on it. "Now I know that you're not a big fan of Paul, but here is an important quote from Romans, chapter eight, which gives us reason to pause. King James reads, *'The Spirit himself testifies with our spirit that we are God's children.'* But compare that to the Aramaic."

He handed it to Maureen, who read it aloud. " *'She, the Ruacha, gives testimony with our spirit that we are God's children.' "*

Peter produced the final documents from his morning research session. "Now take a look at this from the Gospel of Philip, which we are very concerned with in our quest for the Book of Love. I think this passage is the smoking gun."

Maureen looked at the copy from the Gnostic Gospel of Philip. At the top of the page, Peter had Xeroxed the original scroll in Coptic, indicating that these critical lines came from page 57, plate 103. Peter's English translation was next to it. It read:

Some say that Mary was impregnated by the grace of the Holy Spirit.
But they do not know what they say.
How can the feminine impregnate the feminine?

Maureen and Peter looked at each other for a moment, allowing the passage to speak for itself in its simple, pure power. Maureen ultimately broke the silence. "Is this really all about something completely different than we ever suspected, Pete?"

"Meaning?"

"Well, I used to think that this was entirely about vindicating Mary Magdalene, making people realize and understand who she was and why she mattered. She was the wife of Jesus and she was his best friend and his partner and his chosen successor. She brought Christianity to Europe and she and her children risked everything to see that it flourished and endured. That in itself is a fairly tall order."

"But . . ."

"But . . . what if that isn't the point at all? Oh, I mean it matters, of course it does, it is *a* point, and a significant one. But maybe it's not the ultimate point."

"Go on."

"Maybe Magdalene is emblematic of a larger issue. Maybe what she represents, even more than the wife of Jesus in his human aspect, is the wife of Jesus in his divine aspect. He is God and she is the beloved of God. His other half. On earth as it is in heaven."

"The feminine aspect of the divine?"

"Yes. But not in the traditionally considered pagan form of a goddess or some minor deity. But as an aspect of God. The equal, female face of God, if you will. The feminine half that completes the male half of God. In this case, seen in the guise of the Holy Spirit."

Peter was considering this as he looked through the notes he had made earlier that morning. "Let me read you something I found very interesting. 'It has even been speculated that the name of God, *Yahweh*, may have evolved from Ya-hu, which means "Exalted Dove" and was the name of an ancient creation goddess who was the wife of God, who was called El. The two, El and Ya-hu, blend into one and are ultimately called by the singular *Yahweh*, which later becomes known to be simply male.' Now to be fair, there are many other theories about the origins of *Yahweh*, and this is just one of them, and certainly not the accepted one by many scholars."

Maureen laughed at this a little. "Lately, I find that I often prefer theories that are not accepted by scholars. You know, the French esoteric writer Louis Charpentier once said that when history and tradition disagree, you can be sure that history is wrong. I'm with him on this. I'll take the living traditions that have endured in France and Italy for thousands of years over a set of academic principles which were designed to support power structures over the truth."

She walked to the window, threw it open to let in the late spring air, and gazed out at the Isis obelisk. To her right, by a few hundred yards, was a piazza and church dedicated to Mary Magdalene. To her left the same distance was a church dedicated to the Virgin Mary and built over a temple to the goddess of wisdom, in the case of the Romans, Minerva—but also known as Sophia, the Lady of Divine Wisdom. Ahead of her was an obelisk in honor of Isis.

"Notre Dame," she said suddenly.

"What about it?" Peter's mind went immediately to the Gothic monument in Paris.

"Not *it*. *Her*," Maureen corrected. "Notre Dame. Our Lady. For two years I've been building a case that all the churches in France that are dedicated to Notre Dame were dedicated to Mary Magdalene, right?"

Peter nodded. He had helped her with that very convincing research. It was clear to both of them that the Notre Dame churches, and churches that contained statues of "black madonnas" all had associations with the Magdalene heresy.

"Well, they are, I'm certain of it, and so are you. But what if that's not the end? What if all of 'Our Ladies'—whether they be Magdalene, or the Virgin, or Isis or Minerva or Sophia—what if they're all the same? And what if they are just telling us that God has a female aspect? Or that God has a wife and a beloved? Could all these shrines have been built to restore that balance? We know all the Gothic cathedrals—all of which are called Notre Dame—were temples to the glory of God. But were they temples to the glory of the female aspect of God? She is Notre Dame. She is Our Lady. In all her guises. Because they all matter, regardless of which personification she takes on earth."

Peter was struck by an idea. "The time returns?"

He didn't have time to complete his thought, as they were interrupted by a knock at the door. It was Lara from the front desk. An envelope had been delivered to Maureen by a courier, which Lara had brought up thinking that it might have been something about Maureen's missing bag and computer.

Maureen thanked Lara and returned to the room. She immediately recognized the card stock and the strange monogram. The "Hail Ichthys" clues had been on identical stationery. This note was very simple:

Genesis 1:26
Genesis 3:22
Amor vincit omnia,
Destino

Maureen spoke first. "Look at the second verse number. Three twenty-two."

Peter was way ahead of her. It was the first thing he had noticed. Since Maureen had relayed her dream to him that morning, he had been fixated on the "coincidence" of Lucia Santos's date of birth, which was the same. "Your birth date."

She nodded. "Do you know the verse?"

"Well, I can't quote Genesis verbatim, but chapter one is creation and chapter three is the expulsion from the garden. I do carry my small Bible with me for reference. It will only give me the English, but we can look up earlier versions and ancient phrasing later."

"Start with the first verse on the list. Genesis one twenty-six."

Peter found it quickly. "Creation. 'Then God said, "Let us make man in our image, in our likeness, and let them rule over the fish of the sea and the birds of the air, over the livestock, over all the earth, and over all the creatures that move along the ground." ' "

He flipped ahead quickly to the third chapter, locating verse twenty-two. "This verse follows the place where Adam and Eve partake of the fruit in the garden. 'And the Lord God said, "Behold, man has become as one of us, to know good and evil; and now, lest he put forth his hand and take also of the tree of life and eat, and live forever." ' "

Maureen was laughing. "Well, I don't know who Destino is, but I want to thank him for doing my work for me."

Peter wasn't there yet. "Meaning?"

"Both of those passages refer to God in the plural form. Let us make man in *our* image, in *our* likeness. Behold, man has become as one of *us*. I had every intention of looking into all the places in scripture where we could argue God refers to himself in the plural, and now I don't have to go searching for that information."

Peter found the synchronicity more unsettling than comforting, and he still wasn't convinced that the mastermind behind the clues wasn't also the criminal with the gun. "Let me see that card again."

Maureen read the Latin motto first. "And it also says *Amor Vincit Omnia*. Even I know that one. Love conquers all. And it shows up on most of the Book of Love material that Matilda quotes in her memoirs. But isn't that from Virgil? Are we to believe that Jesus was quoting ancient Roman poetry? Because that's a stretch even I can't make."

"I'm not so sure it's that much of a stretch," Peter countered, surprising Maureen. "Look, I know I'm supposed to be the voice of reason here, but it is fascinating. If Jesus had a classically influenced education, he could have known about Virgil, who was only a generation ahead of him. Further, Virgil is often credited with predicting the coming of Jesus in the same work, the *Eclogues*, that uses the phrase *Love conquers all*. Eclogue Four is sometimes said to be about the nativity. So there is a strong connection, and perhaps even a deliberate effort to attach yet another messianic prophecy to his legacy. Or it could just be that this concept of *Love conquers all* is completely universal and archetypal and continues to return and recycle with different generations across the globe."

Maureen caught it immediately. "Making yet another aspect of what *the time returns* could mean." She nodded her understanding as she glanced down to catch the signature at the bottom of the card.

Destino.

Maureen paused before asking a question she already knew the answer to. "Pete, what does *destino* mean in Italian and Spanish?"

"*Destino*? It can mean either destiny or destination, or both."

Before Maureen had time to consider the correlation between Peter's revelation and her dream of Easa, the phone rang.

Father Girolamo di Pazzi needed to see Maureen on urgent business.

Vatican City
present day

"Do you know what this is?"

Maureen looked at the yellowed manuscript pages on Father Girolamo's desk and shook her head in reply to the old priest's question. She did not, legitimately, know exactly what it was, so she wasn't lying.

"Look closely," he rasped. "In fact, here." He handed one of the pages to her, and she took it gently. "Hold this and see what you think."

Maureen jumped a little when the paper made contact with her hands. There was power in these pages. Real power. She looked down at the verses, more curious now than wary. "They're in French. I'm sorry, but I'm not fluent."

"It doesn't matter. These verses are not to be translated verbatim with your mind. They're to be translated with your heart. Try."

Maureen read the first line in French. *Le temps revient.*

"The time returns," she said softly.

Father Girolamo nodded. "You do know what it is."

Maureen was quite sure that she was holding a piece of the Libro Rosso, or at least an aged translation of it, in her hands. But she couldn't admit that. To do so would be to give away that they had Matilda's manuscript, and she wasn't going to do that for anyone at this stage. There were too many questions. While Peter was certain that Father Girolamo was trustworthy, Maureen trusted no one within the walls of Vatican City. And Peter hadn't been allowed to accompany her, which was suspect. Girolamo insisted that the meeting was limited to the two of them.

"It's . . . poetry?" Maureen replied lamely.

The old man tried not to let his growing irritation show and spoke to her gently. "It's prophecy. Written in quatrains. Can you read more?"

Maureen looked at the verses, her hands shaking now. *Yes!* She wanted to scream at him. She could read them, and she knew exactly what they said, what they meant, and who wrote them. The page she held in her hands reverberated through her body.

"*Choisi . . .*" Maureen muddled through the literal French, which appeared to be medieval, or early Renaissance. "Something about being chosen. There are a lot of words here about love . . . that's really all I can translate. I'm sorry."

Father Girolamo patted her hand softly. "Do not rush, my child. Take your time, and just relax. I did not mean to put such pressure on you." He pulled out another page; this one appeared to be the very first in the manuscript. "See what you think of this."

It was a dedication page, and she could decipher that it was made out to Pope Urban VIII. But she stopped short as she saw the next line.

Les Prophéties de Nostradamus.

"Nostradamus?" Maureen asked, confused now.

"Yes, yes. These have all been attributed to the famous Frenchman."

Maureen could not shake her head or protest, did not indicate that she knew these were not the work of a French doctor from Provence in the sixteenth century. But she didn't have to.

"But as you already know"—Father Girolamo winked at her conspiratorially—"these prophecies are not the work of the famous Frenchman. Tell me, what else do you think *Les Prophéties de Nostra Damus* could mean?" He separated the syllables in the name deliberately, causing Maureen to gasp in spite of herself.

Hiding in plain sight. *The Prophecies of Nostra Damus.*

"The Prophecies of . . . of Our Lady."

✻

Maureen called Tammy on her cell as she walked across Saint Peter's Square in search of her own Peter.

"We owe Nostradamus an apology," she quipped as her friend answered from the château in Arques.

Maureen went on to explain the events in Father Girolamo's office. "Nostradamus wasn't a plagiarist. He was preserving the prophecies. Protecting them and providing a way for his generation to begin to understand them. And he couldn't exactly come out and say, 'These are the prophecies of the daughter of Jesus,' when the Inquisition was lurking just across the border from him. So he hid them in plain sight, within his name—the name his family adopted intentionally when they converted to a particular Order of Christianity. And that's *Order* with a capital *O*."

She signed off as she saw Peter approaching her, promising Tammy to call her later and fill her in on all the details as they were rapidly unfolding in Rome.

❀

Father Girolamo was very pleased with the interview. While he knew that Maureen was holding back, he had also seen her genuine reaction to the manuscript pages. He would be patient and gentle with her, and wait. He was quite certain that her sheer curiosity would eventually bring her back for more.

Salerno
1085

GREGORY VII WAS DYING.

The last years of his life had tested the limits of his faith. Had he been given the chance to be near Matilda during these trials, he could have endured anything that God put in his path, but they had been apart for eight years since that last night in Rome. How strange that, somehow, they both had known it was their last night together. When Matilda sent the portrait upon her return to Tuscany, it was her way of acknowledging that they were not destined to meet again in the flesh, at least not in this place and time. For all her warrior queen nature, Matilda was a deeply gifted mystic. She knew that their parting would be permanent.

She also knew, as did he, that their parting was only physical. Their spirits were united, their hearts and dreams were one and the same. Matilda had proven herself time and again to be the most loyal and devoted of souls. When Henry IV marched on Rome, Matilda sent every man she could muster from Tuscany to defend Gregory. When there were not enough men left in Tuscany, she sold everything she owned and purchased mercenaries from all over Europe. She even melted down her personal jewelry, everything except the ring she had been given on her sixteenth birthday. She raided her own monasteries and churches, liquidating anything that could be used to buy support for the papal cause. Over the last two years, Matilda of Tuscany had completely devastated her personal wealth and position in defense of the man she loved and in support of their mutual cause. That it wasn't enough, that she was unable to save him, was her ultimate heartbreak.

After a lengthy and bloody struggle, Henry IV had succeeded in deposing Gregory VII and installing a puppet pope on the throne of Saint Peter. Rome was in Chaos. Gregory was forced into exile in the coastal town of Salerno, where his family owned a sizable estate. He tried to rally support from Norman allies, but Henry's stronghold was now too great in Italy. Gregory's papacy was over, and with it, his life. In his exile, Gregory was unable to write to his beloved, and he was unable to save Rome and his church from the tyrant who would call himself king. He had lost the will to carry on, and a wasting sickness was overtaking him.

He called in one of the few men he trusted and asked him to write a final letter, one that he prayed would find its destination across the war-torn plains of Italy. He gave the man one of the few treasures he had left, a ring in gold with a carnelian intaglio of Saint Peter, and asked that he take a vow to see that this package reached its destination. That the messenger was an honest man, and intrepid, was God's final gift to Gregory VII before he left this earth for heaven on May 25, 1085.

In his final words, taken by a scribe, Gregory VII whispered, "I have loved justice and hated iniquity. Therefore I die in exile."

Canossa
June 1085

THE NEWS of Gregory's death was carried to Matilda by Conn, although it did not come as a surprise. She knew when it happened, down to the very minute on the very day.

"You do not lose the other half of your soul without feeling it in every piece of your being," she said quietly. "I have been mourning him for weeks. Long before the news arrived in Canossa."

Conn nodded. He had been away on one military crisis after another and had not been here to stay with her and comfort her as he would have liked. She was regal in her grief, like a queen who had lost her king but knew she had an obligation to carry on for the sake of her people.

"Tilda, a messenger brought a package today. It is from Salerno."

She swallowed hard; she had not expected this. To get any messenger from Salerno, past Rome, and into Tuscany in the current climate of all-out war was nearly impossible. That it had arrived safely was surely an act of divine protection. She took the package from Conn and opened it carefully, saying a prayer of thanks for the arrival of anything that would perhaps give her one last moment with her beloved.

The package contained the portrait of her and Guidone, the image in blue painted as a madonna and child that she had sent to Gregory four years before. She read the letter that accompanied it:

My beloved, my perfected one, my sweet dove—

How I miss you, how I have ached for you in these trying times. While God has chosen to give us terrible trials, none is harder for me than knowing that I cannot tell you how much I appreciate all that you have done, given, and sacrificed for our vision of love and equality. I know the toll that it has taken on you, and on your people. I pray many times a day that God will care for you and that your faith will bring you peace.

As my days left on earth grow short—indeed I shall likely be with our father and mother in heaven by the time you receive this—I wanted to return this portrait to you. For it is the single item that has kept me alive over the terrible period of exile. It was this image of your strength, and of Guidone's promise, that gave me hope when I had none. It was this reminder of your beauty, and of the sacred nature of our love, that gave me strength. This portrait is the single most valuable possession of my life, and as I die I do not want to see it lost. And so I return it to you, that you may know what it has meant to my heart and spirit for these years that it has been in my possession.

My final words to you, my beloved, are these: do not mourn for my passing. Celebrate it. For now, I will be able to stand beside you every single day, and nothing—no force of man or earth—can keep me from you. And I will fight by your side for truth and justice.
Semper. Always.

Conn, standing behind her as she read, left her alone as he watched her body begin to convulse. As he hurried down the hall to give her the privacy she would need, he heard the explosion of her sobs echo across the ancient stones of Canossa. Never, in all his eventful lifetime, had he heard anything more heartbreaking than Matilda's ultimate mourning.

I say unto you that there are only two commandments that must concern all men and women at all times, and they are:

Love God, your Creator in heaven, with all your heart and all your soul.

Love your neighbor as yourself, knowing that all men and women are your neighbor and that in loving them, you are loving God. So many search the earth and do not realize that they gaze into the face of the divine every day, for the divine is in each of us.

If all mankind lived by these two commandments at all times, there would be no war, no injustice, no suffering. These are not laws of diet or practice or sacrifice. They are laws of love.

How simple is the true will of God!

For those with ears to hear, let them hear it.

FROM THE BOOK OF LOVE,
AS PRESERVED IN THE LIBRO ROSSO

CHAPTER SIXTEEN

Mantua
1091

The metallic stench of blood filled Matilda's nostrils, causing her to hold her breath to keep from retching. Henry's troops had decimated most of Tuscany, looting, burning, and raping with a fevered vengeance that was beyond the imaginings of decent human beings. Matilda's childhood home was desecrated beyond recognition. Blood puddled in the streets where carcasses of her cherished Tuscan citizens were strewn in gore-dripped pieces; entire families, from grandparents to toddlers, were left hanging from the external rafters of their homes as emblems of hatred. Henry had been determined to make Mantua, Matilda's greatest and most valuable stronghold, the ultimate victim of her disloyalty to the king.

If she had any doubt of that, she did not after what she witnessed next.

Walking through the smoldering wreckage, Matilda and Conn, with a retinue of their most intrepid men, searched for survivors. They approached one of the larger houses on the outskirts, one attached to a fair amount of prime farming land. Matilda's heart was in her throat. She knew this house. It belonged to one of her distant cousins on the Lorraine side, a woman called Margarethe. Matilda had not had the time to get to know this cousin well, although she had intended to, as her duties called her away so frequently. She now had cause to regret that she had not stopped by this house to visit in the past, to talk with her kinswoman and know her family. It was one of life's harshest lessons that most people do not realize how many opportunities for love and friendship are missed until it is too late to reclaim them.

Matilda was aware that both Margarethe and her husband had long been loyal supporters, as Beatrice had mentioned them through the years. Matilda could hear her mother talking about the precious loyalty of friends as she approached the house. Strangely, Henry's soldiers had not burned this to the ground as they had the others. The door was smashed in and there was visible vandalism and obvious looting, but the structure itself was intact. Matilda wondered why the house had been spared and sought to enter, praying all the while that there would be some sign of life or hope here. Conn, ever suspicious and protective of her, insisted on preceding her into the dwelling.

Conn was a man hardened by the ways of war, but even for him the sight that awaited upon entrance was beyond bearing; he doubled over to catch his breath. Two female victims, apparently Margarethe and her daughter, were tied like livestock, naked, with their throats cut. Both the woman and the girl, who was no more than ten or eleven, had deep purple bruises across their thighs, a silent and horrific testament to what had happened here in the wake of a war in which men lost their humanity. Conn turned to stop Matilda from entering but was too late. She stood behind him, staring at the horror before her and weeping openly. Despite the overwhelming anguish she felt, or perhaps because of it, she did not fail to notice that both these tragic victims were the bearers of red hair.

"Pray with me, Conn. Let us pray for these, our sisters, that their souls are together in heaven and that they will never again know pain."

Conn nodded, but the voice that replied was not his. It came from a dark corner, raspy and soft. "I will pray with you."

Matilda startled, and Conn's hand flew to his sword in reflex, but both waited, holding still, to see what would come next.

A man emerged then from the shadows, hunched and broken. He had once been a tall and strong lord of this manor, but the violence that had been inflicted upon him and his family was beyond bearing. It was clear as Matilda saw his eyes that this man's spirit was as shattered as his body. More accurately, Matilda saw one eye. The other had been gouged out by a German dagger.

⁂

The man, who was called Ugo Manfredi, was carried back to Canossa on a litter, and the bodies of his wife and daughter were wrapped gently in linen cloth and pulled behind them on a cart for proper burial. Matilda nursed Ugo herself, focusing on his spirit as much as his wounded body. In the course of his rehabilitation, the man recounted the nightmare that he had endured at the hands of Henry's forces.

The soldiers had surrounded the house and kicked in his door. He had seen them coming, but not in enough time to secure his family. Although the women hid beneath a mattress, they were ultimately discovered as one of the German scouts had seen them in the fields days before. He remembered them because of their unusual hair color—remembered them because his commander provided bonuses to men who found such exquisite and particular spoils of war. Ugo reminded Matilda that his wife was from a noble family in Bouillon, and that her father had come here in the service of Bonifacio when she was a child. Matilda listened distraught to the rest of Ugo's horrific story.

Ugo was captured first. He was asked to declare his loyalty: was it to the harlot of Tuscany or to their divinely appointed King Henry? Ugo was Tuscan by blood and spirit and would never take a false vow, and certainly not one against the woman who ensured the peace and prosperity of this land as her father did before her. He declared for Matilda, knowing that only death could await him. But they did not kill him. They beat him severely, but they allowed him to live. After what he was forced to witness next, he wished that they had given him the blessing of death. Ugo stopped a number of times during the telling, as the events were nearly beyond his ability to recount them.

When his wife and daughter were found, they were stripped and bound as the commander of the forces was brought in to inspect them. The leader, obviously a man of some importance, demanded that both women swear their allegiance to the king. But Ugo's wife considered herself a kinswoman and was unerringly loyal to their benevolent countess. Neither would swear against Matilda, and Ugo's eye burned with tears as he recounted his little girl's bravery in asserting that she was a Tuscan and the kinswoman of the countess.

The arrogant, imperious leader of the troops had his way with them first, then threw them to the remaining soldiers, of which there were fifteen. Not all the men wanted to assault the women, but the leader insisted on it, determined as he was to debase them in the most violent way possible. The soldiers were clearly terrified of their leader, and they followed his orders. All the while, Ugo was kept in the room, forced to witness the horror inflicted upon his precious wife and child.

If God had any mercy left for Ugo, it was that both women were unconscious by the time their throats were sliced open. Most likely they were dead. Hugo was nearly certain that his daughter had died during the beatings that accompanied the rapes because the leader had considered taking the girl with him for his further entertainment later in the evening. He declined after closer inspection, as she was too damaged to be of any use to him. The orders were given to kill them like pigs at the slaughterhouse. At the same time, a second command was given to "mark" Ugo in a way that would show the world what happened to those who were fool enough to declare loyalty to Matilda and deny Henry.

The last thing that Ugo remembered, just before the dagger blade approached his eye, was the leader of the troops standing before him. The arrogant man spit in his face before making his pronouncement. "I have allowed you to live so that you can deliver a message to my bitch of a cousin. Tell the whore of Tuscany that I will desecrate every town that she claims as her own, and every women who claims loyalty to her, in just this way until she begs for my forgiveness on her knees before me. This is the only reason I will leave you your tongue, traitor."

The imperial leader of the troops who had raped and murdered the

Manfredi family then gave the signal for his soldier to end this chapter by maiming the lord of the house. King Henry IV stomped out of the dwelling, anxious to inspect what other spoils of war awaited him in Mantua.

His next target was equally personal, and one he was looking forward to looting himself: the Monastery of San Benedetto de Po. It was Matilda's spiritual sanctuary, her "Orval of the South," and a monument to Bonifacio's family. Taking it from her would be so very sweet.

More than a thousand years before the birth of our Lord, there rested in France a carving of a woman cradling an infant upon her knee. The pagan people of this place had received a great prophecy, a revelation from their druidic priests that a perfected young woman would give birth to a God, and that God would bring light and truth to the world. These pagan peoples were called Carnutes, and they gave their name to the town that would eventually grow from around this place: Chartres.

The sculpture of the perfected lady and child was believed to have magical properties, carved as it was in the hollowed-out trunk of a pear tree and perched on a mound of earth that was known to be sacred. For this hillock covered what the Carnutes called the wouivre, *a powerful and purifying current of energy that surged through the earth under its surface and found its pinnacle in this very place. The Carnutes understood that the* wouivre *was the artery that contained the life-blood of the planet. Thus the holy mound that marked the very pulse of the earth itself became a place of spiritual initiation for peoples all across the expanse of Europe who traveled here to feel the current run through their own veins. The essence of this flow stimulates the divine in every man and woman. It cannot be explained, but once experienced, it equally cannot be forgotten. The spirit is awakened here, and it is in this place that humans become fully* anthropos, *which is to say fully realized and integrated in their body, mind, and spirit.*

Adding further to the sanctity of this rare locale was a holy well, a chasm reaching deep into the land that filled with the magical womb-waters of the Woman Who Was the Earth. The Holy Mother of Us All was worshipped here in this place for as long as there is memory in man, and she was worshipped under many names. To the Carnutes she was Belusama and it is in this guise that she gives us the story we have come to hear. Belusama was the wife and partner of God, who the Carnutes called Belen. It was a name in keeping with the vernal equinox, the time when the day and night are in perfect balance, thus the name equi-nox, which means night is equal to day in length; dark and light live in harmony.

Belen had at his side a sister-bride, sister in that she was the other half of his soul, and bride in that she was his beloved. This was the glorious Belusama. Belen was known to rule the sky and the air, while this wife ruled the land and the sea. For the male sky God covers the female earth God in a natural occurrence of sacred union. Together, they were whole. Lands were consecrated in their name, many lands, and for this story it is necessary to know that the region where Chartres was founded, and where the magical wouivre wound through the ground with its healing and sacred current, was long named for the wife of God. Through the mists of time, this region was called Belusama, then La Belusa, and finally in the current French tongue it evolved into what we call it today: La Beauce. Thus in the ancient etymology, Chartres is "the sacred land of the Carnute peoples who lived within the holy region of the Mother of Us All, La Beauce."

Was the carving in the pear tree a representation of Belusama, the perfected wife of God who would create new life in the form of a human child? It was that, and it was more. It was a representation of the divine female principle in creation, and it ever will be.

It is the female face of God.

THE LEGEND OF THE SACRED LAND OF CHARTRES AND
LA BEAUCE, AS PRESERVED IN THE LIBRO ROSSO

Canossa
1091

THE LIBRO ROSSO was safely in Canossa, and so was the Master. He had been visiting at San Benedetto Po, involved in the instruction of Matilda's son, when Henry began pushing toward Mantua. The Order had enough time to secure what was left of their precious objects, those that had not been melted down or sold in the last defense of Gregory VII. Matilda's child, along with several of the brothers, escaped to safety in the hills south of Florence, where a new order had been founded decades earlier by a holy monk called Giovanni Gualberto. The order, called the Vallambrosans, were Benedictines of the strictest reforms who were recognized by the abbot of Cluny as the most saintly of God's brothers. As such, King Henry IV did not dare accost them, and the monastery at Vallambrosa was declared neutral territory and became a safe haven for those of Matilda's brothers who chose to find sanctuary there.

These brothers of the Order would ultimately blend with the Benedictine Vallambrosans, creating a secretly hybrid philosophy of strict monastic rule and heretical principle that Matilda would fund until her death. It was the Vallambrosans who would take over the Florentine properties of Santa Trinità, where she had spent her teenage years within the teachings of the Order. Four hundred years later, the importance of this—Matilda's financial support and the endurance of the Order's most sacred teachings—would become apparent as Santa Trinità evolved into the womb from which the Renaissance was born.

Matilda had spent this morning crafting a writ of dedication to Santa Trinità, a legal document that would ensure continued financial support to the Order from Rome in the event of her death. Drafting it had taxed all her knowledge of the law, and she was mentally exhausted from the exercise. She did not have the luxury of time to rest when her lands and people were in so much danger, so as soon as she put her pen aside to allow the ink to dry on the document, Matilda went out in search of Conn to discuss current military strategy. Henry IV had sacked San Benedetto de Po as he looted and destroyed the remainder of Mantua. Canossa was all they had left of safety, and they needed to be confident that it was secure at all times.

One of Conn's men came to advise Matilda that his captain was last seen heading for the chapel. She noticed that Conn was spending a lot of time in there since the massacres in Mantua. As Matilda reached the chapel, the door was ajar and she was able to see that Conn was on his knees in prayer, before the Libro Rosso and beside the Master. She watched quietly, waiting until both men appeared to be stirring to rise before entering the room.

The Master had to be ancient at this time in his long life, and yet he did not look so very much different than he did when Matilda first met him as a child. He appeared tired and perhaps a bit worn, but he was in remarkably good physical form for a man of his advanced age. And nothing of the years impacted his spirit, or his mind.

"Come in, my dearest child, come in."

Matilda entered her chapel, bending her knee to the beautiful life-sized statues of Jesus and his most beloved, Maria Magdalena, before reaching up to kiss the Master on his scarred cheek. She glanced up at Conn, who was looking sheepish, as if he had been caught doing something that was somehow inappropriate and definitely embarrassing.

"My two favorite men in the world." Matilda smiled, adding with a note beyond curiosity in her voice, "But what on earth could they possibly be doing together?" She knew there was some planning unfolding here—she just wasn't sure what it was.

The Master looked at Conn, who turned a shade of red that matched Matilda's hair. "Before I tell you the decision that the Master has come to, and I with him, I need to tell you a story, little sister."

It was just like Conn to have a story when times were toughest, so Matilda wasn't surprised at this answer, but she had an inkling that this would be a tale unlike any other he had ever told. The Master excused himself and left the pair of them to the chapel and the stories that it contained.

After nearly twenty years of secrecy, the man named after the ancient Celtic warrior, Conn of the Hundred Battles, told Matilda the story of his long journey to a new life in Tuscany.

❈

Conn, who was born and christened Conchobar Padraic McMahon in the province of Connacht, left the west of Ireland as a boy of fifteen summers after an invasion by the Northmen had brutalized his village.

He had willingly entered a monastery three years prior and was committed to the study of language and religion. He loved it, lived for it, and as he was one of seven sons, Conn's vocation as a monk had been accepted readily by his father, who now had one less child to worry about. As it happened, when the Northmen invaded, Conn was on a supply mission to a monastery further north up the river in Galway to gather more ink and parchment for the manuscripts that the novices were learning to illuminate. He was out of harm's way when the vicious storm blew in from Scandinavia.

While the majority of Vikings had been driven from Ireland by the great king Brian Boru in 1014, there were still scattered regions where the violent warriors of the north would come to raid. They most often struck the richer communities along the rivers, as they not only possessed the greatest spoils but also provided the easiest escape routes for the narrow and swift Viking ships. It was one of these raids along the River Shannon that had razed Conn's hometown and led to the brutal deaths of most of the villagers, including his parents, sisters, and brothers.

The monastery where Conn lived was looted and burned to the ground; the gentle and learned brothers who had become his second family were hacked to pieces. Conn was now truly an orphan. Worse, he could not bear the sight of his desecrated village and violated monastery. He buried his family and his brother monks with his own hands over the next days, then set out with a determination to leave Ireland. He could no longer remain in a place where such violence was a daily possibility, when all he craved was solitude and learning.

Remembering happier days with the brothers, Conn's thoughts turned to a visiting monk who had come from Gaul. The monk was the most learned man Conn had ever met. He was fascinating and full of wisdom. He was also very gentle and loving, unusual qualities in a scholar. Conn loved all the brothers at the monastery, even the stringent abbot who beat him periodically when he was caught delving into the Celtic pagan mythologies that were preserved in the library. But this French monk was the first truly holy man Conn believed he had ever met. The monk, who told Conn that he had no name, talked of his education in a place called Chartres, where there was a school of the spirit unlike any other on earth. When the elder monks were long in their beds, Conn would stay up and listen to the Frenchman speak in terms that were clearly heretical. And yet he wasn't shocked by the stranger's point of view. He was fascinated, recognizing a strange truth in the startling perspective, and each revelation left him hungering for more information.

The visitor told Conn of the man called Fulbert, who was the bishop of Chartres as well as the force behind the great school associated with the cathedral. When a tragic and possibly intentional fire burned part of the cathedral to the ground in 1020, it was Fulbert who rebuilt it in a solid, traditional Romanesque style. He took great care to hire the finest craftsmen, focusing on the sacred crypt under the cathedral. The crypt covered a primeval well—said to be the holiest on the planet—and the sanctified pear-wood carving of Notre Dame, called Our Lady Under the Earth. Fulbert protected and preserved all these items with utmost care.

The French monk spoke of the teachings of the great Greeks, specifically of Plato and Socrates, and of a teaching method called *dialectic*, which was one of the acknowledged liberal arts. Dialectic was the method of civilized argument, and it was through this teaching that men were made to think and thoroughly analyze a proposition and a counterproposition. It was through this dialectic teaching that Fulbert's greatest student emerged, the man who would be known to history as Berengar of Tours. While Berengar would eventually inherit the leadership of the Chartres school at the passing of his mentor, Fulbert, it was his vitriolic battle with the Church that made him infamous. Berengar proposed an opposition to the doctrine of transubstantiation, the Church's belief that the sacramental bread and wine of the Eucharist physically becomes the body and blood of Christ once it is consecrated. He put forth that this was meant to be a spiritual concept rather than a physical one, citing earliest Church fathers and a "mysterious ancient text" to lend credence to his argument.

It was the secret and mysterious text, which the monk referred to as the Book of Love, that obsessed the young Conn as he listened to the Frenchman's stories. The brother whispered for Conn's ears alone that this great book had been written in the hand of the Lord himself and brought to France by Maria Magdalena following the crucifixion. It was her descendants who had protected the teachings that came from it through the millennium. But the religious climate in France was changing, becoming less tolerant and more dogmatic, and these secret truth teachings were suddenly dangerous. Followers of the Book of Love, the pure Christians who would become known as the Cathars, were forced underground and found secret ways to carry on their teachings. It was through Neoplatonism and the revival of Greek philosophy and dialogues that the heretical teachings continued in the region of La Beauce. Many of the more controversial principles from early Christianity were re-dressed in Greek thought so that they could be argued as scholarship rather than heresy.

It was in one of these dialogues that Berengar of Tours first raised the challenge to transubstantiation. Explaining this to Conn, the monk quietly imparted a teaching from the Book of Love, reciting from this heretical document:

What is my flesh? My flesh is the Word, the Truth of the Logos.
What is my blood? My blood is the Breath, the exaltation of the Spirit
that animates the flesh.
Whosoever welcomes the Word and the Breath has truly received
sustenance and clothing,
For this is food, drink, and raiment.
This bread is my flesh, and it is the Word of Truth.
This wine is my blood, and it is the Breath of Spirit.

Conn was transfixed. While the verses were undoubtedly heretical, they were also beautiful. And most of all, it simply made sense to him that Jesus was possibly using the flesh and blood, the bread and wine, as metaphors.

The Church, however, did not find this perspective beautiful in the least. The outcry from within France and subsequently Rome very nearly destroyed Berengar, who was imprisoned by the French king for his heresy and spent the remainder of his life in a constant struggle with Church authority.

Conn dreamed of the day that he could meet more men like this French monk and his extraordinary teachers, who challenged everything in the name of truth and wisdom. He vowed that one day he would see this school for himself, and it was this that he was determined to accomplish following the Viking massacre. Perhaps he would find the peace that he sought in the school at Chartres.

The young Conn traveled south and sold the costly ink and paper to a monastery outside Tralee. With the money he bought his way aboard a ship sailing to the place of the Normans in Gaul. From there he would make his way to Chartres, either by horse or by foot. He prayed for God to forgive him for using the monastery's supplies to support himself, but he had no other means at the moment and he pledged to do good works as his penance. Thus he arrived at his destination, on the doorstep of Fulbert's cathedral, recently reconstructed over the damaged ninth-century edifice—itself constructed over a site considered to be holy ground for thousands of years.

Conn studied at Chartres for nearly ten years, applying his naturally swift intellect to becoming expert in Neoplatonism, Greek language and thought, all aspects of religious theory and doctrine, and European history. But it was the heresy that reached into his spirit and took root. It was the teachings from the Book of Love that became Conn's raison d'être. These teachings were not offered to everyone. They were part of the mystery school that was attached to the formal cathedral school. One had to earn admission into the mystery school through good works and strong intentions toward wisdom. Conn, an astonishing pupil, became a master of the material in record time.

The associated teachings of the labyrinth were critical to the mystery school of Chartres, and Conn walked the eleven circuits each day before beginning his studies. There was not, at this time, a labyrinth in the cathedral. There was a garden labyrinth built of stones, which was nonetheless effective. This labyrinth was based on the Solomon design with a rounded center for the initiate to pray in upon arriving in the heart of the circle. It was in the center of this garden labyrinth, in the shadow of Fulbert's rebuilt structure, that Conn received the vision that would change the course of his life.

It began as a vision of the archangel Michael, the messenger of light who defeats the darkness. Michael carried his flaming sword of truth and righteousness with him as he hovered over the labyrinth and over Conn. The angel reminded him that his name, Micha-El, meant "he who is like God." Then Conn saw a little girl, perhaps nine or ten years old, with coppery red hair and an extraordinary energy. She was under attack by unseen forces, and Michael swung his sword over the girl's head to dispel the darkness that threatened to encroach upon the child. He then turned and spoke to Conn.

"Behold, your promise. It was to protect this girl, this daughter of God, above all else and for as long as necessary. You will become her brother and her knight protector, you will be as I am to you, an angel of light that defeats the darkness. But make no mistake, this is a battle of good versus evil, and you will be called upon to fight the evil.

"This child awaits you in Tuscany. Go to where the duke of Lorraine lives in Florence, and there you will find your calling to protect her."

Conn was dumbfounded. Here was without a doubt a vision of such clarity, such pure message, that he could do nothing but obey it. He had devoted a decade of his life to intensive spiritual training in order to receive just such messages clearly. But the warrior's life was not for him, surely. While he was strong and athletic, and had already grown into his enormous frame at this stage, he did not desire to be a soldier. Why did God not give him the chance to stay at Chartres and ultimately become a teacher there? Why did he have such desires if it was not his destiny? This was a spiritual crisis for Conn, because the Book of Love teaches that our dreams as humans are not accidental, they are not random. They are our soul's means of reminding us what we are here to do to fulfill our promise to God. Then why did he crave the solitude and peace of the school when he was told that his calling was war? Why did he love Chartres beyond all reason and want nothing more than to live and die in the shadow of the blessed cathedral and its wisdom school?

It would take Conn many years to understand the answer completely, and this in itself was a critical piece of the teaching. For it is true that we often discover meanings and reasons for things many years after they mattered quite so much to us.

Conn had made a promise to his Lord, and he intended to keep it. But before he could be worthy of defending this petite princess, he would need to hone his warrior skills. Thus it was that Conn became a mercenary, hiring himself out across Europe to gain skill and experience from the greatest captains on the continent. It was after he had earned the nickname "of the Hundred Battles" that he determined he was ready to find Matilda in Florence. Taking a commission with Duke Godfrey, Conn bided his time, watching the petite countess surreptitiously until the day that Godfrey sought him out and requested that he become her weapons master.

Tears streamed down Conn's face as he told Matilda how much he loved her, how she was truly his sister of the heart and spirit and that defending her was the most sacred and honorable duty he could have asked for. And then he told her the rest, and she realized the reason for his tears.

Conn was leaving her to begin the next phase of his destiny, and to realize his ultimate dream. He was returning to Chartres and taking the Master with him. Together, they would bring the Libro Rosso to a place of ultimate protection, where it would be safely out of Henry's destructive reach once and for all.

❁

In honor of the Lucchesi traditions that surrounded the *Volto Santo*, a cart was constructed to transport the Libro Rosso in exactly the same way that the Holy Face had once been pulled across Italy. Matilda provided two snow white oxen to drive the cart on which the Ark of the

New Covenant would be carried to its new home. These travelers would have to be very careful crossing through the war-ravaged region of northern Italy with their precious cargo. The ark was encased in a simple wooden covering so the gilded and jeweled majesty of the true container would be obscured. A false bottom was installed in the cart to hide the Libro Rosso, and another "relic" was devised to be stored in the ark. An artist created a rendition of Veronica's veil, made to appear as an impression of the face of Christ on a silken white cloth. It was a spiritual pun of sorts for the Order, as the face imprinted on Veronica's veil was sometimes referred to as the *Volto Santo,* as was their sacred treasure in Lucca. This manufactured relic was placed within the ark as a safety measure: if they were stopped by German troops, they would tell the story of this holy veil and how they were carrying it out of Italy and into France for its protection in the abbey of Cluny. For all their barbaric violence in this war, it was unlikely that any German soldier was going to accost monks who were carrying such a holy relic. Besides, they were leaving Italy, not entering it.

Finally, in order for Conn to appear utterly convincing as a monk, he shaved his head. When Matilda saw him for the first time, she burst into tears.

"Oh God, you really are leaving me." She threw herself into his arms and cried like a child. Conn hugged her and stroked her hair, singing to her in his Celtic language for the final time.

"I am only leaving you temporarily. *Le temps revient,* little sister. You know that the families of spirit are never truly separated. I will see you soon, wherever God decrees." He pulled away from her and cupped her chin with his huge hand. "You will be well cared for. Arduino is a better strategist than I have ever been, the best military leader in Italy. If anyone can help you reclaim your lands from Henry, it is Arduino. And you have a new watchdog, don't you? One who will protect you fearlessly."

He was referring to Ugo Manfredi, the maimed husband of Matilda's murdered cousin. Through his rehabilitation, Ugo had spent time with Conn. While he had lived most of his life as a farmer, that work had also made him strong and hearty. And he was clever. The combination would turn him into an effective warrior, the kind who was utterly without fear as he had nothing whatsoever left to lose. Once recovered, Ugo became a physical force to be reckoned with, and that force was fiercely devoted to the Tuscan countess who had applied the healing unguents to his eye socket with her own hands.

Matilda did not begrudge Conn this mission. Far from it, she was grateful that the Libro Rosso and the Master would have the most effective protection in Europe. She handed Conn a little bundle as a final gift. "Take her with you. She has been with me since I was born and I have always felt that she watched over me. Now she will watch over the two of you."

Conn pulled away the cloth that covered the faded but still exquisitely beautiful little statue of Saint Modesta. His eyes welled as he whispered, "Modesta. We are both going home."

Matilda grasped his free hand in hers and began the sacred recitation that is applicable to love in all its guises, a sacrament that he knew as well as she.

I have loved you before
I love you today
And I will love you again
The time returns.

They choked through it together for their final time in this life, through their tears.

CHAPTER SEVENTEEN

Vatican City
present day

*M*aureen walked into Saint Peter's with a different purpose now, and that was to pay her respects to the woman she had come here originally to meet and now felt that she knew intimately—the miraculous, inspiring, and completely larger-than-life Tuscan countess, Matilda of Canossa.

The complete version of Matilda's autobiography ended with the departure of Conn and the Master for Chartres. It was as if Matilda lost interest in the details of her life after that. Gregory was dead, and her spiritual adviser and best friend had left her for France. Anselmo had also passed away, and Isobel was running the Order in Lucca. Matilda carried on and continued to fight against Henry and for Tuscany, and most of all to secure the throne of Saint Peter against secular influence. She did all these things because she had made a promise to do so: a promise to God, to herself, and to her people. And she would never rest until that promise was kept.

There were more pages in Matilda's autobiography, but these were akin to basic diary entries that marked major events of significance. One that stood out for Peter said, "Letter from Patricio, who is leaving Orval and going to Chartres." It did not indicate why Patricio was abandoning his cherished Orval, but Matilda would have been struggling to hold on to her territories in Lorraine, and it was likely a dangerous place to be her ally during the wars.

Peter was driven to do the research into Matilda's later life, so that he could bring closure to the story for Maureen, who had become obsessed with the Tuscan countess. Maureen was desperate to know if Matilda ever saw any real justice where Henry IV was concerned, and Peter was very happy to tell her that she did. It took many years, but Matilda eventually won the war for Tuscany and against Henry. Henry's wife and his own son even defected to Matilda's camp eventually, seeking refuge in Tuscany from the tyrannical Henry, who had physically abused his wife with such violence that she sought legal action against him. Historical documents indicated that Queen Adelaide, a former Russian princess, begged Matilda for asylum as she recounted horrors of Henry's sexual proclivities, including orgies and black masses.

Maureen was struck by this amazing aspect of Matilda's story. She was an icon of women's rights, hundreds of years before such a term was ever popularly understood. Matilda was possibly the first woman to demand a prenuptial agreement, just as she was the first woman to shelter victims of domestic violence and protect them from the perpetrators—even when the abuser was a king.

Slowly and carefully, with the strategy of a master chess player, Matilda rebuilt Tuscany. Her political strength and her wealth returned gradually, and when it did, she went after Henry's strongholds in Italy. In the autumn of 1092, while wearing her now legendary copper armor, Matilda led an army against Henry's troops who had held the region surrounding Canossa for far too long. It was, by all historical accounts, an example of military strategy at its most ingenious. Matilda, with Ugo Manfredi and Arduino della Paluda at her side, routed the Germans. With their base of operations recovered, the Tuscan armies eliminated the German presence from the majority of Matilda's territories over the course of the next three years, and she reigned unopposed for the remainder of her long life.

With Matilda's return to political power, she supported the cause of a new pope who was committed to Gregory's memory and their shared determination to separate the papacy from the influence of secular power. He was a fierce defender of Rome's independence and a staunch opponent of royal interference in spiritual matters. Matilda maintained a close relationship with this new pope, Paschal II, for the remainder of her life.

Paschal. The similarity between this pope's name and her own were most certainly not lost on Maureen. The connections within this story were never-ending.

Maureen approached the marble tomb with a new awareness. The magnificent woman depicted here held the papal tiara and the keys to the Church because she had lived here and ruled here with her own beloved. Together they were the manifestation of Solomon and Sheba in their time, and perhaps even a reflection of Jesus and Magdalene, El and Asherah. They were the embodiment of their own holy concept: the time returns.

And Bernini, the great Baroque master who inherited the designs for Saint Peter's from Matilda's descendant, Michelangelo, knew it. He created a powerful and elegant design that would preserve the truth in marble, for those with eyes to see.

Art will save the world.

Running her hand along the cold marble, designed by an artist who knew more than he was telling, Maureen examined the depiction of a scene from Matilda's life that graced the facing of the tomb. It would not have meant anything to her before. Here was the event in Canossa, with Henry on his knees, begging forgiveness. Pope Gregory VII held central focus on his throne. Matilda, of course, stood beside him as she had literally and figuratively throughout their eventful years together.

Matilda's story inspired Maureen more than any other she had ever investigated, with the possible exception of that of their shared ancestress, Mary Magdalene. Matilda, with her unprecedented commitment to equality for all men and women under God, her passion for charity and for improving the lot of the poor, had contributed to the demise of the Dark Ages by allowing in a new era of light. She was, in many respects, the first modern woman.

Most of all, Matilda kept her promises. She never stopped fighting for the reforms Gregory had attempted to implement. A thousand years later, reforms put into place by Gregory VII, with Matilda by his side, were considered critical to the foundations of the established Church.

Matilda dedicated her life to the people of Tuscany and their prosperity, and she built and restored centers of spiritual learning all over Italy, while managing to get her sweet bishop Anselmo canonized and remembered by posterity as a saint. She designed bridges and buildings and beautified existing structures with artworks: paintings, mosaics, and sculptures, thus becoming the first official patron of the arts in Tuscany. She would be the forerunner of the great artistic patrons of the late Middle Ages and the Renaissance who nurtured and supported artists. Matilda insisted that her artists and sculptors sign their works when such a thing was unheard of, because she believed that posterity should remember the names of those who created such beauty.

As a gift to her beloved Lucca, she designed and financed a magnificent bridge across the Serchio that would facilitate both trade and travel for the people. She called the bridge Ponte della Magdalena, Magdalene's Bridge, and it was a feat of art and engineering worthy of the great Lady's name and legacy. The bridge was constructed of semicircles that seemed to rise out of the river. When viewed from a distance, the shapes reflected in the water create geometrically perfect circles. In their reflection, the circles were whole.

And Matilda of Canossa remained committed to the teaching of the Way of Love throughout her extraordinary reign. She implemented equality and tolerance among her own people at a time in history when there were no words for such concepts. She was a most unique woman with an epic life and legacy.

She was, quite simply, Matilda. By the Grace of God Who Is.

When Adam, the first man, lay dying, he begged for the archangel Michael to visit him upon his deathbed. Micha-el, the angel whose name means One Who Is Like God, came to Adam and offered to grant him his last request. Adam asked that a seed be given to him from the Tree of Life, the symbol of Holy Mother Asherah, that he might possess all her wisdom and know the answers to life's mysteries on earth before he left this place, and that perhaps—just perhaps—the life-giving properties of her great divinity might save him.

Michael granted this wish and placed the requested seed directly into Adam's mouth. But upon ingesting it, the first man drew his last breath. Rather than saving him, the Tree of Life brought about his demise. There was too much knowledge to be contained within one man. Adam was buried, and the following spring a sapling burst forth from the seed in his mouth, splitting the earth and growing into a new and mighty tree. It flourished for many centuries, before it was cut down with an axe by ignorant men who did not believe in its powers or its sanctity. The wood from the sacred tree was used to build a bridge that would cross the waters and lead to Jerusalem.

When Makeda, the Queen of Sheba, first came to Solomon on her long trek from Sabea, she crossed this bridge on the final day of her journey. It is said that in her grace she recognized immediately that this bridge was built of a special wood. The wood cried out to her and told her it had once flourished as the Tree of Life, before men without wisdom destroyed it. The beauty of Asherah, once a living and vital element on earth, had been hacked to pieces by the ignorant.

The Queen of Sheba fell to the ground in awe and worshipped the wood, realizing as she did so that she had been given a divine gift. But her sadness at this great loss tore at her heart, and she wept. As her tears struck the wood, the wisdom which had been trampled upon for so long was released to her and she was further bestowed with a vision from God. Makeda was shown that a new order, a new covenant, and a new messiah would come forth from the line of David and Solomon to change the world. Sadly, she also saw tragedy in the vision. This messiah of light would be killed for his beautiful beliefs, killed by the very same wood upon which she now knelt.

During her time of communion with King Solomon, the Queen of Sheba told him of this experience. Solomon was alarmed by the vision and believed that it had been given to her so that they could take precautions to save this descendant of prophecy. He ordered the bridge destroyed, and the wood buried outside Jerusalem. In his faith and wisdom, Solomon hoped that by his returning the wood to the earth, the Tree of Life might flourish once again. If this could not happen, then perhaps he would eliminate the possibility of its use in the destruction of this forthcoming holy man. This was done, and the wood remained underground for fourteen generations.

During the reign of Pontius Pilate, the wood was discovered by chance when a battalion of Roman soldiers were digging mass graves for Jewish insurgents. They brought the wood to Jerusalem, where it was used to create the beams of the cross upon which our Lord met his divine fate atop the hill of Golgotha.

A man's destiny cannot be denied when it is written in the stars.

It is further said that the place where Solomon and Sheba had their first fated meeting would become the exact location of the Holy Sepulcher. It would seem that there are areas of the earth that have their own destiny, chosen by God as places of power.

For those with ears to hear, let them hear it.

THE LEGEND OF THE TRUE CROSS, PART ONE
AS PRESERVED IN THE LIBRO ROSSO

Rome
present day

BÉRENGER AND MAUREEN strolled toward the Piazza della Rotonda, hand in hand, on their way back to the hotel. The Pantheon gleamed under the spotlights, and the fountain gurgled, all in harmony with the bustle that occurred every evening in this ancient plaza. Vendors sold flying toys and cheap souvenirs to tourists who weren't already jaded from paying too much for mediocre pasta at the cafés perched on prime real estate. Maureen had learned quickly that to walk a few paces away from the grand spaces in Rome was to find far more appealing cuisine at prices that didn't include rent for such a historic view. Tonight they had dined in the quiet nearby piazza dedicated to Mary Magdalene, where a beautiful portrait of their Lady was preserved in a large, cameo-shaped frame at one corner of the square.

Maureen and Bérenger skirted the bustling piazza, as alive on a late spring night as the Trocadero in Paris or Times Square in New York City. As they entered the sanctuary of the hotel lobby, the night porter recognized Maureen and signaled to her.

"There was a package left here for you. One moment."

He scurried to a back room and emerged with a container the size of a shoe box, wrapped in brown paper. The plain package made Bérenger immediately suspicious.

"Did you see who left this package?"

"A courier. From a local service. I had to sign for it."

Maureen thanked him and took the package. She briefly hoped that the package might at least contain her missing notebooks; it was too small to hold her computer. As they waited for the elevator, the pair of them inspected it. In the upper left corner, handwritten in a scrawl on the brown paper, was a single word: *DESTINO*.

"Bloody hell, who is this guy?" Bérenger growled his irritation. The mystery was getting to him, although he wasn't inclined to let Maureen know just how disturbed he was. He was a man used to being in charge at all times, and he was beginning to chafe at a game where he was not in control of the players, or the rules.

"He knows too much about our comings and goings; he knows your history. He knows something about me, clearly. And . . ."

"And he knows what I dream about. How is that possible?"

They placed the box on the bed and sat on either side of it, opening it together. As she removed the brown paper on her side of the box, Maureen cried out.

"Ouch!"

It was simply a paper cut, albeit a particularly vicious one that ran across the inside of her middle finger and began to bleed. And it hurt disproportionately, as paper cuts are wont to do. She got up to wash her hands and held a towel around the offended finger for a moment until the bleeding stopped. Then she returned to Bérenger to finish un-wrapping the parcel. He first kissed her wounded finger gently and in-spected it to be sure it wasn't too deep.

While the exterior of the package was addressed very simply to Maureen, the interior was filled with two smaller boxes, each individu-ally addressed. One was to Maureen, one was to Bérenger.

"You first," Maureen said, handing Bérenger the small box with his name on it. It was the same size as a gift box for a small jewelry item, and when he opened it, he saw that it was very definitely something rare and valuable, like a jewel. The box contained a small silver reli-quary, oval in shape and made like a locket, but with a cover that slipped over the top, like the lid on a tiny box. The lid covered the red wax seal that is used to both protect and authenticate religious artifacts. In this case, the seal was so ancient and deteriorated that it was impossible to determine what the original image looked like in its entirety, but there were tiny stars visible in what appeared to be a circular pattern, embed-ded in the wax.

While smaller than Maureen's thumbnail, the casing was, con-versely, highly detailed and well preserved. Embossed into the silvered cover was a miniature crucifixion sequence. At the foot of the cross, a long-haired and kneeling Mary Magdalene clung to the feet of her dying beloved. Strangely, the only other element—carefully crafted—was a columned temple perched on a hill behind them. The temple looked distinctly Greek, resembling the Acropolis in Athens, the shrine built to honor feminine wisdom and strength.

Bérenger recognized it immediately. "It's a temple that symbolizes the Sophia element in spirituality," he said. "Divine feminine knowledge. Artists affiliated with the bloodline used it when painting Magdalene to indicate that she was the keeper of the knowledge, as have the secret societies affiliated with bloodline traditions for centuries. You can identify the Sophia temples specifically, as they have rounded rooftops representing female curvature."

Maureen looked at the image and nodded. In her research into Magdalene art, she had seen a number of Italian depictions of the crucifixion with similar configurations: her Mary at the foot of the cross, usually clutching it. In several cases, there was a structure that resembled a classical Greek temple in the background. Some artists depicted the temple in ruins, symbolic of the loss of the divine feminine wisdom in their contemporary spirituality.

Bérenger turned the case over to see the relic itself. It was minuscule, so tiny as to be nearly invisible, but it was there. A speck of wood was held in place by some type of resin, glued into the center of a golden flower. Beneath the relic was a sliver of paper, handwritten in painstaking script: *V. Croise.*

It was an abbreviation that both understood, even in the antiquated French, *Vraie Croise.* They looked at each other and said in tandem, "The True Cross."

There was a time, even in the last week, when Bérenger Sinclair would have scoffed at any relic that claimed to be a portion of the True Cross, particularly if the provenance of the item could not be established. But given recent events, and Maureen's presence in Rome, he knew there was no room for skepticism. The minuscule splinter's tiny size gave credibility to the authenticity. If a villain were going to create a forgery for the sake of a black-market relic sale, wouldn't he at least create a splinter that was wholly visible to the naked eye?

Maureen jumped suddenly and let out a little squeal.

"What is it?"

She had been holding the reliquary in her open palm. When she jumped, it fell on the bed. Bérenger leaned over to pick it up.

"Feel it," Maureen said.

Bérenger's eyes grew wide as he picked it up. "It's hot."

Maureen nodded. As she had held the relic in her hand, the metal had begun to grow warm, finally heating up to such a degree that she dropped it.

It was cooling now, so Bérenger returned it to its resting place in the box.

"Bérenger, look. My paper cut. It's . . . gone."

She held out her hand to show him. She had held the reliquary in the same hand that was injured. The cut, an inch in length, that she and Bérenger had both witnessed just minutes before, was gone.

He nodded silently, then reached for the accompanying card on the now familiar stationery with the strange monogram, the A tied to the reversed E, and read it aloud to Maureen.

This once belonged to another Poet Prince, the greatest who ever lived. You are charged to wear his mantle. Do so with grace and God will reward you just as the prophecy promises.
Amor vincit omnia,
Destino

For the first time in their relationship, Maureen saw Bérenger Sinclair at a loss. The blood had drained from his face and he looked stricken. Haunted.

She reached out and took his hand, gently. "What's wrong? What does it mean?"

He reached up and kissed her hand to soften the blow of his evasiveness. "It means . . . that there is something I need to tell you. But not quite yet. Let's look at the other items in this mysterious Pandora's box first."

Maureen didn't want to let it go, but she would respect his wishes for the moment as she was equally curious about what was left within the treasure box. Reaching in for her own package, Maureen extracted another container designed for jewelry, larger than the one addressed to Bérenger. Hers was lined with an exquisite indigo-colored satin, a rich fabric and hue falling somewhere between deepest blue and violet. Sitting atop the satin was an ancient-looking medallion of hammered copper. Bérenger recognized it instantly.

"The labyrinth in Chartres Cathedral."

Inscribed on the reverse, in what appeared to be a more modern engraving in French, were the words:

Marie a choisi la meilleure part, et personne ne la lui enlèvera.

Bérenger, who was fluent, translated it aloud quicker than Maureen could have, although both recognized the passage immediately. "Mary hath chosen the better part, which no one will take from her."

"Luke ten forty-two," Maureen replied simply. All devoted students of the Magdalene knew this passage by heart. It comes after Martha complains that she is doing all the housework while Mary sits at the feet of Jesus and listens to him. Jesus replies in support of Mary with this enigmatic phrase.

"What do you think it means?" Maureen spoke first. "Because we both know it's not going to be an obvious, scriptural interpretation."

"Of course not. It's on the reverse of the Chartres labyrinth image, and it's in French, so those elements are obviously connected. Read the card."

Maureen extracted the card, not bothering to disguise her shock as she read.

> *The Book of Love is in Chartres Cathedral. This is your destiny and destination on June 21. Window 10.*

While the first line had significant impact—could it really be possible that the Book of Love was in Chartres Cathedral?—the lines that followed left her speechless.

> *Behold, the Book of Love. Follow the path that has been laid out for you, and you will find what you seek. Once you have found it, you must share it with the world and fulfill the promise that you made. Our truth has been in darkness for too long.*
> *Amor vincit omnia,*
> *Destino*

The words were verbatim to those spoken by Jesus in her dreams about the Book of Love. Was the author of this card, this Destino, a messenger of divine providence? Or was he the thief who had stolen her laptop and notebook, taunting Maureen with her own notes?

Following the sacrifice of our Lord on the Black Day of the Skull, the honorable Joseph of Arimathea, along with the most blessed Nicodemus and Luke, collected all the items that were instrumental in his destiny. The beams of the cross, the nails, the thorns, and the titular written by Pontius Pilate were removed to the property of Nicodemus, where they were kept in hiding by the Order of the Holy Sepulcher in a subterranean chamber. Following the resurrection, the holy shroud that once wrapped the body of our Lord was also taken by the Order to this protected place. The chamber was sealed by enormous boulders that required the strength of many men to remove them. These most sacred relics were highly protected, as their power

was deemed too great and intense for the average man or woman to gain exposure to them.

Most sacred of all were the beams of the True Cross, for the wood carried the entire history of our people within it. It represented the spirit of Asherah entrapped and downtrodden, and it symbolized the persecution of all who would restore her, and the truth, in the form of our Lord who came to show us the Way of Love, which is the Way of El and Asherah.

Access to the relics was granted only to the closest members of the Order, the family, and the original followers once a year, on the commemoration of our Lord's sacrifice, which is the Holy Friday, through to the day of his resurrection. The relics were carefully concealed at all other times.

When the blessed Saint Luke came to Italy, he presented a detailed map to the brothers of the Order of the Holy Sepulcher in Calabria, a guide to the exact location of the relics. As there was great unrest in Jerusalem, Luke was afraid that the relics would be endangered, or perhaps forgotten by future generations if the surviving members of the Order were forced from their homeland. And as it happened, the wicked Titus destroyed the Temple in Jerusalem and attempted to eliminate both the Jews and the earliest Christians in the year 70, and the relics were abandoned as the people fled for their lives or died fighting.

Two and a half centuries later, the map created by Saint Luke was entrusted to the mother of the emperor Constantine as a gift for her generosity and protection of the Order. Santa Helena enlisted a noble group of warriors and converts to take an unprecedented journey to the Holy Land on an expedition to find the treasures of our people. Utilizing the map drawn by Luke, the members of Helena's troop were able to identify the cavern that held the treasure by the large letter X that was carved on the exterior. X has since been used to mark the location of the treasure that comes with enlightenment. In addition to the relics of the Passion, the crèche that once held both the Lord and his holy daughter in their sleep as infants was also recovered from the cavern.

These sanctified relics of our Lord Jesus Christ were carried back to Rome and preserved by the great lady. However, in honor of those who protected them, splinters of the True Cross were given to the leaders of the Order of the Holy Sepulcher in Calabria, Rome, and Lucca. These are the most holy and potent items in the history of mankind. As such, the relics of the True Cross were divided into tiny splinters in order to share their sanctity with the many families in Italy who preserved the true teachings of the Way. These fragments contain the wisdom of Asherah, the breath of Adam, the tears of Sheba, and the blood of our Lord.

While the nonbelievers may scoff at the validity of such relics, anyone who has had the joy of holding even the smallest piece of the True Cross will never forget the holy experience. The healing powers are miraculous and should only be placed in the hands of the worthy.

For those with ears to hear, let them hear it.

THE LEGEND OF THE TRUE CROSS, PART TWO,
AS PRESERVED IN THE LIBRO ROSSO

CHAPTER EIGHTEEN

*P*eter stopped working as he was interrupted by Maggie Cusack. A courier had delivered a package for Father Healy, telling her it was urgent that he open it right away. Maggie placed the parcel, wrapped in plain brown paper, on his desk. She left the room shaking her head. The return address on the package was blank, except for one word scrawled in the upper left corner: *DESTINO.*

Peter opened his own package, unaware as he did so that Maureen and Bérenger were experiencing their own version of Christmas across the Tiber. Peter's box contained a small statue of a madonna and child, carved out of a very dark wood. This madonna, while somewhat rustic, was enthroned, crowned, and commanding. In her right hand she held the globe of earthly dominion. The infant was delivering the sign of the benediction confidently from his mother's lap. The front of the base of the statuette was inscribed "Notre Dame de Montserrat"; the back of the base was carved with a Latin motto, *Nigra sum sed formosa.*

Peter recognized the Latin. It was a much-debated line spoken by the bride in the Song of Songs: "I am black but beautiful." It was significant in what was known as Black Madonna worship throughout Europe.

He opened the enclosed card to see what further clues awaited him. It contained a single line.

WHY DID YOU BECOME A JESUIT?

He considered the question for a moment. It did not ask, Why did you become a priest? It asked, more specifically, Why did you become a Jesuit? And this madonna was also specific. It was the madonna of Montserrat, the mystical monastery high in the mountains north of Barcelona. Peter had been there on several occasions. Like many of his brothers before him, he had taken the funicular, rather like a large version of a ski lift, up the steep rise to the monastery. This was sacred ground for members of the Society of Jesus, who were better known as the Jesuit order. Sacred for many reasons, but chief among them was that their founder, Ignatius Loyola, had discovered his faith in this very monastery and in the presence of this very same Black Madonna.

I am black but I am comely, O daughters of Jerusalem.

So sings the Shulamite woman in the Song of Songs. For she is the springtime bride, the representative of Asherah's grace in human form. She shares with the women of Jerusalem her secrets and welcomes them into her fold. Those who enter become priestesses in the Nazarene tradition, which is to say the hidden tradition. They become known by the sacred name of Mary. The leader amongst these women, the one who is perfected in her wisdom and grace, is the tower of the flock. One woman alone shall be given this title of the Magdalene, whilst all the other Marys shall serve at her side.

Black is the color of her wisdom, as it has been obscured and hidden behind the veil, made completely unavailable to the uninitiated.

A garden enclosed is my sister, my spouse;
a spring shut up, a fountain sealed.

My beloved is the Black Madonna, the hidden lady. Yet she hath chosen the better part, she is the embodiment of compassion on earth, she is the Comforter. My bride is trapped in the enclosed garden, her wellspring of wisdom dammed and sealed by the closed minds of men who have turned their hearts away from the Holy Spirit, the Sacred Dove. It is not until she is released that there will be peace on earth.

This is the apocalypsia *that is approaching, which means most literally the unveiling of the Bride. To save ourselves, we must understand the true interpretation of the* apocalypsia. *And we must welcome it.*

The veil must be lifted, and the face of the Bride revealed. For She is Asherah, the beloved of El, as she returns through time in all her guises, to unite with her Bridegroom. She is Sheba, she is Maria Magdalena, and she is all women who would stand for the harmony that comes with reunion: male and female, on earth as it is in heaven.

O my dove that art in the clefts of the rock
hidden in the secret places of the mountains,
Let me see thy countenance, let me hear thy voice
for sweet is thy voice, and thy countenance is lovely.

It is the charge of all men who would serve the Lord God with all their hearts and all their minds and all their souls to lift this veil. It is upon us to allow the Bride to show her lovely countenance and let her voice, which is a melody of union, be heard. We must awaken while in this body for everything exists in it. We must allow the Bride to open to us, to receive us, and to share her perfected wisdom through our reunion.

I was asleep, but my heart was awake.
It heard the voice of my beloved, who knocked.
Open to me, my sister, my love, my dove, my perfect one!

The Song of Songs, our gift from Solomon and his beloved Sheba, is the salvation of mankind. It contains within it the joyous reunion of our Father and Mother in heaven, through their cherished children on earth. It contains within it the ultimate seeds of wisdom and love.

My beloved is mine, and I am hers.
She hath chosen the better part
And no one shall take it from her.

THE SONG OF SOLOMON AND SHEBA,
FROM THE BOOK OF LOVE,
AS PRESERVED IN THE LIBRO ROSSO

Rome
present day

IT WAS well after midnight, and the Piazza della Rotonda was quiet. The vendors had packed up their wares an hour or so earlier, and the tourists were back in their hotel rooms. From time to time, a few younger couples strayed through the plaza on their way from a late meal, but overall it was quiet save for the eternal gurgling of the central fountain. It was here that Maureen and Bérenger sat, alone now in the moonlight. They were settled on the stone steps, backs to the obelisk and facing the majesty of the Pantheon. Bérenger made his explanation softly and reverentially.

"What is the one thing we have all learned in following this magical path, with the Magdalene as our guide? She has taught us so many things, but for me nothing is as important as the lessons about balance and harmony. And I believe that is what he was showing us too, wasn't it?"

Maureen nodded but said nothing, not wanting to interrupt him.

"Think about this for a moment. There is a prophecy that is left to us from Sarah-Tamar, who is the perfected child of two perfect prophets. You know this prophecy intimately, as it has shaped your life. It is the prophecy of women who will come at various intervals and perform important spiritual functions in order to ensure that the truth of our people does not die. It is the legend of The Expected One, but it also incorporates the philosophy of the time returns, doesn't it? Now, remembering what we know of harmony and union and balance, let me ask you something. If there is a prophecy about a woman who must come and restore harmony, what must exist to counterbalance that?"

Maureen didn't have to think about it. She had already come to this conclusion while they were still in the room. She just wanted to hear it from his own lips, with his explanation. She replied, "A prophecy about a man who will do the same thing, who will complement her own work."

He smiled at her, not at all surprised that she was already there with him. "Yes," he replied quietly. "It is called the prophecy of the Poet Prince, and it also comes from our little Sarah-Tamar."

"Will you recite it for me?"

He nodded, took a breath, and gave it a poetic recitation, allowing the Scottish burr of his accent to roll over the words of the prophecy. It made Maureen's spine tingle.

The Son of Man shall choose
when the time returns for the Poet Prince.
He who is a spirit of earth and water born
within the complex realm of the sea goat
and the bloodline of the blessed.
He who will submerge the influence of Mars
And exalt the influence of Venus
To embody grace over aggression.
He will inspire the hearts and minds of the people
So as to illuminate the path of service
And show them the Way.
This is his legacy,
This, and to know a very great love.

He looked at Maureen pointedly as he completed the final line of the prophecy, and they said the closing, which had become so familiar to them of late, in unison.

"For those with ears to hear, let them hear it."

They sat in the silence of it for a moment before Maureen asked, "The realm of the sea goat?"

"Capricorn," Bérenger explained. "Those who know little about astrology think of Capricorn as just a standard farm goat, but it is, in fact, a mythical creature. A sea goat is a spirit of both the earth and the water."

"Like the male version of a mermaid? Which is one of Asherah's symbols, and later the symbol of the bloodline?"

"Right. And the prophecy is specific about other astrological elements as well. A predominance of planets in earth signs and water signs. And submerging the influence of Mars is believed to refer to that planet in a water sign, specifically Pisces. So you see, like The Expected One, the Poet Prince has to fulfill certain qualifications of birth and blood."

Maureen was taking it all in, awestruck by the impact of this revelation. Her reply was just above a whisper. "All of which you have."

"Yes."

"And I am assuming, that like The Expected One, you have a number of historical brothers who have fulfilled this prophecy? Destino's note said that your True Cross relic was once owned by the greatest Poet Prince."

"Yes, and I am trying to figure out which one he is referring to. I'm guessing it refers to René d'Anjou, as he was the king of Naples and Jerusalem, and the count of Provence. History refers to him as Good King René as he was the quintessential fairy-tale prince, and also Joan of Arc's mentor and benefactor. And he was the father of Marguerite d'Anjou, who was also an Expected One, and a very powerful woman in history. His baby Marguerite grows to become the queen of England and the champion of the Lancaster faction in the War of the Roses."

"Really? You mean there were two women at one time who fulfilled The Expected One prophecy, Joan and Marguerite? Good King René must have had his hands full."

Bérenger laughed. "Quite. The other aspect I have observed is that each of the men who fulfilled the Poet Prince prophecy were surrounded by very headstrong—but also highly inspirational—women, women who changed their thinking and their lives while shaping their destinies."

"So . . . are The Expected One and the Poet Prince always alive at the same time?"

"From all the examples that I know of, that seems to be the case. But they have different relationships. Sometimes they are father and daughter, sometimes brother and sister, other times not connected by family, but there is a mentor relationship. Of course, the most legendary tend to be the lovers, but it is not the only blueprint. I think it is God's way of showing us the many guises that divine love can take. They are from the same family of spirit."

"Whatever is necessary to get the work done, I think. Keeping the promise?"

"Yes. And in the fifteenth century, there was certainly much to get done. It was a very powerful period of history, truly an era that embodied the concept of *the time returns*. God was taking no chances in the fourteen hundreds, it seems."

"Who was the other Poet Prince at that time?"

"Lorenzo de Medici, the godfather of the Renaissance."

Maureen considered this. "Was he one of us? Really? I never would have guessed."

"I believe he had to be, if he inspired men like Sandro Botticelli and Michelangelo. But I confess I know far more about the French side of the family. Perhaps this Destino will fill us in as it appears we are going to meet him—or someone—on the summer solstice."

They had discussed this earlier with Peter, and all three had agreed that they would travel together to Chartres, and meet Roland and Tammy there as well. If all of them were together, the chances of anything unsettling happening were lessened. There was safety in numbers. It wasn't lost on Bérenger Sinclair that "Destino" was emulating his own actions. Two years earlier Bérenger had enticed Maureen to meet him in precisely the same way, requesting her presence at a church in Paris on the summer solstice. Clearly, Destino, whoever he was, was well versed in their history together. It was as intriguing as it was disconcerting.

Maureen remained focused on the revelation of the latest prophecy. "Why didn't you tell me this before?"

"Because I was waiting for the timing to be right. But obviously Destino made that determination for me, forcing my hand. Yet I'm glad he did; I'm relieved that you know now. I don't feel like I'm hiding anything from you anymore."

Maureen swallowed hard, but the words she was going to speak would not come out. Her eyes filled with tears, glittering emeralds in the moonlight that reflected off the marbled Pantheon.

He took both her hands in his, gently stroking them with his thumbs as he spoke. "And so, my dear Expected One . . . I just want you to know that I understand all that you are, and all that you've been through. As I too know what it's like to live in the shadow cast by such a potent prophecy."

"How long have you known about the Poet Prince?"

"All my life. I was the golden child as a result, you know. My grandfather's prized possession. That's why I spent so much time in France growing up, while my siblings stayed in Scotland. Old Alistair watched me closely until the day he died, to see what I would accomplish, if I would fulfill his prophecy."

"He must have been very proud of you."

Bérenger shrugged. "I don't know that he was. I didn't really accomplish anything while he was alive. Even today, I still need to determine exactly what it is that is expected of me. Finding you . . . well, it was the first time I ever really felt like I might actually have the ability to fulfill my destiny." He stopped for a moment to catch his breath as he was unexpectedly overwhelmed by the flood of the past years' disappointments and desires. He composed himself quickly and continued.

"Maureen, I know you think I rushed into this with you, and now I hope you see why. The truth is, I am normally a very careful and calculating man in all other aspects of my life. But with you, I simply cannot be that. When I look at you and see what is in your eyes, I see someone

I have waited for. Not just in this life, but in others. Maybe for hundreds of years, maybe for thousands. But it was you I have waited for, you and only you. Of this I am certain."

She was crying openly now as she listened. She replied through her tears, "I'm so sorry. I put you through so much when you have been so patient with me. And . . . I think I have been asleep for a very long time."

He reached up gently and cupped her chin in his hand. "It's time to awaken, my Sleeping Beauty. My dove."

They were both beyond speech. Maureen's reply was to lean in closer to accept the touch of his lips against hers. In the center of the piazza, with the fountain of Isis flowing behind them, these lovers of prophecy and scripture shared in the warmth of the *nashakh*, the sacred kiss. Their souls merged through this sweet blending of their breath. No longer were they two; they were One.

The Eternal City seemed a singularly appropriate location for such an epic reunion.

✵

The following morning, Peter rose early to take on the day ahead of him. He knew where this was leading even if he didn't know why. He would go to the church dedicated to Saint Ignatius, the church that just happened to be located a few hundred yards from Maureen's hotel. He had the strangest sensation that he would find some answers there.

Peter had spent most of the sleepless night researching Montserrat, and the Black Madonna specifically. What he discovered was somewhat disconcerting. He reflected on how interesting and often shocking it was when information you have had for years suddenly takes on a very different meaning based on a shift in perspective. For while he remembered some of these details about Montserrat, they would not have struck him in the past as they did today.

Montserrat, like Chartres, had been a place of worship long before Christianity, recognized as it was by the ancients to be a location of extraordinary natural power. Since the earliest Christians, it had been some type of religious settlement dedicated to Mary, and the current monastery was referred to as Saint Mary's. What Peter found disconcerting was that there were strong local legends indicating that Mary herself performed great miracles there. Looking closely at early Christian history and folklore, he could find absolutely no reference to the mother of Jesus coming to Spain. But there were plenty of legends linking Mary Magdalene to this region. This was the southern border of heretic country, and it had been for two thousand years. For Peter, there was only one conclusion. The miracles that were so firmly recollected here in Montserrat were Mary Magdalene's. This was her place, her monastery, and that was her image carved in the ancient wood.

Through the Middle Ages, the monastery became known as a center of learning as well as a sophisticated cultural center visited by royalty and aristocracy. High-ranking noble families sent their sons here to study from all over France and Italy. Peter had found records in the archives and paged through the family names, which was something of a who's who in terms of European wealth and privilege, but also in terms of heretical family ties. He had learned to recognize these family names over the last years of working on this subject around the clock.

Montserrat was widely referred to as the Grail Mountain, and there were theories that the Grail Castle of Parsifal's legend was once nestled amid these rugged, barren peaks. The affiliation with the Grail, and the idea that the "container that held the blood of Christ" was an allegory for the Lord's wife and his children lent further credence to the possibility of Montserrat as a sacred location for descendants of the Magdalene and her teachings. *Their* teachings. And if all this wasn't enough, Montserrat was famous for a red book. In this case, what was called the *Llibre Vermell* was a book of sacred songs written in 1399 and bound carefully in red velvet some centuries later to protect it. But like so many legends, it was predated by earlier stories of a mysterious, secret book that was hidden in the monastery and known only by the highest initiates.

Reigning over all this mystery was the ancient sculpture of the madonna of Montserrat. She was nicknamed "La Moreneta" by the local people, a phrase meaning "little dark one." While official records claimed it was carved in the twelfth century, the legend in Catalonia indicated that this petite yet powerful image of Notre Dame had been created in Jerusalem during the first century, either by Saint Luke or by Nicodemus. The same mythology indicated that the entire monastery was built around this statue when it was discovered, as it could not be moved by any number of men. Like Matilda's favored sculpture, the *Volto Santo*, the Madonna of Montserrat had chosen the place where she wished to reside and was firm in her resistance to change.

Peter was struck by another strange similarity between the Holy Face in Lucca and the madonna in Montserrat. These two works of art represented an interesting pattern he was secretly exploring in the Church. Here were two carvings, both artistically beautiful and having strong legendary connections to the first century. And yet in both cases, the Church was emphatic that neither was original. Each piece was declared a copy from the Middle Ages. This would be easy enough to understand if it were true. What Peter found fascinating was that there was more information to substantiate that these items were potentially first-century originals than there was "proof" that they were copies. In his opinion, the case for both of these items being originals was quite a bit stronger. The *Volto Santo*, for example, had been considered original in Matilda's time. If the current sculpture were a medieval forgery, what happened to the original? And why was there no outcry about its removal from Lucca if such was the case? Why does nothing in history indicate the removal of the Holy Face from the site that was chosen by God for it to rest in perpetuity? Peter believed that it was because the original had never been moved. The *Volto Santo* in Lucca today was, in fact, the original carved by Nicodemus. And he was beginning to think that the same was true of the madonna in Montserrat.

But why? Why wouldn't the Church want the faithful to know that these items were authentic? This knowledge could only make them more valuable, and yet there seemed to be a concerted effort to convince the public that many of these sacred items from the first century were forgeries, and that all the originals had simply disappeared into the mists of time. He had yet to understand it, but he would pursue it. Could this also be true of the Shroud of Turin? Did the Church, for some reason he hadn't figured out yet, want us to believe that the Shroud was a fake when they knew that it was truly a holy relic of immense power? Just how big was this issue?

Peter had recently visited the Church of the Holy Stairs near the Lateran Palace. It was named for the staircase that the sainted Empress Helena brought with her to Rome, the twenty-eight white marble steps that Jesus climbed on his way to judgment by Pontius Pilate. Peter climbed the stairs on his knees, as is required of the faithful, to view the treasure that awaited him at the top. Installed in a vault was a legendary painting of our Lord, credited to Saint Luke but often called *acheiropoieton*, which means "not made by human hands." Like the *Volto Santo*, it was believed that angels guided the artist's hand that created the face of Jesus to ensure that it was perfected.

The last pope to display this painting in public, prior to its modern restoration, was Leo X, the son of Renaissance godfather Lorenzo de Medici. After the death of Pope Leo, the painting disappeared for several centuries. When it reemerged into public view, portions of the work had been covered permanently with silver and jewels, as if to obscure a number of details on the original board. In fact, the majority of the painting had been concealed by these late-addition papal decorations, leaving only the face of Jesus entirely visible. Was there some element of this original painting of our Lord that the Church did not want us to see? Otherwise, why would anyone tamper with such a holy object? Did they declare that it was a copy by an unknown artist with little value simply because they didn't want the faithful to ask questions? Peter scoffed at this notion. In his experience as a priest, he had come to realize that the faithful rarely asked questions of their religious hierarchy, even when they were desperately necessary. If more questions were asked by parishioners, if more real answers were demanded, the Church might not be immersed in scandal at the dawn of the twenty-first century.

This painting was on display under the most heavily protected security system in Rome. Peter had been in nearly every church in the city and had never seen security like this around any other piece of art. This painting of Jesus was set back from the viewer by at least ten feet, behind thick walls of protective and bulletproof glass and what appeared to be an impenetrable network of iron bars. Yet the Church declared that this painting was only a copy of the original, made by an unknown artist in the Middle Ages.

Really? Then why the iron-clad vaulting? The Hope diamond didn't have security like this. Nor did any of the relics in Rome that were claimed to be authentic and priceless have security like this.

Peter found the whole thing puzzling, but when he listed the works of art that he believed were authentic, and that the Church claimed were not, he did find one important thread that connected them. All had an association with one of the original members of the Order of the Holy Sepulcher, either Luke or Nicodemus, or both. Could he make the leap that, subsequently, each of these items had potentially come into contact with the Book of Love?

Peter crossed the Tiber as he contemplated this idea, walking toward the section of Rome that contained two churches significant to the Jesuit order. The Gesù, the largest and most well known, had been the official headquarters of the superior general of the Jesuit order for hundreds of years. It was said that Michelangelo was so impressed with the power and purity of Loyola's conversion that he offered to design his church, the Holy Name of Jesus, for free. Now, knowing what they did about Michelangelo's lineage, Peter wondered if there wasn't some greater connection between the great artist and Ignatius Loyola—a connection that somehow involved the Book of Love.

While the Gesù was imagined during the lifetimes of both the saint and the sculptor, construction began after their deaths. Peter passed the Gesù and bowed in respect to it but continued to the smaller church that was his destination, Sant'Ignazio. In Peter's eyes, this was the church of the working Jesuit, as it had once been the official center of worship for the Roman College, also known as the Pontifical Gregorian University. This, one of the oldest universities in the world, was believed to be named after Pope Gregory XIII, who was a primary benefactor of its construction. But Peter was struck by another concept that had just occurred to him. A superior had told him a story once that the university had been called Gregorian also in deference to Gregory VII, a great reformer of the church. Matilda's Gregory.

He entered Sant'Ignazio, not entirely sure what he was searching for here, but standing in the faith that it would find him in this place. He moved to stand near one of the details that made this church unique—the golden disk in the floor that marked the perfect spot to view what appeared to be a beautifully vaulted dome, covered in elaborate frescoes. But the dome was a trick of the eye. It was painted by a brilliant Baroque craftsman, the Jesuit brother Andrea Pozzo, using a perfect trompe l'oeil technique. Legend said that the neighbors in Rome refused to allow a dome to be built that would block their afternoon sun, and the brothers were forced to create a false dome. Rather than becoming irritated by the restriction, they took it as an artistic challenge and created something truly memorable. When one stood on the golden disk, it was nearly impossible to tell that the dome was a trick of unequaled and illusory painting.

"The Church is full of grand illusions, isn't it?"

Peter jumped at the voice behind him, then turned quickly to see who had made the same observation that had been running through his head for the last two years. Standing behind him was Cardinal Barberini, his brother on the Arques council. Barberini put his finger to his lips and pulled Peter around to sit in one of the pews.

Peter asked him simply, "Are you Destino?"

Barberini smiled. "No, no. Not even close."

Peter considered for a moment before asking a follow-up question. "Is Destino a Jesuit?"

Barberini shook his head. "Destino is many things. He does not fit into any category that you have reference for. Yet. But that is for later. For the moment, I came here to tell you why you became a Jesuit, other than the reasons that you think you already know."

It was a strange position that Peter found himself in. Here was a senior ranking member of the Church who had obviously followed him. Barberini had inside information on very serious and secret matters—and evidently quite a lot of it—but he was still something of an enigma. Cardinal DeCaro, whom he trusted implicitly, had introduced Barberini as an ally, and yet this clandestine behavior was strange. And unnecessary. Or was it? Was Peter being watched? He had always suspected he was, but this was potential confirmation. Was DeCaro being watched as well? The more conservative factions within the Vatican were in open conflict with Tómas's progressive stance, particularly on the Magdalene material, but was there something deeper going on here?

Barberini was reading Peter's thoughts apparently, as he continued, "You will simply have to trust me until I can tell you more, my boy. For now, I have come to talk to you about our founder. The great and very holy Saint Ignatius de Loyola."

Peter's gut reaction to the question "Why did you become a Jesuit?" had been one word: knowledge. The Jesuits had always been the great educators and educated, and his personal passion was studying the history of religion and spirituality and of ancient language and wisdom. He lived to teach and had missed his true vocation terribly since relocating to Rome to participate on the Magdalene committee. Ignatius de Loyola was the founder of the university here, and he was a pillar of education, both religious and humanist. As such, Peter knew his biography well, as all good Jesuit priests did. Loyola came from a Basque family in northern Spain, where he was born on Christmas Eve of 1491, the youngest child of thirteen. He was low-level nobility but high enough to live an early life of leisure. He was something of a playboy and a gambler in his youth, becoming an army officer at the age of thirty.

At Pamplona, Ignatius was struck by a cannonball in the battle to save the territory from the encroaching French. One leg was broken and the other injured by the blow. The broken leg healed so badly that it had to be broken again and reset, all of which was done with no anesthetic. Loyola healed, but the broken leg was shorter than the other, and he walked with a terrible limp for the rest of his life. His descent into disability inspired a new interest in intellectual pursuits, with reading and acquiring knowledge above all others. During his rehabilitation, he read every book that was available at the castle in Loyola; they were all religious in theme.

There is some mystery surrounding Ignatius during his time in Loyola. Who supplied him with the books and what, specifically, was he reading? There were rumors that during this period he fell deeply in love with a mystery woman, a woman with copper hair and royal blood who nursed him tenderly and had an enormous impact upon him during his lengthy convalescence. By the time he recovered enough to walk and travel in March of 1522, he was an entirely new man, fueled by a feverish spiritual intensity.

Loyola's first act upon his rehabilitation was to make a pilgrimage to the Monastery of Saint Mary of Montserrat, high in the mountains north of Barcelona. It was said that, obeying the rules of chivalry in regard to Our Lady, he knelt in all-night vigil before the altar of the Black Madonna. Some accounts said that he did this for three consecutive nights in honor of the trinity. At the end of his vigil, he placed all his weapons on the altar before the madonna and pledged that he would become a new warrior for her Way.

Barberini interrupted Peter's thoughts with an abrupt question. "When did Loyola go to Montserrat?"

"March 1522."

"Correct. What day in March?"

"The Feast Day of the Annunciation. March twenty-fifth."

"Wrong."

Peter was startled by this. Every Jesuit knew that date. Barberini acknowledged this, and continued. "He made his pledge to Notre Dame on March twenty-fifth, that is true. But this was after three days of prayer and meditation. He arrived on a specific date for a specific reason."

Peter answered, trying to make it all fit in his brain as it was happening. "March twenty-second."

Barberini nodded.

"But why?" Peter understood, in theory, that this date held heretical importance in terms of births and prophecies. But he wasn't sure what the connection was specifically here. Barberini prompted him.

"Are you aware of anything—a controversial and priceless document, perhaps—that may have come to the monastery of Montserrat?"

It hit Peter like a blow to the back of the head. Montserrat was the final known resting place of the authentic manuscript of the Book of Love, the document that was written in the very hand of our Lord and delivered to Europe by his wife and beloved—his beloved Mary Magdalene, who was depicted in the image at Montserrat, holding his child. Peter knew this, but he certainly hadn't connected the Book of Love to Loyola before. He had assumed their dual association with Montserrat was . . . a coincidence. He knew better, but how could he have possibly put these two potentially conflicting ideas in the same place?

Peter nodded his understanding as Barberini continued.

"The final massacre of the Cathar stronghold at Montségur happened on March sixteenth, 1244. It took the surviving four refugees six days to reach Montserrat and safety. March twenty-second is the anniversary of the arrival and installation of the Holy Word of Jesus Christ at the monastery. Loyola's vigil—and his indoctrination—began on that night for a reason."

Peter asked the next question very slowly and carefully. "What are you saying? Are you telling me that Loyola was a heretic? That he founded our order for entirely different reasons than anyone understands? That he . . . had access to the Book of Love?"

"He called it the Society of Jesus, didn't he? Of course, that could mean anything, but it's a trifle unimaginative otherwise, isn't it? Does Loyola strike you as a man who would create a revolutionary new religious order and then give it a name that did not perfectly represent what he stood for? But if he was working from teachings that were directly from Jesus and not from other sources, well . . . that would account for it, wouldn't it? And remember at all times these words that were immortalized in the writings of his closest friend, Luís Gonçalves de Câmara. He said, '*Ignatius was always inclined toward love. Moreover, he seemed to embody all love, and because of that he was universally loved by all. There was no one in the Society who did not have much great love for him and did not consider himself much loved by him.*' Strangely, the Church does not preserve this portrait of our Loyola, do they?"

Peter was stunned. The traditional perspective on Loyola's character was that he was a stern, harsh, and taciturn man. He may have been brilliant and devout, but *loving* was not the first adjective that sprang to mind when one studied his biography. To be reminded that the closest person who ever wrote about Ignatius Loyola wanted to preserve just how much he was inclined toward love, that he "seemed to embody all love" was a revelation.

"So does this mean that Loyola had the Book of Love? Was it in Montserrat as late as 1522?" This would certainly be valuable information, given that all other references to the original document disappeared after 1244.

Barberini leaned over to pat Peter on the shoulder and then used him as a crutch to stand up. "My bones ache from the walk across the river, my boy. So for now we shall have to end this chat, but I'm so happy that we had it. Oh, and one more thing . . ."

Peter helped Barberini lift his aging, pudgy body out of the pew as the elder man delivered the last shock. "The committee is going to make an announcement about the Magdalene material. It will happen in the next week. But you must go to France with your cousin in the meantime, so Tómas and I will keep you posted as the developments occur.

"They are going to authenticate the Arques Gospel and release it to the public, or so they tell me. Maureen shall be vindicated if this happens. And so, my boy, shall you. But most of all . . . our Lady's story will finally be told, and it will be told in its truth and its entirety. May God grant that it be so."

Watching the older man waddle out of the church, Peter whispered in echo of Barberini's parting words.

"May God grant that it be so."

CHAPTER NINETEEN

Chartres, France
present day

Chartres Cathedral can be viewed from more than twenty miles away, perched as it is atop its sacred hillock, with the mismatched spires on either side of the western portal rising over the plain of La Beauce. Maureen, Peter, and Bérenger remarked on the beauty of it when they arrived via chauffeur-driven car early on June 20. Bérenger had arranged for them to be picked up upon arrival at Orly Airport just outside Paris.

Maureen was first to comment on the power of the place, as she could feel it in her bones when they were still miles away. There was indeed a magic that radiated from it. The two men in her company had been to this place before and were not experiencing it from the same fresh perspective. Maureen ran her hands over her arms as the goose bumps covered her flesh.

After they checked into their charming hotel on the edge of the town square, they set out to make the short walk up the hill toward the cathedral. Their goal was to get the lay of the land, to determine where, exactly, window 10 was located, and to get a first glimpse of the labyrinth. Tammy and Roland were driving up from the Languedoc to join them.

Maureen caught her breath as she stood before the cathedral for the first time. It was the most majestic building she had ever seen. She insisted on walking around the cathedral in its entirety before going inside, taking in the enormity of the place and the exquisite decoration that covered virtually every inch of the exterior in elaborate bas-relief and statuary. It was breathtaking. Here was a monument of unequaled beauty, a testament to the power and grace of human accomplishment born out of heart and spirit. Bérenger Sinclair acted as impromptu guide, knowing a fair amount about the esoteric nature of Chartres from his own studies. He took Peter and Maureen around to the left of the cathedral, to the northern side, called the Door of the Initiates, and showed them some of the more famous statues—those of the patriarchs. But it was not the sculptures of Moses and Abraham and David that grabbed Maureen's attention. Instead, it was her immediate observation that this church was covered with women. Some were obvious; there appeared Judith, the Old Testament heroine who saves her people, there was Mother Mary in the annunciation and with her cousin Elizabeth in the visitation, and there was a sequence of the Queen of Sheba coming to Solomon, each crowned with an elaborate sculpture of the original Temple. Others were not easily identifiable, but there were sequences with women covering much of the northern façade.

Bérenger informed them, "There are several hundred images of women on this church, and over one hundred seventy believed to be of the Great Mary, the Mother Mary. No other church in the world has so many depictions of females; nothing even comes close."

Maureen was mesmerized by all that she saw but stopped in admiration before the magnificent sculpture of a woman that was installed on an external pillar of an arch on the far right of the door. She was young and beautiful and carried a book in one hand, while the other, though damaged by eight hundred years of weather and war, appeared to be raised in benediction.

Bérenger smiled at her. "I knew you would love her. So do I. Of the thousand or more images on this cathedral, this is the one I obsessed over from the very first day I arrived here. And now that we know

Matilda's story so well, I am beginning to see why this particular lady has always been special to me. Maureen, meet Modesta. She is the patron spirit of this place."

Maureen felt an unexpected surge of tears behind her eyes at the mention of Matilda. She knew that her heart and spirit would be inextricably connected to her Tuscan countess forever.

"Modesta's is a tragic but important story," Bérenger said, pointing up at the saint.

"Of course it is." Maureen went and stood under the statue of Modesta, whose feet hit above Maureen's head. The scale and size of Chartres was deceptive owing to the expert use of perspective. It was easy to lose sight of just exactly how enormous—and exquisitely detailed—all the artwork was unless it was examined very closely.

Modesta's face was lovely and serene; her long hair flowed beneath a veil. The book in her left hand appeared beautifully bound. Maureen commented, "I am noticing that many of these figures are holding books."

Peter explained, "Traditionally, that symbolizes the Word. Scripture. The gospels. It is common in Christian art."

Maureen tried not to be irritated when Peter gave her typical, obvious explanations, automatically recited from his entrenched perspective as a priest. She knew, of course, what the traditional symbolism of the book was. She also knew that it was necessary to look at all these works of art with new eyes, given that they had fresh information regarding them. Could there be another reason that these characters, particularly so many women, were holding books? Could this be a different book, a specific reference to the Book of Love? She rolled her eyes at Peter and turned to Bérenger.

"Tell me what you know about Modesta."

"The common legend in the guidebooks says that she was the virgin daughter of a very cruel and intolerant Roman governor called Quirinus, who was sent to Chartres specifically to quell the growing cult of Christianity. But by all accounts Modesta was a loving young woman who was horrified by the persecution of the Christians and began to help them. For example, she would alert them when her father was going to raid their secret places of worship, one of which was here where the cathedral is now. It is said that during this time Modesta fell in love with a young man named Potentian, who converted her wholly to Christianity. When Governor Quirinus discovered that his daughter had converted and was betraying him to her Christian brethren, he had her publicly tortured as an example of his zero-tolerance policy. Even the governor's own daughter was not safe from the might of Rome. She was decapitated and her body was thrown into the deep well that is in the crypt here, and this is why she is often called the guardian spirit of this place. It is said that she can be heard in the crypt, whispering secrets from its depths for those with ears to hear."

Maureen shivered at the story, sensing immediately that there was more to Modesta's biography than she was currently grasping.

Bérenger noticed. "What is it?"

Maureen looked back up at the sculpture of the serenely beautiful woman clutching her book. She shook her head slowly. "There's more. As important and tragic as that story is, it isn't the whole story. I just know that somehow."

The mention of the crypt, with its well, had her attention at the moment. Perhaps if she could get in there, Modesta would whisper its secrets to her.

"Can we go into the crypt?"

Bérenger shook his head. "Unfortunately not. It is not open to the public, except once a day when a very brief guided tour is given in French at eleven a.m. I have often wondered why, precisely, the Church doesn't want average citizens in the crypt. The well is covered, so it cannot be for safety reasons. The black madonna that is on display in the crypt, Our Lady of Under the Earth, is a copy of the one that was burned during the Revolution, so it is not to protect any ancient relics. But for some reason . . . the crypt is off-limits to the general public."

They continued to explore the perimeter and Maureen lost count of all the female figures on the exterior of the church, while noticing that Saint Anne, the grandmother of Jesus, was also well and prominently represented. Most significantly, she held a place of power at the grand Door of the Initiates. Walking around the back and up along the south entrance, where the doors were bolted shut, they found that the primary, central figure was a beautiful thirteenth-century statue of Christ, a sculpture known as *Christ the Teacher*. In his left hand he held a beautiful and ornate book. Maureen shot Peter a look but said nothing. Funny that Christ was shown holding books so often, yet the Church contended that he never wrote one of his own.

Maureen was busy taking mental notes of elements that had esoteric meaning. The apostles were depicted here in statuary, perched upon beautiful, twisted columns. She had learned in reading everything she could get her hands on about Solomon and Sheba that the wise king himself had created the first twisted columns to decorate his own legendary temple, and that such architectural details were a nod to his genius. Also on this side of the cathedral, on the archivolt over the portal, were the signs of the zodiac, in order. Maureen sighed as she looked at these. It was frustrating trying to grasp the details of Chartres in such a short time. It would literally take years to see and appreciate every single detail on the exterior of this place, so vast was it and so grand the art that covered the exterior. Maureen observed to no one in particular, "I think the greatest art gallery in the world just may be outside for all to view, and has been for eight hundred years."

They walked full circle now, back to the front of the cathedral. This was the western entrance known as the Royal Portal. There were several men who appeared to be homeless on the steps, holding out scallop shells and requesting offerings. One was standing at the top of the stairs and singing in French; another was huddled close to the door, looking the worse for wear. Bérenger dropped euro notes discreetly into both shells as he passed. Maureen noticed, and she added her own contributions. The singing man pulled a wildflower from his pocket and handed it to her with a wink.

Both Bérenger and Maureen paused, Peter behind them, to examine the statuary that greeted them on the right of the western door. Was it a coincidence that the primary entrance doors to Chartres Cathedral contained sculptures of King Solomon and the Queen of Sheba? It seemed that the epic lovers were quite well represented here.

The three of them entered the narthex through the enormous doors and went immediately to the gift shop on the left to purchase a plan of the cathedral, which would identify window 10 in the stained glass. The shop was full of books and art prints of the sculptures and the windows, but the superstar of Chartres Cathedral was the Blue Madonna, the twelfth-century stained glass masterpiece known as Our Lady of the Beautiful Window. She existed here in posters, greeting cards, and bookmarks. And yet despite her omnipresence in the gift shop, she was not diminished. There was something intense and powerful about the image, something in the purity of the art that transcended the commerce.

Maureen did not begrudge the cathedral its merchandising. That this monument to the love of God was available to the public every day at no charge was a gift to the world. If selling postcards and posters of the artwork helped to maintain and preserve it, so much the better. The three of them made their contributions to the coffers, buying guidebooks and maps. Peter set out to find window 10, leaving Bérenger and Maureen alone at the entrance to one of the great shrines of human history.

Maureen took a deep breath and allowed herself to enter the nave of this, the grandest cathedral in the world. It was awe inspiring in its enormity, and yet there was a strange and beautiful intimacy about it. While the lofty vaulting and the hundreds of tons of stone should have been completely overwhelming, the overall atmosphere of Chartres was welcoming and warm. It was also entirely . . . holy. That was the only word that Maureen could think of as she allowed herself to be dazzled by the colors of the stained glass that lined the nave in two stories, one on top of the other. She read in the guidebook that Napoleon's famous comment, upon entering this cathedral for the first time, was "Chartres is no place for an atheist."

No place indeed.

"Look behind you," Bérenger said. "And up."

Maureen sighed over the beauty of the sight. The enormous western rose window and the three lancet windows below it, installed originally in the twelfth century along with the ubiquitous Blue Madonna, glittered in the afternoon sun. These were the oldest original windows in Chartres, and they were special. While the glass throughout is magnificent, these specific windows predated the others by almost a century. Their grace and color were unequaled by anything that Maureen had ever seen in any other church. The rose windows in Notre Dame de Paris were gorgeous and grand, but there was something happening here in Chartres that was exceptional. The three lancets below the rose all radiated the same powerful essence.

Bérenger explained in hushed tones, "It's the blue. It has never been duplicated in any other church in the world. It's called Chartres blue because it is unique to this place. No one has ever been able to determine just exactly what it was that the glaziers used when they were creating these windows. The other window from this time period was recently restored. It's the Blue Madonna. She's over there . . ."

Bérenger did not complete his sentence as he saw the stricken look on Maureen's face. Immediately he understood and nodded solemnly. As they were viewing the windows over the door, they had walked between several rows of moveable chairs. Maureen looked down and realized that they were standing in the middle of the labyrinth, that most sacred symbol created by Jesus' and Solomon's combination of extraordinary wisdom and faith.

The sacred symbol that was completely obstructed and damaged by the rows of chairs that covered it.

Maureen sat down, quickly, thinking she was going to be sick. She was suddenly very, very dizzy.

"Are you all right?"

She nodded, but there were tears in her eyes. The impact of seeing the labyrinth littered with chairs was something she was unprepared for. She knew to expect it, but she had no frame of reference for how it would make her feel—the anger, the indignation. She said simply, "How could they?"

Bérenger had no answer. He had spent most of his eventful life asking that same question over and over again.

Peter approached them, waiving the guidebook. He stopped when he saw Maureen's face and nodded.

"I know," he said. "Oddly, I have always felt that way about the labyrinth being covered like this, even before I knew just exactly what it was and why it mattered so much. But on a happier note, I have found window ten."

Maureen rose to follow him, happy enough to get away from the tragedy of the labyrinth's disgrace. Peter led them to the south transept and pointed out the first window on the right. It was dedicated to an Italian saint who was the first bishop of Ravenna, Saint Apollinaris.

"He was a disciple of Saint Peter, credited with a number of miracles, which are depicted here in the glass. But I don't think it's the specific saint here that we are concerned with," he explained. "Rather, it's that circular hole in the window, right up there."

A circle of white light shone through the darker colors of the window via a hole that appeared to be cut deliberately on the right edge.

Peter pointed to the ground just a few feet away from where they were standing. "See that flagstone there in the floor? The one that is set at an angle from the rest?"

Bérenger nodded. "It's a different color, lighter than the others. And obviously set differently. It's meant to stand out." He hunkered down to run his hand over the stone and smiled. "And look at this, there's a brass spike hammered into the stone. *X* marks the spot."

"Which means?" Maureen wasn't following entirely.

Bérenger explained. "Do you remember when we met for the first time in Saint-Sulpice?" The question was rhetorical; the day they met had changed both their lives indelibly and neither would ever forget it. But that meeting had also been arranged specifically to occur on the summer solstice, on June 21, because Bérenger wanted to demonstrate to Maureen just how precise the builders of the church at Saint-Sulpice had been. Those architects had marked the solstice through a brass line embedded in the floor. At midday on the solstice, the sun shone through the windows and illuminated the brass.

"A similar event occurs here. At midday tomorrow, the sun will shine through that hole in the window, specifically illuminating that brass nail in the slantways stone, marking the high point of the longest day of the year."

Maureen understood now. "Which means it is a celebration of light, marking the moment of strongest sunlight in the entire calendar."

"Illumination," Peter said softly, causing both of them to turn and stare at him. There was profound insight in that simple word. "It's a celebration of the illumination which can occur in this sacred space."

They all stood together for a moment, in quiet appreciation of the architects, masons, and astronomers who must have worked in extraordinary unison to create such an anomaly over eight hundred years ago.

"The orchestration of such a thing is phenomenal," Maureen observed. "Every aspect of this cathedral had to be created with absolute intention. Nothing in here is random. Nothing. I can feel that in my bones; it screams from every inch of this extraordinary, holy place."

They sat in the pews adjacent to window 10, facing the northern rose window and the lancets below it. The central figure was an enormous image of Saint Anne, depicted in the style of a black madonna.

"Like that. That's specific. Saint Anne as a black madonna, and she is centric. She's all over this cathedral, and in each case she is represented in a position of authority and important placement. That cannot be an accident."

"I can't vouch for the presence of Saint Anne, but I can say this." This was Peter again. "The Gothic movement begins not long after Matilda's death, roughly in 1130, and it just appears out of nowhere. But it's not really Gothic, is it? It doesn't come from the Visi*goths*, who were by most accounts a barbaric and warlike people who were hardly given to delicate artistry in stone and glass."

Bérenger jumped into a topic he had some background in. "That's because the phrase *Gothic art* is a translation error. The original phrase that applied to what we call the Gothic cathedrals wasn't *art gothique* but rather *argotique*. *Argotique* is a word that means 'slang,' and refers to a specific lost dialect. The great alchemist Fulcanelli said that *argo-*

tique was a 'language peculiar to all who wished to communicate without being understood by outsiders.' "

Peter nodded his understanding. "So you're saying that this cathedral isn't the 'art of the Goths' but rather art encoded with a special and secret language."

"For those with ears to hear," Maureen added.

"Exactly. *Argotique* was also called the language of outlaws, which certainly describes the heretic cultures."

Peter continued, even more animated now. "It all fits beautifully. Suddenly in the twelfth century, there are over twenty Gothic cathedrals under construction, and just as suddenly, there appear stonemasons, mathematicians, architects, and glaziers who know exactly how to execute these previously unheard-of masterpieces of architecture— and art that is encoded."

Maureen and Bérenger were both listening closely now. Peter rarely dissertated like this; when he did, it was necessary to pay close attention. It was obvious that this was something he had been thinking about a lot in his recent research.

"This movement in architecture springs up, almost overnight, and flourishes," Peter continued. "Yet no one knows how or why. Equally, no one knows who financed these cathedrals, particularly not this one. There is intention here, as you pointed out, Maureen. There is will. And a strong one. But why, and why here? There is something privileged about Chartres, and it goes beyond anything that the guidebooks and the traditional Church will tell us."

"So what do you think the answer is, Pete?"

He paused for a moment, very serious, before turning to smile at his cousin and answering with a single name. "Matilda."

Maureen was floored by the unexpected answer. "Matilda?"

Father Peter Healy nodded. "She was devoted to architecture. Look at how much she loved building Orval, at how she challenged the architects and builders of her time with the size and shape of the arches. And what do we know about the Libro Rosso? It contained secret architectural drawings. Where did those drawings come from? From Jesus. Where did Jesus get them? They were passed down through his exalted family lineage, from none other than Solomon himself, and perhaps Sheba as well."

Maureen added, thinking out loud, "In Matilda's retelling of the Solomon and Sheba legend, she reminds us that the Sabeans were known as the People of Architecture and that the queen was the founder of schools for sculptors in stone."

Peter nodded his agreement; this was his precise point. "And we have seen on the exterior that both Solomon and Sheba are well represented with at least two life-sized sculptures, as are elements of the original temple."

The enormity of it hit Bérenger first. "So are we saying that Chartres—and in essence the entire Gothic movement—was potentially started by Matilda? And that it was based on original drawings from Solomon's Temple?"

"As preserved by the Order in the Libro Rosso," Maureen jumped in, brimming with excitement over the idea. "And . . . brought to Chartres. By Conn and the Master? My God . . ."

Peter continued the thought, speaking very fast now, proving that he had been devising this theory for some time. "It all works. Remember that Fulbert rebuilt the cathedral after the fire in 1020. But there is another fire, even more catastrophic, that destroys everything but the crypt in 1134. Maybe it was an accident, maybe it wasn't. But the cathedral was completely rebuilt on a new and unprecedented model and becomes the masterpiece of art and architecture that it is today. The height of this vaulting has never been matched, anywhere in the world."

Maureen instantly felt guilty about her earlier annoyance with Peter. He had come a long way in two years. This was a stunning theory, and a progressive one.

Bérenger continued to build upon the idea. "So it's about thirty years from 1100, which is roughly when Conn and the Master come to Chartres, to 1134, when reconstruction begins here. We know they were eventually joined by Patricio, who was the architectural mastermind, along with Matilda, of the magnificent Orval. They would have had enough time to perfect the techniques, the plans, and the geometry, to begin construction on an entirely new type of temple. And perhaps even to train an entire generation in those principles and techniques. Then there is another fire in the next century, after which even more elaborate ornamentation is created for the new elements."

Maureen finished the thought. "Because now the residents here were truly expert in all the architectural modalities needed to create this kind of perfection."

They were strolling slowly through the cathedral now, talking, thinking, allowing the vastness of the place and its history to sink in. Bérenger stopped them in front of the famous window in the south ambulatory. "Here she is, the queen of Chartres," he explained, pointing at the lovely madonna and child that towered over them. "She is called Notre Dame de la Belle Verriere, Our Lady of the Beautiful Window, and you can see why. She is the oldest surviving piece of stained glass, here since 1137." The magnificent madonna, which had been called "the most beautiful stained glass in the world," was entirely regal in her golden crown, set with jewels and topped with fleurs-de-lis, and gowned in the most exquisite blue, the famous Chartres blue that could not be duplicated, which was set off by an intense red background. Photographs did not do justice to the hues that shone through the glass in the morning sunlight. Behind her and atop the throne was a fortress-style castle, and an enormous white dove, the emblem of the Holy Spirit, hovered over the figure of the madonna and her son.

"The official Church position is that this cathedral is dedicated to the Virgin Mary, and that all the madonna images in here are her in various guises. But I think we can all agree among ourselves that there are several Marys depicted," said Bérenger.

"Agreed," Peter added. "But at the risk of Maureen kicking me in the shins, I need to say something else." They continued to walk around the curvature of the ambulatory until Peter stopped them before a chapel on the northeast side that held a large and exquisite reliquary. Within the panes of clear glass, a draped length of white silk was displayed. "The *Sancta Camisa*. The Veil of the Virgin. This is one of the holiest relics in Christendom, and it has been here in Chartres since the ninth century. Everyone will tell you that this is why the cathedral is dedicated to the Virgin Mary, which is as it should be."

Maureen responded. "I wouldn't dispute that for a moment. I've said it before but it bears repeating. It has never been my intention to diminish the importance of Jesus' mother. Far from it. I think she was chosen to give birth to him and to raise him because she was singularly brilliant and strong and pure of heart and spirit. I'm just saying that it doesn't end with her, does it? And based on all the images of her mother, Saint Anne, here in the cathedral, I'm also willing to say that it didn't begin with her. And she, of all people, probably wouldn't want us to think that it did."

❁

Each year on the twenty-first of June, the archdiocese of Chartres allowed the labyrinth to be uncovered. Knowing this, Maureen, Bérenger, and Peter met Tammy and Roland for an early breakfast and planned to get to the cathedral shortly after it opened. All of them were anxious to see the labyrinth and to walk its eleven circuits. Tammy and Roland had arrived the night before, in time for a late dinner. Thankfully, the French tradition of lengthy evening meals allowed time to catch up on recent events.

As the five of them arrived at the steps of the western entrance, Maureen noticed that there was a different man standing on the steps today. He also held out a scallop shell for his contributions, and he too was singing. But as they grew nearer, she stopped to listen to him, tapping Tammy, who was speaking to Bérenger, on the shoulder. "Shh. Listen."

The man, who appeared spry enough despite his aged appearance, was standing sideways, visible only in profile as the little group approached the steps. This appeared to be intentional: he was deliberately not looking at any of them. He was singing, softly yet clearly, and Maureen got a chill as she heard the song in accented English.

Mary had a little lamb
its fleece was white as snow
And everywhere that Mary went
the lamb was sure to go.
It followed her to school one day
which was against the rule
It made the children laugh and play
to see a lamb at school.

But it was the second verse, the one seldom heard in the school yard, that grabbed Maureen in the heart every time. It made her cry, it always had. Only recently did she understand why.

"Why does the lamb love Mary so?"
The little children cried.
"For Mary loves the lamb you know,"
The teacher did reply.

As the man sang the last line, he turned to face Maureen full on, causing her to stop dead in her tracks.

One entire side of his weathered face was puckered in a scar that zigzagged from the top of his cheekbone into his neck.

"Destino."

Maureen said it as the old man smiled at her and nodded. The others, coming up behind her, were beginning to understand what had just transpired. But while all of them had their own reasons for being here, the man they would call Destino was clearly focused on Maureen. The others stood back and allowed them to talk, waiting on the steps of the cathedral in the growing warmth as the first day of summer approached.

"I have . . . so many questions," Maureen said, at a loss to know where to start.

"We have time, Madonna. Plenty of time. I will answer one now but the rest will have to wait as we must all go inside. There is something we must do together and we must do it soon."

Maureen noticed the specific cadence of his accent and commented on it. "You're Italian?"

"Is that the one question you want me to answer now?"

"No! Give me a second." This was like having a genie ask if you were certain of your wish. Maureen had to be sure she chose wisely. After a moment of thought, she asked, "How did you know what was in my dreams? And know it exactly? How did you know the exact words that Easa spoke to me?"

The old man shrugged. "Do you think you are the only one he speaks to?"

His reply threw Maureen. It was not what she expected. "Is that the answer?"

"It is the only answer I shall give you. Come now, my child. And bring your friends. We have sacred work to do."

Maureen gestured for the others to come inside, and they followed Destino into the cathedral. They were all surprised when they saw that the labyrinth was still covered with chairs. "But I thought they opened the labyrinth on the summer solstice," Maureen said.

Destino shook his head sadly. "No. This is a great sacrilege, a terrible lack of understanding that causes this . . . I shall never get used to it and I have seen it for more years than I can tell you. You see, they—the Church—will allow the labyrinth to be opened on certain days of the year, but theirs will not be the hands that do so. Ours must be. It is our duty to remove the chairs. But do not regret it. It is sacred. You shall see."

Destino gestured to Roland and the two of them demonstrated the technique for moving the chairs. They were attached in rows and were bulky, if not as heavy as they looked. But moving them without scraping the floor and causing further damage to the ancient stones that made up the labyrinth was tricky. Destino showed them where to place the chairs, behind the additional pews and along the sides of the nave.

They worked together in pairs: Maureen and Bérenger, Tammy and Peter, Roland and Destino. The labyrinth was forty-two feet across, and the job of removing the chairs was somewhat daunting. But as they began to remove them and the labyrinth came into view, Maureen and the others began to understand what Destino meant when he said that this was a sacred duty. It was liberating, and the metaphor of releasing the labyrinth from that which attempted to obscure it was powerful and felt by each of them.

It was cathartic. Maureen thought for a moment about that word. *Cathar-tic.* Pure and purifying, through the true teachings of love.

Roland looked up at his comrades as they worked and grinned at them. "One for all and all for one. That is our motto, is it not?"

As they performed their sacred task in harmony, a group of enthusiastic students on a pilgrimage from Belgium entered the cathedral and asked to help. They pitched in, obviously feeling the same euphoria that came with releasing the spirit of the labyrinth on this, the longest day of the year, when there was more light shining through these special windows than at any other time. There was a sense of community and solidarity as the labyrinth was eventually cleared. Everyone stepped back to admire the handiwork of the master craftsmen who had installed this work of spiritual art eight centuries ago. Destino gestured that they should allow the students to walk the labyrinth first, as he had a few details to show them before they entered.

Turning from the west-facing entrance of the labyrinth, Destino hobbled with his funny, ancient gait away from the labyrinth and toward the western door, stopping abruptly in the aisle of the nave. He pointed to the ground, indicating that he was too old to kneel and stress his weary joints, but that they should all look to the floor. Embedded in the stone was an iron plate.

"Madonna Ariadne," he said by way of explanation, indicating that there had once been an iron ring here. Destino gestured to the stained glass window that was aligned with the iron ring, the window nearest to the entrance of the labyrinth.

"There were one hundred eighty-six stained glass windows here when the cathedral was completed in the thirteenth century. Do you think it is by chance that the one nearest the entrance of the labyrinth tells the story of Mary Magdalene? Do you think also that it is a coincidence that this window has twenty-two panels? Come." He gestured, and the five of them followed to get closer to the magnificent Magdalene window. Destino explained that stained glass windows were read like books, but in a very specific manner. The reader begins at the bottom left corner and reads the images from left to right, working upwards one line at a time. The bottom row of the window had three images, all of them showing men carrying jugs and pouring water.

"Water bearers? Is that a reference to Aquarius?" This was Tammy.

Destino shrugged. "Yes. And no. Everything in Chartres has layered meanings. Everything. And often there are several explanations, all of which relate to each other. You cannot grasp all the lessons here at once. This is the home of layered learning, and the more you come to see the art that is here, the more veils will be uncovered. Every inch of this monument was considered by the men and women who created it. And yes, I said women. For this place . . . it is a monument to love, a temple. Can you not feel it? And to give it this feeling, there had to be balance in the design and the building. But to your question . . . yes. Aquarius. Because it heralds that we enter the Aquarian age, perhaps? But think deeper."

Peter offered up the Church explanation, which he had read last night while poring over the literature from the cathedral. "It says that the water carriers who helped to build the church, by supplying the workers with the water they needed from local wells, were the patrons who paid for this window and that is why they are depicted at the beginning of the story."

Destino nodded. "Yes, yes. But there is a flaw in that version, no? You see, the men and women who worked as water carriers, they were the poorest of the people. They had no skills or artistry, and were unable to work on those details of this holy temple. All they could do was to carry the water. Now I do not diminish their contribution, for every person who used his hands and hearts in the building of this place is equally blessed. No man's job was more exalted than another. The poor, illiterate girl or boy who carried water was equal in the eyes of God to the educated man who was the architect. This is not the point. The point is that the water carriers did not have the wealth to donate such an elaborate window. That explanation is preposterous. And as you are a special group of seekers, I will expect you to interpret this. Go on. I'll wait."

And he stood patiently, staring up at the window, determined not to say another word until one of his students proved worthy of his time with a correct answer. They discussed it aloud, together.

"The man in the middle is actually immersed in water," Bérenger observed. "The underground stream, secret knowledge."

Destino nodded. "Yes. More."

"The *wouivre*," Roland offered. "Water sometimes represents the telluric current which runs through the earth, and it is strongest here in Chartres as it runs from here all the way to the Languedoc."

"Yes, yes," Destino encouraged him. "We will see more of this current very soon, as midday approaches."

"Water carriers. They could be symbolic of . . . cup bearers?" This was Tammy.

"And another way to interpret *cup* in our esoteric world"—Maureen this time—"is *Grail*."

Destino beamed at her. "We in the Order have always called it the Grail window. Now, see here. It is commonly believed that Madonna Magdalene is washing Jesus' feet with her tears, that she represents the unnamed sinner from the gospel of Luke. But this is a true blasphemy, to call our Lady a sinner. Instead, she is anointing the feet of her beloved with oil, and the symbolism of her unbound hair around him shows that they are preparing for the bridal chamber, which occurs in the gospel of John. For anointing the feet is the beginning of the *hierosgamos*, the preparation of the bridegroom by the bride. It is the first step in the sacred marriage, which is why it is the first window in the Magdalene's story."

Maureen and the others were certainly aware that Mary Magdalene was not the unnamed sinner in Luke's gospel, and that the Church had combined these stories in the sixth century to create a vision of her as a repentant prostitute. But outside of Matilda's autobiography, they had never heard this specific accounting of the anointing with spikenard as a ritual for the bridal chamber.

"The next windows show Magdalene's presence and participation in resurrection. For it is love that is the key to life over death, and here we are reminded that love comes in many guises, and all of them are strong enough to conquer death. See here first, she is present at the resurrection of her brother, Lazarus. Above that, she is the first to see the risen Lord, and here he is telling her that it is her mission to inform the others of the Good News, and that it is now her responsibility to spread the word of the Way of Love. If you look closely, you will see that she carries a scroll, a symbol of her authority given from him, as she approaches the others to tell them that she has the Book of Love and will teach from it. And here above, you see her on the boat, heading for France. This central diamond depicts the blessed Saint Maximin establishing the first church in Provence. But look to this final window, for it is most important. This represents the earthly death of Madonna Magdalene. You will see at her feet there are three mourners—one older man, a woman, and a younger man. Her children. Standing over her is Maximinus, her great companion who loved her beyond all, and he reads from a book that rests upon a golden stand. I should not have to tell you which book this refers to. It is visible in the connecting panel, where our Lady is mourned and buried. Here at her feet are representations of the sacred lovers, Veronica and Praetorus. The Roman Praetorus is depicted in priestly dress to show you that he has converted to Christianity. Now, do you see this other man here, he who carries the cross? You will not guess who he is, so I shall tell you. That is the formerly wretched Roman centurion called Longinus."

Peter jumped at this. "Longinus Gaius? The centurion who stabbed Jesus with his spear?"

"The same accursed Longinus. As you must know from your recent studies, he became a devoted Christian at the merciful hands of Madonna Magdalene, and he served her until her death. Longinus is the perfect example of how the most desperate of lost souls can be redeemed through love that does not judge. He earned his place of honor in the telling of this story."

Destino pointed to the final panel at the top of the window, which showed Jesus in heaven, awaiting the delivery of Mary Magdalene's pristine soul. "Here she is, her spirit painted in white to show her holiness, carried aloft by angels to be reunited with her only beloved."

Maureen was crying again. The window was beautiful to her beyond words, depicting as it did the version of Mary Magdalene's story as she knew it to be true, knew it from the Arques material and from everything she felt in her own heart and spirit. Destino put his hand on the back of her head in a fond, paternal gesture. "Now, my child, you see how we pay our homage to the ladies of the labyrinth before we begin our walk. I believe we are ready. You will go in first, and the rest of us will follow. Go. Your Creator awaits you. *Solvitur ambulando.*"

Destino had explained that there was no right or wrong way to walk the labyrinth, there was just your own way. But there was an etiquette, and that was to allow the person ahead of you ample time to get into the maze before following him or her. If you passed someone on a circuit coming in or out, you stepped aside silently and allowed the other to pass. When there were multiple people walking at once, the labyrinth became a type of dance with a communal spirit. Each person had his or her own journey, and yet each journey intersected with others along the way. The labyrinth was filled with metaphors for life's pathways.

Maureen approached the labyrinth, awestruck by the artistic beauty and geometric perfection of the structure. Destino had encouraged her to remove her shoes, advising that the sensation of her feet against the stone was an important part of the ritual, and that she would be wise to observe it. All five of them removed their shoes and left them along the edge of the labyrinth. Maureen entered first, staring down as she walked, observing the elegant twists and turns along the path. She looked up periodically, marveling at the way that light from certain stained glass windows fell upon the labyrinth. She was certain that none of it was accidental. As several wise men had already pointed out, every inch of Chartres Cathedral had been carefully considered.

The light continued to swirl around her, and the specific, magical indigo colors that shone from the enormous western rose danced across the floor, causing Maureen to feel dizzy as she took another turn in the circuit. Her vision blurred as she caught a glimpse of the pile of empty shoes that littered the edge of the labyrinth.

Empty shoes.

Maureen was suddenly overwhelmed by the symbolism as she contemplated the women in this great story that was unfolding through history. Mary Magdalene, Matilda. Both women were left behind for many years following the deaths of their beloved partners. They were left to continue the work, to carry on and ensure that the message would continue. They both faced the challenge of filling those empty shoes. And yet both had been forgotten by history for their true contributions, which were of inestimable value to humankind. Which was the greater tragedy? Maureen knew what each of these women, noble and loyal and full of faith and love, would say. They would say that facing the empty shoes was far harder than any other challenge that their eventful lives had presented to them.

She reached down to touch the copper amulet around her neck with the inscription from the gospel of Luke, "Mary hath chosen the better part, and it shall not be taken from her." Perhaps this was the true meaning of "the better part." It was a choice to carry on against all odds, to ensure that the sacred teachings endured, to be the living embodiment of the Way.

As she had this thought, Bérenger Sinclair entered the labyrinth, passing her at a turn in one of the circuits. He looked at her in that moment with so much love that Maureen stopped walking for a moment. Here was one of the lessons for her in the labyrinth, and this was the reminder to enjoy the great love that had been given to her while she was able to do so. Here, now, and without fear.

Maureen approached the center of the labyrinth and silently said the Pater Noster within the six petals, just as Matilda had taught her through the telling of her story. As she completed the prayer, Bérenger entered the center of the six-petaled rose, where she awaited him. Silently, he took both her hands and they stood, facing each other, in the center of the labyrinth where the dazzling first light of summer filtered through ancient glass, to cast bands of blue into the ancient temple of love.

✦

Just before midday, the little group of pilgrims made their way to window 10 to await the arrival of the beam of light that would illuminate the brass spike in the tilted stone. It came, as it always had, right on time. The beam of sun shone through the perfectly round hole and rested on the brass, long enough for it to glitter in the light.

"The *wouivre*." Destino smiled, and the scarred side of his face puckered with the explanation. "Its heart is in the earth, beneath us here in the place within the crypt that covered the original mound. This place"—he pointed at the brass spike—"is the precise wellspring of the current. It is nothing less than . . . the heartbeat of the planet Earth."

Destino left them with that piece of extraordinary information and the cathedral. Before leaving, he invited them to spend the following day with him in the French headquarters of the Order of the Holy Sepulcher, located on the outskirts of Chartres proper. He explained that it was a sprawling property along the river Eure with a magnificent view of the cathedral from the lower lands. All of them were very much looking forward to seeing this man in his natural habitat and finding out more about him. He was enigmatic, he was mesmerizing, and he was clearly a brilliant source of information. Then there was that little matter of the scar on his face. Could it be possible that as late as the twentieth century, the leaders of the Order were still taking that terrible scar upon themselves? Clearly, this was the case. Maureen wondered at what stage a successor was chosen for the Master, and when the scar was inflicted. Would it be an appropriate question to ask? She wasn't sure, but she was terribly curious about these old ways that were still handed down in the most ancient of secret societies.

CHAPTER TWENTY

Chartres
present day

They were discussing Destino as the group of five walked back to the hotel to rest for a while before dinner. Peter's cell phone rang, and Maureen could see by his face that the news he was receiving had him agitated. When he snapped the cover shut, she asked him, "What happened?"

He stopped walking for a moment and the others stopped with him. "I don't know what to say. That was Tómas DeCaro. He said that the Arques committee has announced that they are going to hold a press conference tomorrow morning regarding the Magdalene material. We think they're going to authenticate it."

"But that's fantastic!" This was Tammy.

Peter shook his head. "Is it? I'm afraid to be optimistic. I have worked with these men for two years, and I am finding this hard to believe, as is Tómas. Barberini is here in France, and they have asked me to come to Paris tonight for an emergency meeting. That's all I know, other than I have a train to catch in an hour."

❈

Maureen pleaded a headache and went back to her room alone after seeing Peter head to the train station. Bérenger was tired too, and he also knew that he needed to give her time and space to process all that had happened today. He was learning to understand her moods and rhythms and had often seen that she required time to write and to think; those were her processes, and he gave them to her.

Realizing, however, that she was too tired to do either, Maureen decided to take a nap before dinner. She closed her eyes and was asleep almost instantly. She slept hard for the remainder of the afternoon. She was jolted awake by the ringing of the phone in her room two hours later.

"Maureen, is that you?"

The voice on the other end was Irish. And female. Maureen rubbed the sleep from her eyes as she tried to gather her wits. "Uh-huh," she said, semicoherent.

"I'm so sorry to bother you, love," the brogue continued. "It's Maggie Cusack."

Peter's housekeeper. Maureen was instantly awake. "What's wrong, Maggie?"

"Nothing's wrong, nothing at all. It's just that Father Healy rang and he said there is an urgent matter that he needs you to attend to. He wouldn't tell me much, mind you; he can be very secretive in his way. Not that I ask questions; sure, it's none of my business."

Get on with it, Maggie, Maureen was dying to say, but she remained politely quiet.

"Well, here are the directions that he gave exactly. He said you are to go to the door to the crypt at the southern side of the cathedral at eight o'clock precisely and that you are to tell no one—not even Lord Sinclair—that you are going there. He said secrecy is of the utmost importance, and that you will understand it when you get there. But he was most insistent that I convey to you the importance of this. Someone will meet you there, and will tell you more. In the meantime, because the good father is on his way to meetings in Paris, it will be very hard to reach him over the next hours. He did tell me that the authentication is happening and it has to do with that, and that you would understand it all."

Maureen considered this. It was strange, as Peter was very rarely so clandestine, but this phone call today about the Magdalene material had shaken him visibly. Something of great importance was happening, and if he needed Maureen at the door of the crypt for some reason, she would be there. And he said it was related to the authentication, which made her pulse race with the possibility. She was a little uncertain about lying to Bérenger—because she was due at dinner at 8:30 and would have to make up some kind of excuse to get out of it—but there was nothing else she could do. Eventually she would tell him the truth and apologize for the deception. He came from the world of secret societies; he of all people knew that sometimes these secrets were necessary.

Maggie was pleading on the other end. "Please, Maureen. Don't let him down on this, or I'm afraid he will have my job. This is terribly important to him."

"Okay, Maggie, thanks." Maureen hung up, wondering what on earth was going on.

Maureen was a terrible liar. She realized that she couldn't effectively fabricate with Bérenger, so she called Tammy and Roland's room as an alternate strategy. Pleading the fear of an oncoming migraine, she asked Tammy to inform Bérenger that she was going to bed and would see them all in the morning at breakfast. Tammy didn't sound completely convinced, but she accepted the explanation and rushed off the phone. Maureen had the impression that Tammy and Roland were . . . occupied. All the better. Tammy asked far fewer questions than usual.

The hotel was large enough that Maureen could slip out unnoticed for her eight o'clock rendezvous. As she climbed the hill toward the cathedral, she hit the speed dial, number two, to see if Peter was available yet in Paris. The call immediately hit his voice mail, indicating that his phone was either turned off or he was out of range. She left a message.

"Hi, it's me. I talked to Maggie and I am on my way to the crypt. Not sure who is meeting me there, but dying to find out what is happening in the authentication process. Call me when you can."

She walked around the Royal Portal to the right, along the south side of the cathedral, where the heavy and ancient entrance door to the crypt was located. It was shut, but as Maureen approached it to knock, she heard the hinges creak as it opened slowly. She didn't see anyone at first; she saw only some candles flickering in the darkness. They threw shadowed light on the stone steps that led down into the crypt.

Maureen nearly jumped out of her skin as an unseen figure reached out to touch her. She turned and saw that the man was dressed head to toe in a dark robe and was virtually invisible in the lightless room. He gestured to the stairs, and she saw as he drew closer to the candlelight that his head was completely covered in a hood, with stitching over the eye sockets. The color was a deep, midnight blue. Maureen realized in a flash, too late, that this was one of the same ominous men she had seen in her dream in Orval. The hooded men to whom her stolen book had been delivered.

The slamming of the exterior door, and the sound of a heavy bolt thrown behind her, punctuated Maureen's complete understanding of this predicament. She was trapped in the crypt of Chartres Cathedral. And that could only mean one thing: her abductor was a high-ranking member of the Church.

"Enter, Signorina Paschal." It was a command rather than an invitation, made by an accented voice, raspy with age, coming from down the hallway. Maureen did not see the owner of the voice in the darkness as the hooded figure behind her urged her forward. They had walked another fifteen to twenty feet when the hooded escort grabbed her elbow and stopped abruptly. He snapped his fingers, and another man, identically dressed in his ominous robe and faceless hood, came around a corner carrying a thick beeswax candle in an iron holder. He leaned forward to illuminate the wide semicircular cistern that appeared to be built into the wall.

The man behind Maureen grabbed her by the hair, yanking her head over the well, as the other figure moved the candle down below the rim of the stone surface. Maureen panicked, thinking he was going to throw her in, and grabbed the edge of the well as she let out a scream. Her assailant let go of her hair to cover her mouth and stifle the sound but didn't attempt to harm her further.

"The fate of Saint Modesta. It will be yours if you do not cooperate in full." The man who covered her mouth spoke, and she recognized his voice immediately. She would never forget it. It was the voice of the gunman who had robbed them at Orval. "You realize, of course, that no one would ever find your body, should it be necessary to duplicate Modesta's demise."

Maureen was led around a corner into a surprisingly large subterranean chapel. There were more candles in this space, and she was able to get a glimpse of the ancient decoration on the wall. Celtic in appearance, it was the oldest art in Chartres, and it added to the mystic intensity of this place. To Maureen's right was the statue of Notre Dame Sous Terre, Our Lady Under the Earth, but the present company had chosen not to illuminate it. Instead, the candles were reserved for the space at the altar where a plain wooden crate was waiting. Next to the crate sat another man, dressed in the strange hooded costume. He removed his hood as she approached, and Maureen's heart sank.

Father Girolamo de Pazzi gestured for Maureen to sit in the empty chair beside him.

Maureen said nothing and waited for the old man to speak. His hooded henchman stood closely behind Maureen, a constant reminder of her captivity—and of the fate of Modesta.

"Tell me, my dear. What did you come to Chartres to find?"

Maureen was mute. Her only defense at this moment was silence. They obviously wanted something from her, some piece of her knowledge or even of herself, and she was not going to give it freely.

"You do not wish to tell me? There is no need. You came to find the Book of Love because somebody told you it was here at Chartres Cathedral, no? Well, they did not lie to you. The Book of Love is here."

Maureen tried not to show her surprise, or her curiosity, as de Pazzi continued.

"And not the copy, either. This is not the Libro Rosso and its patch-work of heresy." He spat the last with contempt. "This is the authentic Book, the original. The document written in the hand of our Lord Jesus Christ. It is here because I brought it here. Come now, you cannot pretend that you would not give anything to see this Book. It is your destiny to do so."

Maureen remained still. Even if the original Book of Love was here, even if she could see it or touch it, she could not imagine that she would ever be allowed to live long enough to tell anyone about it.

But Girolamo de Pazzi was not a foolish man. He had been stalk-ing this prey for a long time and had studied her kind and character for all his adult life as a singular obsession. And after reading through her stolen notebook and observing her carefully in their last meeting, he knew what she would respond to: knowledge, information. The truth.

"You must know by now, Signorina Paschal, that I am not here to harm you. It doesn't mean that I won't if it becomes necessary, and as you have seen, these men are perfectly willing to do just that if you do not cooperate. But the truth is, I need you and it is to my benefit, and the benefit of my Church, to gain your cooperation. And so I would like to make a bargain with you. I will tell you a secret, a very great se-cret. And I will show you the greatest treasure in human history. But in return, you will do something for me."

"What do you want me to do?" she asked with greater calm than she felt. Internally, she was praying to Easa for his strength and protection. If the Book of Love was really here, perhaps his presence would some-how protect her.

"First I will give you a hint as to the secret. Lucia Santos."

Maureen paused, thinking fast and trying to figure out where this was going. She asked, "The real secret of Fátima. Is that what you're going to tell me?"

He nodded.

"Why?"

"Because"—Father Girolamo paused, and for a moment she saw something other than bitter determination behind the old man's eyes, something that looked almost like sadness—"I need your help."

Maureen remained mute as he continued. "You want to know the true secret of Fátima? Here it is. The Blessed Immaculate Virgin came to tell the children of Fátima that we, the Holy Mother Church, were holding the Book of Love and had been doing so since Ignatius Loyola brought it with him to Rome. Yes, that is correct. When Loyola left the monastery of Montserrat, he revealed its hiding place in exchange for the right to study it and the freedom to create a new order with its own set of rules. This was granted, and the book was brought to our Eternal City and has been in our possession ever since."

Maureen was taking it all in, committing it to memory on the off chance that the menacing men in the hoods really did let her live long enough to take this information out into the world.

"But you see, we had an unexpected complication. While the Book itself is intact, and it contains the words and diagrams as committed to the paper by our Lord, there is another layer of learning and teaching within this book. This is what we discussed once before. There are teachings within the Book that are only for those chosen to know them, those with eyes to see and ears to hear. But they cannot be accessed by most; even our Holy Fathers have not been able to break the seal that protects all that is contained within the Book of Love. Our Lord used something of his divinity to encode his holy teachings within these pages. No one has been able to reach them . . . except Lucia Santos. And even she could not do it all the time."

"And was that one of the mysteries of Fátima? Was Lucia told how to unlock the secrets within the Book?"

The old priest shook his head. "She did not need to be told. It is not something you can teach." He spat the next sentence as a grudging admission. "It is something that . . . you are."

The realization fell on Maureen, hard. "An Expected One."

"Yes. While I cannot understand why it is that our Lord would entrust his most holy teachings to females, it appears that he has done just that."

The power in de Pazzi's revelation struck Maureen hard. *The Book of Love could only be unlocked by a woman.* In that instant, Maureen understood why. Jesus encoded his teachings in such a way that *women could not be extricated from the process of teaching and leadership.* It was a brilliant and exciting concept.

The old man surprised her by reading her thoughts. "I know what you are thinking, but you are wrong. The Libro Rosso is a copy of the Book of Love, and it was made by Philip. A man."

Maureen shook her head. "No. It was *transcribed* by Philip. He wrote it down. But *she* translated it for him. The Libro Rosso itself says that Philip made the copy while visiting the pregnant Mary Magdalene in Alexandria, and that he created the copy under her instruction. She read it. He wrote it down."

De Pazzi waved off this theory with annoyance, moving directly to the issue at hand. "And now you will be a good and obedient child of your Lord, and you will unlock this book for me. And we will have no more pretending, as when you viewed the prophecies."

"Is this why you kept Lucia Santos in solitary confinement for almost eighty years?"

Father Girolamo wasn't the least bit bothered by the question. His reply was matter-of-fact. "Yes."

"And she wasn't able to give you everything you needed over eight decades?"

"She wasn't always successful. And she certainly wasn't always cooperative, which is why we had to isolate her so completely. Those born under your stars are . . . headstrong."

"Why do you think I can give you what you want, here and now? Why do you think I will, even if I can?"

"Because you're as curious as we are. And even if you die finding out what is in that Book, you won't resist the opportunity to see it. How can you? You were born for this day, and you know that to be true."

"And how do I know you won't try to lock me up as you did Lucia? Or worse?"

"You don't know that. But it is a risk I think you will take."

"My friends will figure this out quickly. They'll find me, no matter what you decide to do."

"Perhaps. But your work is controversial and you've made many enemies, haven't you? You've run afoul of any number of fundamentalist groups and various crackpots. You have recently reported being robbed and followed in Rome to the authorities there. The death threats you receive have been widely reported in the media. It would be easy to the point of effortless to convince the authorities that one of those came to fruition. Checkmate, signorina. You cannot beat us at a game we play better than anyone in the world, and have done for nearly two thousand years. We will do with you what we will, just as we have done with all the women who preceded you."

"But the truth . . ."

"Truth? What is truth?" He was suddenly impatient with her, as if he realized that he was embarking upon an argument with the enemy, and snapped to control the subject. "The truth is that it is possible for you to avoid the fate of Modesta. If the information you provide is of value, it will impact our decision regarding your fate. For example, if you were to determine that the Book of Love confirms our established and holy doctrine, and were willing to write such a thing, your circumstances could be entirely different."

Maureen was momentarily speechless. She found her voice after a moment of hesitation. "Are you . . . are you offering me a . . . deal?"

For all of his earlier bravado about their omnipotence, Girolamo de Pazzi had a painful admission to make. "The Church is at an impasse. For the first time, we are fighting a battle in which we may ultimately be outmatched, and that is the war of words. We cannot control the information that is flooding out into the world any longer. So we must find new ways to impact it. Young people are listening to you. Your work is in languages all over the world. If you used this growing platform to affirm our position rather than oppose it, it could beneficial to you, to your friends, and to your cousin. Think of the impact if you, the heretic, recanted because you have seen the light. Think of the impact if you were to come back to the one true religion. It would be a tremendous collaboration, and a positive force for everyone involved."

Maureen wanted to understand completely. "Are you asking me to write a book that says that traditional Church doctrine is the truth, and everything I have ever written and stood for in opposition to that is a lie? How can I do that?"

"You will have to recant. You will have to say that you created the Arques gospel as a forgery to make a fortune, and that you have repented. We will then come forward and offer you our forgiveness as you return to the embrace of Holy Mother Church and abandon your search for heresy."

Maureen was stunned into silence by the offer. She thought of the plaque in Bérenger Sinclair's library, the one with the quote from Joan of Arc, *"I would rather die than do something I know to be against God's will."* Thinking of Bérenger at that moment gave her strength.

She remained silent, causing de Pazzi to revert to his more tried tactic. "But should you choose otherwise . . . there is no telling what could happen. To any of you."

Maureen's mind was spinning with the possible outcomes of this situation. It was very hard to think under the heavy breathing of the men in the dark hoods, the ancient priest with his raspy voice and his outrageous proposition, and the somewhat ominous presence of the wooden crate on the adjacent altar. She gestured to the box.

"Is it in there? May I see it now?"

Girolamo de Pazzi, for all his arrogant intolerance and twisted thinking, still believed himself to be a holy man. He knelt before the crate and said a prayer under his breath, genuflecting, then rising. He reached into the crate, which had no lid, and removed from within another, smaller box. This was ancient and elegant, a bejeweled reliquary made specifically to contain the most sacred documents in Christendom, and beyond. The gilding of the hinges glittered in the candlelight, and Maureen let out a little squeal against her will as she saw the lid of the case. It was inlaid with jewels in the shape of a six-petaled rose, identical to the center of the Chartres labyrinth.

De Pazzi opened the jeweled casket and placed it before her, but she noticed that he did not reach in to touch the book itself. He seemed to be careful not to make physical contact with the actual item as he pushed the box in her direction across the altar. "Take it out," he ordered. "And . . . follow your instincts. Or your voices. Or whatever comes to you. Lucia heard the voice of Our Lady when she held the book, but you may respond to it differently. You are a very different creature than the others." He said this last as if looking at an insect—a particularly abhorrent and poisonous insect—under a microscope.

Maureen, as petite as she was, had to stand to see inside the box. She saw that the cover was plain, apparently a type of animal hide—perhaps the pergama skins she had read were used in ancient Greece. She touched the cover and felt nothing for a moment, but as she rested her palms flat on the skin, they began to tingle. The sensation ran slowly up her arms and moved through her entire body. She closed her eyes as this happened, and saw behind them the vision of Easa from her dream. She heard him then, as she had heard him before:

> You are my daughter in whom I am well pleased, but your work is not yet finished. Behold, the Book of Love. You must share it with the world and fulfill the promise that you made. Our truth has been in darkness for too long. And be not afraid, for I am with you always.

The fear drained from Maureen's body as she lifted the Book from its resting place in the jeweled casket. She could hear Easa's voice in her head, speaking rapidly now, in phrases from his own writings.

> Fear and faith cannot exist in the same place at the same time. Choose one.

Maureen chose faith.

She opened the book, determined to cherish this moment of holding something so sacred, in spite of the circumstances that surrounded her. Ignoring the old priest and his henchmen completely now, she ran her fingers over the faded pages in reverence. She could not read the ancient writing: some of it looked like Greek; some of it appeared to be Aramaic; some of it was definitely Hebrew. But it didn't matter. This was not a question of reading the words, for something else was happening as Maureen held the Book of Love. As in her dream, the pages began to grow brighter, letters shimmering with indigo light, blue and violet patterns on the heavy, linenlike paper. The light grew brighter as it emanated from the Book, filling the room now, seeming to swirl with special intensity around the statue of Our Lady Under the Earth. The light penetrated Maureen's body; she could feel its heat and radiance filling her. And as it did, she was absorbing the Book of Love. She did not need to read it or to see it in translation. She was becoming it, embodying the teachings in their entirety as the vibrant blue light ran through her.

Visions came in rapid succession: Solomon and Sheba, Jesus and Magdalene, his mother Mary and his grandmother Anne, his daughter Sarah-Tamar. She saw the little girl in Orval—*I am not who you think I am*—followed by the ethereal and ultimately feminine apparition of the Holy Spirit in Knock. And then came an understanding so clear that it brought her to her knees, clutching the Book to her heart. Jesus had written this Book of Love as a celebration of the women in his life, their wisdom and grace. This was his tribute and his monument to the lost feminine principle of spirituality that had brought him to this truth: that our father and mother in heaven are One in their union, that they love us, their children, and that as the time returns, we come back in all our forms as our Creator made us in their holy image, male and female, to experience love over and over again.

It was the Nazarene mission of Jesus and his followers to bring the balance back, to restore Asherah to her throne beside her beloved El, and to reunite humankind in an understanding of that love here on earth. Jesus died trying to make the world understand the power of love, while resurrecting the divine element of feminine spirituality in balance with the divine masculine.

The light grew brighter, the room spun faster, as Maureen clung to the Book, listening, feeling, understanding everything that Easa was conveying to her: Love, and only love, is real. Everything else is an illusion that keeps us from the purity of the experience that our parents in heaven created for us. And Jesus did not mean for us to create a new religion *about him*. He meant for us to reclaim the truth as it had been distorted over time. A truth that was simple and beautiful and about love in all its forms: romantic, parental, filial, neighborly. It wasn't so much a New Covenant as it was the *original* Covenant coming back to us in his hand, with him as the messenger: him, and his family of spirit. Us and our families of spirit.

The time returns.

She heard him whisper it, and now the phrase reverberated with new meaning. The time returns was the most sacred of the prophecies because it foretold the second coming. But the second coming was not the physical return of Jesus. It was the return of his message and his teachings through a global effort of love and service.

We are the very people that we have been waiting for, and we always have been. We are the second coming.

Maureen was lost in the visions as she came to another understanding: that she had seen this specific, beautiful, radiant blue light very recently—in the stained glass right here in Chartres Cathedral. She knew then without any doubt that the builders of this temple to love had seen this light themselves and reproduced it so that it would shine on each individual who entered, blessing them with a fraction of what she was experiencing now.

Her mind was spinning with all she had seen on the exterior of the cathedral. Solomon and Sheba, the tragic and lovely Modesta, the many Marys, Saint Anne, the countless, nameless women who were celebrated in bas-relief. The sculptures flashed through her consciousness in rapid succession. What did they all have in common?

Maureen saw now, in her mind's eye, the filtered light from the stained glass in the main cathedral as she had walked the labyrinth earlier that morning; it shimmered around her as she was lost in the vision. When she took this turn, she could see the window of Mary Magdalene with her true story told in elaborate and careful detail. All the while, the great western rose shone its sacred blue light into the center of the labyrinth. She walked faster now, in rhythm with the escalating beat of her heart, as other windows in the cathedral came to life: Saint Anne was aged and wise; the majestic Blue Madonna was strong and compassionate; lives of saints and martyrs danced around her as she continued in the circuits of the labyrinth. She was being drawn to the center by a force that was extraordinary and magnetic. Her pace quickened and her heart pounded as the blue light pulled her into the central temple, into the tabernacle, into the place where the voice of God can be heard for those with ears to hear.

Oh, sweet Easa. Is this what you've been trying to tell us all along? Could it have always been this simple?

She saw him now, standing in the center of the labyrinth with his kind, dark eyes. In his hands he held the tools of the master mason, the compass and the square. Easa held them out together so that they formed the elongated diamond shape that represented the sacred union of beloveds. Behind him now appeared his own beloved: Mary Magdalene, a vision of auburn hair and ethereal beauty, arriving at his side.

They looked at her in the vision, across time and space, and Easa said once more, as he gestured around him to indicate the entire, massive structure of the cathedral, *"Behold, the Book of Love. You must share it with the world and fulfill the promise that you made. Our truth has been in darkness for too long."*

The sob that broke through Maureen's body echoed through the ancient stone of Chartres. She raised her head and the kaleidoscope of stained glass prisms from her vision swirled past her through her tears. Finally, she understood.

It wasn't that the Book of Love was in Chartres Cathedral. It wasn't that the Libro Rosso was in Chartres Cathedral. The most holy teachings of Christianity, perhaps of all humanity, weren't hidden *in* Chartres Cathedral.

They *were* Chartres Cathedral.

The cathedral had often been called "a book made in stone" by the many writers through history who had celebrated its grandeur. How right they were.

Maureen saw clearly now the master architect in her vision, and this time he was a man with a terrible zigzagging scar across one side of his face. He was guiding the sculptural program that would encase the Book of Love in stone for all humanity to learn and celebrate for all time. The teachings of the Order lived on here, and the tradition of the Master lived with it.

The entire Libro Rosso had been built into the façade and the stained glass of Chartres Cathedral, an eternal book in stone that could never be destroyed by the Church, as the Church would never destroy itself. It was an utterly brilliant strategy. The labyrinth was installed at its center as the starting point of initiation for all pilgrims who would have eyes to see and ears to hear. Walking the labyrinth allowed the heart and spirit access to the codes that enshrined the Book of Love within this unparalleled temple.

Maureen was still on the ground, on her knees with the Book of Love clutched against her. She was reeling with the light and the visions but beginning to feel that she was coming back into her body once more. She had to get out of here, had to find a way to let the world know that the Book of Love was embedded in the stone and glass of this astonishing monument to the truth, that it was available to anyone who wanted to view it, experience it, feel it—and it always had been. The most valuable wisdom in human history had been hidden in plain sight for eight hundred years. And the Church knew it. By covering the labyrinth, they hoped to obscure the tool that was needed by the average person to crack the code and read the book.

She looked up and saw that the henchmen were still in place, although they stood back from her more than before. Because of their menacing hoods, it was impossible to determine where their eyes were, but they both appeared to be looking at the ground, not at her. As she climbed slowly to her feet, Maureen caught a glimpse of Father Girolamo de Pazzi. He was staring into space, past her, with a most haunted expression on his face. Maureen heard Easa one final time as she came into her full, waking consciousness. His melodic voice in her ear said simply, *"Love conquers all."*

She looked down at the priceless item in her hands, feeling its power recede back into the Book. The final page held a perfect drawing of Solomon's labyrinth, the eleven-circuit model that graced both Chartres and Lucca; it was the symbol of geometric perfection that allowed men and women to access God in their own temple space, wherever that might be in the world. The blue light faded here last, the remainder of its power absorbed back into the Book of Love.

Maureen glanced at the old man who had brought her here under such menacing circumstances. He looked at her now with rheumy eyes that were filled with tears. When he spoke, this time, his raspy voice was a whisper. "That did not happen with Lucia Santos."

Whether Father Girolamo de Pazzi had seen the same visions or had been granted visions of his own, Maureen would never know. But by the look on his face, it appeared that he had been changed by what had occurred in the crypt.

The sound of pounding, a loud thumping from above, startled everyone in the room. Through the ancient stone, a male voice shouting Maureen's name could be heard, muffled somewhat by the thickness of the walls. But not so much that Maureen could not tell whom the voice belonged to.

Bérenger Sinclair. He sounded like he was going to break down the door of the crypt.

The henchmen looked at Girolamo de Pazzi, who shook his head slowly. He said to Maureen simply, "Go."

She looked at the miraculous book in her hands for a final time. Putting it down was the hardest thing she had ever had to do in her life. She knew that holding it had changed her for eternity. In her own way, she had become the human embodiment of Chartres Cathedral during these moments, and of the Book itself. She had taken all of it into her body, mind, and spirit while here in this place.

Later, Destino would help her to understand just how perfectly the stars had aligned when she released the energy of the Book of Love. Where she stood in the crypt was directly over the *wouivre*, the pulse point of the planet. It was the summer solstice, the longest day of the year. She had started the day in the labyrinth, and done so with her family of spirit as well as her most beloved. She was in a singularly powerful place to unlock the secrets of the Book of Love and release them in the place where they most belonged: in Chartres Cathedral, the temple that was built specifically to express them.

Maureen Paschal kissed the cover of the book, the singular, perfect document that had been created by the hand of Jesus Christ, and returned it to its resting place in the jeweled casket. She turned her back on Father Girolamo and simply walked away. She paused as she passed the ancient well, certain that she heard whispering from its depth. An ethereal female voice floated up, and Maureen was almost certain she heard it say, "*Merci, merci beaucoup,*" before releasing a contented sigh. Maureen said a little prayer for the spirit of the tragic Modesta, hoping that she was now at rest, before climbing the stairs and opening the door to the man who had been chosen by God at the dawn of time to be the twin of her soul.

❁

Girolamo de Pazzi remained motionless as he watched Maureen retreat. He would never understand why it was that the Lord had chosen to reveal his light to such women, or why he remained outside this special love that females like Lucia Santos and Maureen Paschal were so easily able to access.

And now, he understood the meaning of the prophecy that had haunted him for so long. The time returns.

He reached into the deep pocket of his robe and pulled out the crystal reliquary that contained the lock of Saint Modesta's hair. Through all the centuries, its red-gold color had not faded. He gazed at it for a moment, then lowered his head and sobbed.

Chapter Twenty-one

Chartres
present day

Back in the safety of her hotel room, Maureen allowed herself to relax in Bérenger's embrace. He let her cry, long and hard, as he held her gently and stroked her hair. When she quieted, he sat back and looked at her carefully.

"What's wrong?" she asked him. "I'm a mess, aren't I?"

He laughed softly. "No, you're just the opposite. I didn't think I could ever find you more beautiful than I already do, but you're positively radiant."

She shared with him all that had transpired in the crypt, struggling to find words that could express the depth of what she had experienced. "I wish you could have seen it, Bérenger. I wish you could know what it is like to hold something so sacred."

"But I already do," he whispered, as he pulled her back into his arms, and blended his spirit with hers through the depth of his kiss.

Paris
present day

PETER LISTENED INTENTLY as Marcelo Barberini and Tómas DeCaro took him through the missing pieces of the larger puzzle. There were moments when he was stunned, and others when he could not believe that he had missed something so obvious. Pope Urban VIII was the mastermind behind the rebuilding of St. Peter's, and the primary patron of the genius of Gianlorenzo Bernini. He was the man who was determined to relocate the remains of Matilda of Tuscany to a place of ultimate power and authority in the middle of the Vatican, where she belonged, across from the masterpiece created by her descendant, Michelangelo Buonarotti.

The birth name of Pope Urban VIII was Maffeo Barberini. The Cardinal Barberini in Peter's presence was descended from the same exalted Italian family and was a grandnephew many generations over of that Tuscan pope who hailed from a powerful Florentine dynasty. He was the pope who lived and worked in the heretical regions of France as a papal nuncio, the pope who was educated by the early Jesuits, the pope who canonized both Ignatius Loyola and his right-hand man, Francis Xavier, for what they brought with them from Spain. He was the first pope to work within the presence of the Book of Love and all that it contained.

"Urban the Eighth was driven to redesign elements of St. Peter's Basilica in emulation of what occurred in Chartres Cathedral. So he brought Bernini in to create such sculpture, to preserve the legacy of our people within the very walls of the Vatican."

Cardinal Barberini went on to explain that the legend of the Libro Rosso had obsessed this pope throughout his career. The secret nature of the Book of Love, and his inability to unlock it, was a driving force behind his papacy and his life. Believing that Matilda of Tuscany held the key, he had her remains brought to Rome with the hope that they would serve as holy relics; he interred them intentionally in the center of St. Peter's for that reason, and because he believed that she was as rightfully a part of the Church structure as her beloved, Gregory VII, had been.

Peter was connecting the dots. "So there has long been a faction in the Vatican that knows the truth of the Book of Love? And protects it?"

"Protects it as best as we can." Barberini shook his head sadly. "It depends on the power and how it shifts. My own family endured years of exile following the death of Maffeo, Urban the Eighth, as his successor was a conservative who opposed the true teachings."

"And my family, of course, endured the same." This was Tómas De-Caro speaking. Peter smiled at him, aware as he was that this man was a descendant of the infamous Borgia family, a family with their own stories to tell about lies and truths.

DeCaro continued. "But we are at critical mass, as I think you are aware. Peter my boy, what will transpire tomorrow will force all of us to make critical decisions about our careers and our future. We convened here in Paris to create safe distance from Rome, in the event that we have to make a counterannouncement regarding the Arques matrial."

"Anything could happen tomorrow," Barberini explained. "And we need to be prepared to go public if there is a cover-up. Are you with us?"

Peter had never been more certain of anything in his life. "Yes," he replied, shaking each man's hand firmly in turn. "The Truth Against the World."

Chartres
present day

THE PHONE WOKE Maureen—and Bérenger beside her—very early the next morning. It had been an extraordinary night of revelations and confessions. Maureen had discovered that Peter, receiving her voice mail, had realized quickly that something suspicious was happening in Chartres. He had called Sinclair and sent him in search of Maureen at the crypt. Maureen and Bérenger had spent the rest of the night together, through her tears and explanations and apologies, through his forgiveness, and ending blissfully in an ecstatic union of passion and promises.

"Maureen, turn on the television." Peter's voice over the cell phone was highly agitated. "There is a press conference on live, from Rome. Regarding the Arques gospel. Prepare yourself."

"For what?" Her heart was in her throat.

Peter sighed heavily across the airwaves. "I'm not certain. None of us are. That's the problem. I'll call you back in a few minutes."

Maureen found the remote and handed it to Bérenger, unfamiliar as she was with French television. He quickly found the live broadcast on a BBC affiliate, in English. A reporter with an Oxbridge accent was giving the history of the Arques gospel and its "alleged" discovery in France by an American writer a few years ago. The writer, Maureen Paschal, had written a controversial best-selling book based on the discovery and her often outrageous, and decidedly amateur, interpretation of its contents.

Bérenger growled at the television but said nothing. Maureen was frozen as she watched the reporter continue to synopsize the path of the Arques material over the previous two years. It had been turned over to the Vatican and had been the subject of intense scrutiny by the finest theological minds in the world, working in combination with scientists to date and authenticate the material. Cameras zoomed in on linenlike fragments of paper with Greek inscription, causing Maureen to gasp and grab Bérenger's arm.

"Do you see what I see?"

He nodded, not taking his eyes off the screen. "What's going on, Maureen? What are they doing?"

"I don't know," she whispered back. "But here's what I do know. That document is not the gospel that we found in France."

Maureen wasn't an expert, but finding Mary Magdalene's lost gospel was not something that one forgot. The appearance of those scrolls—their perfection, their preservation—was etched into her memory in perfect detail. And what was appearing on the screen, the documents shown to the press at this media circus, was absolutely not what she had discovered.

The spokesperson for the Church approached the podium and began to speak, as Bérenger and Maureen watched in a combination of horror and shock. They were here today to authenticate this magnificent document, to verify that this gospel was, in fact, written by Mary Magdalene to the best of their ability to authenticate it. But most exciting of all, this document was in essence a beautiful retelling of the gospel of John. Mary Magdalene was indeed a blessed woman and a saint, just as the Church had always said. The proof was all right here, the proof that her word was entirely in accordance with the scriptural teachings of the New Testament as accepted by Catholics since the earliest days of the Church. It was a day to rejoice. It was a day to put to rest all the ridiculous speculations about Mary Magdalene that had become such a part of misguided popular culture over recent years. Mary Magdalene had spoken once and for all, and her words were definitive—and in keeping with Church doctrine in total.

Expert witnesses were then interviewed, and they meticulously pointed out numerous places on the papyrus that were identical to the material in John's gospel.

Maureen had stopped listening. This was beyond anything that she had anticipated. Yes, she knew that the idea that the Church would ever actually authenticate the true Magdalene material was unlikely, maybe even impossible. But she thought, at worst, that they would ignore it, bury it, or—the most likely outcome—call it a forgery. But this . . . to fabricate an entire gospel in order to lie about it at this level was beyond any expectation she could have ever had.

"You realize what this is about, don't you?" Bérenger found his voice, his utterly outraged voice. "This is about discrediting your work entirely by making you look like a complete liar."

Maureen nodded. "I know." She took a deep breath, and added, "But I also know that it's not about me, and it's not even about Mary. It's about the Book of Love. They know that I will write about it, that I will tell the world everything I know. And if they can destroy my credibility before I do that, then perhaps nobody will care about the truth."

Maureen forced herself to breathe. She would weather this storm as she had all the others. Hadn't Easa told her that faith and fear could not exist in the same place at the same time? In this situation, she would, as she always had, choose faith.

❁

Maureen and Bérenger walked with Destino along the picturesque river called the Eure, on the edge of the property that had belonged to the Order for eight hundred years. Destino lectured them gently.

"You should not be upset about this new development. The opposite is true. You should embrace it as God's will. It is good that the Church does not authenticate the Arques Gospel, just as it is good that they will repudiate the existence of the Book of Love."

Maureen was shocked by this stance, and more than a little confused. "What am I missing here? How can this possibly be a good thing?"

"Faith," Destino said simply. "You see, if the Church authenticates the Arques Gospel, or the Book of Love, nobody has to think about it. They don't have to let it into their hearts and their spirits and decide for themselves if it feels like the truth or not. They don't have to push themselves to operate from a place of absolute faith. There is no risk, and therefore no spiritual gain. All that is taken away from them, which is a tremendous disservice. We want people to think and feel for themselves, not to be led like sheep into what they believe. Be grateful for this day; God has given it to you for good reason. And he has given it to the people of the world for good reason, that their faith will be tested. And those who recognize the truth in spite of all the opposition will be greatly rewarded in their hearts, minds, and spirits."

Maureen nodded her acceptance of his wisdom. She knew he was right, but it might be a while before she could accept this most recent encounter with the Church as a positive force in her life. Destino looked at her knowingly and shook his finger at her. "Thy will be done, Madonna Maureen. You need some practice in the second petal of the labyrinth. It is that will," he said, pointing heavenward, "and not ours at work here. Surrender to it, and you will find the peace that eludes you."

They walked in silence for a moment before Destino began to speak again. He filled in the history for them, of how Conn and the Master had come here to Chartres with the Libro Rosso, had joined forces with the existing Cathedral school, and had been the masterminds behind the extensive design of the cathedral, passing on their passion and knowledge to the succeeding generations, who were responsible for the magnificent monument that existed today. He pointed toward the north, where the two enormous spires rose to the sky.

"Do you know why the spires are mismatched? Do you think that such a thing was an accident or caused by lack of intention? Of course you do not think this, as you are initiated. You know that every aspect of this temple is in harmony with the true teachings. So here I will tell you just one of the thousands of secrets about Chartres Cathedral. The spire on the left is known as the Spire of the Sun, or the Spire of El. It represents God in his male creator aspect, as that spire is three hundred sixty-five feet long. Thus each foot correlates to a day of the solar year. The spire to the right is known as the Spire of the Moon, or the Spire of Asherah. It represents God in her female creator aspect, and as such it is twenty-eight feet shorter than the other, twenty-eight representing the days in the lunar month. When you enter the Western Portal at Chartres, you walk between the complementary principles of our father and mother, on earth as it is in heaven."

He went on to explain that Chartres endured yet another catastrophic fire in 1194, one so terrible that the lead from the structure melted and destroyed the stone walls, causing them to split. Yet despite the devastation, the entire western façade, with its two divine towers, was spared, as was one other element of the cathedral: the stained glass window of the Blue Madonna. The people of Chartres, realizing that this was a sign from the heavens, dedicated themselves to the reconstruction of this monument to the divine in its purest and most balanced form, and worked from the Libro Rosso to create it as it stood today, telling each of the stories in stained glass and sculpture.

"The Blue Madonna, you know who she is, no?" Destino asked them.

"Notre Dame," Bérenger replied.

"Yes, but which one?"

"It doesn't matter," Maureen said. "They're all one, aren't they? Whether it's the original Notre Dame, who is Asherah—the Holy Spirit—or the Mother Mary, or Mary Magdalene or Sarah-Tamar or any of their saintly descendants, they all represent the divine female essence."

"Yes, yes, you are correct. But I have a little surprise for you as this is a trick question. Come inside and I will show you something."

They followed Destino into a large bungalow-style building that they had not entered upon arrival. It was an ancient structure, part of an old monastery that once stood on these grounds. The interior was stunning, as the walls were covered from floor to ceiling with what appeared to be medieval tapestries, tapestries that illustrated the hunt for the unicorn.

"Are these copies of the famous tapestries?"

Destino laughed. "No. The famous tapestries are copies of these. There were two sets made, one for the Order and the other for Anne of Brittany. She is an important woman in our history, but one we will speak of later. We have many biographies to write, Maureen. I shall keep your pen busy for the rest of your long life, if you will allow yourself to become the new scribe of the Order's history."

Maureen smiled at him warmly. "I look forward to it. It will be an honor."

Maureen walked toward the first tapestry to get a closer look. It was one of the most magnificent pieces of art she had ever seen. The detail was exquisite. How it was possible to achieve such texture and color through the weaving of threads was beyond her capacity to comprehend.

"You know them, of course. And you know the allegory?"

Bérenger answered, "The unicorn represents Jesus?"

"The unicorn represents the true teachings of Jesus. It is a rare and beautiful creature that represents the Book of Love and the Way of Love that stems from it. Or that should have, had it been allowed to flourish. But no, it was hunted down and destroyed, as is depicted in the tapestries."

"Oh!" Maureen was listening, but her attention had been caught by the proliferation of symbols on the tapestries. In no fewer than five places on the first tapestry alone, the strange combination of the letter *A* and the backwards letter *E* was found, in all cases tied together by a rope with tassels. "This is on all the cards that you sent! What does it mean?"

Destino approached the first tapestry with his aged, hobbled walk and began to trace the initials with his finger. "See the rope? It is called a *cordeliere*, and it was used in ancient times to bind the bride and bridegroom in the handfasting nuptial ceremonies that preceded divine union. Now, the knot that you see here is a bridal knot, also known as an Isis knot. And the letters . . . Well, the *A* is for Asherah and the *E* is for El."

Maureen was thrilled by the explanation. It was so elegant, so beautiful. But she had one question. "Why is the *E* backwards?"

"Because each beloved is the reflection of the other. They are mirror images, which is why small mirrors were given as gifts in the wedding ceremonies of our people. So in the case of the monogram, it is a celebration of the divine and sacred union of Asherah and El, and a reminder that we will always see our reflection in the eyes of our true beloved.

"A very wise man once said that 'art will save the world,' and the members of our Order have believed and practiced that since the days of Nicodemus and the *Volto Santo*. But it is not just the symbolism that matters," Destino continued. "It is the intention of the artist. For this is the great secret of art. True art is imbued with the spirit of the artist; this is what creates a masterpiece—love for the subject and an intense desire to convey that love. An initiate can observe a piece of art and take the meaning of that piece directly into his heart and spirit. It is not about seeing the art, it is about feeling it. This is why there are some authentic pieces that the Church claims are copies. Because they do not want people like you to spend too much time in their presence. Believe me when I tell you that the *Volto Santo* is a living, breathing piece of art. It contains the passion of Nicodemus, his memory of the crucifixion. But most of all, it contains his memory of the true teachings of Jesus."

"That's why it spoke to Matilda," Maureen observed.

"Yes, of course. And she was a child and pure, so she heard the voice of the artist very clearly, just as the children in Fátima heard Our Lady. But if the Church tells us that it is not really the *Volto Santo*, that the masterpiece of the Holy Face created by Nicodemus was somehow lost with no explanation and that this is a copy, perhaps no one will try too hard to hear what it is actually saying. And yet they keep it locked up at the Cathedral in San Martino in an iron cage that makes it quite difficult to view. The same is true of the painting created by Saint Luke that is now at the top of the Holy Stairs in Rome. It is kept behind many inches of thick glass and bars so that you can never be in the presence of it completely. And for extra protection, they say it is a forgery, so you will not be too inclined to look at it closely."

Both Bérenger and Maureen were speechless. The idea of art containing the truth in so many layers, even beyond the basics of symbolism, was thrilling. "You must remember," Destino continued, "that this idea of art saving the world reached its peak during the Renaissance, and that, my dear, is what we must approach next. When you are ready, I will ask you to meet me in Florence and I will tell you a tale of the most beautiful men and women who ... who have ever lived." Destino's voice caught in his throat for a moment. He allowed the pause in honor of these great people of the past. "They embodied the understanding of *the time returns,* and they used it to create a rebirth of human understanding. I promise you that once you know the truth about Lorenzo de Medici, his friends, Sandro Botticelli and Michelangelo Buonarroti, and the marvelous women who inspired them all, you will never look at art the same way again. Nor should you."

Destino ambled with them through the town and up the hill to his be-loved cathedral. Against his body he clutched a battered messenger bag, which he patted periodically as he walked. He wanted to show them something, a specific detail on the exterior and another on the interior, before the day was over. It was the twenty-second day of June, and he reminded them that extraordinary things were known to happen on the twenty-second day of a month. He winked at Maureen when he said this, and she smiled back, thinking all the while that for such an old and weathered face, and one with a fearsome scar, there was some-thing about Destino that was incredibly beautiful.

The man was holy. Of that, she had no doubt.

They followed Destino at his slow, hobbled pace, content to let him lead while he filled them in on the history of this marvelous town that covered the pulse point of the earth, a town that gave birth to the most important and spectacular shrine in the Christian world. They came around the western entrance and passed the spires to walk toward the lovely sculpture of Saint Modesta.

"You know her story?" Destino asked.

"Modesta? She was martyred by her Roman father," Bérenger replied.

"Not literally." Destino shook his head. "Everything about Modesta's story is symbolic. Modesta was a daughter of the prophecy, an Expected One, at a time when the Book of Love resided here in La Beauce. All threats to the power of the growing Church had to be eliminated in the wake of Constantine and his councils. And Modesta—indeed all women of the prophecy—represented a great threat. What could her 'Roman father' be a symbol of?"

Maureen got it immediately. "A patriarch in Rome. The pope or the Church. So Modesta was executed as an example to any woman who would challenge the newly established Church doctrines? A Christian killed by her own 'father'?"

"Partially, but her true crime was this." Destino gently ushered Maureen and Bérenger around the pillar and pointed up at another, parallel sculpture of a man. "Potentian. Her husband. They were executed together because they represented the couples model of preaching that came from Jesus and Madonna Magdalena. Beloveds teaching from the Book of Love was more dangerous than anything and it always will be."

In response, Maureen grabbed Bérenger's hand, and he squeezed hers. They paid their respects to Modesta as they passed, and Destino stopped, pointing to one of the pillars. "Look closely. This is deteriorated but important. Most miss it, even those who would be able to recognize it for what it means."

The pillar showed a cart with wheels, and atop the cart was a casket of sorts.

"An ark," Bérenger said.

"The Ark of the New Covenant," Maureen added. "Matilda's ark?"

Destino nodded, the smile pulling at the weathered scar. "Yes, Matilda's ark indeed. And this lettering here, it provides the instruction for the artisans and architects at the onset of the rebuilding of this, the Door of the Initiates. It says, *Hic Amititur, Archa Cederis.* It is flawed Latin by modern standards, but the translation is roughly '*Here things take their course. You are to work through the Ark.*' And this is what they did. They utilized the Libro Rosso, the New Covenant, and translated the entire book into the stone and the glass that have stood here in testament to love and the truth for eight hundred years."

The wonders would never cease, of this Maureen was certain. She saw the answering wonder in Bérenger's eyes too, as they followed Destino through the door and into the church. He paused and pointed first to the western rose window high in the church, then down at the floor, where the labyrinth was once again littered with chairs in the age-old act of vandalism. "Here is something you will not believe, even though you are here and looking at it. The diameter of the rose window and the diameter of the labyrinth are exactly the same."

He was right. Standing on the ground and looking up many stories to the rose window, it was impossible to understand that it was forty-two feet across. It was another amazing feat of architecture. Destino wasn't finished boasting about the astonishing accomplishments of the architects at Chartres. "It is geometrically perfect. If the rose window were on hinges, it would fall down right here and cover the labyrinth perfectly. Can you imagine such precision?"

He did not wait to answer before moving them along. The old man was positively giddy as he led them across the transept and to the left, to stand before the majesty of the Blue Madonna, Our Lady of the Beautiful Window. He was beaming at them as he leaned in, whispering.

"This . . . this is only for those with ears to hear. And for me, it is most exciting as I have had so few occasions in which to share this secret. You were both correct when you identified this window as Notre Dame, and all that this title carries with it. But here is what you do not know. There was a human model for this window. The most appropriate model in the history of our Order."

Destino reached into the messenger bag and very carefully removed a piece of aged, painted parchment. As he revealed it to Maureen and Bérenger, they both grasped his meaning immediately. The parchment was a portrait of a medieval woman in a gorgeous gown of azure silk, a white wimple and veil, and the crown of the royal lineage of Charlemagne on her head, the crown inset with fleurs-de-lis and five specific jewels. Seated on her lap was a little boy with dark hair. Destino pointed to the fortress depicted above the madonna and child in the window and said, "Canossa."

For Maureen, this would become the most beautiful and poetic aspect of the extraordinary temple that she found herself in. The Madonna of the Beautiful Window, known as the most famous and most glorious stained glass in the world, represented the female aspect of God—but wore the face of Matilda of Canossa, Countess of Tuscany.

Destino turned to Maureen, and she noticed then that there were tears in his ancient eyes as he said in a whisper, "You are . . . so much like her."

Maureen's tears echoed his, and she whispered in return, "Thank you, Master."

"And like her," the old man said, eyes gazing into a very distant past, "you are a credit to God."

CHAPTER TWENTY-TWO

*I*t was a dream that Maureen had had before, once in her sleep and once in a waking vision in the Cathedral of Notre Dame de Paris. It had caused Sinclair and the others to be sure that she was, in fact, The Expected One of her time, and it had led ultimately to the discovery of Mary Magdalene's gospel.

But tonight, the dream had a twist that Maureen could not possibly have expected. Tonight she was given the glimpse of a truth that, even after all she had endured in the last two years, she was completely unprepared for.

✸

It was starting to rain now, and Maureen was out of the crowd, but she could see her lady, Mary Magdalene, just ahead of her in her red veil. Lightning ripped through the unnaturally dark sky as she stumbled up the hill with Maureen behind her. It was a strange sensation of both participating and observing. Maureen could not tell if she was experiencing her own feelings or Magdalene's feelings, as they were all blending together in the experience.

She was oblivious to the cuts and scrapes—hers, Magdalene's, it no long mattered. She had only one goal, and that was to reach him.

The sound of a hammer striking a nail—metal pounding metal— rang with a sickening finality through the air. As she—or they—reached the foot of the cross, the rain escalated into a downpour. She looked up at him, and drops of his blood splashed down on her distraught face, blending with the relentless rain.

Maureen looked around, removed from Magdalene now and once again an observer. She could see her lady at the foot of the cross, supporting the figure of the mother of the Lord, who appeared to be nearly unconscious with her grief. There were other women wearing the partial red veils around them, the other Marys, huddled together, supporting each other. One younger woman in a white veil in the midst of them caught Maureen's attention. This, she knew, was Veronica. There was a Roman centurion standing next to the women, but he appeared to be protecting them rather than terrorizing them. There was something kind in his face, something in his remarkable, light aqua eyes that appeared to be as tormented as the suffering family. Once, this man may have been a puzzling presence to her, but she knew him well from his deeds in the Arques gospel. He was Praetorus, who would one day share in the sacrament of the sacred union of beloveds with the lovely Veronica. Together in the future, they would spread the teachings of the Way.

Another Roman stood nearer the cross with his back to the mourning family. Maureen could not see his face at first, as he snapped orders at the other soldiers in the retinue near the cross. She could not hear his words, but there was a cold arrogance to his voice that was unmistakably dangerous. And she knew what came next, which made it that much worse. For this man could only be the accursed centurion Longinus Gaius. He was about to seal his own wretched fate to wander the earth in search of death and redemption.

A scream shattered the scene, a wail of absolute human despair that had come from the lips of Mary Magdalene. As Maureen looked up at her Easa on the cross, she saw immediately what had happened. The dark centurion, Longinus Gaius, had shoved his lance into her Lord's side, as she knew he would, until blood and water flowed from the wound.

The sounds of Magdalene's grief blended with the harsh laughther of the evil Roman, as he turned and looked directly at Maureen. Maureen had just enough time to see the livid scar that zigzagged across the left side of his face as he shook his weapon in defiance. The weapon known to history as the Spear of Destiny.

In Italian, the spear was called il giavellotto di destino.

Destiny and destination *came from the same root, and that root was* Destino.

She had just enough time to realize that, in the twenty-first century, she had recently come to know this wretched face rather well.

❁

Destino awoke with a start. He gasped desperately for air as he struggled to sit up in his bed. He was not shaken by the nightmare, but rather because tonight there was no nightmare. For the first time in his nearly eternal memory, the man who now called himself by the word that meant both *destiny* and *destination* had spent one night in peaceful slumber.

Was it possible? Could it be . . . over?

He did the only thing he could think of to do. He fell to his knees and began to recite the Pater Noster in Greek, the way he had first learned it. The way that *she* had taught it to him in her infinite mercy, all those centuries ago.

Tears slid down his ancient face, unbidden and uncontrolled. The man who had been known by so many names over so many centuries rose slowly.

It took some time for him to reach the antique mirror that had graced this chamber since it had been given to him by his own beloved so many years ago as a wedding gift. For the greatest curse of immortality was watching those you loved disappear, over and over again. Upon reaching the weathered glass, he met his own gaze steadily and viewed his face as it changed. Here first he was Destino, the wizened keeper of the greatest stories never told, the man who must not fail his final challenge—to ensure that the complete teachings of the Libro Rosso found a modern storyteller to restore them for a new millennium; that the true history of the people would never be lost. He believed now that he had succeeded in this.

Going back further, he was the architect who orchestrated the masterpiece that was Chartres Cathedral. Then back further still, to a time that brought him great happiness in the memory of his favorite pupil, the miraculous Matilda of Canossa. If ever there was a woman worthy of her bloodline, it was she. Even today, the thought of her could make him smile, particularly when he thought of both Matilda and Maureen in tandem. How alike they were despite the fact that nearly a thousand years separated their lives and times; how much they proved together that the time returns.

Through his tears he watched in the mirror as the planes of his face took on the characters he had assumed through time, characters who worked tirelessly in search of a penance that never came. He reached up to touch the one element that did not change—the jagged scar on the left side of his face. It was the one constant of all these figures; all possessed the scar, because it was the same scar, on the same face of the same man.

He allowed himself, finally, to go back to the time that started it all, to the time when he received that scar in the service of Pontius Pilate. The recollection of that pain was not what tormented him now, rather it was the memory of his own misdeeds that had enslaved his mind and spirit for the past two thousand years of living hell. Every night of his interminable life was haunted with the memory of those actions: his own sadistic laughter rang in his head as he ripped the flesh from the Son of God with his scourging arm; he drowned nightly in his own disdain as he shoved the point of his spear into the side of the dying Jesus.

Closing his eyes now, he allowed himself to recall the great blessing and curse that had been placed upon him by his most heavenly father:

"Longinus Gaius, you have most offended me and all people of good heart with your vile deeds on this day. Your punishment shall be one of eternal damnation, but it will be an earthly damnation. You shall wander the earth without benefit of death so that each night when you lie down to sleep, your dreams will be haunted by the horrors of your own actions and the pain they have caused. Know that you will experience this torment until the end of time, or until you serve a suitable penance to redeem your tarnished soul in the name of my son Jesus Christ."

He had indeed been driven to the brink of madness by this sentence, until the day that he went in search of Maria Magdalena to beg her forgiveness and receive her grace. She shared with him the glory of God to be found through the teachings of the Way of Love. And on the day that he stood at her gravesite as an accepted member of her family, beside her mourning children and her great companion and protector Maximinus, alongside Praetorus and Veronica, he took a vow before all of them. He would spend every waking minute of his eternal life teaching the lessons of the Book of Love. He would share the beauty of the Way as it had been taught and lived by his Lord Jesus Christ and his beloved wife, Maria Magdalena, and their holy children.

There was no man in the world who could understand the transformational power of love and forgiveness better than Longinus Gaius, the accursed centurion.

The preservation of the Book of Love became a greater hardship through history than he could have ever imagined when he first took that vow. In those days, they all still believed that the authentic New Covenant would be readily heard and accepted by the children of the world. It was a task that had challenged his physical and mental stamina through two millennia. He had watched in horror as the most beautiful souls were martyred for their belief in love, torn apart in horrific ways by the unconscionable laws of men and power, men who violated every true law of Jesus Christ in his own sacred name. He endured the atrocities of the Inquisition; he had lived the anguish of watching the truth die a wretched and unjust death, of watching the most miraculous teachings become twisted beyond recognition in the pitiless hands of liars and powerbrokers. He had witnessed the intentional and systematic desecration of Mary Magdalene's sacred name.

How could any of them have ever known that, two thousand years later, the world would still not have access to the true teachings of the Book of Love? And that such simple teachings of love and faith and community would be considered more dangerous today than they were even then? Of all the horrors he had witnessed, this was the greatest hell he had endured on earth.

As a part of his self-imposed penance, he began to record for posterity the glory of those who had lived and died for the true teachings of the Way. Who better to keep the records of history than a man who cannot die and remembers it all exactly as it transpired? Thus was the Libro Rosso born in his early refuge in Calabria. And now, it appeared that it could be resurrected for a new age and a new time, that the children of a fledgling millennium were ready to read it in its entirety.

We were entering a new era for those with ears to hear.

"Please . . . let them hear it," he whispered to himself and to his Lord before rising again. He realized that there was very little time to do what must be done. And now that it was finally here, he was struck deeply by the sadness of it all. For there was truly great beauty in this world, in what God had created and in what man had created in his image, and hers. This longed-for death would be bitter in its sweetness.

But as Destino lay back down in what, he believed, was his preparation to die, he saw a vision of his Lord. It was Easa with his kind, dark eyes, whispering to him across time and space.

"You are my son, in whom I am well pleased. But your work is not yet finished."

Destino smiled. Death would not claim him yet, and that was all the better. He had so many more stories to share with Maureen. Just as soon as she was finished with the book she would be charged to write about how, precisely, to read the Book of Love as it had been preserved within Chartres Cathedral.

Chartres
present day

MAUREEN HAD HER WORK cut out for her. There were over a thousand pieces of art in Chartres. The task of interpreting it all through the lens of the Book of Love and the Libro Rosso was gargantuan, one that could take years. But she would not have to do it alone. She would do it surrounded and assisted by those she loved, as there were many around her who had ears to hear and eyes to see. This was the greatest blessing that God had given her in a very blessed life—to have beautiful friends, a family of spirit, the most remarkable mentor in history, and an extraordinary man who had gifted her with the greatest sacrament of their people: the sacred union of beloveds.

Together, they would all prove the truth of the prophecy that the time returns. They would create something as beautiful and as enduring as the extraordinary men and women in history who had come before them with the same mission. They would invite the world into an understanding that all men and women who wish to be a part of the prophecy already are. For *the time returns* referred most of all to creating heaven on earth, and this would require the participation of the entire human race, because everyone is a prophet and everyone is one with God, just as all men and women are created equally in love.

On earth as it is in heaven.

This was a gargantuan and utopian task, perhaps, but Maureen had learned to believe in miracles over the last years of her life.

But first, she would add to the Libro Rosso herself. It was, after all, her destiny as an Expected One. Like Matilda before her, she would create her own monuments to the teaching of the Way and to the great men and women who had lived and died for so important a cause. Her twenty-first-century monuments would be in print and on paper, rather than stone or stained glass or canvas, and published around the world in many languages. She would add to the Libro Rosso by chronicling the lives and loves of Matilda and Brando, and the comrades who populated their story. They, more than anyone, deserved to be remembered for their contributions to the Way of Love. And there would be others. Destino had told her as much, and she looked so forward to exploring the lives of the other extraordinary men and women who awaited her in the past—and in the future.

Maureen was already planning to meet Destino as soon as possible in Florence, where she would begin formal training in the ways of the Order, the same training that Matilda had—under the same teacher. Bérenger would join them, as he had his own mission and prophecy to fulfill. They would work together to fulfill their destinies and their prophecies; they would work together to bring the Way of Love back to the people, under the guidance of a most extraordinary teacher.

And perhaps, one day, Destino would allow her to tell his own story. Most of all, Maureen wanted the world to know of the great and tormented man whose name meant both *destiny* and *destination*. For his was the story of the human race. It was the story of redemption, through the power of faith and forgiveness. But most of all, it was the story of rebirth, through the power of love.

For those with ears to hear, let them hear it.

❀

Maureen had one final dream before leaving Chartres. Destino had warned her that after her encounter with the Book of Love, her dreams and visions would increase at an alarming rate. She would have to learn to live with this, and it would take adjustment. But she felt indescribably different since her encounter with the Book of Love. Something within her had changed, a door to the divine had been opened within her mind and her heart, making the dreams more vivid than ever before.

❀

She was an observer in this dream, rather than a part of it. A low drone of chanting swirled in the darkness around her as she watched a strange procession work its way through the narrow, cobbled streets of a medieval Italian town. It was night, and the men who marched in the procession carried torches. She thought they were men, but there was no way to tell. They were dressed head to toe in robes, with separate hoods that covered their heads completely. The robes were pristine in their snow white fabric. On the sleeves of each robe was an emblem, embroidered in scarlet thread—an alabaster jar to symbolize Maria Magdalena and the Order to which they were devoted.

The procession wound through the streets. At the center of the parade, two hooded figures carried a banner, painted with a life-sized image of the Magdalena enthroned, depicted with grandeur as the female aspect of God.

As the devotional procession passed her, Maureen was now able to see two figures standing at the side of the road. They were not hooded and did not participate in the parade. Maureen saw that one was an older man, gray-haired, yet very tall and strong, and definitely aristocratic. He had the air of a king. Beside him was a teenage boy with glossy black hair and keen, intelligent eyes. This child was noble and wise beyond his years.

Like Maureen, they were observers, and yet they were deeply connected to the events that they were witnessing. Tears streamed down the boy's face as he watched the procession pass them. There was a light in his eyes as he spoke to the older man.

"I will not fail you, Grandfather. Nothing will stop me. I will not fail our Lord or our Lady, and I will not fail the legacy of the Medici."

Maureen was swept up in her visceral reaction to this boy and his declaration. She was overwhelmed by the mixture of love and fear and sadness and awe that she felt as she watched. Destiny radiated from him. His was tangible with the promise of a life that would be filled with both triumph and tragedy.

The older man put an arm around the boy and smiled at him. "I know that, Lorenzo. I know that more than I have ever known anything. You will not fail because it is your destiny to succeed. You will be the savior of us all."

The older man's final words were the last thing that Maureen remembered.

"You will not fail because you are the Poet Prince."

✳

Maureen awoke to find Bérenger beside her. He smiled as she opened her eyes.

"You cried out in your sleep. Were you dreaming?"

Maureen nodded sleepily. "Mmm-hmm."

"About what?"

Maureen reached up to run a finger lightly over Bérenger's aristocratic features. "I think I was dreaming about you."

"About me? It must have been a magnificent dream."

She laughed with him. "Magnificent? Yes, I believe you were. And I also believe . . . that I have loved you before."

"And do you love me today?"

"I love you today. And I have no doubt that I will love you again."

Maureen reached up to touch Bérenger's lips gently with her own, and then snuggled into his arms.

"Good night, sweet prince. The time returns."

He laughed into her hair, as he pulled her close. "The time returns. Thank the Lord and his beautiful wife."

And the lovers of scripture came together yet again. No longer were they two. They were One.

THE HISTORIES OF THE BOOK OF LOVE AND THE LIBRO ROSSO

The Book of Love (original)

First Century: The original manuscript is written by Jesus Christ. Following the crucifixion, it is taken by Mary Magdalene first to Alexandria, and then to France.

Mary Magdalene teaches from the book, handing it down to her daughter, Sarah-Tamar, as her successor upon her death. While other traditions from Sarah-Tamar and the bloodline families are preserved within the French culture, they are not immediately documented as they will be in Italy. In France, the Book of Love remains in its pristine and untouched format, although it is bound in leather to protect it.

Second to Thirteenth Centuries: The Book of Love in its original form is protected by bloodline families in France, who continue to teach from it. It is the foundation of a "heresy" that is preserved in France to this day, most commonly referred to as Catharism.

Thirteenth Century: Maureen's ancestress, La Paschalina, saves the Book of Love from the Crusaders at Montségur and smuggles it to safety, taking it to the Cathar sympathizers at the monastery of Montserrat, on March 22, 1244.

Thirteenth to Sixteenth Centuries: The Book of Love remains hidden by the bloodline families in Catalonia (northern Spain).

Mid-Sixteenth Century: Ignatius Loyola discovers the secret of the Book of Love and reveals it to the pope. The Book is taken to Rome, where it becomes the highly protected and secret property of the Church. It is never spoken of publicly, and all historical records that refer to it are destroyed.

Seventeenth Century: Pope Urban VIII rebuilds St. Peter's to honor the secret traditions of the Book of Love, in emulation of the decoration of Chartres Cathedral.

The Libro Rosso (copy)

First Century: A copy of the Book of Love is made by the apostle Philip, at the request of Mary Magdalene during her confinement in Alexandria. This copy goes to Jerusalem, where it is protected by the Order of the Holy Sepulcher, a secret society formed on the first Easter by Saint Luke, Nicodemus, and Joseph of Arimathea.

Luke takes this copy to Italy, where he installs it in a monastery in Calabria. A tradition is born, wherein Calabrian scribes begin to chronicle the lives and deaths of the holy family and their descendants. The Calabrians add the prophecies of Sarah-Tamar to their manuscript, and along with their copy of the Book of Love, they begin referring to this as the Libro Rosso after it is bound in red leather.

Second to Eleventh Centuries: The Libro Rosso moves to Lucca in the second century as the Order of the Holy Sepulcher creates a base in Tuscany.

Eleventh Century: Matilda sends the Libro Rosso to Chartres in France, where it is the inspiration for the rebuilding of the Gothic masterpiece that is Chartres Cathedral with its enigmatic labyrinth, designed by the hand of Jesus.

Twelfth to Fifteenth Centuries: The Libro Rosso is in the hands of the French royal family, until it is returned to Italy by King Louis XI as a gift to the Medici family.

Mid-Sixteenth Century: The Libro Rosso is in the possession of the Medici popes, Leo X and Clement VII, and remains in the Vatican until the Barberini family smuggles it out following the death of Urban VIII. It disappears from history at this time.

Seventeenth Century: Pope Urban VIII moves Matilda's remains to St. Peter's Basilica and, with Bernini, also honors Longinus and Veronica for their roles in protecting the holy teachings that came directly from Jesus.

AUTHOR'S NOTES

The subject matter of this book is one that, to my knowledge, has never seen the light of publication anywhere in the world. As such, the research required to put all the pieces together was years in the making and paralleled my search for Mary Magdalene as chronicled in the first novel in this series, *The Expected One*. As a result of the multiple layers of time and history, the first draft of this book was well over 1,400 pages and completely unruly for both this author and my future readers. With the aid of a team that features a gifted agent and editor, I made those tough choices that most writers dread—cutting entire storylines and characters, and hundreds of pages of historical detail. These author's notes could easily run half the length of the book itself. But as space (and trees) will not allow that, I invite those who are interested in exploring this world in more depth to visit my Web site at www.KathleenMcGowan.com, where I will share extensive annotations, anecdotes, and addenda.

All history is conjecture. All of it. It is the height of folly and arrogance for anyone to say that he or she knows definitively what happened in the past. We piece it together the best we can, with the shreds of evidence that exist. When we are very lucky, the pieces come together to form a beautiful and cohesive collage. The difference between the mosaic that a historical novelist creates and that which a historian constructs occurs in the chasm somewhere of what we accept individually as evidence. I tend to think that novelists prefer to work in Technicolor, whereas academics choose to work strictly in the realm of black and white. Both have merits in the worlds of entertainment and education, and I hope that one day we will all learn to complement each other on our mutual search for the glories of our human history.

About the Book of Love

I first heard about the Book of Love while touring the Languedoc in the early 1990s. I was fascinated by the fleeting references to a "mysterious gospel" that was used by the Cathars in their most sacred and secret traditions. Initial attempts to understand what, exactly, this Book of Love was were largely unsuccessful. Requests for information in the Languedoc turned up coy and elusive replies—that is, when they received replies at all. More often than not, I was told that the Book of Love was an alternate version of the gospel of John. This sounded like a cover story to me. I would find over the course of ten years that it was most definitely a smoke screen to protect the truth.

Readers of *The Expected One* are likely aware that my own spiritual quest has mirrored Maureen's in many ways. Like my fictional heroine, it was my immersion into the cultural and folkloric traditions of France, and later Italy, that changed my thinking, my faith, and my life. As I was blessed with access to extraordinary teachers—and "perfect heretics"—I was told a different version of the true origins and contents of the Book of Love. I have done my best to present these lost teachings within the preceding pages. While the words of the Book of Love in these pages are entirely my own, they are an interpretation of the moving and powerful traditions and teachings which I believe have been passed down for two thousand years.

At the time when I first became aware through the oral histories of the Book of Love and its contents, I had not studied the Gnostic Gospels. Thus it was a shock for me to discover that the Gospel of Philip was identical in numerous places to the "heretical" teachings as they had been given to me. The Gospels of Thomas and Mary Magdalene also contained notable similarities to the traditions from the Book of

Love. Certainly, the erotic and passionate nature of the Philip material was a revelation, as was the clear indication that the Holy Spirit was feminine. I absolutely believe, as Peter conjectures in the preceding pages, that the Gospel of Philip was at least a partial attempt to reconstruct the Book of Love—for those with ears to hear.

For those who wish to tune their own ears to hear and who desire to study this subject in greater detail, I would enthusiastically recommend taking a very close look at Philip. While there are many great interpretations and commentaries available, I am personally fond of the writings of Jean-Yves le Loup, which are available widely in English translation. Newcomers to the Gnostic Gospels should begin their search with Elaine Pagels's classic of the same name for a more thorough foundation.

About Matilda of Tuscany

I first encountered Matilda physically while touring Italy with my husband in the spring of 2001. We were in St. Peter's Basilica, and I had just turned around from Michelangelo's masterpiece, the *Pietà*, when I nearly crashed into her enormous marble shrine. That there was a monument to a woman in the center of the Vatican was astonishing to me. That the woman in question held the papal tiara and the key of Saint Peter in her hands was nearly beyond my comprehension. Who was this woman, what was she doing in the middle of St. Peter's, and why didn't anyone I asked have the answer to those questions? I had to know.

Researching a woman who has been dead for a thousand years, and who lived in a time when uppity women were not beloved by the monks recording history, is a tremendous challenge regardless of background or approach. Factor in what I am certain was Matilda's commitment to the Cathar heresies in Tuscany, which were by their nature secret and protected, and you have what I refer to as a historical blackout.

An important note here on Cathar history: academics will happily throw stones at me for referring broadly to all these heresies across time and through Europe as "Cathar" because history recalls Catharism in a very specific time and defined space. However, this tradition of "pure Christianity," which is the very essence of the word *Cathar*, dates back two thousand years. Thus I unapologetically refer to all of these "perfect heretics" as Cathars.

Like most French Cathars, these "pure ones" in Italy lived a quiet existence that was found to be entirely unthreatening to traditional Catholics for nearly a thousand years. The persecution of these original followers, declared dangerous heretics by the Inquisition, would happen in earnest by the thirteenth century, when the Italian Cathars would endure the same hardships as their brethren in France. Also, like the French Cathars, their history was entirely misunderstood and perhaps intentionally misrepresented by the Catholic Church and subsequent historians. These people were not descendants of other, later heretical sects that had migrated from elsewhere in Europe to oppose Catholic doctrine, as has long been purported in histories derived from Inquisition sources. The Cathars of Umbria and Tuscany, like the Cathars of the Languedoc, had been there since the foundation of Christianity, holding their traditions and their teachings in quiet strength as they always had. That the Church did not recognize them as such was a canny strategy and instrumental in their successful persecution.

My sworn mission as a writer, and my own promise, is to uncover the stories of extraordinary women who dared to change the world and risked everything to do it, yet have been forgotten or misrepresented by history. Matilda of Canossa exemplified this more than any subject I have ever studied besides Mary Magdalene. I learned so much from her! While many are aware that the south of France has been home to heretical history for two thousand years, the prevalence of these traditions in Italy is a new idea for most. Yet it has been hiding in plain sight there for centuries, as we have seen here in Matilda's life story. I have just come from visiting her territory in Tuscany with my family, where we viewed the Ponte della Maddalena, the bridge that Matilda created just outside Lucca. It is breathtakingly beautiful, how the stone semicircles reflect perfectly in the water to create a complete circle, particularly visible at night. We stayed there for hours because we couldn't leave the place, it was so . . . magical. It is clear that the designer of this bridge had a spiritual intention as well as a practical one. That the structure was named for Mary Magdalene and that there was once a statue and a chapel dedicated to her at the foot of the bridge is, I think, highly indicative of Matilda's devotion to her lady. That there have been several attempts to change the name of the bridge over time and obscure its origins is also significant. But Mary—and Matilda—will not be ignored; and the name Ponte della Maddalena endures and is recognized officially in Italian government documents.

There is very little written in English about Matilda, and, given her huge historical impact, not an awful lot more written about her in Latin or Italian. Matilda is subsequently one of history's great mysteries. The Donizone manuscript that resides in the Vatican is the key source of information on her life to be found on record. However, I truly believe she manufactured it as a public relations exercise with the help of the Church to protect her holdings and her reputation. Often, what Donizone *doesn't* say is, I believe, far more important than what he does. The alternative manuscript that Maureen is given is rumored to exist, but I can't prove it and for our purposes it is fictional. Matilda's sarcophagus in San Benedetto was opened on several occasions prior to the rule of Pope Urban VIII, and for the record I believe that members of the Medici family did find this alternate version of her life written in her own hand. The Medici and their methods—and how they transformed the world through the Renaissance—will be revealed in my forthcoming book, *The Poet Prince.*

I must honor the esteemed author Michèle K. Spike for her excellent book, *Tuscan Countess*, which is the definitive work in English on Matilda and highly recommended reading for those who would know the complex historical details of her world. Ms. Spike's book is written with a passion that is rare in an academic setting. I am grateful to this learned woman, whose interest in Matilda sent her on her own journey through the Middle Ages and ultimately aided mine as I also trekked through Italy in search of this near forgotten heroine. So while I necessarily draw different conclusions in terms of many of Matilda's motivations (and motive is the one element of human nature that we can truly only conjecture), I remain in debt to the richness that was produced through her work.

Ms. Spike also helped me solve the riddle of Michelangelo's claim to be a descendant of Matilda and was ridiculed for the claim! While I came upon sources that hypothesized that this could have been possible if the baby Beatrice had not died, I knew there was another explanation. I had long suspected that there was a second, hidden child in this story, and it was Michèle Spike who led me to him with her discovery of the three documents that mention Guidone and Guido Guerra, most significant of these the Vallambrosan "adoption decree." Let me emphasize that Ms. Spike does not draw this conclusion about the identity of Guidone as Matilda and Gregory's child. That assertion is entirely my own. Based on the surrounding evidence, I am certain that these are Matilda's son and grandson and that they are Michelangelo's ancestors. This concept will also be explored in more detail in the forthcoming sequel, *The Poet Prince*.

I will ask that medieval scholars and experts cut me some slack for condensing and abbreviating the complicated events of Matilda's time to make her extraordinary life more palatable to the average reader. There were periods of months at a time when I was in despair of ever finishing the Matilda chapters, as it was so difficult to distill the feudal politics and papal intrigues. While I have tried to remain as faithful as possible to the historical backdrop, there were necessary abbreviations for the sake of which I plead poetic license. Indeed, at least ten popes and their histories ended up on the cutting room floor as I worked through this story. Again, those who are interested in delving deeper are invited to my Web site, where they will find more historical details of Matilda's world.

There is no definitive recording of Matilda's birthplace. Several noted scholars, including Michèle Spike, advocate for Mantua, as that is the first recorded city of activity in her childhood, and the place she chose to be buried. However, I came across several sources along my path that named Lucca as a "possible" or even a "likely" location. For me, and with all due respect to my friends in Mantua, this was a gut choice: it feels right. Certainly, Matilda's commitment to Lucca and the people within it never waivers, even when Henry IV does his damnedest to alienate her own people from her. And the events I describe—her dedication of San Martino's, the decree of protection for Lucca in 1099, and the great bridge built in the name of Maria Magdalena—are all historically based.

Several guide books that I possess, published and obtained locally in Lucca, indicate that Matilda was present at the time that San Martino's was rededicated. However, they place this date as 1070, which is impossible. One of the few things we know about Matilda definitively was that she was in Lorraine in 1070, married to the hunchback and building Orval. While scholars have theorized that it may have been Beatrice who was present and not Matilda, I disagree. I think it is highly unlikely that anyone in Lucca, particularly during her time, would confuse Matilda's unforgettable and legendary presence, certainly not with her mother's. And I believe that Matilda would have insisted on being present to rededicate the church that housed her beloved Holy Face. I think it is far more likely that the date may have been mistaken or incorrectly recorded.

While I used the Italian version of Brando's given name, Ildebrando, he is most often referred to in historical sources by the Germanized *Hildebrand*. The accomplishments of his reign are often referred to as "Hildebrandian reforms." I chose the Italian pronunciation to emphasize his Roman background. And I thought that Brando was a sexier name for such a complex, masculine character—ironic, certainly, in that he also strengthened the cause of celibacy in the priesthood. It is urgent to remember historically, however, that celibate priests did not produce offspring. Therefore, Rome was their sole heir. The decision to keep the clergy celibate had far more to do with economics than it did with morality.

My interpretation of the Brando/Pope Gregory character is largely colored by the vast number of letters he left as part of his legacy. It is clear while one reads through them that he was strong, smart, ambitious, fearless, and very, very passionate about Matilda. I also think that Brando did sincerely believe that the end justified the means, and that he was overall a good and just man who cared about real reform. I also believe that he was brilliant, cunning, and absolutely ruthless when necessary. Anything else would have put him at a decided disadvantage in the political mire of his time. He had to operate on a level playing field in order to survive, and he was more than capable of creating that field by any means necessary. I believe he was Matilda's greatest teacher in this regard as well. So it has been in politics since the dawn of time.

Certainly, there is great controversy historically over whether the intense relationship between Brando and Matilda was, indeed, romantic and consummated. Obviously, I do not hesitate to assert my perspective on this. I refer readers to a letter from the pope to his beloved where he writes of his yearning to run away to the Holy Land with her, to a place where they are not under scrutiny and able to pursue the true work of God. It is a letter of such desire that it could only have been written by the most ardent of lovers.

Knock and the Holy Apparitions

I visited Knock with my family during the final edits of this book. I had not been there since I was twenty years old. My view of it now, knowing what I know, is very different than it was then. I believe with all my Irish heart that Knock is a holy place, possibly the only place where the Holy Trinity has appeared for a prolonged period of time for mortal viewing. It is highly sacred ground. I also believe that Saint Patrick saw a similar vision there when he proclaimed that Knock would become holy in the future.

I extend my apologies to anyone I may have offended with my perspective on the Holy Apparitions. I know this is sacrosanct territory for many. I do believe that all these children viewed something extraordinary, and that many of them were mystics. I certainly feel this is true of Lucia Santos. Like Maureen, I wept while reading her story of isolation. I only wish we knew, in her own words and her own voice, what she truly experienced throughout her long and inspired life. I do not, in any way, wish to diminish the miracle of Fátima. I simply wish to inspire people by giving them a different perspective on the circumstances and their outcome so that they may meditate on it as they will.

The priceless document of prophecy that is in the possession of Father Girolamo de Pazzi and attributed to Nostradamus exists and was indeed given in dedication to Pope Urban VIII. It was discovered hidden in plain sight in a national public library in Rome by an Italian journalist in the 1990s. A book and documentary, referring to it as the "lost book of Nostradamus," were created to chronicle the discovery. But as I indicate here, there is far more to this book than all the traditional Nostradamus commentary would indicate. I am studying it in depth and hope to publish my findings in the near future.

On Chartres and the Labyrinth

I write this as I sit on the steps of Chartres Cathedral, beneath the exquisite statue of Saint Modesta on the north portal, the entrance that is often referred to as the "door of the initiates." In all my travels, there really is no place on earth that inspires me like Chartres. It is a most astonishing monument to God built by human hands: magnificent in its grandeur, yet humble in its faith.

There are legends that surround the building of this place, stories of faith and dedication and human strength, that are unlike any I have heard before. Historians have never been able to account for the financing of such an enormous endeavor, but the folklore here says that if they are searching for ledgers and accountings, they will be left wanting. Chartres was built by people of faith, as a tithing to God. I believe that most of the labor was given freely and with grace. Some say that the reconstruction of Chartres after the terrible fire in 1194 was undertaken by those who opposed the Crusades—they were the medieval version of conscientious objectors. Parents dedicated their sons to the building of the monument to God's love instead of enlisting them for war—they chose to create for God rather than kill.

There are other legends, stories of prayer rituals that were required for purification before anyone was allowed to begin work for the day on this eternal monument to love and faith. If a laborer was having a bad day and did not come to work in the spirit of the endeavor, he was simply asked to return when he felt restored to the communal mission. No intention that was not based in love was permitted.

Are these legends true? Is there proof of any of this? They endure for eight hundred years in the stones of this place, and that is enough for me. I know, when I see the spires of Chartres from the approach on the road from Paris, that this place is special. I believe its unequaled beauty and grace artistically, architecturally, and spiritually was accomplished by an extraordinary effort based in a community founded on the principles of love and faith, all of which were celebrated through prayer. I believe that Chartres as it exists today was and is a monument to the Book of Love.

As such, the labyrinth at Chartres Cathedral is, for me, the most sacred space on earth. Like Maureen, I weep when I see it covered by chairs. When I first began visiting Chartres years ago, the labyrinth was never uncovered. Most visitors had no idea that there was as much glory beneath their feet as there was in the stained glass high above them.

There has been some progress over the last few years in terms of accessing the labyrinth. As I write this, I am in Chartres, where I have just spent an entire, blissful afternoon in the labyrinth. The Church now opens it once a week, on Fridays, from approximately April to September. I pray—literally and often—that this is the beginning of an opening of minds and that these limited hours will expand into a more regular access to this unique spiritual tool that the architects installed here over eight hundred years ago, a tool that I believe was designed by the collaborative efforts of no lesser beings than King Solomon, the Queen of Sheba, and Jesus Christ. I invite you to pray with me that this unique place will one day in the not too distant future be recognized and honored for its sanctity and that the destructive practice of concealing it while damaging it with unneeded chairs will end once and for all.

There is a growing labyrinth movement worldwide as humankind rediscovers this beautiful opportunity for a walking prayer that leads them directly to God. Resources on the Internet, including labyrinth locators, will aid you in your search to find one close to your home. And if you cannot locate one in your area, well, perhaps you are being called to create one there!

As I write, one of the local guardians of the cathedral arrives for his morning ritual and pledge of faith. He brings flowers daily to Notre Dame; today, he gives one to me as well. The spirit of this place and the souls who created it endures as a beacon of light on this planet for those with eyes to see and ears to hear, and perhaps even for those who have yet to develop such senses. I come here annually because it restores me. I come with the hope of taking some small piece of it with me, back into the world to share in this marvelous vision of what humans can accomplish. I come because my own promise was to uncover and reveal the stories that have been lost to history, the truths that have been hidden so long below the surface, awaiting their time to be revealed once again.

That time is now. And there is no other place that I know of on earth with as much to reveal to the human spirit as Chartres. This book is my own monument to those who inspired and created that holy place, that we may attempt to emulate them, each in our own ways. I pray that I have done them justice with the work and that this might inspire others on their own path.

Chartres, France
May 17, 2008

Acknowledgments

While writing is a most solitary endeavor, the process of completing a book and preparing it for publication is a highly collaborative one. It takes a village to publish a book. There is not enough space or time to thank everyone individually for the generous inspiration, support, and encouragement that has been showered upon me through the often challenging period of completing this one. I hope that all who are with me along this path know just how much I love and appreciate you, even if space does not allow me to name each of you individually.

The Time Returns, of this I am certain, and the following people have proven that to me with their magical, powerful presences in my life and work. I believe that all of them are members of my own "family of spirit" and hope they view me in the same light. As the Book of Love says, *those who remember and recognize each other are blessed beyond belief.* My literally eternal gratitude goes out to all of them, as they have indeed blessed me in such a way.

My personal life is centered on family, and it is my own that make this work possible on all levels. My passion and appreciation go to my husband, Peter, who will always be first: my first love, my first reader and critic (an often thankless job), and my first line of support. Our three beautiful boys are living proof of the power of love; they are a credit to God. To my parents, who are there for me every single day of my life and give me everything, I offer all my love and gratitude, which I also extend to my brothers, Kelly and Kevin, and their families, whom I love as my own.

I truly could not have done this without:

Larry Kirshbaum, who supports me with such unconditional patience and grace that I'm not sure what I did to make God love me so much that he sent such an angel in my direction, but I am grateful beyond words every day for his presence in my life.

Trish Todd, an editor who is as patient as she is gifted, for making sure I always put my best words forward and for giving me such a safe place to be completely who I need to be on the page.

Patrick Ruffino, for remembering, believing, and living the truth so fearlessly, and for providing magical artwork in record time, thus instilling his own spirit into this book, and for never coughing up the red pill; extra love to his beautiful wife, Julia, who shares him with me so generously.

And thanks will never be enough for:

Stacey Kishi, for every minute of the countless years we have been on this path together, but special mention this round for discovering the little madonna in Orval, and for putting up with me while I sobbed after walking every available labyrinth in France. And thanks to her men, Michael and Elliott, for sharing her with me.

Ampy Dawn, who taught me with her generosity and loyalty that God did not give me biological sisters because he wanted me to choose my own, and I have chosen her.

Olivia Peyton, because as the time returns, I thank the Lord and his beautiful wife that she agrees to be there with me every step of the way. Her genius is beyond my comprehension.

My own Issy, Isobel Denham, who taught me so much in so little time, not the least of which was that beautiful song, the one in French, about love, and what it really means to be a "perfect heretic" through her loving and compassionate example of the work she does with women and children in Bosnia.

Larry Weinberg, for his warmth and widsom.

Acknowledgments

Lovely Laurence Rabe, for her help with French.

Gary Lucchesi, who became my most unexpected (and most reluctant) muse, by giving me a living example of the noble legacy of Lucca.

My newest little sister, Mary Ann Parent, for jumping into the journey and adding her own uniqueness to the work and my life.

Special mention goes to Sarah Symons, the founder of the Emancipation Network, for her daily dedication to the cause of ending human trafficking in our suffering world. Sarah's commitment to humanity is one of the great inspirations in my life. I can only hope to emulate her devotion to service, and in an attempt to do that, I am donating a percentage of my royalties from this book to her work and to projects that support this worthy cause. For more information on how Sarah and I are combining our efforts to protect women and children, visit www.MadeBySurvivors.com or www.KathleenMcGowan.com, my own Web site.

Danke to Tobi and Gerda (my equinox sister!), for all the wonderful times in RLC and beyond, but most of all because they embody the teachings of the Book of Love, just in the way they live every day.

To my friends and associates who are authors and artists in the trenches, I give thanks for the camaraderie and conversation that we writers require like oxygen. I have learned much from all of you, on the page and in person: Jeffrey Butz, Ani Williams, Nancy Safford, Shannon Andersen, Flo Aveia Magdalena, Angelina Heart, Phil Gruber, Victoria Mary Clarke, Henry Lincoln. As I was finishing this book, Jean-Luc Robin, a custodian of the soul of Rennes-le-Château and the author of the definitive book on that mystical, heretical village, passed from this world to the next. I pray that Jean-Luc now holds the key to all these mysteries from his place in heaven.

My love and gratefulness abound for the miracle that was and is Destino, because *destiny* and *destination* do indeed come from the same root. And of course, for Easa and Magdalene and their legacy of love that changed the world once before and will again.

Most of all, this is for all of you, my readers, who are my brothers and sisters on the path—past, present, and future—for the thousands of you who have written me from all over the world in support of my work and research. I read every single letter, and most of them make me cry with gratitude that there are people out there like you. It is my fervent hope that what you read here may help you to *remember*, as that is certainly one of the greatest goals of our quest, together and separately. There is no thrill to match that which comes with rediscovering our need to seek, the aching hunger to search for something mysterious and divine—and to live in the wonder of it all as we do so. Perhaps the Holy Grail that awaits discovery looks different for each individual soul, but for me the ultimate treasure is the truth of our own magnificent legacy and history as human beings. It is God's great game for us, this quest, and there is immense joy in deciding to play it with all our heart and spirit. Easa said, *Whoever searches must continue to search until they find.* The search is the destination, the finding is the destiny.

And finally, in homage to the Lady Ariadne, I have attempted to weave a "clue" for all of you to follow in and out of the labyrinth. As such, I have written this book using the ancient mystery school technique of "layered learning." The more you read it, the more veils will be removed and the more truths will be revealed. So there! Now you can go back and read it all again . . .

As for me, one truth remains after all is said and done, and that is this:

I have loved you before, I love you today, and I will love you again. The time returns.

For those with ears to hear,

Kathleen McGowan

Acknowledgments

In chapter two of the Book of Love, Maggie Cusack sings a traditional hymn to Jesus in the Irish language. My husband, Peter McGowan, comes from a village in Ireland where legend says that Saint Patrick preached this same message: a hundred thousand welcomes, Jesus.

As indicated in the previous pages, I believe that Patrick was a descendant of Jesus and Mary Magdalene and that he preached from the original teachings as found in the Book of Love. To celebrate this, Peter and I developed a song utilizing Patrick's own words. Saint Patrick was a Poet Prince in his own right, and we think his words are a beautiful illustration of the early teachings.

The refrain of the hymn is ancient, and arguably the words of the saint himself, as is the chorus melody. The song can be heard in its entirety by visiting my Web site, www.KathleenMcGowan.com.

Céad Mile Fáilte Romhat, a Iosa

I arise today through the strength of heaven's bliss
And the warm ray of the sun
To the splendor of fire, to the speed of lightning,
Through the swiftness of the wind I run.

This day I call to me
God's hand to uphold thee
So we will spread the truth that no one can deny.

Through a mighty strength, invocation of the Trinity,
I arise, I arise today
Through the belief in the Threeness,
The confession of the Oneness, to the Creator of all Creation.

I believe, I believe
In predictions of prophets and preaching of the Way,
In the strength to direct me, in the power to sustain me,
In the wisdom to guide me, in the path before my eyes.

Acknowledgments

This day I call to me
God's hand to uphold thee
So we will spread the truth that no one can deny.

God's hand to guard on me,
God's wisdom to guide me,
God's ear to hear me,

God's eye to look before me,
God's might to uphold me,
God's word to speak through me,
God's love to sustain me,
God's shield to protect me.

Céad mile fáilte romhat, a Iosa